Praise For
Tracy Brogan

The New Normal

"Brogan's voice is distinct and irresistible, offering both laugh-out-loud scenarios and moments of poignancy as Carli and Ben wade through the murky waters of divorce and single parenthood. Supportive neighbors enhance the hilarity and add a sense of community sure to tug at the heartstrings. This sweet romance is a joy."

—*Publishers Weekly*

My Kind of Forever

"[An] adorable contemporary . . . This charming sequel successfully continues threads from its predecessor and deepens the community and character relationships . . . Will provide satisfying comfort for both new readers and returning fans."

—*Publishers Weekly*

My Kind of You

"In this relaxed contemporary, Brogan (*Love Me Sweet*) creates a charming small town where even the scandals and secrets are relatively wholesome. Events sweep readers along, making them long for the idealized community Brogan portrays."

—*Publishers Weekly*

"Recommend this romantic story to fans of women's fiction."

—*Booklist*

"This story is filled with lively characters who jump off the page. The author knows how to capture her readers' attention. The scene where the hero tells the heroine that she's 'the kind of woman a man wants to make promises to' was romantic and sweet."

—*RT Book Reviews*, 4 stars

Crazy Little Thing

WALL STREET JOURNAL BESTSELLER

RWA RITA® FINALIST, 2013, BEST FIRST BOOK

"Heart, humor, and characters you'll love—Tracy Brogan is the next great voice in contemporary romance."

—Kristan Higgins, *New York Times* bestselling author

"Witty one-liners and hilarious characters elevate this familiar story . . . Readers will love the heat between the leads, and by the end they'll be clamoring for more."

—*RT Book Reviews*, 4 stars (HOT)

"Brogan shows a real knack for creating believable yet quirky characters . . . The surprising emotional twists along the way make it a satisfying romp."

—Aleksandra Walker, *Booklist*

"*Crazy Little Thing* by Tracy Brogan is so funny and sexy, I caught myself laughing out loud."

—Robin Covington, *USA Today, Happy Ever After*

"Tracy Brogan is my go-to, laugh-out-loud remedy for a stressful day."

—Kieran Kramer, *USA Today* bestselling author

The Best Medicine

RWA RITA® FINALIST, 2015,
BEST CONTEMPORARY ROMANCE

"With trademark humor, lovely, poignant touches, and a sexy-as-sin hero, *The Best Medicine* is Tracy Brogan at her finest. Charming, witty, and fun."

—Kimberly Kincaid, *USA Today* bestselling author

Love Me Sweet

RWA RITA® FINALIST, 2016, BEST CONTEMPORARY ROMANCE

"An upbeat, generous message about finding yourself, standing up for yourself, and living an authentic life . . . A sexy, slightly kooky romance that should please Bell Harbor fans."

—*Kirkus Reviews*

Jingle Bell Harbor: A Novella

"Brogan's hilarious voice and wordplay will immediately ensnare readers in this quick but satisfying small-town romance."

—Adrian Liang, *Amazon Book Review*

"*Jingle Bell Harbor* is a fun, funny, laugh-out-loud Christmas read that will surely put you right in the mood for the season."

—*The Romance Reviews*, 5 stars

"This was an incredible read! I was definitely surprised by this book and in a great way."

—*My Slanted Bookish Ramblings*, 4.5 stars

"*Jingle Bell Harbor* by Tracy Brogan is about discovering what you want, deciding what you need to finally be happy, and rediscovering a love of the holidays. It's a quick, easy read filled with laughter and enjoyable, quirky characters. If you're in the mood for something light and funny, I would recommend *Jingle Bell Harbor* by Tracy Brogan."

—*Harlequin Junkie*, 4 stars

"This is a really cute, uplifting Christmas novella. It's quick, light, and gives you warm fuzzies just in time for the upcoming holidays. There is plenty of humor to keep you entertained, and the quirky residents of Bell Harbor will keep you reading to see what else is in store."

—*Rainy Day Reading Blog*, 4 stars

Hold on My Heart

"Successfully blends a sassy heroine and humor with deep emotional issues and a traditional romance . . . The well-developed characters and the sweet story with just a touch of heat will please readers looking for a creative take on romance."

—*Publishers Weekly*

"Launched in hilarious style by an embarrassingly cute meet, this delightful romantic comedy will keep the smiles coming."

—*Library Journal*

Highland Surrender

"*Highland Surrender* features plenty of action, romance, and sex with well-drawn individuals—a strong yet young heroine and a delectable hero—who don't act out of character. The story imparts a nice feeling of 'you are there,' with a well-presented look at the turbulent life in sixteenth-century Scotland."

—*RT Book Reviews*, 4 stars

"Treachery and political intrigue provide a well-textured backdrop for a poignant romance in which a young girl, well out of her depth, struggles to reconcile what she thinks she knows with what her heart tells her. *Highland Surrender* is a classic sweep-me-away tale of romance and derring-do!"

—Connie Brockway, *New York Times* bestselling author

My Kind of Perfect

Other Books by Tracy Brogan

Trillium Bay Series

My Kind of You
My Kind of Forever

Bell Harbor Series

Crazy Little Thing
The Best Medicine
Love Me Sweet
Jingle Bell Harbor: A Novella

Stand-Alone Novels

Highland Surrender
Hold on My Heart
The New Normal

My Kind of *Perfect*

A Trillium Bay Novel

TRACY BROGAN

 Montlake

Text copyright © 2021 by Tracy Brogan
All rights reserved.

Published by Montlake, Seattle

www.apub.com

Amazon, the Amazon logo, and Montlake are trademarks of Amazon.com, Inc., or its affiliates.

ISBN-13: 9781542094399
ISBN-10: 1542094399

Cover design by Laura Klynstra

Printed in the United States of America

For Webster Girl and Tenacious D

Chapter 1

"And just like that, Gigi O'Reilly-Callaghan-Harper-Smith died the way she lived. With a martini glass in each hand."

My sister Brooke performed a lazy, single-fingered sign of the cross as our grandmother, the *very much alive* Gigi O'Reilly-Callaghan-Harper-Smith, tripped over a calico house cat, swayed on one foot before bumping her gray-haired noggin against the doorframe, and yet somehow managed to not spill a drop from either of the glasses she held aloft. Not a dribble nor a droplet. Nary a ripple. The olives didn't even wobble.

"This is designer gin," Gigi responded matter-of-factly, lurching forward and plunking the drinks down on the red-and-white-checked cloth that covered the old pine table in her kitchen. "It was a parting gift from Gus."

"Does Gus know it was a parting gift from Gus?" Brooke's tone remained as dry as the hint of vermouth Gigi typically waved over her drink of choice, but our grandmother just scoffed good-naturedly. She was a tiny dynamo in faded jeans and an extra-large blue-plaid flannel shirt that swallowed her to the knees. The sleeves were rolled up a half dozen turns and were still cuffed just above her wrists.

"After what I put up with at his place, I think I earned myself a few door prizes on my way out. And anyway, he shouldn't drink so much."

I locked eyes with my sister, who shrugged off the comment with practiced resignation. There was no point in telling Gigi that she *also* drank too much. Every time the topic arose, she'd just tell us she was pickling herself to ward off old age, and she might be onto something. At seventy-plus years old, she was as vivacious as ever and showed no signs of slowing down—as evidenced by the fact that, until two weeks ago, she'd been shacking up with a much younger man—one Mr. August Mahoney.

Their surprise affair had rocked and shocked the Wenniway Island community and kept the winter population of six hundred inhabitants busy gossiping and speculating and tsk-tsk-tsking, but—like a firecracker—their relationship had been loud, painful to the eyes, and blissfully brief.

They'd lived together just long enough for Gigi to discover that the hard-of-hearing Gus was a nocturnal TV watcher of true-crime documentaries who ate potato chips in bed while wiping greasy fingers on the sheets, habitually left up the toilet seat, and needed pruning shears to clip his freakishly fast-growing toenails. It was all a bit too much, even for a scrappy, adaptable gal like Gigi, who'd been widowed not once, not twice, but thrice. So she'd informed Gus it was over and moved back to her own house, where she could drink his designer gin in peace and quiet.

I'd caught up on all this information, along with a few more salaciously repellent details about Gus and Gigi's romantic exploits, while sitting in my grandmother's homey, cinnamon-scented kitchen. It was April, and a late-season northern Michigan snowstorm was blowing against the windows, but the house was cozy inside thanks to a fire crackling in the fireplace. I'd missed that sound of a wood fire burning, just as I'd missed the wind howling and sleet pelting against the glass panes. After spending the past several months in warm, sunny Sacramento in a $2 million house with glossy glass-stone fireplaces that were sleek and silent and really just for show, I found myself appreciating these quaint, familiar sounds of home.

This *was* home. Trillium Bay on Wenniway Island, and in spite of the questionable subject matter at hand, I was very glad to be there. And very glad that one of those martinis was for me because I'd arrived just two hours earlier, and the travel from California had been exhausting, both physically and emotionally. Like my grandmother, I, too, was flailing in the wake of a doomed love affair, but unlike in Gigi's situation, no one on the island knew yet that my relationship with John Taggert was teetering on the brink of disaster. My family thought I was there for a short visit, but it looked to me like I was home to stay.

I'd have to explain things to everyone eventually, of course. They'd notice if I never left, but the situation was complicated, and I wasn't entirely sure what to tell them. Tag and I were sort of . . . on a break, but I suspected it was the irreconcilable sort of break that couples didn't recover from. And while no one would technically judge me for this, a long line of people were waiting to say, "I told you so, Lilly," because I'd been cautioned—repeatedly—that the relationship was a mistake.

"She's all set, you guys! Oh my gosh, are you ready?" my niece, Chloe, called out excitedly from the top of Gigi's stairs, where Emily—the middle Callaghan sister and Chloe's mother—was waiting to model her bridal gown. She was getting remarried in a few months, and this big-reveal moment was exclusively for me because Gigi, Brooke, and Chloe had already seen it. I'd missed the wedding dress shopping excursion because I'd been in California with Tag, and the regret still stung. I hadn't been home when my sister had gotten engaged, either. I'd missed Christmas with my family because we'd been on a Caribbean vacation. Even the courtship of Brooke and her boyfriend, Leo, who was now a deputy with the Wenniway Island Police Department, had blossomed without me around to share in the joy of it, but still, it was the dress shopping that seemed to rattle me the most. I'd missed all the *feels* and the *aahs* and the *oohs* and the giggles and the cheers and the *saying yes to the dress*, and for some reason that really bothered me.

Emily's first marriage at nineteen had been a spontaneous runaway elopement, so the entire family had missed out on that one. I was only fifteen at the time, and there'd been no dress shopping or cake tasting or bridal shower attending. No bouquet toss or champagne toast or vision of my father walking her down the aisle—a point of contention that had created a fair amount of friction between the two of them that they'd only recently resolved. So *this* wedding was meant to make up for *that* wedding. Emily tying the knot with Ryan was going to be an *event*, with all the matrimonial fanfare, frothy tulle, fragrant white roses, and tuxedoed harpists that my sister could wrangle together. And of course, most importantly, there would be the Perfect Dress. The dress I hadn't helped choose but was eager to see nonetheless.

"We're ready!" called out Brooke, and Gigi began to hum a pitchy version of the "Wedding March." Thirteen-year-old Chloe's laughter preceded her as she bounded down the wooden stairs in sneakers, sounding more like a basketball player galloping across center court than the slender girl she was. She rounded the corner and skidded to a halt, shoes squeaking and hair swirling, before turning back toward my sister.

Emily descended with far more grace and solemnity, the swish of chiffon nearly drowned out by Gigi's off-key humming as my sister floated her way down the steps and into the kitchen. She did a slow Cinderella-quality turn with one hand holding out the soft white fabric of the gown. She smiled at me, her cheeks pink with excitement. Her red-gold hair was twisted up in a simple knot, her blue eyes sparkling. I pressed my hands to my own instantly warm cheeks as fat tears full of mixed emotions puddled in my eyes.

"Well?" she asked tentatively. "How'd I do?"

"Yeah, how'd we do?" demanded Chloe, the mini-version of her mother right down to the red hair and smattering of freckles.

It was well established that I was the most fashion conscious of the three Callaghan sisters, although admittedly the bar was low. Dark-haired Brooke lived in jeans and sweaters, even though she was the mayor of our town, and strawberry-blonde Emily leaned more toward *nicer* jeans and *nicer* sweaters, but I was the one who paid attention to the latest trends. Thanks to a brief (and disastrous) stint in the pageant world, I knew how to play up my assets, accentuate my best features, and pose to look five pounds lighter.

But Emily didn't need any of that.

"Oh my gosh, Peach," I said on a big exhale. "You're so beautiful."

"Am I?" she asked, laughing.

"You are stunning. The dress is perfect, and you are gorgeous. Oh my gosh. Give me another twirl," I said, rising from my chair. I needed to get a closer look. Her gown was snowy white with a sweetheart neckline and cap sleeves trimmed in just a hint of sparkly rhinestones. Just right for her.

Emily obliged my request, turning a full spin and then rotating back in the other direction before stopping to face me. Her grin was wide and blissful—for about five seconds. Then she burped, slapped a hand over her mouth, rushed to the kitchen sink . . . and puked.

I gasped in stunned surprise, but Gigi just admonished her to not get any on the dress, and Brooke calmly took a sip of her own martini. Even Chloe didn't react. They seemed not the least bit concerned, which was my first clue. Actually, it was the second clue, the puke being the first.

Emily gingerly picked up a towel from the kitchen counter and dabbed at her mouth before turning, slowly, back around to face me. Her expression was more sheepish than shocked.

"So," she said. "Guess who's pregnant?"

Half an hour later we'd gathered once more around the table. Emily had replaced her gown with fleece pajama pants decorated with sloths drinking coffee and an oversize sweatshirt bearing the image of the island's own Imperial Hotel. "Of course Ryan and I are thrilled," she said. "We knew we wanted to add to the family soon, like right after the wedding, but I guess we jumped the gun a bit. Turns out there's no grace period after going off the pill. The only downside is that it took Dad almost fifteen years to forgive me for running off with Chloe's dad, and now here I am, finally getting remarried to a wonderful guy, properly this time, in a church, with the veil and the dress and the priest, and now I have to tell him I'm already knocked up."

"Harlan isn't that observant," Gigi said. "I don't think we need to tell him."

"You've been engaged for a while, so at least no one will think this is a shotgun wedding. And with that empire waistline, you picked the perfect dress. No one will even notice," Brooke added.

"Unless she throws up in her bouquet," Chloe murmured.

Emily, to her credit, chuckled. "The wedding isn't for a couple of months yet. The morning sickness should be gone by then, but there will be no hiding my belly. Ah, well. Ryan and I figured we'd wait a few more weeks but then probably just tell everyone anyway. In the meantime, though, this is a *secret*." She glared at Gigi because if anyone was going to let it slip, it would be our grandmother—except it wouldn't be an accident. Gossip was social currency around here, and this was a valuable piece of intel. Family loyalty only went so far.

"Mum's the word," Gigi replied, twisting an imaginary lock over her pursed lips. "Or should I say, *mom's* the word?"

"You're funny." Emily then turned to me and added, "A secret from *everybody*. No one outside of this room and Ryan knows about this baby. He hasn't told his family yet. Got it?"

"I got it," I said.

My sister rested her chin in her hand and said wistfully, "I sure wish I could have one of those martinis."

∽

A baby.

A wedding *and* a baby.

That was good news all the way around, and my sister deserved this for sure. *I* was so happy that *she* was so happy, but it threw my current situation even more firmly under the microscope. The news brought into focus the importance of creating the future you crave and not settling for less. Of course, not every relationship was meant to lead to marriage and children, but what if I was ready for those next steps? But my boyfriend had already been there and done that?

Last spring, when widower John Taggert showed up in Trillium Bay, we fell hard. It was instantaneous attraction, and we were all in, right from the start. But everyone said that at fifty-nine he was too old for me, and that at twenty-six I was too young for him. Emily had warned me that his family thought I was just after his money, and that he was only interested in my body. No one believed we were really in love. No one except for us.

So we'd taken our show on the road. Tag retired from his role as president of Taggert Property Management, and we headed off to explore the big, wide world. We trekked through the Saadian Tombs in Marrakech, went "black water" rafting in the Waitomo Caves of New Zealand, and gazed out over the Atlantic Ocean from a sun-dappled courtyard of the Monserrate Palace in Portugal.

It was a dream. A glorious dream full of sunshine and rainbows and good sex and delicious food, but like every wonderful dream, eventually you have to wake up. The constant travel left me feeling adrift, more of a voyeur than voyager in my own life, and let's face it: once you've ridden one Moroccan camel, you've ridden them all.

After a few months of living from suitcases, work beckoned Tag back to Sacramento, and that retirement of his turned out to be just a temporary leave of absence. Projects multiplied, and as our time in California increased, I was left with little to do except wander around *his* house, looking at framed photos of his adult children—who were all older than me—and wonder if I *had* made a mistake in leaving behind everything I'd ever known just for the sake of a man.

Survey says . . . maybe?

Tag texted me at two o'clock that morning as I lay awake in Gigi's guest room staring at the ceiling. Given the hour, I thought maybe his message would say something about missing me terribly and wondering if we should reconsider our breakup. But it only said:

WANTED TO MAKE SURE YOU ARRIVED SAFELY. TAKE CARE.

Ten minutes later he texted again.

SORRY. FORGOT ABOUT THE TIME DIFFERENCE. HOPE I DIDN'T WAKE YOU UP.

Of course he hadn't woken me, because my brain was still on California time. And besides that, it was full of rioting thoughts. All the happy, buoyant, effervescent thoughts about my sister and about being home, but also all the soul-crushing, emotion-twisting, domino-tipping, spaghetti-tangled, cyclone-swirling thoughts about Tag and our past. And about Tag and the future and whether we might figure out a way to share one.

Deep down I already knew my answer. Tonight, seeing Emily's bride-to-be, baby-on-the-way joy had solidified it for me. I needed more than he was willing to give.

And then Tag sent one final text.

I LOVE YOU.

Yep, that one was the clincher. There'd be no decent sleep for me tonight. Because it would have been so easy to say it back, but what good would that do? I knew he loved me, and I loved him, too. I also knew it didn't matter. Love wasn't our problem. Timing was.

Chapter 2

"So this is the seat of power, huh? Are you drunk with it?" I asked as I stood in the center of the mayor's office—my sister's office.

Like her, it was tidy, well organized, and lacked any unnecessary adornments. I'm not saying she was boring. Brooke was just pragmatic and sensible and efficient to the point of being bossy. That didn't bother me, though. With Brooke, you always knew where you stood and what was what. She was calm where Emily was far more emotional and unpredictable. At least on the outside. I liked to think I fell somewhere in the middle. Not too staid, not *too* irrational.

"Yes, drunk with power," Brooke answered smoothly. "Every morning I insist Gertie bring me coffee at precisely 199 degrees with exactly fifteen drops of creamer. Otherwise she knows it's off with her head." She made a flicking gesture with her hand, and her black-haired, waif-like assistant, Gertie, chuckled from the other room, obviously not intimidated by this threatening piece of information. Probably because my sister was the least pretentious person imaginable and far more apt to *get* someone a coffee than to demand one.

I looked around, taking in the pale blue walls and framed photographs of Petoskey Bridge, our greatest local landmark besides the island itself, and the Imperial Hotel and its six-hundred-foot-wide front porch that sat on a bluff overlooking Lake Huron. There was a series of lilac photos, another claim to fame our island was known for. So much so that each June we held a festival to celebrate their blooming season, along with a parade and picnic and evening fireworks. I was voted Miss Lilac Festival as a senior in high school, my own personal claim to fame which, unfortunately, came with absolutely zero perks—other than getting to ride in the first carriage of the procession.

Above a black metal filing cabinet was a serious picture of Brooke wearing a navy-blue suit and white silk blouse. I'd never seen her in a suit, and her lack of smile in the photo made me smile back at it, as if to prompt her image to respond. It didn't.

"Is it weird to sit in an office with your own portrait staring at you?" I gestured toward the wall.

Her gaze rolled over it. "I don't really notice it anymore, but I made sure we chose the least flattering shot, just to keep me humble. You know."

That was Brooke, downplaying everything and treating compliments like flies: something to be swatted away without much acknowledgment. She was the eldest of the Callaghan sisters and had all but raised me after our mother died. I'd been five at the time. Everyone around here felt sorry for me about this tragic turn of events, and sometimes I did, too. It was strange and complicated to miss someone I barely remembered, but I'd had Brooke and Emily and Gigi and all the ladies from Saint Bartholomew's Church fussing over me throughout my childhood, so in a way, I gave up one mother but gained about twenty, and I didn't know any different. Still . . . I wish we'd had her longer.

"It's a great photo, Brooke," I said, settling into the burgundy leather chair near her desk. "And it's beyond kick-ass that you're the mayor. I can't believe you toppled Harry Blackwell's regime. I also can't wait to see the new community center and all the other stuff everyone has been working on. Honestly, I've only been gone for five months, but it feels like five years."

Brooke nodded, giving her shoulder-length chestnut curls a little bounce. "The community center is coming along. Thank goodness for Ryan. I couldn't have done it without his construction expertise. Nice of Emily to marry him, too, because I've got a half dozen more projects lined up, and with you keeping Tag busy with all that travel, he's no use. When is he coming back here, anyway?"

I glanced away and Brooke, ever astute, was onto me in an instant. Her brows furrowed. "What's that look for?"

"What look?" I responded, slinking down in my chair like an errant middle schooler waiting in the principal's office.

She eased back, the soft leather giving a quiet whoosh as she crossed her arms. "Spill it. What's up with you and Tag? Trouble in paradise?" This would be the bossy, efficient side of Brooke. No easing into the question. No hinting at curiosity or leading me to divulge my secrets. If she hadn't been a science teacher before becoming the mayor, Brooke would've made a good detective.

I got up, gently closed her office door, and sat back down. "I think we broke up."

"You think? You're not sure?"

"Well, technically we're on an indefinite break to reevaluate, but more realistically, we've reached an impasse that can't be overcome unless one of us changes our mind."

"That's generally how an impasse works, but what's the topic? I mean, what don't you agree on?"

"For starters, he thinks I should move to Sacramento permanently, but he was supposed to retire and move to Trillium Bay. That's what he told everyone he was doing last summer, and that's why Ryan and his brothers got so hot and bothered by our relationship, remember?"

She nodded again, and while it might seem strange that Ryan— my future brother-in-law—would care anything at all about my dating habits, the thing was . . . Tag was his father.

My sister was marrying Ryan *Taggert*, the son of my boyfriend, John Taggert.

It's not nearly as hillbilly, banjo-twangy, cross-eyed in-breedy as it sounds. I met Tag and we started dating, but when his adult sons, all vice presidents of Taggert Property Management, discovered this, his son Ryan was dispatched to Trillium Bay to try to break us up because they thought I was, as they so gently put it, *a gold-digging bimbo*. Instead, Ryan fell in love with Emily and never went back home.

We Callaghan women *are* pretty irresistible.

"But instead of retiring," I continued, "he's working all the time. Probably because Ryan is here instead of in Sacramento, so maybe it's Emily's fault." I knew it wasn't, but it would be nice to have someone to blame. "But honestly, it's not so much the moving. It's the babies." I couldn't contain my sigh.

"The babies?" Brooke's left brow arched. "Emily's baby?"

"No, my babies. I mean, the babies that I want—eventually—and that Tag doesn't want ever. He's already raised his three sons, and he says that's enough for him."

"Ah." That earned me a sympathetic head-tilt/slow-nod combo from my sister. "I think you hinted at that issue when you were home for Thanksgiving. Sounds like you've discussed it?"

"We have. He's got two grandsons and he loves when they visit, but after about an hour, he's done. I can't very well be angry at him for not wanting more kids, but I also can't see my life without some. I'm a preschool teacher, for goodness' sake. I love kids!" I did love kids, and Tag had known that when he met me. In fact, he'd seemed to *love* the fact that I loved kids. It was all very frustrating.

"I'm sorry, Lilly. I have no good advice for that. I mean, he's sixty years old, so I can see his side, but I also think you'd be sorry to never have any. It would be a shame if you didn't. It does indeed sound like an impasse."

That was the nicest *I told you so* I could hope for.

"It is. We've gone round and round, but now, even if he said he wanted a baby, I wouldn't believe him, and I wouldn't want to have one that he wasn't sincerely excited about. Plus, there's that little issue of us, you know, not being married. I don't think proposing was anywhere on his radar, but then Em and Ryan got engaged, and that sort of propelled us into having conversations about the future. It seemed like the kid topic needed to be discussed."

Truthfully, I may have underplayed my interest in matrimony when we first started dating, just as any sensible woman would, but I'd never been less than forthright about my interest in children. "It was easier not to think about it when we were traveling because at least then we were *doing* something, but I didn't quit my job and leave my family behind so I could sit in Sacramento to be his girlfriend and be treated shitty by his friends."

"His friends treated you shitty?"

"Kind of. Sort of. I think they didn't know what to make of me, which is exactly what Emily said would happen. The men assumed I was dumb and only good for sex, and the women thought I was opportunistic. The only person I got to be friends with was Tag's daughter-in-law, Trish. She was okay. Maybe because we're the same age."

That earned another nod from my sister, along with a *well, whadda ya gonna do* expression on her face. "Still no good advice for you. I wish I had some, but maybe a little time apart will help you clear your head and figure out what's most important. And you probably ought to tell Emily before Ryan does."

"I know. I didn't want to dump it on her my first day back, especially with her in her wedding dress puking into the sink. That was something, by the way. Thanks for the warning." I shook my head to dispel the vision. "Anyway, Tag agreed to not say anything to anybody until I'd talked to her. And just so you know, we are both committed that, no matter what, we will not make the wedding stuff awkward. We're adults. We can be mature."

Brooke straightened some papers on her desk. "Well, that's more than I can say for most of the people who'll be there. Emily still has the same raggedy work crew she had last summer, and I'm sure they're all invited."

Emily was a house-flipper turned cottage-remodeler and was working her way through all of Gigi's rental properties with the help of an assortment of local mutants, but not cool X-Men-style mutants with helpful superpowers like drills for hands or laser-beam eyes that could cut drywall in a jiffy, but rather the kind of mutants with X-rated taste in websites, clumsy social manners that sometimes landed them in hot water, and questionable decision-making skills that sometimes landed them in jail.

"Sounds like it'll be a fun reception," I said. "Where's she working today? Maybe I should go tell her next and just get it over with."

"I would if I were you," Brooke responded. "You know how secrets around here have a way of growing exponentially."

"But so far you're the only one I've told," I said.

"Exactly, and you know I can't hide anything. Please don't leave this burden on my shoulders. I've got enough on my mind already."

"Such as?" I prompted. "Everything okay with Leo?"

Her insta-blush was the only answer I needed. "Everything with Leo is good. No issues there. I'm just busy with work stuff. You know, being the mayor and all." She lifted her arms and gestured around the room as if a multitude of tasks were floating in the air above her head. "And with the movie people coming, it's just one more thing to deal with."

"The movie people?" How had I not heard about movie people?

"Didn't I tell you? We have a production crew showing up next week. They're filming some kind of ghost story, or love story, or ghosts in love or something like that. I can't remember. Anyway, they'll be doing some stuff at the Imperial, on Main Street, and maybe over near Potter's Pointe, too. The location details are still being worked out."

"Wow," I said slowly. "Nice job, Madam Mayor. That's quite an achievement for your first year in office."

Brooke laughed. "I'd love to take credit for attracting them here, but I think we just got lucky."

"Well, regardless, I assume this means a nice influx of cash for the locals, right?"

"Absolutely. Between the cast and crew, they've got one whole floor of the Imperial Hotel filled up, along with rooms at a few other hotels, plus half the rental cottages, including Gigi's. Not sure who is staying where because some of them are using fake names, but one of the movie guys talked to the chief about extra security, so I'm guessing these people might be some very VIP VIPs."

The chief she was referring to was none other than our very own father, Chief of Police Harlan Callaghan. He'd held the job for almost thirty years and led a crew of six officers, with Brooke's boyfriend, Leo Walker, being the newest. She'd recently admitted to me she got a kick out of the fact that our father was her boyfriend's boss. This island pretty much ran on nepotism.

"Fun stuff," I said. "I wonder who'll show up. Maybe it'll be one of our sexlebrities."

She squinted at me. "What's a sexlebrity?"

"You know, a celebrity you'd have sex with if ever given the opportunity. No strings attached and your significant other can't get mad at you. Like, if Idris Elba showed up right this minute, you could rip off all your clothes and do it right here on this sturdy desk, and no one could judge you for it." I patted the mahogany surface with gusto, just to tease her, because this was so not her thing.

She stared at her desk for a moment, as if trying to figure out how to have sex on top of it without messing up any of her papers. Then she remembered herself and gave a shake of her head.

"Uh, first of all, I don't know who Idris Elba is. Second, I don't have that kind of list. And third, if Leo's got one, he'll just have to forgo acting on it in the event that his fantasy dream girl shows up. No hall passes for him." Brooke was so practical even her fantasies had rules.

"If you knew who Idris Elba was, you might change your tune, but anyway, who is Leo's fantasy dream girl?"

She frowned. "I don't know. Our conversations veer toward topics other than who he'd rather be sleeping with, but anyway, they're having a cattle call for extras, you know. Maybe you can work your way onto the set and find your own fantasy hookup."

"There's a cattle call? When?"

"Late next week at the Imperial. Or maybe the week after that. I'm not sure, but according to Dmitri, they need people for some street scenes and some other stuff. Then again, I got this from Dmitri, so who really knows?"

In a community full of genuine eccentrics, Dmitri Krushnic was one of our more exotic of the species, an individual prone to wearing a beekeeping hat as a fashion statement and known for his complete inability to maintain a confidence. It was often said that the best way to get news around the island was to whisper it to Dmitri and tell him it was a *secret*. The only drawback being that he was also known for hyperbole and, in some cases, outright misinformation and fabrication. I'd paid him twenty bucks last summer to keep my relationship with Tag a secret, and that had bought me exactly fifteen minutes of silence.

"I saw him on my way here," I said. "He gave me some song-and-dance number about you guys having had a jewel thief hiding out on the island while I was gone. What's that about?"

Brooke's smile was enigmatic as she shook her head. "Oh, you know Dmitri. You can't believe a word that guy says."

"True, but the cattle call is a real thing, right?"

"Yep. Just know you'll be up against about ninety-eight percent of our population. So far I haven't talked to anyone who isn't hoping to get a spot."

"Even you?"

"Except for me. Someone has to run the town while everyone else is playing dress-up."

Chapter 3

I texted Emily from Brooke's office, inviting her to meet me at Joe's Cuppa Joe Coffee Shop on Main Street, and had a vanilla latte waiting for her when she arrived.

"I got you a decaf," I said as she joined me at a table in a sunny spot near the floor-to-ceiling windows. Last night's winter storm had passed, and today the sun was shining brightly, working hard to melt away the remnants. Spring was late but it was on its way.

"Decaf?" she asked, shedding a periwinkle-colored scarf from around her neck that perfectly complemented her complexion. Brooke and I were both brown-eyed brunettes, so Emily was the outlier in our family. The random redhead who'd been nicknamed Peach as an infant because of her full baby cheeks and fuzzy orange hair. Legend had it that Brooke arrived with a full set of dark curls and a stoic disposition. No one ever really talked about me as a baby per se, but throughout childhood I'd often heard myself referred to as *the pretty one*, which was ridiculous because both of my sisters were pretty, too, and I'd grown up wishing that just once someone would say I was *the smart one*, but everybody knew that was Brooke.

"Yeah, decaf because of the . . . you know." I discreetly pointed at my abdomen, and she chuckled.

"Ah, yes. That. I usually drink herbal tea these days anyway, but coffee sounds good, even if it is decaf."

My sister was typically a *give me java intravenously* kind of person. I guess that baby was already changing her life. "When did you start drinking herbal tea?"

"Matt has us all drinking it. I resisted for a while, but I confess I haven't had a headache since I gave up caffeine a few months ago."

"Matt?" I took a sip from my cup and was grateful that I had not, in fact, switched to herbal tea. My sleepless night was catching up to me, and I was exhausted. I needed every jolt I could get from this coffee.

"Yeah, you remember Matt. The guy on my crew who teaches yoga? The one Dad always calls Yoga Matt?"

Oh, that guy. I definitely remembered him. Matt Eastman had moved to the island last spring and joined my sister's construction crew just a few months before I'd left town. He was very appealing in a man-bunned, granola-sexual kind of way. In fact, my sister had even tried to use him as bait to lure me into forgetting all about Tag, but I wasn't going to remind her of that until I'd had a chance to fill her in on the latest details. Instead, I let out a chuckle, and the foam in my cup rippled.

"Oh, that guy. Sure. I remember him. Is he still hot?"

"Smoldering. Too bad you're taken."

"Well . . ." I paused, and my sister slowly set down her cup.

Her eyes locked with mine. "Well . . . what?"

It was dumb to be so nervous, but I wasn't just talking to my sister about *my* boyfriend. I was talking to her about *her* future father-in-law. Fortunately, as my story tumbled out, I spared no detail, yet Emily seemed neither surprised nor disappointed. Only sympathetic.

"Honestly, hon," she said, giving me a gentle smile and a pat on the wrist, "you guys lasted way longer than anyone thought you would. I'm not trying to be mean or anything, but the age difference was pretty substantial. Plus, Ryan says his dad is a total workaholic and very much used to being the boss. I've kind of been expecting this, but I'm proud of you for standing your ground and coming home when things started to go south."

"You are?" Another gentle *I told you so*. My sisters were being very nice and not at all judgy about this. Not that they were prone to judginess, but the drawback of being the baby of the family, as well as having all those substitute mothers cluck-cluck-clucking over me all my life, was that I felt like my recent choices had somehow let them all down. Maybe my ego was at play in there somewhere, too, because I'd been so adamant that I knew what I was doing, but I'd been duped by my own foolish heart. "I still feel kind of stupid, though. I was so sure we could make it work. True love defying the odds and all that. It seemed so romantic, but it was just a mirage."

Emily's smile was patient. "Look at it this way. It did work, for a bit. You had fun together and took some great trips, right? Just because what you had didn't last forever doesn't mean the stuff you shared has less value. And if he's not able to meet you halfway so you both get at least some of what you need, then that's not fair to you."

"I suppose."

She stared at me for a long minute before saying, "Can I be really, seriously honest with you?"

That was a scary question. "Um, okay."

"I'm relieved that you're taking a break, and for what it's worth, I think you should make the break permanent. You deserve better from a man. I mean, sure, he's rich and good-looking, but the more and more I've heard from Ryan about his dad, and what his parents' marriage was like, I think you would've been miserable if you'd stayed. His dad completely neglected his mom, and it sounds like he's starting to do the same to you. Old dogs don't learn new tricks, you know? And he is an old dog."

She couldn't resist getting one age-related jab in there, but I guess I had that one coming. I almost felt the urge to defend him, but my sister's words hit close to home. I had felt neglected, and when I'd tried to point that out to him, Tag had said I was being *childish*. That was the last fight we ever had, because I booked my plane ticket home the very next day.

"So," she said, placing both hands on the table, "the good news is, Gigi's place might not be as cool as some palace in Tibet or bungalow in Bali or wherever the hell you've been lately, but it does have something that none of those other places have."

"What's that?"

"Me. And Chloe. Since you're staying at Gigi's, we'll have lots of time to visit before she and I move out."

Emily and Chloe had been living at Gigi's house since last summer, but after the wedding, they'd be moving into the back portion of a bed-and-breakfast they'd bought and were renovating. They'd named it the Peach Tree Inn.

"You *are* going to stay at Gigi's, aren't you?" she asked.

"I'm not sure what I'm going to do. I know I have to find a place to live, and I have to find a job. I'm hoping she'll let me hang around, at least until I can afford a place of my own."

"You know she will. She'd love to have you. Or you could move in with Dad."

"Oh gosh. Let's hope it doesn't come to that." I loved my dad, but he was so set in his ways, a tornado riding wild horses couldn't make him budge. "I would just cramp his style."

"Maybe, but he'll be ecstatic when he finds out you're home for good, not that he'd ever admit it. I'm sure you can imagine he was no fan of Tag's." She picked up her coffee cup and leaned back in the chair. "As for work, what are you thinking?"

"Not sure. I plan to call Mary Lou Baxter to see if I can get my old job back at the preschool for next fall, but in the meantime, I'm open to suggestions. Got any?"

"I heard they're hiring guides for the nighttime ghost tours."

"Wow, I can't imagine anything I'd enjoy less than walking around at dusk when the midges are swarming and telling tourists a bunch of stories about ghosts that don't exist."

I didn't believe in ghosts. I'd wanted to for a long time because I figured if my mom was out there somewhere in the ether, it might be nice for her to send me some little sign, just to check in once in a while. Like maybe leave a penny in my path with her birth year on it or have a butterfly land on my shoulder or something. She never did, though. And any rattling doors or knocks from the attic were pretty easily explained away. When you spend most of your life in buildings that are 150 years old, there's some serious creaking and thudding and whistling and moaning going on. Wind in the eaves. Moisture making wood shrink or expand. Birds, bats, squirrels in the rafters. Just that. No ghosts.

"Really? I think the ghost tour might be kind of fun," Emily said. "And certainly not worse than working at Judge's and having to smell them making fudge all day. Or being a salesclerk in one of Sudsy Robertson's T-shirt shops. Worse yet, how about working with Old Vic and being a street cleaner?"

"Ah, agreed on all counts. I guess ghost-tour guide would be the fourth-worst job on the island. I think street sweeper might be at the top of the bottom-worst jobs, but hopefully I can find something that doesn't involve fudge, tourists, ghosts, or horse shit."

One of the more unique and charming aspects of Wenniway Island, aside from an overabundance of Victorian architecture and candy shops on every corner, was our complete and total absence of cars. Back in 1889 they'd been dubbed *noisy, stinking machines* by the town council and banned, and no one had ever tried to change that. We Wenniwagians got around on foot, by bicycle, or by horse-drawn carriage. I'd spent my entire life waking up to the soothing, rhythmic sound of harnesses jangling and the soft clap of horses' hooves on the pavement, another thing I'd missed while away from home, but the profusion of ponies also meant a profusion of poo. Old Vic and his street-sweeping team had their work cut out for them each and every day.

"Well, maybe if none of those jobs appeal to you, you could join my work crew," Emily said with a coy smile. "The pay sucks and the hours are terrible, but at least there's no benefits."

"Way to sell it."

"I support truth in advertising, but the real truth is . . . I could use an extra set of hands right now. Ryan is occupied with our remodel at the Peach Tree, and I need someone I can trust to help me organize things and keep projects on track. With all the wedding stuff coming up and the you-know-what giving me the queasies all the time"—she mimicked my earlier gesture of pointing at her belly—"I'm having a little trouble keeping up with things. I could use a personal assistant for a couple of weeks. Can you hang wallpaper?"

"Maybe. Probably. The sticky side goes against the wall, right?"

Emily chuckled. "You're hired."

"Seriously?"

Her eyes widened in surprise, and her cup went *clack* against the table. "Are *you* serious? Would you really come and work for me? I'd love that."

See? Nepotism. It was so rampant that working with family was practically an obligation. I was handy enough with a hammer and nails, I was organized to a fault, and Emily and I had always gotten along well. She'd be an okay boss, and maybe, hopefully, keeping busy would prevent me from self-medicating with copious carbs and fretting endlessly about the fact that I currently had no plans, prospects, or purpose, either personal or professional. I literally had nothing going on in my life. Maybe this was just what I needed, and I could kid myself into believing I was doing a favor for her, instead of the other way around.

"Tell you what," I said. "Since I'm technically homeless with an income of zero and have nothing but time and heartbreak on my hands, I can't be that choosy. If you need an assistant, I'm all yours. It'll be fun, but I should warn you, I'm going to audition for the movie coming to town, and if they cast me as an extra, I will blow you off without a moment's notice."

"I think the same could be said for my entire crew," Emily said with a smile. "They all want to be in this movie. So, when can you start?"

"Um. How about now? I do have one request, though."

"Sure. What's that?"

"Can you please fill Ryan in on our conversation? I don't feel like going over it again, and I don't want him thinking mean thoughts about me for potentially breaking his father's heart."

She nodded emphatically. "Absolutely. I've got you covered. And I promise he'll be neither surprised nor offended. Now, coffee break is over. Let's get to work."

Chapter 4

Main Street on Wenniway Island was like a picture-perfect postcard from a bygone era. All the shops and restaurants had Victorian charm, with lots of scalloped shingles, pastel colors, and vintage signage. There was an old-time photography studio and shops that looked like old fur-trading posts. The brilliant turquoise library was at one end, with Trillium Pointe off to the side, and at the other end of the street was an expansive lawn that led up to Fort Beaumont. Basically, if you stood in the center and looked in any direction, there was something beautiful to see—the marina full of graceful sailboats and luxury cabin cruisers, the five-mile-long Petoskey Bridge, the elegant white steeple of Saint Bartholomew's Church, and, in the spring and summer, lilacs everywhere. The scent was even more delicious than the ever-present aroma of fudge.

Yes, it was beautiful, but today, walking down the wooden-planked sidewalks with my sister was no quick trek. Word had spread I was home for a visit, so I had some stops to make. I popped into the post office to say hello to our beloved postmaster, Shari, then moved on to O'Doul's grocery store so Emily could buy saltines, since Baby Taggert was threatening to upset her stomach again. I said a quick hello to a handful of others, but we avoided Link & Patty's Breakfast Buffet, since the cantankerous old Mahoney sisters were there. April, May, and June were a fearsome threesome I was not ready to encounter. Now or ever.

On down the street, past the boat dock, where I greeted no less than a dozen old friends and neighbors who'd gathered around to watch as the horses were led from a ferry. It was always a cause for celebration when our four-legged workers returned to the island for the summer after spending their winter relaxing in Manitou. They were shaggy and round, their hooves all needing attention, but it signaled the reawakening of the island as everyone prepared for the onslaught of summer tourist season.

Since our only export was fudge, the community relied heavily on visitors to keep our economy afloat. They'd buy candy and sweatshirts and tacky souvenirs like snow globes with a tiny Fort Beaumont inside. They'd rent bikes to ride the eight-mile circumference of the island, or maybe get a pony from Colette's Riding Stable and try their skills at being a vacation equestrian. They'd comment on the lovely view of Petoskey Bridge or mention the pervasive scent of lilacs in the air. And inevitably, they'd speculate about what it might be like to live in such a place all year round. They often acted as if we were aliens living on a different planet, or as if Wenniway Island were some kind of amusement park and we were just characters wandering around for their enjoyment, but we were used to that.

I spotted Percy O'Keefe, who waved and shouted a greeting before disappearing beside a gray, speckled mare. Percy was my first kiss. My first and worst. In fairness to him, he hadn't seen it coming. I'd planted one on him when he'd least expected, and mostly what I remember is the look of surprise in his eyes right before my mouth landed half on his lips and half off to the corner. He'd tasted like salt and red licorice and smelled like a barn. From the looks of things, he probably still smelled like a barn, but I had no interest in finding out how he tasted these days. Some people thought Percy hadn't lived up to his full potential . . . but I was pretty sure he had.

"There's Dad," Emily said, pointing toward a cluster of three men, two of whom he towered over, although he wasn't particularly tall. The chief, in his light brown police uniform, had a good six inches over Judge Murphy and Father O'Reilly, both of whom boasted almost as much width as they did height. The three men had grown up on the island, raised their own share of hell, and then settled down nicely to become pillars of our community.

"There she is!" Judge Murphy greeted me with ruddy-faced enthusiasm, all but pinching my cheek but opting to pat my shoulder at the last minute. "Welcome home."

"Thanks, Judge. It's nice to be back," I responded with a smile.

"Hello, Lilly," Father O'Reilly added with a beatific nod. "Nice to have you with us for a bit. Hope to see you on Sunday."

Always the salesman. I hadn't been to a church service since leaving the island last fall—not that I had anything against going. It just wasn't something Tag and I had made a part of our routine, but it might be nice to settle into the pew at Saint Bartholomew's and confess a few sins, get a little absolution. Maybe a little time in church and some divine intervention would help me figure out what I was supposed to do with this next period of my life.

"Hi, Daddy," I said next, leaning in and giving the chief a big, squeezy hug. I was the only one who ever called our father "Daddy," and for the most part, I was the only one who ever gave him big, squeezy hugs. Brooke just wasn't demonstrative that way, and he and Emily had too much baggage between the two of them to show much physical affection, but he and I had a groove. We'd lived together the longest, because after Emily had run away and Brooke was already living on her own, it was just the two of us. We'd spent a lot of evenings playing backgammon or watching *Everybody Loves Raymond* and *Frasier*, probably because my dad could relate to those TV dads, all grumpy and gruff and surrounded by flakes.

"Hello there," he said, returning my squeeze. "Are we still on for dinner tonight?"

"Yes, absolutely. Six o'clock at Brooke's house. Can't chat with you fellas right now, though. We're on the way to Em's work site."

I would've stuck around and spoken with my father a bit longer, but Emily was tugging on my jacket. She looked a little green around the gills, and it was a truth universally acknowledged that it's bad form, and probably bad luck, to reveal your out-of-wedlock pregnancy by hurling all over the shoes of a priest. We made it around the corner of the library just in time for her to return that latte into a lilac bush.

"This is getting very old, very fast," she said as I handed her a tissue and started digging around in my purse for a mint.

"You need ginger, girlfriend," said a familiar voice, startling us both.

We turned to see our friend Gloria Persimmons-Kloosterman lumbering toward us like a gal on a mission. Her white-blonde hair was teased and poufed and immobilized by the unseen force of some powerful hairspray. She wore a lavender wool coat that barely contained her because, like my sister, she was pregnant. Only Gloria wasn't just a little pregnant. She was hugely pregnant. Her belly was like a striped jersey-knit-covered freighter bearing down on us at full speed. She reached Emily's side and produced a bottle from her green-and-white polka-dotted bag, tipping it into her palm and procuring a beige capsule. "Here. Take this. In fact, take the whole bottle, because I haven't had morning sickness in months."

"Oh, I don't have morning sickness," Emily responded wanly. "I think I just ate some bad shrimp last night."

"Buh-and-may-I-say-loney, Peachy-keen. Your secret is safe with me, but I know morning sickness when I see it."

Emily sighed and leaned against the side of the building. "It's totally a secret right now, Glo. No one knows."

Well . . . no one except for me. And Brooke. And Gigi. And Chloe. And Ryan. And now Gloria. And if Emily came to dinner at Brooke's tonight, Harlan and Leo were bound to figure it out. This was exactly why trying to keep secrets on this island was so pointless. My sister may as well just take out an advertisement in the *Island Gazette*.

"In that case, let me be the first to say congratulations!" Gloria's smile was wide, accentuated by frosty plum lipstick. She pulled a bottle of water from her bag and handed that to Emily, too. "I think it's only fair that I be in the loop since you did get engaged at *my* wedding reception. We're practically sisters, right? And speaking of sisters, hello there, Lilly-vanilli." She grabbed me for an effusive hug. "I heard you were back on the rock for a visit. I can't drink alcohol, of course, but I'm still hosting Drunk Puzzle Night soon. Marnie and Eva will be there, so you sure better come by and tell us all about your amazing trips! How are things with old Mr. Hottie McRichGuy?"

Emily twisted open the water bottle and looked at the capsule in her hand. "What's this stuff? Tell me how this works."

Emily probably knew the answer but was trying to deflect Gloria's attention so I wouldn't have to get into the details about Tag.

Again. Secrets. Little point in trying to keep them, but it seemed like Ryan should find out from me or his father, and not from Tiny Kloosterman's wife or Brooke's assistant, Gertie, or Shari at the post office, who was very astute and probably also guessed that my sister had a teensy little bun in her oven and may have somehow discerned that I'd broken up with my boyfriend.

"It's ginger powder and it'll settle your stomach. You can also eat regular fresh ginger, but I don't have any of that in my bag because that would just be silly. Oh, wait, I do have this, though." Gloria pulled out a bottle about the size of a lipstick tube and took off the top before abruptly grabbing Emily's hand and pulling it toward her. She rolled the tip against my sister's wrist.

"There. Smell that. It'll help, too. It's Earth Harmony essential oils. I'm selling them now, so if you want to buy some, you'd better get them from me and not from Xavier Price. Just because he started selling them first, it doesn't mean you shouldn't buy them from me, right? Practically sisters, remember? Plus, you know how much Tiny earns working for you." She arched a heavily penciled brow to indicate that whatever my sister paid him, it clearly wasn't enough.

Tiny Kloosterman was Emily's foreman. He was six foot six and three hundred pounds of good intentions and poor execution, but everyone loved him.

Emily sniffed her wrist. "That smells nice. What is it?"

"A proprietary blend that I'll reveal to you should you make the wise decision to become an Earth Harmony representative. You too, Lilly-vanilli. You could start a kick-ass team in Sacramento and make hundreds of dollars a month. I'm working my way up the corporate ladder. I just need four more sales pioneers for my power posse to become a tier-three diamond-plus district manager. I'm hoping to win a trip to Tahiti."

She said that last part in a whisper, as if Xavier Price might be lurking around the next corner waiting to snatch away her new recruits, but in no way was I interested in joining some multilevel marketing scheme, especially on an island of just six hundred people, because inevitably, we'd all have to take turns buying from each other, just as we had when Flickering Nights Candles had hit Wenniway. Or Pretty Woman cosmetics, or Eco-Ware Storage Solutions.

I had more of that stuff than I could use in a lifetime, and I'd officially disavowed any future involvement with home sales companies after attending a Wild Hearts Lingerie party and watching Vera VonMeisterburger, our oversexed spinster librarian, model a sheer, fur-trimmed ensemble that allegedly came with crotchless panties.

"Here's how you put the dewy in his Dewey decimal system," she'd said, and then went "Rarrrrr" along with making some clawlike hand motions that were probably supposed to represent . . . a cougar? Regardless, I hadn't been back to the library since.

"Tahiti?" I said to Gloria. "That sounds awesome, and may I say you are glowing, Glo. You look amazing. When's the baby due?"

She patted her round, protuberant belly with both thick hands. "That's not glowing. I'm sweating. This baby makes me run at about 150 degrees. I'm ready for him to vacate the facility, but I'm not due for another two months."

Seriously? If that baby had much more growing to do, Gloria wasn't going to fit through the doors of the hospital. She was what you might call big boned, and since Tiny was roughly the size of a toolshed, that baby was going to come out looking like a twenty-pound turkey.

"Well, either glowing or sweating, I think you look beautiful, and I'm so happy for you guys." In truth, Gloria never really looked beautiful exactly. Her teeth were a bit on the toothy side, and her fashion choices were less Dolce & Gabbana and more Barnum & Bailey, but today she looked cute and she certainly looked happy, with flushed cheeks and rhinestone-encrusted glasses.

"So how have you been feeling overall? I mean, aside from the sweating?" I asked.

"Better than this one," she said, gesturing toward my sister, who was once again bent in half, taking slow, deep breaths with her hands resting on her knees. "After I got through the first couple of weeks, I felt fine. And married life? Sweet heavenly baby Jesus, it's good! I could not have found a better husband than Tiny. He treats me like a goddess. As soon as I get home, he makes me sit down and gets a pillow for me to rest my tootsies on, and then he gives me a foot massage. It's adorable. I can't wait to see him being a father. There's just nothing sexier than watching a man change a diaper."

I could think of several things that might be sexier than that, but I knew what she meant, and it snapped against my heart like a rubber band because I knew for a fact that Tag didn't do diapers. We'd been babysitting his grandsons a few months ago, and when the baby started fussing, he'd handed him to me and suggested that maybe he needed changing. I was so happy to get my hands on an infant that I'd done it without thinking, but now I realized he was just avoiding it for himself.

And I couldn't for the life of me imagine him getting me a pillow for my feet. He might give me a gift certificate for a luxury day at a spa, but he wouldn't rub my feet. He didn't like feet.

"I'm so glad to hear it's going well," I said. "That's wonderful. I think maybe I need to get Emily home, though. We'll catch up more later."

From the corner of my eye, I could see my sister nodding her agreement.

"Do you need any help?" Gloria asked.

Emily's nod changed to a shake of the head. "I think I'll be fine in a minute, Gloria. Thanks so much for the ginger. And don't forget, we're not telling people yet."

"I totes understand, girlfriend. Your secret baby is safe with me. I'll just be on my way then. I'll draw attention in that direction so no one spots you over here hurling in the shrubberies."

Since Gloria created a wake of attention all the time, that shouldn't be a problem. Meanwhile, Emily and I made our way past the library, onto Marquette Street, and then turned on Cahill. As we walked, Emily seemed to regain the pep in her step.

"I'll be damned. That ginger worked. Or the oils worked. Either way, I do feel better. Hopefully it'll last long enough to show you the plans for our current project. It's that one, right there." She pointed to the left.

For the most part, the homes of Trillium Bay came in three styles. First, there were the elaborate, ornate, three-story dwellings full of Victorian details like fretwork and corbels and scalloped siding that rich lumber barons and industry tycoons of the mid-1800s had built as their summer *cottages*. Then there were the places like Gigi's, two-story middle-class homes constructed around the turn of the century that still had some Victorian flair but were far more modest and boasted smaller front porches. Last—and least—were the bungalows, most of which were clustered in the center of the island north of Main Street, close to the tiny airport and out of sight from the tourists.

Like the one before us, most of the bungalows were unimpressive and nondescript, with space-efficient floor plans that included little more than a basic kitchen, a family room, two or three bedrooms, and a single bathroom. They were typically owned by long-term residents of the island, but over the past few years, more and more had been purchased and turned into long-term rentals for island workers.

"Isn't this Frannie Houlihan's house?" I asked as we stopped in front of the particularly sad little dwelling.

"It was. She moved to Florida last winter to be closer to her grand-kids, and Gigi bought it not too long ago."

We walked past a dray wagon full of construction debris and into the dim interior. Once inside, a cacophony of "Hi," "Hello," "Hiya, boss lady," rang out, echoing and bouncing around in the nearly empty room. There was Tiny Kloosterman working in a green shirt with the sleeves torn off in spite of the cool day outside, his thick tattoo-covered arms flexing as he picked up buckets full of drywall scraps. I spotted rough-and-tumble Georgie Reynolds in her overalls and a dingy blue sweatshirt working on the floor next to her scruffy, scrawny, perpetually sniffling brother, Garth. Though they were twins, she'd gotten the looks, the brains, and the personality, leaving him nothing but the Reynolds overbite and some male-pattern baldness. Horsey Davidson was in the kitchen area pulling nails from a piece of molding.

And then, there in the center of the room, standing on an over-turned barrel like it was his pedestal, was the infamous Yoga Matt. He had on old Levi's and a faded red chambray shirt. With his arms stretched upward, the hem lifted, and I caught a momentary glimpse of the smooth skin of his muscular abdomen before he lowered his hands from the light fixture on the ceiling and smiled down at me like Helios driving his chariot across the sky. Yes, he was Greek-god kind of hot—if Greek gods wore faded jeans and scuffed-up work boots.

"Hey, gang," Emily said. "Everybody knows Lilly, right? I've drafted her into lending us an extra set of hands for a couple of weeks."

There were nods and smiles and more hellos. Matt hopped down from his perch and, lightly touching his fingertips together, offered a little head bow.

"Welcome home, Lilly." His expression was warm, the gaze of his sapphire-blue eyes clinging to me for an instant, and I wondered if he realized how handsome he was. It was jarring, especially in this dim, dilapidated environment. And double especially because my sister hadn't warned me that he'd cut his dark hair. Last summer he'd worn it long, making it easy for me to write him off as a bit too free spirited for my taste. Now his hair was short on the sides but long enough on the top to have some waves. A girl could drown in those waves if she wasn't careful.

Then he winked at me, and I was reminded that Matt was the playful sort. The kind of guy who might steal your heart for an evening but who had no intention of trying to keep it.

Chapter 5

With my family gathered around the oval-shaped dining table at Brooke's house that evening, it took exactly thirteen and a half minutes before my dad turned to Emily and said, "Peach, is there something you'd like to tell me?"

There'd been no preamble or segue; in fact we'd mostly just sat down and begun commenting on how the baked whitefish and green beans looked delicious. I was on one side of the table, in between Gigi and Chloe, while Leo, Emily, and Ryan sat across from us. Brooke was at one end, with the chief at the other, and instead of saying grace, he basically kicked off the evening with, "Pass the salt—is there something you want to tell me?" That's just how we Callaghans rolled. Sometimes it was kind of brutal, but it saved us a lot of time in the long run.

At Harlan's words, my sister looked momentarily abashed, and I could see the mental cogs and gizmos rotating in her brain as she tried to formulate an answer, but after a brief pause, she simply said, "Who got to you first? Was it Gloria? I knew I couldn't trust her."

But the chief shook his head, his expression as enigmatic as usual. There was a minuscule pause as everyone looked at one another, and then Chloe slowly raised her hand, her smile sheepish.

"Sorry, Mom. I'm afraid I let the cat out of the bag about the bun in the oven. Grandpa asked which room would be mine when we moved to the Peach Tree Inn, and I said probably the one in the back because the front room was for the baby. And then he said, 'What baby?'"

Harlan's shake of the head transitioned to an agreeable nod. "I did say that."

"Well, there you have it," Gigi added, tossing up her hands and letting her napkin fly. "Who could possibly withstand that sort of interrogation?"

"Right?" Chloe demanded. "Grandpa's a cop. I had to tell the truth."

And that was that. The conversation proceeded, with lots of excited talk about babies, and weddings, and rental renovations, until at last, as the meal was nearing its end and we'd polished off virtually everything Brooke had served, including blueberry cobbler, the topic of *me* finally arrived. I'd known this was coming, of course, so when my dad asked how things were going with Tag, and how long my visit might last, I took a page from Chloe's book and confessed everything.

"Tag and I broke up, and I'm home for good."

A quick glance at Ryan assured me he'd been filled in by Emily and was fine with this turn of events, and the slow smile on my father's face told me everything I needed to know about his opinion on the matter as well. No surprises tonight. Not really. And in roughly thirteen and a half seconds, it was determined by unanimous decision that I'd stay with my grandmother until I could afford my own place.

"Of course you'll stay with me," Gigi said, as if any other option would simply be an insult to her. "You stored your stuff in my attic when you left last summer, so you're halfway moved in already. Plus, it's good timing. I don't usually have my cottages rented out this early in the season, but with the movie people coming, I have a full roster, and since Geena went and had a hysterectomy, I could sure use your help."

Gigi turned to Brooke and muttered, "Now, why she couldn't have gotten her plumbing fixed in the winter and be properly recovered by the time I needed her, I don't know. But there it is." She turned back to me. "So, can I count on you, Lilly? To lend a hand with my rentals?"

I could hardly say no. It was a small price to pay for indefinite free room and board. I rose from my chair and started clearing away the dirty dishes. "Of course, Gigi. I'd be glad to help."

"Don't forget you're also helping me," Emily added, handing me her plate. "I call first dibs because I hired you this morning."

"You did?" Gigi and Ryan said at the same time.

"Yes, because this spawn keeps making me nauseous," she said, resting a hand on her still-flat abdomen. "And we have a bed-and-breakfast to finish, the nursery to decorate, the Cahill place to completely remodel, and wedding plans to finalize."

Ryan nodded. "Oh yeah. All of that. Maybe I should get more help, too." He stared pointedly at Leo.

Brooke's boyfriend chuckled. "If the chief can spare me, I'm happy to lend a hand. And I'll work for beer."

"I can help with stuff, too," Chloe added. "But you'll have to pay me in cash because of child labor laws."

"Or I could pay you with cookies and your allowance," Emily responded.

"Orrrr . . . ," Chloe volleyed back, "you could reward me by letting me be an extra in the movie. Susie Mahoney found out from Mike Tupper that they're looking for some kids to be in it, too. Just, like, hanging out in the background and stuff."

"You're still in school."

"I know, but this is a once-in-a-lifetime chance, and they haven't even started filming yet. Maybe they won't need us until after school gets out in June." Chloe clasped her hands in front of her, her expression pleading.

"I'll think about it," Emily said.

"Well, I'm certainly going to audition," Gigi said. "This could be my big break. I've always wanted to be discovered."

⁓

"You seem pretty well organized," I said to Emily after we'd spent the next morning together in Gigi's kitchen going over all the various projects my sister was working on. Like me, she was a list-maker. She had a binder for each remodeling location with subfolders for all the different areas needing attention. She had a binder for the wedding, too, and even a separate folder labeled CHLOE'S BEDROOM, which was full of decorating ideas provided by my niece, including a hammock chair suspended from the ceiling, a huge four-poster bed, and faux-furry everything.

"I am organized," Emily said, popping a ginger capsule into her mouth, "but unfortunately being organized only gets you so far if you have more work than time. Some of these tasks are only ten-minute jobs, but there's about a million of them. And then there's the stuff that's easy but time consuming."

"Such as?"

"Such as this. Do you see this knob?" Emily asked, producing a vintage drawer pull from her pocket and waving it obnoxiously close to my face.

"I do see it. You're practically hitting me in the nose with it."

"Okay, well, there are eleven more just like it at Perkins Antiques in Michlimac City, and I need them, but the owner only deals in cash. He's willing to hold on to them for a couple of days, but I have to go pick them up, and by the time I take the ferry there and back, it's a whole afternoon."

"How about I go and get them for you?"

Her smile was instant, her relief palpable. "Would you? That would be wonderful. The last thing I want to do right now is get on the ferry."

"Hey, I'm your assistant. You get to decide what I do, right?"

"Sure, but I hope it's stuff you at least sort of enjoy."

"I don't mind going over to Michlimac. In fact, there's actually a couple things I need to pick up for myself anyway."

"Awesome, and if that's the case, how about getting me this stuff, too?" She pulled a list—suspiciously at the ready—from her other pocket. I may have just been set up. I looked it over. It was expansive and included both business and non-business items. Apparently, I wasn't so much a member of Emily's work crew as I was her personal assistant.

"This is a pretty big list, Peach. I'm not sure I can haul everything back over here by myself. Rolls of wallpaper and paste may be hard to carry."

"Hmm. I guess I could send someone with you. Maybe Matt?"

This sounded just as premeditated as the shopping excursion. "Don't you have other stuff he's more useful for? Or are you trying to play matchmaker again? You've tried that once already. Remember?"

Emily's laugh rang of sincerity. "No, I'm not trying to set you up with Matt. My matchmaking days are over. He's just the best person to send to the hardware store, because every time I send someone else, they come back with all the wrong stuff. And I can't very well ask him to get me the other items on the list—not that he wouldn't be willing to buy me hemorrhoid cream. I'd just rather not cross that boundary unless it's absolutely necessary."

"Understandable." I perused the list one more time and thought about running errands with hot and bendy Yoga Matt. We'd have to go to a dozen different stores, but there were worse ways to spend an afternoon. "Looks like I'm going to have quite an adventure zipping all over Michlimac City. I might have to ask for a raise."

"We'll negotiate that at your first employee review. You're still on double secret probation, but at least you can use the company car."

"There's a company car? You mean Dad's?"

Like many full-time residents of Wenniway Island, the Callaghan family kept a car in a storage facility over on the mainland for occasions such as this. Ours was a pale blue 1976 Chevy Chevette hatchback with 123,000 miles on it that the chief had bought used from Dmitri Krushnic. I'd driven it just enough to be competent, but fortunately there wouldn't be much traffic in the city this time of year. I'd manage.

"No, the Taggert company car. Ryan keeps his truck over there, so you can drive that."

"Um, if I crashed Ryan's truck, I'd feel awful, not to mention being embarrassed. I'll just take the Chevette."

"Suit yourself. Either is fine with me. I'll give you my charge card to pay for all the stuff. Can you leave right now?"

I hadn't exactly dolled up for this meeting with my sister, what with it being in Gigi's kitchen and all. I had no makeup, my hair was in a ponytail, and I was wearing old jeans, Converse tennis shoes, and a Trillium Bay High School sweatshirt that had passed the *throw this out* stage and cycled back around to being *vintage*. But it wasn't as if I needed to get fancy for a trip to Michlimac City, even if Matt was going to be my traveling companion.

"Yeah, I can leave now. Where in the Cahill house are you putting up wallpaper, anyway? It's still in the demo stage."

"This is for the Peach Tree. I want to get Chloe's room all set up as a surprise. There's a lot happening right now, and I don't want her feeling left out, especially with there being a new baby coming."

"I think she's excited. She told me she wants to be a big sister."

"She is, and she does, but it wasn't that long ago that it was just the two of us living in San Antonio, and now we live here, and Ryan is in our lives. Things keep changing. I'm just trying to make sure she doesn't feel like she's getting lost in the shuffle."

"You're a good mom," I said, sliding my chair back from the table.

"Ha! Try telling her that."

C h a p t e r 6

Driving the Chevette proved to be more of a challenge than I'd expected. It was a stick shift, and apparently I'd forgotten how to get from first to second gear. Having Matt sitting quietly and patiently in the passenger seat only added to the pressure, but he never said a word. He didn't fidget or flinch.

"You must think I'm pretty inept," I said after a few noisy, jerky attempts. "I used to be decent enough at this, but it's been a while since I've driven a manual transmission."

His posture was the picture of relaxation, as if riding in a car were supposed to feel like sitting on the hood of a jeep while driving over a pile of boulders. "You're doing fine. Some things take practice, and it's important to find joy in the discovery of learning something new. Or in this case, relearning."

I laughed out loud, although I wasn't sure if he was trying to be clever or just sincere in that earnest, Boy Scout-y way of his. "That must be a yoga philosophy," I said. "Because in my family, the joy is in the *knowing*, not the learning. My dad isn't exactly famous for his patience." Although my father wasn't typically expressive, he had a way of letting you know that you'd let him down or caused him frustration. In fact, maybe that's why he seemingly didn't react—because he was in a near-constant state of mild to moderate frustration with occasional blips of extreme frustration. It was anybody's guess.

"Harlan is definitely a work in progress," Matt replied.

I wondered what he meant by that, but I didn't ask because I was too busy trying not to grind the gears. I finally managed to get the hang of it after we'd driven around the parking lot of the storage facility a few times. Matt offered some gentle coaching, and I had to commend him for his ability to not laugh every time the car burped and stalled. I could never be that Zen, and my frustration was making me sweat. Hopefully he wouldn't notice.

"How about if you drop me off at the hardware store while you fill up the gas tank and then meet me over there," he said. "That way we can divide and conquer this list and save some time."

"That's a good idea, since I just wasted half an hour of our day *enjoying* what a terrible driver I am."

His chuckle was very much the *laughing with you* kind and not the *laughing at you* version, which managed to make me feel a little better about the whole endeavor. Maybe it was all sort of funny, me grinding and stalling and starting and stopping. Maybe. I dropped him off and lurched my way to the Shell station to fill up the tank. At least I remembered how to pump gas.

The sky was gray, with no discernible clouds. Just one big soot-colored layer hiding the sun from the earth, a not-unusual occurrence this time of year, and as I stood next to my little blue Chevette watching the gauge of the gas pump go round and round—because up north we haven't really embraced the whole digital-age thing yet—a shiny black sedan pulled up to the pump next to me. The driver got out. He wore a navy suit and tie and took the time to button his jacket before opening the rear passenger door.

I watched with interest as a young woman eased out gracefully wearing big, dark sunglasses in spite of the overcast skies. She had glossy brunette hair. Her skinny jeans, tucked into knee-high suede boots, were topped with an oversize cream-colored sweater that draped off one slender shoulder, exposing a hot-pink bra strap. She looked markedly out of place at this dingy gas station. She adjusted her glasses, almost as if to adjust her vision because she, too, thought she was simply too glossy for this glum little spot. All that, along with the manner in which she'd effortlessly glided her way from the back of that very nice town car, told me she wasn't from around here. And by *around here* I meant anywhere in the Midwest.

Nudging her glasses back against the bridge of her nose, she let out an exasperated little huff, indicating with a singular breathy syllable, *I'm so bored with all my fabulousness, but one must make do. I am so very brave.*

As the driver shut her door, the other rear door flew open, and a man emerged with far more energy than his ennui-stricken companion. His Ray-Bans were just as dark as hers, and he wore a slouchy gray beanie with a bit of blondish hair escaping from the back. His brown leather jacket was distressed just enough to tell me it was expensive and not actually distressed, and his T-shirt was tucked in only in the front, which I knew from my time in California was called a french tuck and was supposed to look casual but mostly just looked indecisive. Like he was getting dressed but got distracted before he'd finished. Then again, maybe he'd just been fooling around with the brunette in the back seat of that car.

"Good Lord, I can only imagine what the bathroom is going to look like at a grease pit like this. Buckley, do you have any Lysol?" she said.

"My apologies, miss," said the driver. "I don't."

I bit back a giggle at the thought of this drop-dead diva having to plant her fancy ass down on the basic toilet seat at this gas station, but my solidarity with all women came first.

"There's a restaurant right over there," I said, and I pointed to Kandy's Kitchen on the other side of the station. "They'll let you use the bathroom without buying anything, and it's usually pretty clean. And if you're hungry, the food's not bad, either."

The brunette tilted her head down to gaze at me above the rims of her bug-eye glasses, as if she hadn't seen me there and wondered where those words were coming from.

"Food?" the beanie man said, his tone light as he looked toward the restaurant. "Food sounds great. I'm starving. Thanks for the tip." He turned back to me, and his bright white smile was so dazzling it practically came with a trilling sound effect, and my suspicions about this couple doubled. She looked slightly familiar and he looked slightly familiar . . . but behind those dark glasses it was hard to tell. It was probably just my imagination playing tricks on me, but if I didn't know better, I might think I'd just had an encounter with *movie people*. And not just any movie people but undoubtedly the stars. It couldn't be a coincidence that two such beautiful creatures were just a ferry ride away from Wenniway Island. And it couldn't be a coincidence that she bore a striking resemblance to Skylar Tremont, and he had the dimples and jawline of none other than Jayden Pierce. My heart gave a little flutter inside my chest. Jayden Pierce wasn't on my sexlebrity list, but I would certainly be willing to add him to it.

"Do they have anything that's gluten-free?" the woman asked. "Or paleo?" It didn't seem that she was asking me so much as she was just tossing the question out to the Universe and expecting an answer.

"Um . . . that I'm afraid I don't know," I said. I also couldn't anticipate what they'd think about the fact that Kandy of Kandy's Kitchen was actually a six-foot-four, neck-tattooed ex-con wearing a perpetually greasy apron who used the same spoon and spatula for everything he cooked, so sometimes your plate would have a little piece of something you hadn't ordered. Like a sliver of grilled onion along with your pancake, or a smidgen of hash browns resting atop your yogurt parfait.

The man turned to her and shook his head. "Does it really matter what's on the menu, babe? You know you're only going to drink a Diet Coke anyway. Buckley, would you mind picking us up over there at that place after you get the gas?"

"Certainly, sir."

Mr. Probably-a-Movie-Star took a few steps forward before halting and slowly turning back around. I thought for a second he was looking at me, because the dark glasses obscured his eyes, but then he took them off and hung them on the neckline of his ninety-dollar T-shirt, and I realized two things. One, he was absolutely, positively, most definitely Jayden Pierce. And two, he wasn't staring at me. He was staring at my car. Embarrassment washed over me, which was dumb because I had no reason to be ashamed of my car. Why should I care what some Hollywood hotshot thought about my humble little vehicle? But then that dazzling smile returned to his face. Cue rippling sound effect.

"Oh my God," he exclaimed slowly. "Is that . . . a Chevette?" It was a simple enough question, but he said the words the same way an enthusiastic paleontologist might say, *is that a newly discovered* T. rex *skull?* He stepped closer still and reverently ran a long-fingered hand across the pale blue hood.

"Um . . . yes, it's a 1976 Chevette. Why do you ask?"

"Oh my God," he said again. "My dad's first car was a Chevette and he loved it. He must have told me a thousand stories about adventures he had in that car. Will you sell it to me? How much do you want for it? Can I see the engine?"

"Excuse me?" I asked, surprise giving my tone a nasally little squeak. That and the fact that Jayden Pierce was so ridiculously handsome up close that he practically looked computer generated. The breath had left my lungs the moment he'd removed his glasses, and the way he continued to lovingly stroke the car made my thighs sweat. I would gladly pop the hood for this guy any day of the week.

He looked at me, bright excitement in his luminous blue eyes. "I'll buy it from you," he said again. "How much do you want?"

Clearly, he didn't realize I would willingly hand over the keys for nothing more than his autograph. Or at least I would have if the car was mine to trade. But, alas, it wasn't. "Um . . . well, it's not actually my car to sell. It's my dad's. And to be perfectly honest, I have no idea what it's even worth."

"Jade!" the woman called out, doing a little pee-pee bounce on those stiletto-heeled boots. "What are you doing?" She was already halfway across the gas station parking lot on her way to the restaurant bathroom.

"You go on!" he called out with a wave of his hand. "I'll be there in a second." He turned back to me, his face flushed. "Seriously. I would love to buy this car for my dad. It's his birthday soon, and he'd get a huge kick out of it. I'll look up the value and can Venmo you the cash." He pulled his phone from his pocket and started tapping away, his gaze redirected intently at the screen.

I glanced over at Buckley, the driver, but nothing in his demeanor indicated he thought any of this was odd or in any way peculiar. I suspected that was a key qualification for a chauffeur. See nothing, say nothing. Judge nothing.

Still, I paused, thinking any second now Jayden Pierce would laugh and tell me he was joking. What a prankster that guy was! But his furrowed brow said otherwise. So . : . he was serious? Wow. What kind of lifestyle did you have to have that would make you think you could just walk up to somebody at a gas station and offer to buy their car? I mean I knew he was *Jayden Pierce* and a huge star. He'd been in half a dozen blockbusters over the past few years, had a rabid fan base, and left a trail of broken hearts wherever he went—according to the very reliable internet—but still, who did that? Who walked up to a total stranger and offered to buy their car? Yes, I said that already, but it bears repeating because . . . who does that? I couldn't decide if it was charmingly obtuse or annoyingly pretentious.

The handle of my gas pump popped, startling me and indicating that my tank was full. As I put the gas cap back on, he let out a soft chuckle. "Hmm, sorry, but apparently your car is not worth much." He made a sort of comical grimace and held up his newest-edition iPhone so I could see the screen. I leaned forward and caught a whiff of the most glorious cologne. Or maybe it was just his own personal phero-mones. Whatever it was, it was subtle yet luscious enough to dilute the smell of gasoline as well as eliminate the sting of finding out I was driving around in a car worth less than twenty-five hundred dollars.

"Ouch," I said.

"No problem, though. I'll give you twice that."

Five thousand dollars for this piece-of-shit car? One might call that highway robbery, and although I didn't think for a second that the chief had any sort of nostalgic attachment to this junker POS, I also didn't think he'd want to go through the hassle of finding a new car. Especially one that only got driven about five times a year. "Look, I'm sorry. I can't make any kind of deal with you because the car belongs to my dad."

"Jay-den!" called the woman, now standing at the door of Kandy's Kitchen.

He rolled his eyes and didn't bother responding. "Does your father live around here?"

"Damn, you're tenacious." The words were out before I gave them any thought, and I wondered if people ever pushed back at him that way. I guess maybe not, because he looked momentarily surprised, and then he burst out laughing. A full-throated, spontaneous laugh that was such a sexy, happy sound I wished I could turn it into my ringtone.

"I'm sorry," he said between breaths. "I am being kind of pushy, aren't I? I just never know what to get my dad for his birthday, and he'd love knowing I bought this car right out from under somebody in the middle of Nowheresville, Michigan. No offense."

Hmm. Looked like *annoyingly pretentious* might be the winner. He was damn pretty but kind of rude. Judging from the mannerisms of his traveling companion, I shouldn't have been surprised. But this wasn't a movie set or Los Angeles. He was in my backyard now.

"No offense taken," I said. "We here in Northern Nowheresville pride ourselves on being off the beaten path. It's kind of our vibe, and as much as I'd love to be a part of this little origin story"—I made a circular motion with my hand to indicate our surroundings and this non-transaction— "I do have errands to run. My father lives on Wenniway Island. He's the chief of police over there, so if you want to buy this car, he's the one you need to talk to. Okay?"

His smile remained, and he seemed not the least insulted by my response, or the phrase *chief of police*. "Yes, okay. Got it. Sorry to come at you like a crazy person." He lowered his voice and leaned toward me to add, "I've been told I'm excitable."

My opinion nudged a smidge back toward *charmingly obtuse*. I knew enough about his life—according to the very reliable internet again—to know he was a bit of a golden child. The only son of a high-profile, Academy Award–winning actor and a supermodel mother, so he probably didn't know how we simple folk lived. Maybe he thought this was how everyone got their cars? I supposed I should give him the benefit of the doubt.

"That's okay. I never know what to get my dad for his birthday, either." I smiled back, feeling all sorts of clever and cosmopolitan for not caving in and asking for his autograph or to take a selfie together. As far as he knew, I didn't even recognize him, and I had to imagine that didn't happen too often. It gave me the most minuscule sense of self-importance. Too bad I was halfway through my shopping that afternoon before it occurred to me—I should have traded him the car for a spot in his movie.

Chapter 7

Built in 1885, the recently renamed Peach Tree Inn sat on a bluff on the corner of Croton Hill Boulevard and Iroquois Lane. The once-grand Queen Anne–style home had a full wraparound porch and a three-story turret, giving it a fairy-tale castle look that I adored, but these six-thousand-square-foot *cottages* were not cheap to maintain, and a series of owners had let this one fall into a sad state of disrepair—something my sister and Ryan were eager to remedy. Right now, with its peeling lavender paint, broken green shutters, and some ratty, overgrown landscaping, it looked more like something from a horror film, but if the plans I'd seen the day before were any indication, it would make a fabulous bed-and-breakfast. Both Emily and Ryan knew what they were doing, and I had complete confidence in their ability to make this a showcase as well as a successful business.

I walked up the gravel pathway leading to the inn at 8:00 a.m. sharp, pulling behind me my little red wagon full of rolls of wallpaper and paste, along with a few other random items Emily had asked me and Matt to pick up, and I arrived to find him waiting on the front porch. I hadn't expected to see him there. I'd thought I'd be hanging the paper on my own, but that little flutter in my veins must have been relief because my wallpapering skills were as rusty as my driving skills and I sincerely did not want to screw up Chloe's room.

"Hi," I said, a little breathless—probably from the slope I'd traversed and not just because he was there.

"Hi, yourself," he answered. "Looks like I'm your assistant again today." He offered up a warm smile that very nearly, but not quite, equaled the dazzling one I'd gotten from Jayden Pierce the day before. He had on another pair of well-worn jeans and a soft blue shirt that made his eyes just that much more sapphire. It was unfair, really, what pretty eyes he had.

"You're the assistant to the boss's personal assistant?" I asked. "I'm afraid that must feel like a bit of a demotion. I'm sorry you keep getting stuck with me."

"On the contrary," he said, walking down the steps, his work boots scuffling along the wood. "I'm looking forward to spending the day together. Yesterday was fun."

It had been fun, especially as I'd regaled him with the story of my celebrity close encounter and near carjacking. Our errands had gone by quickly, and we'd laughed on the ferry ride home, sitting on the top deck like tourists and letting the wind whip around our hair.

Once or twice over the course of the afternoon it had *almost* seemed as if he might be flirting with me, but then again, Matt was a feel-good, touchy-feely, positive-vibes kind of guy and just so enthusiastically friendly it seemed like he was flirting with pretty much everyone most of the time, so I decided not to read too much into it. Especially since, in spite of how fine Matt was—which was *very fine*—I wasn't ready for anything new. I wasn't over Tag yet, and I had some emotional processing to do, so easy, breezy flirting was perfect, like dipping a toe into the cold water of Lake Huron. You had to take it slow, or the jolt would just be too much to handle.

"Well, I hope you still feel that way after spending a few hours trying to put up wallpaper," I said. "If memory serves, it's a little tedious, but I watched a YouTube video last night and picked up a few tricks that will hopefully make the job go smoothly."

"I've got a pretty deft hand at it. Thanks to your sister, I've gotten lots of practice. She's had me wallpaper a dozen rooms in the past year."

I looked at him in surprise. "Have you been in Trillium Bay a year already? It doesn't seem like that long."

"Maybe because you were gone for most of it." He reached down and picked up the rolls of paper from the wagon. I gathered up the other items, and we climbed the steps in unison. The last of the snow was gone now, and the sun was bright in the sky today. No gray haze. The breeze off the lake was still cool, of course, but it held the promise of gentler weather to come. May was just around the corner, and this time of year was always a guessing game on Wenniway Island. It could go from winter to summer and back again over the course of a day. My dad even had an old, faded photograph on his bookshelf of Emily and me standing in our front yard wearing snow boots and bathing suits.

"Where is everyone?" I asked as I walked inside and realized we seemed to be the only two around.

"Most of the guys are down at the dock picking up supplies, and a couple of them are helping out over at the Cahill house. They'll probably show up in a bit. Looks like it's just you and me for now."

Totally a statement of fact, but the way he said it seemed full of innuendo, like the notion of it being just the two of us was somehow better than it being us along with everyone else. Then again, that could have just been my imagination, because he turned away as soon as he'd spoken and said, "Chloe's room is this way. Let's get to work."

He led the way up two flights of stairs, giving me a nice view of his backside. I tried not to notice, but he was *right* in front of me, and he was very . . . fit. Everyone on Wenniway Island knew he used to be a model, and no one was surprised.

When we reached the third floor, he pointed to the turret room, with a huge circular window overlooking the bay. Certainly one of the nicest rooms in the house and one that would demand a hefty reservation fee.

"This is going to be Chloe's room? Are you sure?"

"I'm positive. She thinks she's getting one of the smaller rooms, but when Emily heard her telling Susie Mahoney she wished she could have *the Princess Turret Room*, she figured Chloe ought to have it."

"Wow, Emily must be feeling really guilty about that ba—" *Ah, shit.*

But Matt just smiled. "She told me yesterday when she asked me to go in to Michlimac for her."

"Oh, thank goodness." I chuckled with relief. "Does the rest of the crew know?"

"I'm not sure. It was just the two of us when she told me."

"Well, if she doesn't get her morning sickness under control, they'll figure out soon enough." I stepped inside the room and scanned the walls. "Oh my gosh. This is going to take forever."

Matt walked in behind me. "Not too many angles, though. We'll be all right." He set to work marking a plumb line while I mixed up the paste. Pretty soon we found a groove, with him measuring and cutting the paper, applying the paste, and then helping me put it on the wall. Basically, he was doing all the complicated stuff, and I was just there to help him slide pieces into place.

"It's definitely more accurate to say that I'm your assistant today," I said to Matt, looking around at the half-finished room. We'd completed most of the trickier angles but still had two more walls to paper. Fortunately, they were mostly uninterrupted, other than a closet door and the door that led to the main hallway, and even though the work had been painstaking while we'd been in the thick of it, the past few hours had moved by in an instant. Maybe that was because, somehow, Matt had made it fun.

As we worked, we'd compared notes about favorite books, a topic on which we did not agree because he liked historical biographies (snore), and I liked stories with dragons and marauders. As for movies, we both liked blockbusters, and surprisingly—or maybe not—Matt confessed a love for rom-coms. As for music, when Matt set up a wireless speaker and played me his most revered playlist, I discovered we were completely in sync. I also discovered, as we sang along, that he had a wonderful singing voice, a kind of husky tenor, and that he—also not surprisingly—wasn't too shy to aim for the high notes, even when he didn't quite reach them.

"No hierarchy here. I'd just say we make a good team," he answered. "And I don't know about you, but I'm ready for a lunch break. Did you bring anything to eat?"

"I brought a granola bar, but I'm happy to split it in half."

He frowned. "That's all? Well, no worries. I figured I'd bring enough for both of us in case we didn't have time to get anything."

That was thoughtful! Matt was a thoughtful guy. We went down to the main level to eat. Wyatt the electrician had come and gone, and the others had dropped off supplies and headed over to the other work site, so it was still just the two of us sitting in a beam of sunshine on the glossy hardwood floor of what would be the main parlor and lobby of the bed-and-breakfast. There wasn't any furniture, so we leaned against one wall, facing the row of windows along the front. It wasn't the most comfortable situation, but the light streaming through a stained glass window cast a decorative pattern near our feet that elevated the ambiance a bit. It was certainly nice enough for a granola bar break.

"Do you like hummus?" Matt asked as he unzipped a red cooler bag and began pulling out one container after another.

"I love hummus. And oh my gosh! How much food did you bring?" I couldn't contain my laughter as the pile of vegetables, dips, crackers, grapes, and other assorted yummies grew in front of me. There were olives and sliced red peppers and a jar of homemade pickles with a pink, lace-trimmed top, which I recognized as coming from April Mahoney's kitchen. The Mahoney sisters didn't like anybody, but apparently, they liked Matt.

"I brought plenty," he said with a broad smile. "I guess it's just a habit. The crew sort of expects me to bring the healthy stuff, so I always have extra."

I lifted up a thermos he'd just set down. "My sister said you'd gotten everyone to drink herbal tea. Is this how you start the process? Luring people in with fresh-cut peppers? I'm not giving up my coffee, no matter how good this hummus is."

"We'll see."

He pulled out a few paper plates and handed me one. It was lime green with dark purple polka dots and said HAPPY 11TH BIRTHDAY.

I held it up. "Um? Nice plates. I assume these are not from your eleventh birthday?"

"Nope. They came with the place I'm staying in, along with some napkins that say HAPPY NEW YEAR 1998, but they make me happy because I think about the celebrations that must have happened there. Plus, I'm all about waste not, want not."

"That is definitely a theme around here. I think we have some plates at Gigi's house left over from my baptism." I helped myself to an olive before asking, "Where are you staying?" As a Wenniway Island lifer, I pretty much knew every home and cottage rental around.

"I'm out by Beech Tree Point. Do you know the Dunnigan House?"

"You're staying at the Dunnigan House?" It was one of the nicest places on the island.

"Hah, hardly. I'm living in the gardening shack right behind the Dunnigans' place. They asked me to convert it into a guest cottage and said I could stay there for free until it's finished. It's actually coming along pretty well."

"Seems like free boarding might be a motivator to not finish very quickly."

His smirk was playful. "Very true, except they did say they'd like it finished by this fall. They understand I'm already working full-time, so they're fine with me making a little bit of progress at a time."

"Well, if you decide to put up any wallpaper over there, let me know. I can stand around and watch while you do all the work."

His soft chuckle made me blush, although I wasn't sure why. I hadn't said anything provocative, and his response was logical and understandable, but for some reason, I just liked the sound of it. I liked the way his chin lifted as he laughed and the way his eyes crinkled in the corners. I refocused my attention to the spread of food before me and added, "This is pretty amazing, Matt. Thank you so much."

"My pleasure." He said it like he really meant it, as if it genuinely brought him satisfaction to do this for someone else, and as we ate our lunch in the sunshine, I found myself wanting to know more about him. Where he'd come from. Where he was going. How he'd ended up on this tiny island in the midst of Lake Huron. Yesterday afternoon and this morning we'd covered most of the basic, superficial topics, so what the hell? I decided to plunge a little deeper.

"So, Matt, can I ask you a personal question?"

He didn't even bat a long-lashed eyelid. "Sure, as long as I can ask you a couple."

That seemed fair.

"How old are you?" I said.

His instant burst of laughter was rich and deep and had a far more stirring effect than I could explain. "That's your idea of a personal question?"

I smiled in response. "I'm just getting warmed up. You know. It's like when you take a lie detector test and they ask you some simple questions up front before getting to the tough stuff."

"Well, I've never taken a lie detector test, but the good news is, I don't bother telling lies. They're bad for your soul and usually cause more trouble than just telling the truth, but to answer your question, I just turned twenty-eight about two weeks ago."

"Two weeks ago? Well, in that case, happy birthday." I held out a cracker so we could toast with it. He picked up one from his plate and tapped it against mine.

"Thanks."

We ate the crackers and I smiled at him again. "That wasn't really my main question, though. I guess what I want to ask is, what makes a twenty-eight-year-old guy who used to be a model decide to come and live in such an isolated community? Are you here for good, or are you just hanging out for a while on the way to something different?" I dipped a slice of red pepper into the very delicious hummus while he considered his answer.

"I tend not to plan too far out in advance. I've found that, for me, the path to happiness is to keep my goals and expectations pretty fluid. So I may stay here for a long time, or I may decide to go elsewhere once I'm done with the guesthouse. Not entirely sure, but I'm pretty content right now. I like my job. Like the people I'm around." He smiled at me, and once again, I tried not to read anything into it. He didn't say the *person I'm with right now.* He just said people in general. I'd seen him in action enough times to know that this seemingly meaningful gaze from him was because of *his* charming personality. Not mine.

"But how did you happen to end up here?" I asked.

"At the Peach Tree? I walked here. Just like you did," he teased.

"Very funny. I mean here in Trillium Bay."

"Oh, that. I got here by plane and then a car and then a boat." His mischievous grin told me he thought he was very funny.

"So hilarious," I said. "Do you not want to answer my question? Because you don't have to tell me if you don't want to. I'm not trying to pry."

"I know. I know," he said. "I don't mind answering. I'm just screwing around. You want the Lifetime TV version of my journey to Wenniway?"

"Only what you'd like to share."

"Do you want the short version or the long version?"

I looked down at the pile of food he'd brought. "Let's go with the long version. Looks like we'll be eating for a bit."

"Okay, let me see if I can make this interesting." He stretched out his long legs in front of him. "I was born in Los Angeles."

My own laughter caught me off guard. "Well, you are going with the long version, aren't you?"

"Hey, you asked for it, and now you have to sit here and listen," he said, his laughter mingling with mine. "And now I have to start over. I was born in Los Angeles. My mom had moved out there when she was seventeen to be an actress, but as you can imagine, things didn't go exactly how she'd planned. She ended up pregnant and working as a waitress. Then I came along, and apparently, I was a very cute baby." His grin was more sarcastic than prideful.

"I have no difficulty believing that."

"I have the receipts to prove it. Anyway, my mom signed me up with a modeling agency as soon as I could sit up. I did a couple baby food commercials that went national, so we lived off of that money for a while. And there were a few other commercials and lots of print stuff. Unfortunately, my mom developed some bad habits along the way. Cocaine to wake up, vodka to sleep. Seems like the more money we had, the more she burned through on shit we didn't need. I kept working, missed a lot of school, but when I was about ten, she ended up in rehab, and I went to live with my grandmother in Traverse City."

He said this all with nonchalance, like he was talking about someone else, or really was offering up the details of a TV movie. No embellishing for drama or self-pity was implied.

"That sounds rough. I'm sorry."

He shrugged. "The past only has power over you if you let it. Anyway, my grandmother was the first person who treated me like a kid instead of a commodity. She has an organic cherry farm and she worked my butt off, but I loved it because it was so awesome being outside and moving around. You know, being a print model usually means having to stand still and smile when you don't feel like smiling, and as a kid, I hated that part of it. To be honest, I hated most of it. Even the money became kind of an evil thing because it sure didn't do my mom any good as she bounced in and out of rehab. She'd stay with us for a few months at a time, but my grandmother wouldn't put up with any of her nonsense, so she never stuck around for long."

"That must've been so hard to be without her." My heart ached for the little kid he'd been, facing those kinds of trials. I'd long ago come to terms with growing up without my own mom, but at least I'd known she'd loved me and wasn't gone by choice.

He shrugged and took a tiny carrot from the container next to my leg. "My grandma was always good to me, so it was probably for the best. Unfortunately, I didn't realize at the time how often people mimic the mistakes of their parents. When I was about sixteen, I started rebelling. Decided I was way too cool to be stuck on some cherry farm and started doing all the same stupid self-destructive stuff I'd seen my mom do. I even went back to Los Angeles to give modeling another try. I landed some jobs, got pretty wild with drinking and partying, living the high life for a couple of years, and I can't deny I had some pretty good times, but when my grandma got cancer, I moved back to Traverse City. I was twenty-one by then and realized I was being an idiot, spending all my money on chasing the next high. So I quit partying. Started doing yoga. Went to therapy to deal with all my mother issues."

He smiled at me. "It's always the mother issues, right? Or the daddy issues?"

I thought he may have been referring to my relationship with Tag, but I didn't say anything. I just took another bite of red pepper, and Matt continued talking.

"Anyway, maybe it was just me finally growing up, but I started working out to *feel* better and stopped worrying about *looking* better, and that was kind of a mental shift for me. I took modeling jobs if they were in cool locations that I wanted to see, and thanks to some good advice from my grandmother, I invested whatever money I could. Turns out I have a head for math. No one saw that coming." He picked up a rice cracker and dipped it in the hummus.

"So what about your mom now? And your grandmother? And your . . . father?"

The cracker crunched as he chewed, and I waited for him to swallow.

"Never met my dad. I don't even know his name. Not sure my mom does, either. She's somewhere in California, I think. I haven't spoken to her for a couple of years. She was pretty pissed I wouldn't finance her drug habit. She knows where I am, and if she ever reaches out, I'll let her back into my life, but I can't fix what's broken in her. Learned that in therapy." His smile was wistful this time, telling me there was still some sadness about that. "And fortunately, my grandma kicked cancer's ass and still lives in Traverse City. She's sixty-eight and slowing down a bit on the farm. She has someone running it for her, but I own twenty-five percent." He crooked an eyebrow and pointed at me with a new cracker in his hand. "And let me tell you, you'd be amazed at how little you earn from owning one-quarter of an organic cherry farm."

I smiled. "I'm sure it's modestly lucrative."

"Very modest. Anyway, as for how I ended up here, I needed a job, wasn't interested in modeling, and I figured a summer on the island might be a nice way to make a little cash. I spent a couple summers here as a Boy Scout, and honestly, those were the best times I've ever had. It's nice that I'm only a couple-hour drive from my grandmother if she needs me for something, and once I found out Emily could keep me busy all year, I decided to stick around, so here I am." Crunch went the cracker.

I pondered all this for a moment, and it was a lot to unpack. "So let me see if I have this straight. You are a model-slash-Boy-Scout-slash-organic-cherry-farmer-slash-carpenter?"

"I guess so. I'm also a vegetarian, an Aries, and a black belt in karate."

"What about yoga instructor?"

"Oh, I just do that for fun. I don't have any formal training."

Even more to unpack. "Well, nonetheless, you are making me feel like a huge slacker. All I have on my résumé is 'preschool teacher.'"

His self-deprecating laughter was endearing, as was so much else about him. "I'm not so sure I'd call my random-ass employment history any kind of a résumé. More like an attention deficit disordered jack-of-all-trades with commitment issues. And don't you undersell yourself. You're also an apprentice wallpaper hanger."

"Right. Thanks. Meanwhile, I have one sister who is the *mayor* of our town and another sister who is *literally* the boss of me. I need to get my shit together and make some plans for the future. I'm hoping a spot will open back up at the school next fall, but that'll depend on how many kids we'll have, and which teachers are sticking around."

With a student population that averaged around eighty across pre-kindergarten through twelfth grade, a teacher shuffle happened every year, depending on the needs. If I wanted to continue instructing the younger kids, my job depended on my neighbors having babies, which was not something I could control. At least Emily and Gloria were trying to do their part. Still, I had yet to get in touch with Mary Lou Baxter, the school principal. I really needed to do that.

"Sounds like you're planning to stick around on the island, at least. What about the guy?" he asked.

"The guy?"

"Yeah, the old guy. What's his name?"

It took me a millisecond to realize he was referring to Tag, and the fact that I'd kind of had to think about who he meant made me feel both guilty and free at the same time. Maybe my heart was more resilient than I'd thought?

"John," I said after another pause. "His name is John, but everyone calls him Tag."

A tiny flicker of Matt's left eye told me just what he thought of that. "And? How's that going?"

"We're on a break."

"Why?"

I paused again. Not because I didn't want to tell him but because I wanted to be careful how I worded it. Like when you're applying for a job and they ask why you left the last one, and you want to paint yourself in the most glowing terms possible without totally slamming your previous employer. I couldn't very well say I was too young and energetic—and fertile—for the relationship to work. Could I?

At my hesitation, Matt said, "Look, I just told you my entire life story. I'm only asking you about the past few months. My turn to ask the personal questions. So . . . ?"

I smiled at his persistence because, quite frankly, I liked that he was asking. "So . . . we wanted different things from the relationship, I guess. Like, for instance, he wanted me to move to Sacramento and be his trophy girlfriend."

"Hmm." He frowned as if he didn't like that for me, and that felt good, too. Like he was standing up for me. "But what do *you* want?" he asked.

I knew it was a standard follow-up-type question, and that maybe his interest was just a part of his natural curiosity about the world in general and the people he encountered, but something about the timbre of his voice and the intensity of his gaze made it feel like a far more intimate question. Plus, he *had* just told me his entire life story, so I felt as if he'd earned a thoughtful and honest answer.

"I guess I want something with deeper roots. It turns out I'm pretty old-fashioned. I want marriage and kids and the house with the white picket fence. I want my family around the table for Sunday dinners and big Christmas parties. I want to be part of a community, like the way things are here. I know that's not very exotic, but it's what I want."

Matt's nod was slow, as if he was contemplating my response instead of just reacting to it. "Exotic is overrated, and honestly, that all sounds pretty nice to me," he said. "The only time I've ever had what you might call a traditional family experience was when I lived with my grandmother. Otherwise I've always felt nomadic and sort of . . . disconnected. Maybe that's what I like about being here. There's so much history to the families, and everyone is so invested in each other. Did you like it here when you were growing up, or did you want to get out?"

"I always wanted to do some traveling, and see parts of the world that weren't just like here, but until last year, the farthest away I ever got from Michigan was a trip to Ohio to visit Cedar Point for a school trip."

We both laughed at that, since a trip to an amusement park could in no way be considered *traveling*. "But my dreams were always about nice vacations. Not moving away, because the truth is, I've always liked it on the island. I did go to college in the Upper Peninsula, but other than that, I was pretty content living here. Until Tag came along."

"Ah, yes. Tag. That's what we were talking about." He didn't even pretend to not roll his eyes, and for some reason that made me smile.

"Yes. Tag."

We were silent for a moment, until Matt brushed away a piece of cracker that had fallen on his pant leg and added, "And plans. We were talking about plans. Now, personally, when it comes to plans," he said, "I think the key is to start with something small."

"Small?"

"Yes, like . . . dinner, for instance."

"Dinner?"

"Yes. Do you have plans for dinner? Because if you don't, you could go out with me."

Why, yes. Yes, I could.

Apparently, his attention wasn't just random, friendly-guy flirting. Yoga Matt was asking me out on what sounded suspiciously like a date. Actually, it was exactly and entirely a date. A dinner date, and the idea appealed to me. Quite a bit. His gaze was direct as he waited for my answer, and my thoughts went all fuzzy, even as my body tingled with a longing that had toyed with dormancy over the past few weeks with Tag. Saying yes would be easy, and it would feel so good, but it hadn't even been a week since I'd said goodbye to Sacramento, and I didn't want my sad breakup emotions to mix in with unpredictable new-fling emotions. It would just get too confusing. Matt was too appealing and too playful, and my heart wasn't ready for that game just yet.

After a pause, I gave up a little sigh. "I would very much enjoy having dinner with you, Matt, and I appreciate the invitation, but I just got back to town a couple of days ago, and I haven't quite decompressed yet. Could I take a rain check?"

His smile came easily. "Sure. I get that. How about you tell me when, because I'm not the type to pester a woman after she's turned me down." He was teasing again.

I decided to tease back. "I'm surprised to hear you've ever had a woman turn you down."

"It's rare, but it does happen. Now, how about we finish that wallpaper?"

Chapter 8

"Matt's a pretty hot commodity," Brooke told me as we sat at Link & Patty's having breakfast. "Bethany Markham has been trying to get Matt's attention since the day he arrived, but he's never asked her out to dinner. Eva Culpepper and Marnie White have both made a play for him, too, but I don't know of anyone he's gone out with, even though virtually every single woman around here would be willing. What's stopping you?"

"I'm not sure," I answered with a big, indecisive sigh. "I can't deny he gives me a serious case of the flutters. But it's too soon. I'm still in mourning, I guess. It seems like I should make sure that Tag's not flying here right this minute to buy a house on the island and surprise me with an engagement ring."

She stared at me, the *WTF* on her face dialed up to about a seven. "And if he did? What would you do?"

That question had been flinging itself around in my brain like a firefly in a jar since the minute I'd landed back on Wenniway Island, but I wasn't sure if it was because I loved him and missed him or because my ego was bruised. I'd thought he'd follow me immediately and was a little humiliated that he hadn't. I'd texted him back the first night, after he'd said he loved me, and just said that I'd arrived safely. Maybe he'd taken that as his cue, because I hadn't heard from him since. Somehow Matt's overtures made me feel like I needed to decide *right now* how I felt about Tag, but I knew something this important shouldn't be rushed.

"I don't know. I guess I just feel like I need to make sure about my decision with Tag before jumping on some other guy."

"I suppose, but if Yoga Matt asked me out, I'd jump on him like a trampoline," she mumbled around a huge bite of pancake.

"Does Leo know that?"

"Leo's seen him. It's implied."

I knew my sister was teasing, and I also knew she was blissfully happy with her choice. Leo was the perfect fit: steady, devoted, and nearly as handsome as Matt. And he was fully endorsed by the chief, so that went a long way in making him Mr. Right-for-Her.

"Will *you* be getting an engagement ring soon?" I asked, causing her to choke a little on that same huge bite. She coughed and took a drink of water. A few diners looked our way.

"I'm not expecting one," she finally answered. "Certainly not soon, anyway. My gosh! We've only been dating since November."

"I know, but those eggs of yours aren't getting any younger."

She subtly scratched her nose with her middle finger and said, "That's ironic, coming from the woman with the sixty-year-old boyfriend. And don't concern yourself with my eggs. They're just fine, and Leo and I are just fine. Why are we talking about me? I thought we were talking about you?"

I'd flustered her. I was only teasing, but her cheeks were bright pink and she was avoiding eye contact, leading me to believe that she and the fabulous Mr. Leo Walker may have indeed discussed the future. I hoped so. I wanted to see Brooke married. Because deep down, I knew that *Brooke* wanted to see Brooke married. You couldn't grow up in a community like this and not recognize the importance of family. And not that many eligible mates wandered onto the island for those of us who lived here. Maybe that was why I'd latched on to Tag. Maybe he wasn't all that awesome after all—but at least he'd been an available option. And now . . . maybe Matt was an available option? A thought which put the cart about fifteen miles before the horse. He'd asked me out for one dinner. Hardly a proposal.

"So guess who I met yesterday?" I said, deciding to change the subject entirely. I'd told Gigi, Emily, and Chloe yesterday as soon as I'd gotten home, so she may have already heard. News like this was social currency, and although Emily had been only mildly impressed, Gigi was all over it, and Chloe had started texting her friends before I'd even finished telling the story.

Brooke picked up a piece of bacon from her plate. "Who'd you meet? Um, the lady who just bought the Island Bookstore?"

"Nope."

"Somebody new on Ryan's work crew?"

"No, and you're terrible at this game."

She frowned at me. "I didn't know it was a game. I just thought it was a question. So who did you meet?"

I leaned forward to whisper. "I met Jayden Pierce, the actor starring in the movie."

"You did? Where?" She took another bite of bacon, seemingly unaffected.

I told her all about my adventures and his offer to buy the car. "You turned down five thousand dollars for that piece-of-shit car? What is wrong with you?"

I could not have picked a worse person to tell. What *was* wrong with me? "You are missing the whole point of my story, Brooke. The fun part is that I met Jayden Pierce."

"I don't know who that is. I mean, I know he's the actor, but have I seen him in anything?"

I sighed with frustration. She was not remotely awestruck by me or my amazing celebrity encounter. "Have you seen *Shangri-La*? *Journey to Tomorrow*? *One Good Soldier*?" I listed half a dozen more movies, but she just kept shaking her head.

"Nope, nope, nope," she said. "But I guess I'll meet him pretty soon myself. We got word last night that the talent are arriving today. That's a new term I learned recently. *The talent.*"

A thrill of excitement rippled through me. "I guess that makes sense, since they were just in Michlimac City. Where are they staying?"

"You know I can't tell you that. And besides, even if I could, I don't know. But that reminds me—are Gigi's cottages all set? I know she's got people checking in this afternoon."

"I told her I'd make sure they were ready after I had breakfast with you. Want to go with me and hide in the bushes to see who shows up?"

"No, and you'd better not do that, either, or Leo will have to come and arrest you. Hey, maybe if you get cast as an extra, you could tell that movie-star guy the car is totally for sale, if he's willing to fork over five grand. Dad would sell it in a heartbeat."

The conversation veered from that to other random things. Details about Emily's upcoming wedding shower. When to host her *baby* shower. Whether or not our wicked, sexually frustrated librarian, Vera VonMeisterburger, would ever find a man to slake her unquenchable lust. You know. The usual stuff. As we finished our meal, a group of non-touristy out-of-towners strode into the restaurant, and my sister and I realized that the movie people had indeed begun to arrive. They were all dressed in various shades of black, and charcoal, and more black, with the occasional bit of gray thrown in. Several of them wore slouchy beanie hats like the one Jayden Pierce had worn, and one man had the brightest orange hair I'd ever seen. It looked like his head was on fire.

"Coffee!" he demanded loudly. "Someone needs to get me a very large coffee."

The young woman next to him, with dark brunette hair, thick-framed eyeglasses, and a headset microphone, shot her arm toward the ceiling.

"Someone needs to get Griffin a very large black coffee!" she shouted to the group around them, and I watched as a skinny guy with ripped jeans hustled his way to the counter and spoke to Patty. My guess was he'd just ordered a very large black coffee.

"Griffin," Brooke murmured. "I think that's the director. His name was on the list they gave me."

I quickly searched for "Movie directors Griffin," and sure enough, the image of a flame-haired man popped up. Griffin Boyle. That explained the posse that moved around him in unison like a school of tuna. Once the procured cup of coffee was in his hand, the whole mass of them left the restaurant just as quickly as they'd come.

Brooke looked at me with brows lifted. "Well," she said, "this is going to be fun."

Chapter 9

The sophisticated, historically adorned lobby of the Imperial Hotel was the scene of mildly contained chaos as Chloe, Gigi, and I made our way across the plush area rugs of moss green and black geometric patterns toward the broad, gilded doors of the Grand Ballroom. Cattle Call Day had arrived at last, and just as Brooke had predicted, at least half the Trillium Bay community was there, each eager for their chance at scoring fifteen seconds of fame.

The ballroom itself was lined with mirrors, and from the high ceilings hung dozens of sparkly crystal chandeliers. Stepping over the threshold, I immediately spotted Tiny and Gloria—an easy task, considering their respective sizes and Gloria's striped turquoise and hot pink dress. They were chatting with Horsey, Georgie, and Garth, leaving me to wonder if Matt was planning to show up. We'd talked about auditioning as we'd finished with the wallpaper, but he hadn't seemed that interested in being an extra, saying he'd already spent enough time standing around in front of a camera. Still, I kind of wished he was here, if only so we could make jokes about how pretentious all the Hollywood people were.

Off to one side of the room I saw my pals Eva and Marnie, along with a cluster of local reenactors who did demonstrations at Fort Beaumont. They were wearing their uniforms of the King's Eighth Regiment, although I had no idea whether this movie required those kinds of costumes. It seemed like that may have been a miscalculation on their part. There was Dmitri Krushnic, without his beekeeping hat; Clancy O'Malley, who owned the Palomino Pub—a favorite Trillium Bay watering hole for the locals—and Percy O'Keefe, who looked as if he may have actually showered for this. In another cluster just to the left of them was our entire town council minus only my sister, who was apparently minding the store as promised, and my father, who was outside at this very moment trying to convince a very determined young woman that she could not, in fact, smoke cigarettes inside the Imperial Hotel. I recognized her as the brunette I'd seen at Link & Patty's, the one with the headset and the singular goal of getting Griffin Boyle a cup of coffee.

As I waved to a few more friends, a frizzy-haired blonde with a frazzled expression on her face strode onto the stage gripping a clipboard. She was five feet tall at the most, but her hair added another six inches to her petite frame, and her dark red lipstick was in stark contrast to her bright yellow top and voluminous black cardigan sweater. She reached the microphone and rapped on it sharply, sending a series of thump-thump-thumps echoing around the room.

"Attention! Attention, everybody!" she said, her deep voice reverberating off the walls. "Thank you all for coming. My name is Monique, and I'll be giving you your instructions today. Everyone needs to fill out an information form, along with the nondisclosure agreement. You'll find them on the tables lined up along the walls. Once you've filled out the form, report to the appropriate table up here."

I craned my neck around the crowd and saw a table on either side of the stage, each with a whiteboard on an easel behind it. One said MEN and one said WOMEN AND CHILDREN, so that seemed pretty self-explanatory.

"Once we have your forms and have verified your contact information, we'll take your measurements. We will not be able to tell you today if you'll be cast as an extra. Those decisions will be made only after we've met with everyone. Bear in mind, this is a long process, and we appreciate your patience. Oh, and if you are under eighteen, you must have your legal guardian with you," Monique said, staring at the clipboard and flipping through some pages.

Chloe turned to look at me, worry crossing her features. "Do I need Mom with me? Should I call her?"

I knew what Emily had on her schedule today and I also knew she hadn't been feeling that great when we'd left the house this morning. The last thing she needed was to be jostled about in this crowd. Especially since there was no telling how long we'd be standing around.

"Let's just do the paperwork and stuff, and if we need to call her to come down, we can. I can sign for you. She won't mind." I didn't actually know if that was true, but Emily had agreed to let Chloe skip school to come, so it was probably okay. Especially since most of her classmates and a few of the teachers were here, too.

Reaching the wall, I gathered forms for myself, Gigi, and Chloe, and we decided to complete them in the lobby, where there was cooler air and not so much mayhem. We settled down into some cushy, red-velvet chairs in the corner, just outside the entrance of the Grand Dining Room.

"I'm not listing my real age," said Gigi. "No movie stars ever tell their real age."

"Can I say that I'm fourteen?" Chloe asked. "I'll be fourteen in a few months."

"Put your actual age. You have to list your birth date on there anyway," I said, briefly wondering if I should make any alterations to my statistics before deciding that would be silly. I was twenty-seven, and if they wanted someone some other age, then it just wasn't meant to be. Most of the other questions were equally as basic. Name, age, address, phone number. *Can you ride a horse?* That one made me laugh, because they'd be hard pressed to find anyone on this island who couldn't ride a horse. *Are you afraid of heights?* That was interesting. I answered no.

I finished my form, but Gigi was still scribbling away.

"What are you writing?" I asked.

"I'm telling them about my previous acting experience."

"What previous acting experience?"

"That time I did *The Sound of Music* for the Christmas charity bazaar."

"You sang one song during a talent show."

"Yes, but I was very good. And convincing. Everyone always says that the song still reminds them of me."

She'd sung a painfully flat version of "How Do You Solve a Problem Like Maria?" and I wasn't sure it was her *talent* that people remembered so much as the fact that the lyrics had suited her perfectly. I'd been twelve at the time, and I still recalled trying to discreetly plug my ears.

"Okay, but hurry up. The longer that takes you, the farther behind in the line we'll be. I don't want to be stuck here all day."

I sat back in my chair and pulled my phone from my purse to check my email, barely noticing a group of people exiting the dining room, until I realized one of them had stopped walking. I heard a voice say, "Hey! Chevette!"

I looked up and for the second time in my life found myself staring into the soul-caressing, crystalline pools of unfathomable beauty that were Jayden Pierce's eyes.

I heard Chloe give an inarticulate little whimper of awe from the chair beside me and saw her slide her own phone from her pocket. This was going to be surreptitiously recorded for sure. And I wasn't at all sorry about that. I'd been kicking myself ever since our encounter at the gas station that my pride had prevented me from getting a photo.

"Oh, hi." Seemed like I should have worked for a more impressive greeting, but yet again, he'd caught me off guard. I stood up and held out my hand. No idea why, but it seemed the polite thing to do.

"Sweet Jesus," Gigi said, popping up beside me and jabbing her hand out over mine. "Hello there, mister! I am Margaret

O'Reilly-Callaghan-Harper-Smith, but you can call me Gigi. Everyone does."

To his credit, Jayden shook her hand and then mine as if he was glad to do so. He was that good of an actor. Chloe eased up next, slowly, as if she thought he might be a mirage that would vanish if she moved too quickly, but he turned that megawatt smile in her direction, and I thought she was about to melt into a quivering puddle of still-thirteen-year-old hormones.

"This is my niece, Chloe," I said.

He shook her hand, and when she drew it back, she stared at like it might turn to gold any second now.

"Hi, Chloe. It's nice to meet you. I'm Jayden."

"Uh-huh," she said, raising her phone once more and not even trying to be subtle about it, but he just laughed and turned back to me.

"You know, I never got your name the other day, and I haven't had a chance to track down your dad, either. But I will. Did you say he's the chief of police?"

"Yes, he is. Are you really still interested in that car?"

The group of people he'd come out of the dining room with were quickly losing interest in our conversation and moved off in the direction of the staircase. I didn't recognize any of them as actors, but then again, my eyes were pretty well trained on Jayden.

"Yes, I am. And what's your name, anyway? If you don't mind me asking. Or should I just call you Chevette?"

My laughter was both polite and slightly deranged. "I'm Lilly Callaghan."

He gave a slight tilt of acknowledgment with his head. Without the beanie I could see that his hair was blonder than it typically appeared on-screen. "Hello, Lilly Callaghan. Are the three of you staying at the hotel?"

"What? Oh, no. We're here for the cattle call."

"The cattle call? Is that today?" He turned around and seemed to notice for the first time the hordes of people taking up space in the lobby. "Ah, that makes sense."

"Can we be in your movie?" Chloe asked, lowering her phone as he turned back to us.

He gave a little shrug and looked completely unperturbed by the request. "Probably. Want me to put your names in with the casting director?"

"Would you do that?" She looked at him as raptly, as if he'd just offered her a lifesaving kidney.

"Sure. No problem." He pulled out his phone. "I'm terrible with names, so I'd better text her right now. Lilly Callaghan." Tap, tap, tap. "Chloe . . . what's your last name?"

"Chambers," she said. "And I'm fourteen."

I gave her the side-eye.

"Um, almost fourteen," she corrected. "My birthday is in September." His smile was indulgent as he tapped away at his phone.

"And that's Gigi O'Reilly," my grandmother said loudly. "I'll keep it short for the marquee."

He glanced at her and his smile grew. "Gigi O'Reilly. Got it." Tap, tap, tap. "And done," he said.

"What's this movie about, anyway?" Gigi asked. "Not that it matters. I'm very versatile."

"The working title is 'Eternal Embrace,' but they'll probably change that. Marketing always does. Anyway, it's about a nineteenth-century couple so madly in love that even death can't separate them. After the woman dies in a suspicious manner, her husband continues to see her everywhere he goes. He's so convinced she has a final message for him that he hires a medium and hosts a séance. But things don't go so well after that. Can't tell you more. You'll have to see the movie to get the ending."

"That sounds awesome," Chloe said. "And maybe they should call it 'Final Message.'"

He looked at her for a few seconds, as if her words were immensely powerful. "They should! Let me text Griff before I forget that." Tap, tap, tap on the phone, then he slid it back into his pocket.

He had on jeans and a brown hoodie, and if it weren't for his face—and maybe his spectacular build—he could have been mistaken for any regular guy just checking out Wenniway Island.

"So," he said, looking directly at me. "Where can I find your father?"

"Actually," I said, "I think he's right outside. He was a little while ago. Want me to go find him?"

"That would be great. I'll come with you."

"Can we come?" Chloe asked. Now that she was on a first-name basis with the star of the show, she wasn't about to let him just walk away. "And . . . maybe could we take a selfie?"

He humored us with a dozen selfies, because Gigi wanted some of that action, too, and it would've just been rude if they'd asked him and I didn't, so we each got our pictures taken a couple of times. Then he autographed Chloe's paperwork and wrote "See you on set!"

In the meantime, I texted my father to see if he was still close to the hotel. He was, so I asked him to come into the lobby and find me.

And that's how we sold our old Chevette to Jayden Pierce.

Chapter 10

After a ten-minute conversation with a movie star, my father agreed to sell him the car, and, true to his word, Jayden Venmo'd the money right then and there. Oh, to have $5,000 you could spend on an *impulse buy*. But he did.

"You said it's in storage over on the mainland?" Jayden asked. "That's perfect. I've got a guy who can fly out here and then drive it back to Los Angeles."

My father looked atypically uncomfortable. "Uh, if the car doesn't actually make it all the way to Los Angeles, are you going to want your money back?"

But Jayden just laughed like that was the funniest question ever. As if my father had been joking, but I was certain the chief was in earnest. That car hadn't hit highway speeds since the Macarena was the latest dance craze, and even then, I'm sure it struggled.

"It's all good, sir," Jayden said, casually placing a hand on my father's shoulder. "Maybe I'll have it moved on a trailer. I'll figure it out."

Again, to have the kind of life that something as complicated as transporting a car from Michigan to California required nothing more than "calling a guy." I needed a guy like that. I was also amazed at the easy way Jayden chatted up my dad. He seemed not the least bit intimidated by the uniform or the gruff demeanor or the monosyllabic responses. He'd even managed to coax a smile from Harlan. A smile! That was some powerful charisma at work right there.

Finally, after a few more selfies at Chloe's request, Jayden left us, the chief went back to work as if there were nothing to see here, and Gigi, Chloe, and I went to take our place in the cattle call line. It moved slowly, but we were kept busy as person after person came up to ask what had just transpired, and I tried to play it off as if that sort of thing happened to me all the time. *"Oh, you mean that car thing with the chief and my dear friend Jayden Pierce?"* But I got the distinct impression my social standing had just increased in value. Some people had thought I was just a little too full of myself for running off with a rich older boyfriend last summer, but this they thought was justifiably cool. Meanwhile, Gigi could hardly wait to brag to April, May, and June Mahoney that her son had just been paid $5,000 by a movie star, and Chloe's phone was blowing up with responses from the pictures she'd posted.

Eventually we got to the front of the line, and I handed over our papers. Behind the table, a thirty-something woman with thick bangs and leopard-spotted glasses perused us as she chomped on her gum. She jotted down a few notes and wrote a big number forty-two at the top before handing me a piece of masking tape with the same number.

"Put that on your shirt, please. Right here." She pointed to a spot above her left shirt pocket, and I obediently complied.

"Good. Now go over there to be measured. Next."

I hesitated for a moment, not wanting to leave Chloe behind as the woman asked, "How old are you, honey?"

"Thirteen, but I'll be fourteen soon."

"Uh-huh. Where's your mom or your dad?"

"Um . . . ?" Chloe looked at me, and I stepped back to her side.

"Her mom had to leave, but I'm her aunt and this is her grand-mother." I pointed at Gigi.

The woman shook her head. "I need her legal guardian with her. You'll have to come back later, sweetheart."

"But Jayden said I could be in the movie," Chloe said quickly, pointing at the top of the forms the woman was holding. "See? It says right there that he'll see me on set."

"It's okay, Chloe," I said. "We can get your mom over here."

"Jayden wrote this?" The leopard-print glasses slid down her nose as she looked at his scrawled note and signature.

"He did, and he just bought my grandpa's car. Look." She held up her phone, which now had a screensaver of her standing there hugging Jayden around the waist like they were the best of buds.

The woman's chuckle held little surprise. "Yeah, that sounds about right. Okay, then. Go on over there and get measured."

She gave Chloe a piece of tape with the number fifty-five on it, leaving me to question what kind of system they were using. Clearly it wasn't chronological. We walked to the far corner of the ballroom, where a cluster of my island mates were standing with arms outstretched like someone was checking their wingspans while a team of production staff swarmed around them with bright yellow measuring tapes. They were fast and efficient, and soon it was my turn.

Once they were done recording the stats of every inch of me, including my head and my feet, I was photographed from the front, back, and both sides. They were so thorough I was surprised they didn't ask for my blood type.

It was while I was waiting for them to finish with Chloe that Monique, the frizzy-haired woman from the stage, approached me.

"Number forty-two?" she asked, her steely-eyed gaze flicking between me and the clipboard she had in her hands. I could see that my forms were on the top as I nodded at her.

"Yes, that's me," I said.

"Would you mind if we took a few more measurements?"

I could not for the life of me imagine what part of my body had not been recorded, and I wondered if they were about to do a strip search. But hey, I'd come this far.

"Sure. Okay."

Fortunately, they measured all the same stuff as before. Height, waist, arms, hips, bust. But they seemed to be a bit more meticulous this time. I wasn't sure if I should feel flattered or violated, and the curiosity was getting to me.

"Was there something wrong with the other measurements?" I asked.

Monique shook her head. "No, it's just that you have nearly identical measurements to Skylar Tremont, and we could use you for her costume fittings, since she's not very enthusiastic about that process. What's your availability over the next few days?"

I was supposed to do a dozen things for Emily, and a couple of things for Gigi, too, but certainly they'd understand. "Um, I'm not entirely sure, but I'm probably pretty available." Yes, Emily would understand.

❧

Actually, Emily did not understand. Well, she *understood*, but she was upset about it nonetheless.

"I really needed your help in getting Chloe's room ready, Lil. And I needed you to order the tile for the Cahill house, and get some paint swatches and a dozen other things I was counting on you doing." As Emily's eyes puddled up with tears, I felt like the worst kind of sister. I'd made a promise to her and needed to keep it. I just hadn't realized how time sensitive some of the tasks would be, or how important they were to her.

"I'm sorry, Em. I can tell the movie people I'm not available after all. It's not that big of a deal."

Then she burst into full-fledged tears. "No, no. Don't do that. Oh my gosh. I'm not even that upset. It's the fricking hormones. I've been crying for two days straight. If this baby is half as much trouble on the outside as it is on the inside, I'm in big trouble. Ryan thinks I'm losing my mind."

We were sitting on the soft green sofa in Gigi's family room, and I moved closer to put my arm around her trembling shoulders. "It's okay, Em. You go ahead and cry if it makes you feel better."

"But it doesn't make me feel better!" she wailed, and then I knew for certain that I was a really lousy sister because I had to bite back a laugh. Not because she was crying but because her reaction was so wildly over the top about something completely fixable. Got to love those hormones. And why, exactly, was I so anxious to have a baby?

"What can I do to help?" I asked. "Do you want some tea?"

She sniffled and dabbed at her tears with the sleeve of her shirt. "Maybe."

"And an oatmeal raisin cookie?"

Emily nodded and sniffled again. "Maybe."

I made her a cup of tea and got her a cookie and then settled back down on the couch.

"So the movie people have asked me to come back to the Imperial at eight a.m. tomorrow morning. I'm not exactly sure who to call to tell them I can't make it, so I'll just go in person and explain the situation. Then I'll come to the Peach Tree right after that. I should make it there by eight thirty. Does that sound okay?"

She shook her head. "No, don't do that. For goodness' sake, I'm being ridiculous. Go do the costume thing. That sounds like fun, and the other stuff can wait. It's only a couple of days, right?"

"I think so." They hadn't actually said, but how many costumes could there be? "What if you told me all the stuff that needs doing, and I'll take care of it in the late afternoon or the evening? It's not like I'll be tired. I imagine all I'll be doing is either standing still or changing costumes."

Emily sipped her tea. "I suppose that would work. Thanks for taking Chloe to the cattle call thing, by the way. She is beside herself with joy over the whole situation. And so is Gigi. The whole thing sounds like fun. If I felt better, I might try to be cast in it, too."

"Maybe Chloe can ask her new BFF to save you a spot."

Chapter 11

"So, as shocking as this might seem, being a live-action mannequin for Skylar Tremont is about a million times more tedious than I'd imagined it would be. I got skewered with sewing pins about twelve dozen times," I said to Matt, Tiny, and Gloria a week after the cattle call as I stood in Chloe's still unfinished room at the Peach Tree Inn. I was there to drop off some paintbrushes, the guys were assembling a white wrought-iron four-poster bed for my niece, and Gloria had stopped by to bring Tiny a second lunch because he'd already eaten his first one at ten thirty that morning.

"I suspected it might be," Matt said mildly. "Just wait until you're doing the actual filming. Hand me that screwdriver, will you?"

I picked up one from the floor and handed it to him. "They're using extras on Friday, and I'm supposed to be there for that, so we'll see how it compares."

"Well, it might be dull as watching paint dry, but it still sounds exciting," Gloria said with a sigh. "And I think it's discriminatory to not let me be an extra just because I'm a little pregnant." She was a little pregnant in the same way that the pope was a little Catholic.

"Maybe they'll call you up for one of the later scenes," I said, but Gloria shook her head, making her silver, maple leaf–size earrings clack against her chunky white plastic necklace. She was wearing a silk, vertically striped dress of red, blue, and yellow that would have, in a pinch, served nicely as a hot air balloon.

"They said something about insurance and liability, but that's just silly. What could possibly happen to this baby when it's all cozy and safe in here?" She rubbed her belly over the silk. "Maybe I'll make my own costume and just wander onto the set. I bet no one would even notice me." The probability of her not being noticed was about negative 100 percent. With her white-blonde hair, bubble gum–pink lipstick, and a guffaw that could be heard from here to Manitou, she was . . . noticeable. Even without the obviously pregnant thing going on.

"That seems kind of risky," I said. "And you wouldn't want to put the chief or Leo in a bad light. They're helping with security, you know."

"I think she's just too glamorous," Tiny said, wiping a sleeve across his forehead to mop up tiny droplets of perspiration while beaming at his wife. "I heard from Delores Crenshaw, who found out from Maggie Webster, that the actress—that Skylar what's-her-name—is a real prima donna. She probably doesn't want anyone on the set who is prettier than her."

I decided not to point out that he'd sort of just insulted me . . . because *I* would be on set.

"Do you think that's it, baby-kins?" Gloria asked, beaming right back at him. "You think that poor little ingenue is threatened by my seasoned beauty?"

Sure. That was it.

"Well, if she isn't, she should be, smoochie-poo." He blew her a kiss, and I saw Matt pressing his lips together as if holding back some mirth. Or maybe I was just projecting. Nonetheless, I'd go along on this little ride for Gloria's sake. It had to be disappointing to not be included—for whatever reason.

"Tiny is probably right, Glo. I heard from one of the movie crew that I was asked to do Skylar's fittings because she's such a drama queen that the costume designer can't stand her. One of the seamstresses does this great impression of her, saying, 'My name is not TREE-mont. It's Trah-MONT.'"

Everyone laughed as Tiny added, "Exactly. Plus, Horsey told me that Georgie told him it's supposed to be kind of a dark, gothic ghost story, and Glo-Glo, since you just radiate sunshine everywhere you go, you'd throw off the whole ambiance."

Again, I thought I'd just been insulted . . .

Gloria patted her artificially blonde curls. "I suppose so. I do radiate sunshine. I just can't help it. What else have you learned from the costume people, Lilly-vanilli?" she asked. "Are you getting all sorts of inside scoopage? Got some juicy deets for us?"

"A few," I answered. "They sort of treat me like I'm invisible, so I've heard a lot about the director, Griffin Boyle, having an affair with the assistant director, Rashida Parker, and how they think they're keeping it a secret, but everyone knows. And they talk about how Jayden is super nice and buys pizza for the crew and stuff like that, so everybody loves him. And then I heard they're trying to do some kind of filming in the woods by Crooked Tree Trail but are having all sorts of trouble getting the equipment where they need it. The horses can't go up the hill and so everything has to be carried, and the crew is not happy about it."

"You know who else is not going to be happy?" Matt said. "Emily, if we don't get this bed assembled." Unlike virtually everyone else in town, Matt was solidly disinterested in the movie and all the fanfare surrounding it. It seemed to be the only topic he didn't put his usual happy spin on, not that he was negative about it—because Matt wasn't negative about anything—but it just didn't seem to fascinate him the way it did the rest of us. Well, him and the chief. Even the sale of that Chevette hadn't made Harlan a fan of the movie people. Except for maybe Jayden. Apparently $5,000 was what it cost to buy my father's devotion.

"I can help if you need an extra set of hands," I said to Matt. I was tired from several long days in a row with the movie costumers but felt immeasurably guilty about not helping Emily as much as I'd promised. I'd managed to handle only a quarter of the stuff she'd asked me to do so far. I'd stopped by the Cahill house a few times for an hour here or there and had spent some time with her and Matt working on some landscaping plans for the Peach Tree, but every day the list seemed to grow longer instead of getting shorter. As soon as I was done here, I had to rush over to Brooke's office and apply for some building permits, and then I had to go check on the linen supplies at Gigi's cottage rentals. Somewhere in there, I needed to call Mary Lou Baxter about a job in the fall. Meanwhile, Gloria wasn't done with her questions.

"What about Skylar and Jayden? Are they an item? I read online that they've been secretly dating since she broke up with Josh Beck."

"If you could hold this post, it would be helpful," Matt said. I reached over and held it steady as I answered.

"No one is certain. He apparently says no, but she plays coy and hints that there's something going on. And he did call her 'babe' when I saw them at the gas station."

"That's just probably a movie-star thing," Gloria said. "You know they're all *Babe this* and *Babe that*."

I wasn't sure where she was getting this information, but I had no reason to question it. We chatted a bit more and finished with the bed, nestling the headboard against the wall; then Gloria and Tiny went downstairs to eat his second lunch.

"So are you all settled in at Gigi's now?" Matt asked once they'd left and it was just the two of us. He sat down on an overturned bucket and indicated I should do the same as he pulled a water bottle from his bag and took a drink.

"I think so. It didn't take much, since all I had were my clothes and a few toiletries. All the stuff I packed up when I left last summer, like knickknacks and stuff, are still in boxes in her attic. I didn't really have all that much. Plus, the furniture I'd been using she's moved into her rental properties, so I don't exactly want that stuff back. How are things at the guesthouse coming along?"

"Pretty good, but there's been a slight delay." He offered the water bottle to me and I took it, feeling a little flicker of something pleasant by accepting. I was about to put my lips where his lips had just been, and that felt personal. Maybe he was just being polite and didn't care about germs, or maybe not.

"A delay? Why? What's happened?" I took a tiny sip and handed it back.

A smile tilted at the corner of his mouth. "I've had an unfortunate infestation."

"Ew! What kind of infestation?"

"Kittens."

"A kitten infestation?" That sounded like the world's sweetest kind of interruption.

"Yeah, some mama cat decided to take up residence under my deck and have her babies, so I can't finish installing the railing until they've all moved on, which could be weeks yet."

"That's so sweet, though. I love kittens." I couldn't keep the *awww* from my voice. I wished I could claim one, but Gigi already had three cats. None of them had names, because she'd never gotten around to that. She just called them all Kitty or Furball or Mr. Whiskers, which seemed fine, because it's not like cats ever came when you called them anyway.

"It's sweet in concept," Matt said. "And I like kittens, too, but she must've gone hunting this morning and left them hungry, because at about four a.m. I could hear all this pitiful meowing that went on forever. I wanted to feed them so bad I nearly started lactating."

My reaction was one part gasp coupled with three parts reluctant laughter, an unladylike kind of snuffle-snort completely appropriate for his comment. "Wow. That's so gross and yet so funny. Did she come back? The mama cat?"

"She must have. They quieted down around five thirty. Just in time for me to get up and go teach my sunrise yoga class. I almost fell back asleep during *Savasana*. Didn't see you there, by the way. When are you going to come take a class? It might help you with your—what did you call it? Decompressing?"

"It might, but I can pretty much guarantee I will never come to your sunrise class. Please don't take that personally, but I like to sleep until the sun is all the way up." I lifted my hand to indicate *high in the sky*.

"How about a twilight class then? It would be a great way to wind down after a stressful day of being Skylar Tremont's voodoo doll."

I laughed at the notion. "Do you suppose that's why they stabbed me so many times? That would explain a lot."

"Exactly, so maybe you need to cleanse yourself of all that negative energy they pushed inside of you. It's worth a try, right?"

For a relaxed guy, he was being kind of insistent about this. I'd gone to only one of his yoga classes last summer, and that was because Emily had coerced me into it. Because she was trying to make me fall for Matt instead of Tag. Oh, the irony.

"Can I be really honest with you?" I said.

"Always."

"I'm more of a *run as fast as you can* kind of exerciser. I like to jog and hike and bike and kayak, but I'm no good at yoga. It's so slow it makes me tense instead of relaxed, and although it's kind of embarrassing to admit, I have zero coordination. In fact, I once tripped over the hem of a strapless gown while walking across the stage during a beauty pageant, and let's just say the results were . . . titillating."

A slow, mischievous smile eased its way across his face, deepening those dimples. "Are you saying what I think you're saying?"

"If what you think I'm saying is that I fell down on stage in front of an audience full of people and both my boobs popped out, then yes, I am saying what you think I'm saying."

His chuff of laughter was both amused and sympathetic, and understandably, his gaze flickered over my breasts as his cheeks took on a flushed hue. I'd made it all but impossible for him not to picture me topless, and his discomfiture was both endearing and flattering. Enjoying this attention, I waved one hand in front of my chestal region and added, "Yep, showed off both of these puppies, and still I lost. You'd think I would've at least won Miss Congeniality. I guess maybe these are just not that impressive."

Matt blinked rapidly as the blush deepened, but his smile remained steady. He took a slow sip of water, his eyes now on mine, and said, "Well, you could let me be the judge of that, but I can pretty much already tell you what the verdict will be."

"Impressive?" I asked optimistically.

"I'm sure of it."

I laughed again, feeling my own cheeks heating up, and I realized that by teasing him, I was toying with my own emotions. Maybe Matt and I should stop talking about my breasts and talk about something else instead. "So anyway. Yoga."

He cleared his throat and, like a true gentleman, decided to let me off the hook. "Yes, yoga. Where you can wear a sports bra instead of a ball gown, should you so choose."

"Sports bra. Excellent point, but I'm sure I'll still be no good at it."

"No one is when they first start. That's why it's called practicing yoga. Because it's not like you reach a point where you ever say, 'Okay, I've done it. I've perfected yoga.' That would be counterintuitive, because the whole point is to be in your own space, focusing on just yourself and staying in that moment without comparing yourself to anyone else. It's just as much about mental and emotional fitness as it is about physical fitness, and it's definitely less intimidating than flashing an auditorium full of spectators."

"I suppose."

"Listen, I'm not trying to cajole you into this, because if it's not your thing, then it's not your thing, but if you decide you want to give it a try and are feeling awkward, we could do some private lessons."

Private yoga lessons with Yoga Matt? Now there was a thought, but at least in a roomful of people I could hide behind Tiny Kloosterman or Vera VonMeisterburger, where he couldn't see me being every kind of clumsy. I mean, how do you maintain your dignity with your ass up in the air, or when you tip over like a drunk? But then again, private lessons . . .

"Um . . ."

He held up both hands as if in surrender. "Again, I'm not trying to pressure you, Lilly. I just think that with all you have going on right now, it would help you feel more centered. I'll leave it up to you, so just let me know if you think you want to give it a try. Once again, I'll stop pestering you."

"You're not pestering me," I said.

"Glad to know that."

"What about kayaking?" I asked impulsively.

"Kayaking?"

"Yes, do you like kayaking?"

"I love kayaking."

"Okay, what would you say about doing a little of that? Maybe this weekend? It'll be chilly, but as long as we don't roll, we'll be okay. We could paddle over to Pine Island and maybe hike a bit? Or just stay in the kayaks. Either way." I had no idea why I'd just invited him kayaking, but apparently, I had.

"I like that idea. I'm working most of Saturday, so how about Sunday afternoon? Around two p.m.? The weather is supposed to stay dry, I think."

"That works for me. Sunday afternoon it is."

I left the Peach Tree Inn wondering if I'd just made a date with Matt Eastman, or if we were simply going on a friendly, platonic excursion.

And I wasn't sure what I wanted it to be. Tag and I used to kayak, and suddenly I was overwhelmed with missing him. It had been hard at the end there, but oh, the beginning was so good. We'd gone on so many adventures, and talked about everything, and kissed for days. But Tag was in Sacramento and I was here. And I wanted more than he could offer. So even though I felt like I'd lost something, I wasn't exactly sure what that was. Maybe the dream of what we could have been? Maybe I was just feeling nostalgic? It was hard to let go of something that had once been so good, even if it wasn't so good anymore.

I called Tag when I got back to Gigi's. I needed to hear his voice and see how it made me feel.

"Hi," he said after the phone had rung so many times that I thought he might not answer.

"Hi." After too long of a pause, I said, "How are you?"

"Busy . . . lonely. How are you?" he responded.

"Busy. Kind of missing us."

"Yeah. Me too." Uncomfortable pause. He cleared his throat. "How are the wedding plans?"

Apparently, he didn't want to talk about us, and I was oddly okay with that because what else was there to say? But at his question, it suddenly occurred to me that I had no idea if Ryan and Emily had told him about the baby yet. Thank goodness I didn't blurt out something about that, which would have been very like me. "The wedding plans seem to be progressing. I'm Emily's new assistant, so she's keeping me pretty occupied. They've got the bed-and-breakfast to finish and then a little house on Cahill. And there's a movie being filmed on the island, so as you can imagine, the town is abuzz."

His husky laughter caressed my ear. "Well, the good folks of Trillium Bay sure love having something new to chatter about. I guess we're old news, huh?"

"Yes, I'm afraid so. You and I are so last summer." I'd meant to make a joke, to say that the gossips had moved on from speculating about our relationship and taking bets on how long we'd last, but it came out wrong. And yet accurate. "I meant . . ."

"I know what you meant." His voice was soft and full of regret. I felt as much as heard his long, deep sigh, as if it had come from my own lungs and my own sad heart. "I'm sorry, Lilly. I wish I could be what you need me to be. I've thought about us so much since you left, wishing I could want what you want, but I just . . . don't."

If one of us had been in the wrong, this would be so much easier. But neither of us was. We were two good people with reasonable hopes for our futures, but that didn't change the fact that our relationship was just a detour, not the destination.

"I know," I said. "I've been thinking about that, too. I wish I could change what I need. But I can't."

"Honestly, honey, I wouldn't want you to. You should have kids. Lots of them, because you're going to be an amazing mother, and you should share that experience and that life with someone your own age. And when you find him, I hope he treats you like a queen."

Tag's words were sweet, and I understood his intent, but I didn't want someone to treat me like a queen. Someone to pamper and spoil me like I was something fragile to place upon a shelf. That was what he'd tried to do, and it had rankled me. It had made me a distant spectator in his life while he protected me from his worries or concerns. While we'd been able to talk about virtually any subject, it took me months to realize he never shared his fears or vulnerabilities, as if he didn't trust me to love him in spite of his flaws. That protected him, but it also shut me out from really, truly knowing him.

That's not what I wanted. Or needed. I needed someone who would see me as an equal, a partner in a relationship where we would take turns being strong, and take turns being weak. But there was no point in trying to explain that. It was simply too modern a take on relationships for him, because my sister was right. Tag was an old dog. A rich, sexy, and generous but old dog.

"I hope you find someone, too, Tag. I don't want you to be alone."

"I'll be all right. And anyway, I'm working all the time, so I'm certainly keeping busy."

"I'm glad. How are things at work?"

We talked for another few minutes, and he filled me in on the latest happenings at Taggert Property Management, but I found my mind wandering. I was too far removed from his daily life now to feel any investment in this. I didn't even feel much when he mentioned Ryan's brothers, Bryce and Jack, or Bryce's wife, Trish, who had, for a brief time, felt like a friend. But even she was hazy in my mind, now. An acquaintance I'd shared a few pleasant afternoons with, but I'd not heard from her since I came home. And I hadn't thought to reach out to her, either. I hadn't even told her I was leaving Sacramento. I thought I should probably send her a text, just to check in, but other than asking how her kids were, I wasn't sure what we'd have to talk about.

I yawned, and Tag heard it. "I should let you go. I forgot how late it is there. But Lilly . . . it was good to hear your voice."

"Yours, too."

"And hey, at least we can see each other in July, right? For the wedding?"

"Of course. I look forward to it, Tag. It'll be good to see you." And I realized even as I said the words that I wasn't sure that it would, in fact, be good. It might be fine, or awkward, or confusing . . . but it probably wouldn't be good.

Chapter 12

It was Friday, the first day of filming with extras, and the Grand Dining Room of the Imperial Hotel was filled with dozens upon dozens of my friends and neighbors, all decked out in Victorian-era finery. Eva and Marnie were there, each wearing striped silk gowns with—as Marnie called them—big-ass bustles. There was Gigi, resplendent in a deep plum-colored dress with black velvet trim and a feather in her hair so enormous it must have come from an ostrich. Chloe wore an age-appropriate pale pink satin gown, and her red-gold hair had been twirled into ringlets, prompting her to bob her head back and forth just to make them swing.

I myself had an elaborate updo enhanced with decorative ivory combs encrusted with fake rubies—at least I assumed they were fake. Gosh, I hoped they were fake! I was sporting a teal-green off-the-shoulder number that squeezed me so tightly around the ribs I could hardly breathe, but it did do amazing things to my cleavage, so, you know, it was a fair trade. Style versus oxygen.

"Well, now, don't you girls look lovely today," Percy O'Keefe said, coming to stand next to me and tipping his top hat. I assumed by *girls* he meant Gigi, Chloe, and me, but given the way he was staring at said cleavage, I wasn't positive. I adjusted the bit of sheer fabric around the neckline, for all the good that did.

"You look mighty dapper yourself," Gigi responded, flipping open her fan with a dramatic flourish. "I wish men still wore hats and suits. Back in the day, Harlan's father always wore a suit. Of course, that was in the 1970s, and it was a lime-green leisure suit." She let out a laugh and thwacked the fan against Percy's arm. "But damn, that polyester sure did something wonderful to his rump, let me tell you."

"Please don't tell us," Chloe murmured.

"Your great-grandfather was a real looker, Chloe. June Mahoney set her cap for him the minute he hit puberty, but he only had eyes for me because I was quite the looker, too, you know. Voted Miss Lilac Festival two years in a row. June's never gotten over it." Flutter, flutter, flutter went the fan once more, while Percy ran a finger around the tight collar of his crisp white shirt.

"How were you Miss Lilac Festival twice?" Chloe asked. "I thought you had to be a senior in high school?"

"Normally that's the case, but there weren't any graduates the year ahead of us, so they picked me from the junior class. It was either me, June Mahoney, or Delores Crenshaw, and even back then, Delores looked like an old woman, and you know how June has that unfortunate nose."

I'd never really given much thought to June Mahoney's nose, but clearly Gigi had. She didn't even try to modulate her voice, although April Mahoney was well within earshot. June's sister cast a dark look our way before jutting her narrow chin upward and flouncing away with a rustle of silks and satin.

"What's wrong with June Mahoney's nose?" I asked, watching April's departure.

Gigi leaned forward as if to make sure April was gone and then grinned at me. "Nothing."

Chloe giggled, and then our attention was drawn to the side of the room as a door opened and in walked a handful of drearily clad movie people. They were fifty shades of gray today. The brunette with the thick-framed glasses I'd seen at Link & Patty's was the first to enter. Just as she had the other day, she wore a headset, but now her hair was twisted into two matching buns on either side of her head that sort of looked like stuffed-animal ears. Not sure if that was the look she was going for, but it's what she'd ended up with. Her T-shirt had the letters *AD* in big block print on both the front and back, and I noticed that all the other movie people had shirts with various letters, too. None of them made immediate sense, but it was easy to guess that they were some sort of job identifier, except that some simply said CREW, which didn't seem all that helpful, since to me, if they weren't actors, they were crew . . .

The bun-headed gal climbed up on a chair and adjusted her headset before clipping a little black something or other to the waistband of her jeans. It turned out to be a microphone.

"Okay, people! Listen up!" she said, her voice bouncing around the dining room and bringing the din of the murmuring crowd down to a hushed whisper. "I am Assistant Director Rashida Parker, and I am in charge of making sure that all of you know what to do today. You may hear me being referred to as the 'assistant director,' the 'AD,' and, more often than not, 'that bitch Rashida.' Does not matter. You still have to do what I say."

Mild, nervous laughter circulated around the room as we all glanced at each other, uncertain of what to expect next. Was she trying to be funny or basically threatening us? Eva made a face at me as if to say, *what's her story?*

"So here are the rules on set, and you must follow them," Rashida said slowly and loudly, somehow managing to emphasize . . .

Each.

And.

Every.

Word.

"Note that if you break the rules, you are out. We do not have time to give people second chances. So, rule number one," she said as she held one finger up high above her head, "and this is rule number one because it is the most important rule. Do. Not. Talk. To the actors. They are here to work. Not to sign autographs. Not to take selfies. Not to listen to your very original story about how much you loved them both in *Shangri-La*. Everybody loved them in *Shangri-La*. They already know that."

Rashida's gaze roved around the room as if to ensure she had everyone's rapt attention as she continued. "Every time you talk to the actors, it is distracting to them," she continued. "And then they have to take extra time to get back into character, and anything that takes extra time costs us extra money. And anything that costs us extra money makes our director, Griffin Boyle, very cranky. Do not make Griffin cranky." She waggled that upraised finger at us.

"Rule number two," she continued, two fingers pointing to the ceiling now, "is just as important as rule number one. When the director calls 'Action,' you must be—and I cannot stress this enough—quiet. On. The. Set. If you are anywhere near a microphone, we can hear you. And if you ruin Griffin's shot because you whisper to the person next to you about how much you wish Jayden Pierce was your boyfriend, or how much you wish Skylar Tremont was your girlfriend, or how much you'd like to have a three-way with the both of them, it will ruin the shot and that will make Griffin very cranky. Do not make Griffin cranky."

"Seems like she's the one who's cranky," Gigi muttered next to me, the ostrich plume fluttering. I gave her a tiny nod. If the *assistant* director was this intense, I could only imagine what Griffin Boyle was going to be like, although I'd gotten an inkling of him when he'd so politely requested coffee the other day.

"Rule number three," Rashida said, three fingers pointed upward now. "Remember where you are standing or sitting at the start and end of a scene. Griffin will do multiple takes, and if you move too far from your original spot, it will ruin the continuity, and that will—say it with me, people—make Griffin cranky. Do not make Griffin cranky."

"Maybe the rule should just be 'Don't make Griffin cranky,'" Chloe whispered from the other side, prompting Gigi and me to giggle and Percy O'Keefe to steal another glance at my chest.

"And one last thing," Rashida said, dropping her arm. "If you happen to be back on set another day when we are doing exterior shots, be aware that the lighting is paramount. Whenever we are outside, we have to deal with sunlight, and clouds, and planes flying by. We have a finite amount of time to get the perfect shot, and if Griffin misses it because you have to run to the bathroom or want to check your phone, you will . . . what now?"

"Make Griffin cranky," we responded in unison.

Rashida smiled for the first time. "Very good! Now, everyone line up along the walls, please, and we will direct you on where to sit." She hopped down from her chair, and the crowd dispersed to the edges of the room while she and two other women walked around and eyed us all up and down like we were outfits they were admiring in the window of a trendy boutique.

One by one we were sent to our designated spots, and eventually, I found myself seated at a table with Chloe, Dmitri Krushnic, and Vera VonMeisterburger. Not too far from us, near the center of the dining room, was a table obviously set aside for the actors, given the row of cameras, technical equipment, and director's chairs lined up off to one side of it. Ten or so crew members were milling around, adjusting things, murmuring into their own headsets, and my excitement built, especially since both Chloe and I were seated such that we were facing the cameras and would be able to watch the actors in motion.

"This is so cool," she whispered.

"Right?" I responded, not taking my eyes off that center table.

"Okay, people! Listen up!" Rashida said once more, pointing to the ceiling again, as if raising her arm made her somehow bigger and louder.

"As I am sure you have discerned, this is a dining room scene. Were this a real meal, you would be eating and drinking and talking. However, this is not a real meal, and although a person may bring you a plate, he is not a real waiter." She paused with a tiny head tilt. "Well, he's probably a waiter, too, but today, he is an *actor . . . acting*. So do not ask him for more bread or to refill your water glass. If you are brought food, do not eat it. You may pretend to eat it. That is because today you are also *acting*. Not staring at the talent, not staring at the cameras, not getting up from your chair. Also, it is not necessary for you to pretend to be talking. Just make eye contact with the people at your table as if you enjoyed their company, and we will dub in conversation sound effects later. Any questions?"

Surprisingly, there were none. Or maybe everyone was just too intimidated by Rashida's brusque manner to dare ask one.

After fifteen minutes of sitting around and waiting while it seemed as if nothing was happening except a lot of people whispering, flame-haired Griffin Boyle finally arrived. He entered from the lobby, strode around the dining room like a man just on the verge of breaking into a run, and gave us all the stink eye before finally flinging himself into a canvas director's chair located behind a monitor. Rashida sat down next to him, and they murmured a bit more before I saw him get on his phone, and the assistant director stood up and moved a few people around. Fortunately, Chloe and I stayed put.

"He looks cranky," Chloe whispered, "but we haven't done anything wrong yet."

I just shook my head, wondering if every scene was going to take this long to get started. Matt was right. So far, being an extra in a movie was nearly as tedious as getting jabbed by Skylar's seamstresses. At least this part didn't include puncture wounds, though.

Off in one corner of the dining room stood a cluster of men I didn't recognize, all wearing tuxedos and holding plates—obviously our waiters for the morning. A few couples were also standing in various spots: Clancy O'Malley and Maggie Webster; Reed Bostwick and his wife, Marissa; and Xavier Price, along with Bethany Markham. They'd been assigned walking roles, and when the director yelled "Action," their job was to—well—to walk. I was glad to be seated. First of all, because I had just about the best vantage point in the room, and second, because I sure didn't want a repeat of my pageant experience. Not that this gown was in any danger of moving.

At long last, Jayden and Skylar strolled in, and everyone erupted with applause, which was technically not against the rules. Or if it was, Rashida had forgotten to mention it. Jayden smiled broadly and waved at everyone with his arm fully extended, while Skylar did a mildly indifferent gesture that was more *don't photograph me, you pesky paparazzi* than it was *hi, glad to see you.* Meanwhile, her friendly counterpart fist-bumped a few crew members, leaned over and kissed another crew member on the cheek, and when he spotted Chloe and me, he gave us another wave that clearly indicated he remembered us. My niece's face turned hot pink in response. "Oh my gosh," she whispered. "I love him so much."

"Get in line, kid," responded Vera VonMeisterburger, who had torqued so hard in her chair at his entrance that I'd heard her corset strings squeak with discordant dismay, like someone learning to play the violin.

The actors spent a few brief moments talking to Griffin before sitting at the table, and my delight quadrupled to see that Jayden was facing us. Long gone was the calm, cool, unfazed-by-celebrity facade I'd been—mostly unsuccessfully—holding together since our encounter at the gas station. I was stupid with anticipation. This was the real deal. I was about to see Jayden Pierce in action. No pun intended.

"Places, everybody! Quiet on the set!" Griffin called, and suddenly all the crew seemed intently focused on their tasks at hand. A man with a furry microphone connected to a long pole moved forward and lowered it just above the table, while another stood between the camera and the table with one of those black-and-white clacker things used to mark the scenes.

"'Eternal Embrace.' Scene twelve. Take one!" He clapped it down and moved quickly from the shot.

Griffin scowled and leaned forward in his chair, as if about to spring. Whatever extracurricular activities he and Rashida were dabbling in had clearly done nothing to calm him down or brighten him up. He seemed as tense as a man with a lit stick of dynamite up his backside who was just waiting for his ass to explode.

"Places. Mark. Camera . . . and action!" he called out.

The moment was like riding a roller coaster.

All morning we'd been tick-tick-ticking up the steep, steady incline, anticipation building, and now at last we'd been released into the satisfaction of free fall. I watched, mesmerized, as Jayden's expression changed and he morphed into a man wildly in love with his dinner companion.

As they moved through the scene, he stared deeply into Skylar's eyes. He held her hand over the table, caressing the back of it with his thumb, occasionally pulling it to his lips to kiss her fingertips. I felt my own hand twitch as I wondered what it might be like to have that be me. Not me as an actress, but me, Lilly Callaghan, having Jayden Pierce gaze at me with such longing in his eyes. Like every person in that dining room right then, I thought it would be incomprehensibly marvelous.

Really, to have any man look at me like that would be heaven. Tag and I had been madly in love, but even when our relationship was at its finest, he'd never looked at me that way. Like the sun rose and set and all the planets aligned just for me. That's how Jayden was gazing at Skylar.

Then Griffin yelled "Cut!" and Jayden dropped her hand like it was unpleasantly hot and leaned back in his chair with a big, casual stretch, and every extra in the room let out a collective sigh.

⌒

After a dozen or so takes of the scene, with cameras moving all around and Griffin pacing and murmuring to Jayden and Skylar and Rashida, and with lines of dialogue being said and resaid until even I was starting to lose interest, Rashida held up her arm. "Okay, everybody, take thirty. There is food set up in the Grand Ballroom. Everybody be back here at twelve thirty sharp."

"Oh my gosh, I'm starving," Chloe said as we left the dining room and headed toward the ballroom. "I've been smelling that roasted chicken all morning, and my stomach's been growling so loud I was terrified the microphone would pick it up and they'd kick me out."

I grabbed us each a turkey sandwich while she got us bags of chips and bottled water, and we were halfway to a table when Jayden walked in. Cue the applause.

He laughed and took a slight yet theatrical bow. "You guys don't have to do that every time I walk into a room," he said to the crowd. "I mean, I like it, but it's really not necessary." He spotted us and came forward just as we'd reached a table and set down our food.

"Hey there, Chloe. Chevette."

I wasn't sure if he was being clever or just couldn't remember my name, but it gave me a thrill either way because I'd just spent the better part of the last hour and a half imagining it was my hand he was fondling. I knew it wasn't real and didn't mean anything special, but it was fun to be singled out, and I could feel lots of eyes on us. Most were just curious, but Vera VonMeisterburger was blatantly scowling. April, May, and June Mahoney were whispering behind their hands, and Dmitri

Krushnic was working his way through the crowd, no doubt to better listen to our conversation and report back to anyone willing to listen.

"Um, I don't think we're allowed to fraternize," I said to Jayden. "The assistant director was pretty emphatic about not talking to the actors."

His expression told me not to worry. "I'll try not to get you fired on the first day, but I think it's okay, since we're not technically on set right now. And because I'm an executive producer." This was said as more of an offhand, throwaway comment rather than a boast, but it elevated him in my assessment even further. "So what did you think of your first day? Are you having fun?" This he directed to Chloe.

"Oh my gosh, Jayden, you were so good. It was all so romantic, and I really believed you were eating during the scene," Chloe said.

He leaned forward and spoke softly, as if he was about to impart an invaluable secret. "I was really eating. I didn't have breakfast, so I was hungry. The trick is to get your dialogue out and not let it look like you're talking with your mouth full. Plus, it annoys Skylar, and I enjoy trying to throw her off her game."

Chloe giggled and he winked at me over her head.

"So are you full in that case, or are you here to have lunch?" I asked.

"Still not full," he said, eagerly eyeing the food-laden craft services table. "I have to grab something, though, and then go talk to Griffin, but hey, I wanted to ask you something." He tugged casually on the satin sleeve of my teal gown as if we were those kind of pals. The kind who casually tugged on each other's sleeves.

"Me?"

He looked around as if to indicate *of course you, because there's no one else around.*

"Yes, you. I keep hearing about this infamous bike ride, or some bike path or something that everyone says you have to do while you're on the island. Do you know anything about that?"

I laughed at the classic touristy inquiry. Next he'd be asking me if the fudge shops really did direct their air vents toward the street so that everyone could smell the fudge, or if we really did ride snowmobiles over the Lake Huron ice bridge during the winter. "Yes. We have a road that follows the shoreline around the entire circumference of the island. It's about eight miles long, and technically it's a highway, but since we have no cars, it's the only highway in the United States that's never had an automobile accident."

He seemed duly impressed by my bit of Wenniway Island trivia. Just wait until I told him about the ice bridge.

"And you can just, like, borrow a bike and ride it all the way around the island on this *carless highway*?" he asked, saying *carless highway* in the same suspiciously disbelieving tone with which one might say *are you sure that rash is not contagious?* At his question I was struck yet again by his complete lack of understanding about how commoners arranged their transportation.

"Well, usually you have to rent a bike, unless you brought your own, but my guess is that any of the bike places in Trillium Bay would gladly loan you one, especially if you promised to post something about it or let them take your picture."

He nodded. "Cool. Do they have those double bikes? You know, those . . ." He snapped his fingers as if to jar his memory.

"A tandem bike?"

One more loud snap, with excitement this time. "Yes! That's what I'm thinking of. Are there any of those on the island?"

Jayden Pierce was simply too precious for this world. "Lots of them," I answered.

"Perfect. Then will you go with me?"

"Me?"

He made a big show of looking around again, even grabbing Chloe by the shoulders to look behind her. "Yes, you," he said, laughing.

"Um, sure. I could do that. Don't you want to go with, like, Skylar or somebody from the movie?"

Chloe was making faces at me like I was a lunatic for arguing with him about who he should take on his bike ride.

"Skylar?" He laughed again. "God, no. I've already had enough of her, and we're only on, like, day six of this shoot. I was hoping to go with somebody from around here. So you can, you know, tell me all about the island. I like to learn stuff about new places. I did get cornered by some lady named Vera Von something-or-other who offered to show me all around, but she had kind of a predatory vibe that made me very uncomfortable."

I laughed at that because he was obviously *not* uncomfortable, even though pretty much every woman in the room, and several of the men, for that matter, were having illicit, if not predatory, thoughts about Jayden Pierce. Myself included, not that I could, would, or should act on them. The rejection would be far too humiliating.

"Yes, Vera is our librarian. She has some issues, and don't let her get started talking about our fruit bat shortage or you'll never get away from her."

"No Vera. No fruit bats. Okay, so great. You and me, then? A tandem bike. Sunday afternoon?"

"Sunday?"

"Yeah, Sunday works, doesn't it? I don't have that much free time."

Chloe glared at me at my hesitation. *What are you waiting for, dumbass?* that glare said.

"Um, yes. Of course. Sunday would work, but could we go in the morning?"

Chapter 13

"So, for those of us keeping score, Lilly-vanilli went from having no boyfriend at all last spring, to having a rich sugar daddy who showed her the world from the deck of his yacht; then she dumped him; and now, two weeks later, she's dating not only the island's sweetest, sexiest yoga instructor but also ultra-mega-movie-star Jayden Pierce. Who had that on their bingo card?" Gloria Persimmons-Kloosterman was all about embellishment. Not just with her wardrobe and her home décor, but with her words.

We were sitting in her turquoise kitchen along with Emily, Brooke, Eva Culpepper, and Marnie White. Officially it was our monthly Drunk Puzzle Night, but since neither Gloria nor my sister could drink, and because I didn't want to, what with my big day tomorrow, it had been—for the evening—redubbed Boring, Sober Puzzle Night. For the first time in ages, we were actually *doing* a puzzle.

"Gloria, that is not at all what I said," I admonished her as I took a sip of my boring, sober lemonade. "First of all, Tag was not my sugar daddy, and he doesn't have a yacht. And second, these aren't dates tomorrow. They're . . . excursions. Jayden just wants to see the island with a local, and Matt and I both like kayaking. It's not more complicated than that."

"Uh-huh," Eva said. "So, in that case, you'll be telling Matt all about your bike ride with Jayden? And telling Jayden you have to cut your ride short so you can go meet Matt?"

She kind of, sort of, had me on that. "Well, I won't make a big production of telling either of them anything, but it's not as if any of this is a secret. You guys are trying to turn this into something scandalous. Honestly, I feel like I'm talking to five Dmitri Krushnics."

Even unimaginative Brooke wasn't going along with me this time. "Is Jayden on your sexlebrity list? I've seen him. He should be on it."

"Oh, for sure," Marnie agreed, nodding so emphatically that her glasses nearly fell off her narrow face and everyone laughed except for Emily. She'd been uncharacteristically quiet for the past few minutes, and I wondered if her allegiance to Matt was influencing her ability to see this for what it was. A big goofy set of circumstances that no one could have predicted. But since she'd assured me her matchmaking days were over, maybe it was something else.

"Of course he's on it," I said. "But let's be serious. Do any of you really think him inviting me to go for a bike ride is Jayden Pierce's roundabout way of getting into my pants?"

They all nodded emphatically this time, and a chorus of *yeses* filled the tiny kitchen. Even Emily, that time.

"You are all being ridiculous. I never should have told you." As if that would've made any difference. Even though I knew that none of this was newsworthy, people were bound to speculate, and hypothesize, and surmise. Maybe I should get a T-shirt that said WE'RE JUST FRIENDS.

"What time are you going biking?" Brooke asked.

"We're going at the super-illicit hour of eight thirty tomorrow morning. I told him I had plans in the afternoon that I had to be back for."

"You seriously told him that?" Eva said, eyes rounding with awe. "You didn't just say, 'I will clear my social calendar for you from now until the day you leave Trillium Bay?' Because that's what I would've said."

"Yes, that's what I said because it's the truth."

"That must mean kayaking with Matt is pretty important to you, too, then," Gloria said, stroking her chin as if deep in thoughtful contemplation—which was impressive because I seriously doubted she was ever truly in deep, thoughtful contemplation about any subject at any time unless it had to do with how adorable and squishy and love-buggy her husband was. Her words. Not mine.

I found a side piece to the puzzle and slid it into place. "Well, since I'm the one who invited Matt, it would've been rude to cancel, and Jayden said he was glad to bike in the morning anyway, because it would be less crowded and because he has stuff in the afternoon, too. You guys are making way too much out of this. Can we talk about weddings or babies or something?" Like a laser pointer and cats, I thought for sure this would redirect their attention.

"Do you want to borrow Leo's bike?" Brooke asked. "He's about Jayden's height, and his bike is way better than anything you'll get from one of the rental places."

Not exactly a redirect, but at least it wasn't about me having two dates, um . . . excursions, in one day. "Thanks, Brooke. That's a really nice offer. I'll ask him in the morning."

"Do you think he'd say no?"

"Well, um . . . seems like he kind of has his heart set on getting the whole Trillium Bay experience. He wants to ride a tandem."

As suspected, this triggered another round of laughter and teasing and innuendo. Emily seemed caught up in it as well, at last, and I was glad her mood had lightened. I wasn't glad that they were all ganging up on me, of course, but all things considered, having your friends and sisters tease you because you had plans scheduled with a movie star and a sweet, sexy carpenter on the same day wasn't such a bad way to pass the time. Fortunately, after that the conversation turned to Emily's upcoming wedding shower and Gloria's approaching due date.

"I think it's a boy," Gloria said, "on account of how I cannot get enough peanut butter. According to Delores Crenshaw, boys make you crave peanut butter, but Tiny is sure it's a girl because this baby makes me burp all the time, and Vera said that meant it's a girl. Then again, Vera told me not to raise my arms above my head because that would get the baby all tangled up in the umbilical cord, so I'm beginning to think both of those ladies are full of Cracker Jacks and don't have any idea what I'm having. Either way, Tiny and I will be thrilled. We still have a bit of organizing to do in the nursery, and he needs to assemble the crib and the changing table, but after that, all we have to do is wait for the stork to arrive."

"You haven't put the crib together yet?" Eva said. "Isn't that cutting it a little close?"

"Oh, it'll be fine. That stuff will only take him a couple of hours to assemble. He's planning to finish up everything next week because we'll be relocating to the mainland once I hit thirty-eight weeks, just to be on the safe side."

The Trillium Bay Medical Center was staffed by two general practitioners and a handful of other medical staff who were well versed in dealing with basic illnesses and injuries, but the facility wasn't set up for labor and delivery. They could handle things in a pinch, but most pregnant women from Wenniway Island chose to spend their last few weeks of pregnancy in Manitou or Michlimac City, since no woman in labor wants to climb into a tiny airplane or take a twenty-minute ferry ride to get to a hospital. The pilots and ferry captains weren't too keen on the idea of having them as passengers, either, which was why the coast guard usually stepped in during emergencies.

"I'll be staying with my cousin," Gloria continued. "But you gals better come and visit me a lot while I wait for the bambino to arrive, because my cousin drives me batshit batty. I shouldn't complain, because she was nice enough to offer me a place to stay, but she's in cosmetology school and always wants to make me over. I've spent a lot of time cultivating my style, and let me tell you, she's not going to mess with it. Anyway, enough about her. Want to come see all the cute baby stuff we have? The nursery is going to be totes fabuloso and so frickin' cute you're all going to want to have a slumber party in there."

When someone asks if you want to come see their new nursery paraphernalia, the answer is always yes, so we filed in, one by one, and nodded adoringly at the pale yellow walls and gingham curtains on the window. The nursery had framed watercolor drawings of fluffy bunnies and playful puppies leaning against a white chest of drawers, and a wicker basket full of cuddly, pastel-hued stuffed animals. Considering the garish colors that usually surrounded Gloria, all this was very subdued and very sweet-baby appropriate. And she was right. I kind of wanted to take one of the super-soft blankies off the shelf and curl up in it. I also wanted to have a baby. Like, right now.

Damn it, Tag. I could have been halfway to motherhood right now if he'd just wanted more kids. But instead, I was single and years away from having a family of my own. For now, I'd have to settle for being an honorary auntie for Gloria's baby and a real one for Emily's baby. Of course, I was already Chloe's aunt, but she was well past the snuggle phase and solidly into the teen-girl phase. Fun, but a bit too knobby and not nearly as sweet.

Our Boring, Sober Puzzle Night ended much earlier than our typical Drunk Puzzle Night, in part because the pregnant gals were tired, and also because Brooke had an early-morning meeting and I had a bike ride to prepare for. My sisters and I walked home together through the dark, quiet streets of Trillium Bay. I'd always loved strolling along the sidewalks after the tourists had left and only a few pubs and restaurants were open. You could see the lights of Michlimac City and Manitou twinkling far away, with the vast expanse of dark water between them and us. This was when the island felt like home.

After Brooke took a left turn to reach her own place, it was just Emily and me.

"So, how are things, Peach?" I asked as we continued on to Gigi's. "You seemed a little quiet tonight."

Her pause told me she did indeed have something on her mind, and once she started talking, it all spilled out. "I guess I'm still feeling a little overwhelmed. There's so much work to do, and wedding stuff to deal with, and I don't feel very good, and to be perfectly honest, Lil, I was hoping you'd be a little more help. You've been so busy with the movie stuff or taking care of something for Gigi. And now all day tomorrow you're going to be busy with Matt and Jayden. Not sure when you're going to fit me in, because I don't see your schedule getting any more flexible. I see it getting less flexible."

There was a hitch to her voice and then the waterworks started, and I knew for certain that this was hormone induced. She'd been a soggy, weeping mess for days, and it didn't take much to set her off. She'd cried when Georgie Reynolds had sung "Always Be My Baby" along with the radio at the Cahill house because wasn't that the sweetest song *ever*? And she'd cried when Horsey was late to work because his mother needed help getting to the dentist, and wasn't he just the best son imaginable to care for his mother that way? She'd cried at breakfast yesterday because Chloe had eaten a Pop-Tart instead of fruit, and surely she was going to get malnourished because Emily wasn't being a good mother. And then, when Matt mentioned the litter of kittens under his deck? I'd thought she was going to hyperventilate herself into unconsciousness over the self-proclaimed solidarity she felt with that mama cat, because really, in the universal scheme of things, weren't they practically the same?

Maybe I *wasn't* actually ready for a baby . . .

"I'm so sorry, Peach. I'll make sure I get to everything on the list this week. I promise, and I don't film again until Thursday, so I'm all yours Monday through Wednesday. I am completely and totally at your disposal."

"You say that now, but what happens after your multiple dates tomorrow, when both of those guys want to see you again?"

Yep, she was delusional for sure. "I'm sure that's not how the day will play out, but if it does, I'll just say no. I'll sing that song to them from *White Christmas*. You know, the one about the two devoted sisters who promise to never let a mister come between them? I'll just tell them Emily comes first."

My frivolous response in no way seemed to ease her crying. I might have to break out into song, but if I did, she'd probably just cry harder because . . . well, because everything made her cry harder. I knew the only thing to do was help her ride it out. Gloria had promised this phase would pass, and once my sister reached her second trimester, we'd have our old Peach back. That day could not come soon enough.

"I promise I'll help you get everything done," I said. "And I know Matt and the rest of your crew are equally devoted to getting the Peach Tree Inn ready for you guys to move into. It's shaping up really well, and everything is going to be fine."

We continued walking, and she sniffle-hiccupped like a toddler who'd just been given a bedtime reprieve. "It is coming along pretty well, isn't it?"

"Yes, it's going to be amazing and beautiful, and you guys are going to be so happy there."

I wove my arm around her elbow and squeezed, and we continued on like this for a moment until she said, "I know Ryan and Chloe and I will be very happy there, and I'm grateful that everyone is working double and triple time, and I know you're helping as much as you can, but then there's the whole situation with this Jayden guy."

I tamped down a frustrated sigh because I was very much over discussing this, and as much as I wanted to be sympathetic to her hormone storms, I was tired. "It's one Sunday-morning bike ride, Peach. I promise I'll get to the list of things you want me to do first thing Monday morning."

She stopped and turned to face me, the security lights from inside the Tasty Pastries Bakery shining on her now-splotchy face. "It's not that."

"It's not? Then what?"

"It's just that . . . listen, I totally get you wanting to go biking with Jayden, but just . . . be careful."

"Careful?"

"Yes. He sounds like a nice enough guy and all, but just make sure you don't do the same thing with him that you did with Tag."

"What?"

"You're getting all googly eyed over some guy who's got a great big life, and he's going to fill your head full of crazy ideas, and it's going to sound so exciting, but it's only exciting if you're in the center of it. If you follow him into his life, you'll just be a glorified groupie circling around him. Everyone is so glad you're finally back home, and Dad in particular would be so disappointed if you left again. Especially when you've got the chance at something really great right here."

"Left again? What are you talking about?" I decided to save that *glorified groupie* insult for later—because that was a whole mood.

She frowned at me like I was being deliberately obtuse. "I'm talking about you falling in love with Jayden Pierce."

I burst out laughing. I couldn't help it.

"I'm being serious," she said.

"Yeah, seriously insane, Peach. Those pregnancy hormones really are doing a number on you. I am not going to fall in love with Jayden, any more than any of the women on this island will. He's a frickin' movie star, for goodness' sake. Totally out of my league. And let's just say, hypothetically, he does want to fool around with me—I'm not going to let that happen. I do have a little self-respect, you know. And still, hypothetically, let's say I did decide to have some kind of fling with him—which I'd be totally allowed to do, what with me being a twenty-seven-year-old consenting adult and all—I'm not so naive as to think it would be about love. It might be a good time, but it wouldn't *mean* anything."

"But it would mean something to Matt." Her frown turned to concern. But not for me, apparently.

Ahh . . . "So you are still playing matchmaker."

She glanced around as if a good response might be posted on one of the nearby shop windows. When none appeared, she looked back to me and shifted from one foot to the other.

"Not playing matchmaker on purpose, but I do suspect that Matt may have a little crush on you, and Brooke told me the other day that you told her he gives you a case of the flutters."

Thanks, Brooke.

I shouldn't have been surprised, and I couldn't really be mad, either. Everyone in town, including Brooke, knew it was no secret that Brooke couldn't keep a secret. She was as bad as Dmitri Krushnic but without the hyperbole and fabrication. And the beekeeping hat.

"Look, I don't know how I feel about Matt. Yes, he gives me flutters and I enjoy his company, but I'm not even sure I'm over Tag yet. Matt knows that, and I think that's a more significant thing to be worried about than whether or not something would ever happen between me and some actor who is going to go back to Hollywood in a few weeks. I'm certainly not going to follow Jayden there, for goodness' sake. Life just doesn't work that way."

"It worked that way for you and Tag. Remember how I kept telling you not to fall in love with him?"

The two situations had nothing in common. My sister's argument wasn't just comparing apples to oranges. She was comparing apples to bacon. "Yes, I do," I said. "And I also remember Ryan calling me a gold-digging bimbo, and everyone thinking I was foolish and going to get my heart broken."

"Right? And see what happened? You got your heart broken." She said that emphatically, as if her predicting my inevitable heartbreak was a real victory on her part. Score one for Peach, I guess.

"Didn't you just tell me last week at the coffee shop to not have regrets about being with Tag? That even though our time together ended, that didn't mean the time was wasted?"

She shifted on her feet again. "Yes, but this is different."

"How?"

"Tag actually cared about you, and this Jayden guy won't. He can get any girl he wants."

"Oh, and I'll just be a glorified groupie?" The term stung, and my tone made that very clear, because it wasn't much different from being called a gold-digging bimbo, which I wasn't, and I couldn't quite tell where my sister's loyalties lay in this situation. Was she worried about me? Worried about Matt? Or did she think I was just too naive and dumb to navigate this territory on my own? The people on this island all had such little faith in me and so little trust in my ability to maturely determine my own fate. Because, after all, I was just the pretty one. Never the smart one.

"Well . . . probably," Emily said haltingly. "That's nothing against you. It's just that he must have opportunities to bag women all over the place, and I can see you wanting to act on your attraction to him, but if you do, I think any chance you might have with Matt will be over."

I wasn't entirely sure why Matt was even a part of this conversation. He and I were flirting, not fornicating. And Jayden and I were biking, not boinking. I knew my sister had a vivid imagination and a propensity to jump to the wrong conclusion, but this time, she wasn't just wrong. Her assumptions were downright insulting, as if I didn't have the finesse to handle dealing with two men at one time. She not only thought I'd be careless with Matt's feelings; she also thought if Jayden expressed interest, it must only be because I was geographically convenient.

"Thanks for the advice, Peach. I'll keep that in mind." I turned and started walking again. To get away from my sister and this conversation, but since we were going to the exact same place, and sleeping in bedrooms right next to each other, avoiding her was going to be tough. She walked three paces behind me. I could hear the scuff of her shoes on the sidewalk. I'm not sure why her words were making me so angry. Well, except for the part about me being a groupie and obviously not captivating and valuable enough to fully capture the heart of someone like Jayden Pierce. I was just little ole Lilly Callaghan from Trillium Bay, Michigan. I wasn't sophisticated or cosmopolitan. I wasn't elegant or powerful. I was the baby of the family, and I should always heed the advice of my wise old elders. Ironic coming from the sister who'd run away and eloped at nineteen, been divorced with a baby just two years later, and now found herself—surprise! Pregnant again. I kind of wanted to say all that, but it would have been just too mean.

But nonetheless, why should I listen to her? Everything she said was exactly what people had said last spring about me and Tag, but he and I *did* have a good run. My current heartbreak was worth it, because I didn't regret a moment of our time together, even though it didn't go where I'd hoped. It was good. Good enough. For a while. And anyway, I had no romanticized illusions about Jayden's interest. I wasn't going to let my casual infatuation get the best of me. I mean, so what if he did want to fool around with me?

Would I do it?

As I stomped down the sidewalk, my head said . . . maybe . . .

But my heart said . . . probably shouldn't.

Either way, it was none of her business.

"Did Matt tell you how he ended up on Wenniway Island?" Emily said from behind me a moment later. I'd gotten several feet ahead of her by now, and her voice sounded far away. Reluctantly I stopped and turned around.

"Yes, he told me he'd been staying at his grandmother's place and needed a job because he didn't feel like modeling anymore."

My sister stared at me solemnly. "That's all he told you?"

"Yes, mostly."

"Did he say anything about Wendy?"

It dawned on me then, thanks to my sister's question and persistent gaze, that he'd told me all about his life without ever mentioning any sort of romantic entanglements, and he must have had some, although

Brooke had said he hadn't dated anyone in the year he'd lived here. I was reluctant to ask, but curiosity got the better of me. "He didn't mention a Wendy. Why? Is she part of his story?"

Emily walked forward and stopped when she reached me. "Yes, but you didn't hear her name from me because it's not my story to tell. And Lilly, I'm not trying to be a jerk or interfere in your life again. Ryan and I were wrong to try to break up you and Tag. We both regret it. And I have no idea if you and Matt would be a good fit. I promise my matchmaking days are over, but I just think it would be a shame to ruin the potential of something good with him because you want to act out on some celebrity fantasy crush with a guy who's going to leave soon. When this movie is over, Jayden will leave without a backward glance, but Matt will still be here, and he's a good person."

I stared back at her. "I'm sure he is, Emily, but you're making a lot of assumptions about me, and they're hurtful. I'm going on a frickin' bike ride around the island. That's all. And then I'm going kayaking with Matt because we are friends. I'm just trying to figure out my life here, okay? How about you give me a little space to do that. I'm not a little kid. And I'm not stupid and I'm not selfish, so give me some credit and keep your opinions to yourself."

Chapter 14

Everyone was up and getting ready for church when I basically sneaked out the back door of Gigi's house. I left a note saying I'd be gone for the day, and they all knew where I was off to, but I hadn't spoken to Emily again last night and didn't particularly want to see her this morning. I'd managed to avoid my grandmother and Chloe, too. Not for any reason, other than I didn't want to discuss the details of my morning bike ride or afternoon of kayaking. I wanted to look forward to my day and not have to dissect all the minutia about where we'd be riding or paddling, what I was wearing (yoga pants and a white fleece jacket over a red T-shirt), or how long I thought I'd be gone. I was going to live in the moment and see where it led.

As for this morning, it led me to the Imperial Hotel, where I'd agreed to meet Jayden.

The sun was golden bright in a cloudless blue sky as I walked up the cobblestone drive of the hotel toward the mammoth front porch. It was lined with tulips and hyacinth that were just beginning to bloom into a profusion of cheerful colors. In the past few days, spring had sprung on Wenniway Island with the enthusiasm of a pack of schoolkids being released for summer vacation, and I decided to take their cue and just be happy today. Emily's words from last night still rang in my mind, but I'd leave them there for now and think about them later. Maybe.

I climbed the red-carpeted steps of the hotel to discover Jayden already there on the porch, waiting for me. He was lounging lengthwise on a delicate white wicker sofa with plush, pink cushions, his baseball hat tilted just so to keep the sun from his eyes and his feet resting on the opposite armrest, extending several inches past the end. He was too big for that bitsy little bit of furniture, like a Great Dane trying to fit his gangly legs into the dainty bed of a bichon frise, and the effect was comical.

A smattering of people on the porch were surreptitiously taking cell phone photos, but no one seemed determined enough to interrupt his early-morning nap. I resisted the urge to take a picture myself and instead walked over and tapped his foot with the back of my hand.

"Late night?" I asked as he slid up the brim of his hat and gave me a bleary-eyed glance. Then he stretched and yawned, and I wondered how someone stretching and yawning could still look so sexy and energetic. Honestly, why was Emily so concerned I'd sleep with him? He was completely and totally resistible, except for . . . everything about him.

He was wearing a light gray jacket and another ninety-dollar designer T-shirt that was pale blue and Hollywood snug, not oversize and sloppy like most of the T-shirts worn by men around Trillium Bay, and with that, he had on basic black joggers with a narrow white stripe down the side. Just like the day he'd worn jeans and the brown hoodie, he could've been just another guy. But he wasn't just another guy. He was Jayden Pierce, and Jayden Pierce made those jogging pants look good. This I knew, and he hadn't even stood up yet.

"Good morning, Chevette," he said, sitting upright. He patted the spot next to him, and so I sat, feeling the warmth of his body retained in the cushion. He rubbed his hands over his face and readjusted his hat. "Yep, late night for sure, but unfortunately it's because I was working. We're shooting this scene in the woods, and it's been an absolute nightmare." He looked around to see if anyone was close enough to hear, but people seemed to be giving us a wide berth, in spite of the cell phones pointed our way. "Did you sign the NDA when you agreed to be an extra?" he asked.

I nodded.

"Well, in that case, let me tell you, Skylar is driving Griffin crazy," he said quietly, but his voice was laced with good humor. "She's afraid of bugs. She's afraid of snakes. She's afraid of bats, and birds, and spiders, and ghosts."

I giggled at that. "Ghosts? Isn't this a movie about ghosts?"

"Yes! And she's read the script, so she knows exactly what's supposed to happen. She knows it's not real, and she also knows how special effects work, so wouldn't you think she'd be brave enough to be in the woods after dark? Especially surrounded by thirty burly crew members?"

"I would think so."

"Yup. Me too. But hey, at least when you're watching the final movie and she looks terrified, you'll know she wasn't faking it."

I considered making a joke about women faking it and how I was sure he was not accustomed to that, but it was too early in the day and too early in our friendship to go that far. I just wasn't that bold.

"Are you afraid of the woods?" he asked.

"No, but then again, I grew up here. I could probably find my way home blindfolded if I had to."

"How about ghosts? Are you afraid of ghosts?"

"Nope. Don't believe in them."

"You don't?"

"No. My grandmother has three dead husbands, and not a one of them has ever come back to haunt her, so I figure we're in the clear." I could mention my mother never making an appearance, either, but again, too early.

"Your grandmother has three dead husbands?" Logically, this seemed to elicit some alarm on his part. Or at least some wary curiosity.

"Yes, she does, but they all died by mostly natural causes."

This time he laughed. "Mostly? Mostly natural causes? Such as?"

"One got struck by lightning, one died from eating a bad taco, and the other . . . well, to put it bluntly, he was crushed by a falling porta-potty."

His blue eyes regarded me for a moment, his smile solidly in place. "You knew someone who died by getting crushed by a falling porta-potty, and yet you don't believe in ghosts? If that wasn't some evil-spirit action right there, I don't know what is."

I'd never really thought about it that way. I just figured it was bad placement and a strong wind. That's what my dad wrote in the police report, anyway. Or so he'd said.

"Are you saying you do believe in ghosts?"

He gave a little shrug. "Kinda. Let's just say I've never ruled it out. I've seen some pretty crazy stuff in LA, and some of it can only be explained by demonic possession." Then he laughed again and assured me he was kidding. At least about the possession part. "Let's just say I don't want to say I don't believe in ghosts, because if I do and they're real, one might show up at the end of my bed just to prove me wrong. I don't like the odds of that."

"There's a ghost tour here, you know. Maybe you should take Skylar on that. It's so cheesy and lame—maybe she'd realize there's nothing to worry about. And maybe you would, too."

"A ghost tour, huh? I'll mention it to Griffin. In the meantime, how about that bike ride? You ready to go?"

"I am."

"Good. Did you eat any breakfast? Because I asked the chef to pack us a little snack, and I think he may have gone overboard." He pulled a soft-sided thermal cooler up from the end of the couch and set it in his lap. It had the Imperial Hotel emblem on it and appeared to be stretching at every seam.

"I had a granola bar, but that'll wear off soon enough," I answered. "How about we bike out to Potter's Pointe and eat there? That's about two-thirds of the ride if we go north from downtown, and there's a little picnic area there. If you want the full tourist experience, that's the best bet."

"Sounds good to me. You're the expert."

Me? An expert? Comical.

"So one last question before we get started," I said. "You could borrow my sister's boyfriend's good quality bike that will be easy and comfortable to ride, or we can go to Earl and Sally's Bike Rental and pick up a tandem. Your choice."

He gave me an *oh, honey, please* look, and I knew our next stop would be Earl and Sally's. Full tourist experience and all.

∽

"These things are a bit tricky to get started on, but after a few tries, I'm sure you'll get the hang of it," said Earl of Earl and Sally's Bike Rental. Meanwhile, Sally stood behind her husband and gave me an enthusiastic but discreet thumbs-up. She, of course, recognized us both, but since Earl wore glasses about as thick as the plexiglass of a clear-bottomed boat, I'm not sure he knew it was me, and I didn't take the trouble to tell him.

"I ride mountain bikes all the time, so I'm sure I can manage," Jayden answered.

Earl scoffed at the irrelevance, as if Jayden had said *I drive a Subaru*. "Mountain bikes are different. This is a tandem, and the most important thing to remember on a tandem is to communicate. Just like in marriage." He tapped Jayden's chest with his forefinger. "You're the captain, and this little gal"—he waved a thumb in my direction—"she's the stoker, and the stoker needs to know what the captain is up to at all times."

"Especially since you'll be blocking her view," Sally added, widening her two hands apart as if to illustrate the impressive breadth of

Jayden's view-blocking shoulders, which I was going to be staring at all morning. Just as I was going to be staring at the muscles flexing under that clingy T-shirt and watching his thighs pump up and down as we pedaled.

I'd be distracted only by the fact that his cologne was going to be wafting past my nose, which would obviously be no help at all. I really should have insisted on him using Leo's bike. At least then I could have kept a modicum of distance between us. Even the addition of the bike helmet didn't make him less attractive.

How was a girl supposed to think under circumstances such as this? Maybe he'd be unpleasant company once he realized that tandems were a nuisance. It was my only hope. Because hadn't I just stood in the middle of the sidewalk last night and promised my sister I'd never do something so foolish as to fall in love with Jayden Pierce? I really, really needed him to be a jerk today. And thoroughly unpleasant.

But no.

He wasn't unpleasant. He wasn't a jerk. He was charming and funny and got a huge kick out of how uncoordinated our first attempts on the bike were. There was tipping over and brakes squeaking and the cooler falling to the pavement, and even a kick in the shin, but at last, after half a dozen tries, we finally found our balance and a bit of rhythm and made our way down Main Street with his jacket and the cooler wedged into the front wicker basket.

"So tell me all about what I'm seeing here," he said, pointing to various buildings. "I'm a bit of a history buff, so give me all the details you have."

I'd taught the history of the island before, but always to kids aged ten or younger, so I was going to have to adapt my delivery a bit, but I managed, telling him about the architecture and the fort and the various eras the community had passed through. For every bit of information I gave him, he asked ten more questions, so I was actually kind of glad to be on a tandem so I wouldn't have to talk and manage all the pedaling myself. And after the first ten minutes or so, I started to grow mostly desensitized to the view of his broad back and his long legs and his movie-star profile. And his glorious buns.

Yep, I was mostly desensitized, but not entirely.

It was almost 11:00 a.m. when we reached Potter's Pointe. The Wenniway Island community was either at church or working, and the summer season hadn't kicked off yet, so only a handful of tourists were there, and all of them were fit, older, retired types who were focused on their biking and probably had no idea who Jayden was.

Even when we managed to clumsily dismount, and he took off his helmet and sunglasses and stretched his arms up to the sky, no one paid any attention—except for me, of course. Meanwhile, Jayden didn't seem to notice that they weren't noticing him because he was too busy noticing the view of the lake.

"I've been a lot of places," he said. "But I like the style around here. It's very . . . authentic. Very . . . real. Very . . . not Los Angeles."

"Yep. It's all real. Real water, real rocks, a real bridge," I said, pointing off to the west, where we could just barely see the peaks of the suspension bridge around the curve in the hillside. "No painted backdrops around here."

"I like it. Let's eat."

We sat at a picnic table and unloaded the smorgasbord of delectables from the Imperial Hotel chef, including shrimp cocktail, gazpacho, smoked salmon with capers and dill cream sauce, skirt steak sliced thin and skewered with blanched vegetables, and angel food cake with strawberry pomegranate sauce. I knew that's what it all was because there was a little engraved menu signed by the chef.

He'd also included a red-checkered tablecloth, sterling silver cutlery, and glass plates that had somehow not shattered when we dropped the cooler. In short, it was an Imperial Hotel Grand Dining Room meal served under the shade of a one-hundred-year-old maple tree next to the sparkling waters of Lake Huron, and I couldn't help but be reminded of the green and purple paper HAPPY 11TH BIRTHDAY plates I'd shared with Matt while sitting on the floor of the Peach Tree Inn eating red peppers that he'd sliced himself.

Two very different lunches with two very different men.

And I wasn't sure which one suited me more.

I'd spent the past seven months traveling with Tag and had experienced fine dining in a variety of gorgeous, exotic settings, and I'd enjoyed it all immensely. I'd felt worldly and adventurous and undeservedly deserving, but I'd also felt a bit like I was playing at something. As if I were a kid at a tea party pretending to be grown up and fancy and maybe not so deserving, after all.

I now knew which fork to use and how to cut a steak and eat it the European way instead of the American way. I'd even gotten quite adept at handling chopsticks. But I'd always felt a bit on display, as if the serving staff knew I was more one of *them*, rather than one of the patrons. I'd chalked it up to still being a little in awe of Tag and all he knew and all the life he'd lived before me.

But I felt that way a bit now, too. I'd eaten at the Grand Dining Room only a handful of times. We went there for milestone birthdays or when someone graduated from high school, but it wasn't my regular stomping ground.

I knew the chef. Sort of. He'd asked me for a light once when he was outside in the back of the hotel sneaking a cigarette and I was taking a shortcut from my place to Eva's, but that was the extent of our history. He'd certainly never written me a personalized menu before. Then again, that wasn't for me. It was for Jayden. I was just the lucky bystander. Emily's words from the night before seeped into my thoughts, but I pushed them away. I wasn't a groupie. *He'd* asked *me* to go biking. Not the other way around.

"So I've told you all about the island; now you tell me all about being a movie star," I said as we settled in to eat, and I decided that Emily was full of shit and too hormonal to be taken seriously.

He waved off my comment with a flicker of his long fingers. "I don't want to talk about that. That's not interesting."

"It is to me. At least tell me about moviemaking in general. Like, for instance, who are all those people milling around on the set? Other than a director and a cameraman, I have no idea what anybody does, but they all seem to take their jobs very seriously."

Jayden laughed and nodded. "They do take their jobs seriously, but most of the crew are pretty good sports about not taking *themselves* too seriously. We work hard, and we play hard. It's a team sport."

"And who does what?" I passed him the shrimp cocktail, and he took a bite of one before answering, as if going through a mental check-list. "Okay, well, you've met Griffin. He's the director and he controls the ultimate vision of the movie. Technically he's the boss, but he does have to answer to the producers because we bring in the money."

"So does that make you his boss? Because you're a producer?"

"Like I said, it's a team sport. For this film, I do have some creative say over the final product, but there are all different kinds of produc-ers. Some just shell out the cash and hope for a big financial reward on their investment, but some are more like project managers making sure that all the finances are being handled appropriately. It just depends on how you set things up at the start. I've worked with Griffin before, so we have a kind of shorthand. He can be a total horse's ass, but I know he'll bring out the best work from Skylar and me when it's all said and done. Wow, this gazpacho is damn good."

He ate for a minute, and I tried not to stare at his jawline as it moved. Or at his cheekbones, or his neck, or his hair. I had an excuse to look at him, since we were talking to each other, but I was walking a fine line between conversational eye contact and stalker-worthy staring. I had the urge to do the latter, so I forced myself to look down at my food every so often, or out over the water.

"Rashida is the assistant director," he continued. "And her job is probably the hardest, although don't tell Griffin I said so. She has to deal with the shooting schedule and making sure everyone else is doing their job. It's a lot. There's also a production manager, but if stuff gets screwed up, it falls on Rashida. That's why she's so cheerful all the time."

"I noticed that about her. She's very intense."

His smile indicated agreement. "She is, but she's also really cool. Give her a few mojitos and a karaoke machine, and you'll see a whole different side. She does a kick-ass Mariah Carey impression. It's impressive, and pretty funny." He chuckled at a memory that he didn't share with me and continued talking.

"Then there's the cinematographer. Don't ever call them a *cameraman* to their face. They take that very personally. The gaffers help with lighting. The grips work on stuff like building camera rigging and stuff like that. Those are the guys trying to figure out right now how to get all the equipment we need up to the top of some hill that Griffin is determined we use. Then, of course, there's the obvious stuff. Costumes, props, makeup. Postproduction stuff like special effects and editing. Like I said. Team sport."

I asked more questions, and he gave more answers as we ate smoked salmon under the dappled sunshine. Then he asked me things about growing up on the island, and I answered while trying to make my life sound a bit more remarkable than it actually was. And he seemed fascinated by all my stories. He was that good of an actor!

A sweet-smelling breeze blew over the lake, sending a sailboat into our view. A few bikers came and went, and, noticing our impressive repast and assuming we wanted privacy, went on their way with a smile and a wave. Jayden continued to eat long after I'd stopped. I'd never seen anyone consume so much in one sitting, unless it was Thanksgiving, although this food was much lighter and healthier than mashed potatoes and gravy.

"This steak is so good," he said, filling his plate for the third time. "Are you sure you don't want more?"

"I'm sure. We still have some biking to do, and it's kind of hard to pedal if you're too full. Careful, or we'll have to walk back to town." I nodded at his plate.

He just shook his head. "No worries. I eat like this all the time."

"Then you must have the metabolism of a vole," I said, not considering that it might sound rude, but Jayden's laughter rang out, and I felt oddly victorious for having elicited that response. Like I'd won a little prize, and it felt good.

"I wish," he said. "It's more a case of my personal trainer being a whip-cracking sadist. I'll burn this off later. I have a nude scene in this movie, so he's working my ass off. Literally."

I'm pretty sure I licked my lips right about then. There was so much I wanted to say to that, but my brain stopped firing neurons the moment he said *nude scene*. Oh, to be an extra on set that day!

A moment passed while he cleaned another plate and then pushed it away with a satisfied sigh. He stretched—with another satisfied sigh—and then ran one hand over his belly like a football-watching grandpa, patting it with contentment. I nearly expected him to burp, but he didn't, and my brain continued to struggle while attempting to merge the *Jayden Pierce of the nude scene* with this *Jayden Pierce of the three-plate lunch and belly rubbing*. The two were incongruent, and yet . . . not. Turns out he was still sexy, and yet incredibly . . . normal.

"I love that there's no paparazzi here," Jayden said as he looked around. "It's very relaxing."

I loved that he was so comfortable and casual on my little island. "There were a few people back at the hotel with cell phones, but on behalf of the Trillium Bay community, let me say we're glad you're here but also want to give you a bit of respectful privacy. I think you're the biggest name we've had here in a very long time, but we do try to mind our manners."

"It's very much appreciated. In LA, I can hardly use the bathroom in my own house without *TMZ* peeking in my windows. It's a pain."

"I would think so. I can't really imagine that kind of scrutiny. Do you ever get used to it?"

He shrugged. "I grew up in that sort of fishbowl. My parents did a pretty decent job of trying to keep me out of the spotlight when I was little, but I started acting when I was twelve, so lack of privacy kind of came with the territory."

"Did they encourage you to act?"

"They didn't necessarily discourage me from it. I think they figured I could give it a try and decide if I liked it, and if I didn't, they certainly wouldn't have pushed me in that direction. But as it turns out, I did like it. They were very involved in my early career, though, trying to make sure I wasn't working too much and making sure I still got to do all the regular kid stuff. I went to summer sports camps and hung out with friends my own age. I went to a normal high school. Well, sort of normal. I mean, it was public, but it was also in the heart of Beverly Hills, so, you know, not exactly typical. We had a sushi chef in the cafeteria lunch line."

I laughed at that, because nothing seemed *less typical* to me than a sushi chef in a school cafeteria. "We did not have that," I said. "We had pizza, macaroni and cheese, and hot dogs. The closest thing we had to sushi was that sometimes we'd fish during lunch and catch a fresh trout." Now it was his turn to laugh.

We talked more, comparing other aspects of childhood and our teenage years, discovering without surprise that our lives had been very different, but I didn't get any sense of judgment from him. Or any kind of condescending fascination. He wasn't measuring my rather ordinary, mundane existence against his fabulous, high-society life. This was just pleasant conversation between two new friends.

And I decided I liked him. As a person. He was curious and self-deprecating and funny, and so very nice to look at. If things were different, it would be very easy to fall in love with him, but things weren't different. Things were what they were, and although a part of me wanted to stay at that picnic table until the moon rose, we both had things to get back to. I had kayaking to do.

After packing the few remaining leftovers into the cooler, we managed to get back on the bike with a bit more ease this time, and the last part of the ride was quiet as we pedaled slowly, digested our lunch, and enjoyed the scenery. When we got back to Earl and Sally's Bike Rental, Jayden gave me the most platonic of hugs. Don't get me wrong. It still felt great and sent a delicious ripple through me. I wanted to smoosh my body as close to his as possible and was struck by how incredibly solid he was, and how he managed to still smell so frickin' good even after a three-hour bike ride, but there was no linger to the embrace. No extra running of his hand along my back or meaningful glance as we stepped apart from each other. Nothing that hinted of sexual tension. Not from him, at least.

"That was awesome, Lilly. Thank you so much for going with me. I had a great time," he said.

It was nice to hear him say my name, since thus far he'd only called me Chevette, but now I kind of missed it. It was like our secret joke. But now he knew me better and knew my name, and the joke was over.

"I did, too, Jayden. That was really fun. And tell the chef I said thanks for lunch."

"I will. When are you back on set?"

"Thursday."

He nodded and touched his index finger against the brim of the baseball hat that had replaced the bike helmet. "Thursday. Good. I'll see you then." And with a smile and a wave, he was gone.

And I had exactly one hour before meeting Matt.

Chapter 15

Yakkity Yak's Kayak Shack was located on the south shoreline just past Trillium Pointe, and somehow I managed to arrive there before Matt. I'd stopped home just long enough to grab a warmer, waterproof jacket, since it would be chilly out on the lake today, and to brush my teeth. And my hair. And to check my mascara and put on some lip gloss . . . so maybe I was looking forward to this afternoon a bit more than I cared to admit. While the morning with Jayden had created a memory I was certain to cherish for the rest of my days, it was like a Petoskey stone. Unique, beautiful to possess, full of sentimental value, but best left on a shelf to be dusted off once in a while and otherwise forgotten.

As I approached the water's edge, Zach of Yakkity Yak's Kayak Shack ambled out from the tiny red hut that served as his business center. He wore a denim jacket that had once been autographed by Bruce Springsteen, but the signature had long since faded. He also wore a dingy green baseball hat turned backward, and since he'd pretty much worn a baseball hat turned backward every single day of his forty-nine-year life, his cheeks and nose were leathery-old-pirate bronze, while his forehead remained Irish baby-bottom pale, except for one little tan spot right in the center where the adjustable brim and hat left an opening. This was only obvious at Mass on Sunday mornings, when Zach was *sans chapeau* and that tan spot looked like the most unfortunate birthmark ever but was, in reality, completely self-inflicted.

"Hiya, Lilly. Glad to see you back home," Zach said.

"Thanks, Zach. It's nice to be back." I looked around but saw no sign of my companion. "Have you seen Matt Eastman around?"

"Nope. Not since sunrise yoga yesterday."

That was not the answer I was expecting. At least not the part about the yoga, since Zach was more of a daily twelve-ounce curls by way of a Budweiser beer can kind of guy.

"You go to sunrise yoga?"

He straightened the frayed lapels of his jacket with obvious pride. "Every Wednesday and Saturday. And Sharon and I do the Tuesday-evening couples' class whenever she's not working."

More information I had not expected, since the only Sharon on the island was Sharon Bostwick, who was not at all, shall we say, Zach's type. Or rather, Zach was not Sharon's type. He wasn't too fussy about his female companionship and would pretty much accept any woman who'd have him, while Sharon, well, she liked men who read literature, dressed nicely, and could do their multiplication tables all the way through the twelves.

"You and Sharon? Are you two . . . together?"

He blushed enough that I could see it underneath the copper hue of his cheeks. "It's new, but yes, and I have Matt to thank for it. He's the one who encouraged us both to try the class, and once you've seen someone do the *happy baby*, well, it moves the relationship forward pretty quickly."

My unbidden laughter came out as an amused snort, but Zach was smiling right along with me.

"Right?" he said, as if to agree with all that need not be said, and giving me another thing to consider while considering those private lessons with Matt. I wasn't ready to *happy baby* for anyone yet . . . but doing the *happy baby* could lead to . . . well, maybe to my own happy baby, in a roundabout sort of way. If I was playing the long game. The very, very long game.

"But sunrise yoga is still my favorite," Zach said. "It starts the day off on the right foot, no pun intended. It gets your blood pumping, clears your brain. It's turning me into a whole new man. You should try it." He fluffed his lapels again, and I didn't have the heart to tell him that he still looked exactly like the same old Zach, right down to the brown target on his forehead. Or that, in spite of his enthusiastic endorsement, sunrise and I had an agreement. I would avoid *it*, and *it* would let me sleep. Because if I really wanted a baby, staying in bed was the way to do it.

"Hi there," Matt said from behind me, and I spun around and felt my own cheeks flush with embarrassment, as if he knew what I was thinking. He couldn't, of course, but my blood vessels didn't understand that.

"Hi," I all but squeaked. "You startled me."

"Sorry. I didn't want to interrupt Zach's sales pitch for my sunrise class. Did he convince you yet?"

"You're as pushy as Father O'Reilly," I said, laughing nervously for no apparent reason. It was just Matt. No reason to be nervous.

"Same good intentions," Matt said. "Different kind of church. So, you ready to hit the water?"

"It's choppy out past Potter's Pointe," Zach said. "Not the best day. I'd recommend staying on this side of the island." Telling us it was not the best day was also not the best business strategy, but I appreciated his honesty. Matt's brows lifted as he looked at me questioningly. "Still up for it? If we stay on this side, we'd have to skip Pine Island."

I'd been looking forward to a bit of hiking on the other island, but in all honesty, this was kind of a relief. I hadn't gotten that much sleep the night before, what with being nervous about the day and the fight with Emily keeping me tossing and turning until all hours, and my morning bike ride with Jayden, although not remotely strenuous, still seemed to have taken a lot out of me. I felt oddly fragile at the moment, and the last thing I wanted to do was get caught by a rambunctious wave and tumble into the lake. The water at this time of the year would be very un-bath-like.

The only downside of this new plan was that I'd hoped during our hike that I could oh-so-casually ask Matt about the mysterious Wendy. We could talk while kayaking, of course, but it wouldn't be as easy, and my curiosity was pretty potent.

"Staying over here is fine," I answered. "I'd rather not risk rolling over and getting dunked in the lake. It's a bit cold for a swim."

"Plus, I didn't bring my flippers or my snorkel," Matt answered, making me smile at the mental image.

"Sounds good. You guys want two singles or a double?" Zach asked as he grabbed keys from the shack. Across the street was a much larger shed where the kayaks were stored at night during the summer months, but since it was still early in the season and not too many adventurous tourists were around yet, most of his inventory was still locked up. Matt looked at me again, another question in his eyes.

"Singles are easier to manage, but it's up to you," he said.

"Singles, please," I said to Zach. He and Matt hauled the kayaks out to the short dock, and after putting on my borrowed life jacket, I climbed in and paddled out of the way. Matt was next to me in seconds, and our *Waterworld* adventure had officially begun.

The sky was still bright and cloudless, but the wind had picked up, and although the water along the shoreline was smooth, the air over the lake was chilly. Much chillier than during my morning bike ride. I should have brought a hat, but on the flip side, the breeze was doing attractive things to Matt's hair, blowing it around and tousling it just so. We made idle chitchat, discussing which direction to head and talking about our favorite spots on the island, the hidden spots that the tourists never found.

"Thanks for showing up today," Matt said after we'd been on the water for about half an hour. "I thought I might get stood up." He had a mild smile on his face, but he was looking straight ahead.

"Why would I stand you up? This was my idea."

"Yeah, but I thought you might get a better offer." This time he did glance my way, and although his expression was neutral, there was something about the look in his eyes that said he'd believed that was a real possibility.

"Why, because I went bike riding this morning?" There was no way it was a secret. He crooked a brow and paused in his paddling so that he wouldn't pull ahead of me.

"That, and I guess I thought with how busy you've been, something else might come up. So, anyway, I'm glad you showed up."

"Of course. And thank you for showing up when you did, too. I don't think I could've talked to Zach about his appreciation of Sharon's yoga poses for much longer. They seem like a very unlikely couple. You must have some powerful matchmaking skills."

Matt's face relaxed as his laughter floated over the water. "I didn't have anything to do with that, other than to invite them both to the class, but maybe I should add that to my long list of non-marketable job skills. I did help teach Tiny how to square-dance so he could win Gloria's heart last summer, but that was definitely a group effort, since I don't actually know how to square-dance."

The wind suddenly got a little chillier—because every Wednesday evening at Saint Bartholomew's Church there was square dancing, and that's where I'd met Tag for the very first time. While Tiny and Gloria were circling each other and testing the waters, Tag and I had fallen in love between the promenades and the wagon wheels, and although I was moving beyond that relationship and storing all those emotions in a locked box somewhere in my psyche, I didn't want to think about that right now. I didn't want to remember how that falling had felt or how it compared to what I might be experiencing now, because although I was certainly attracted to Matt, I'd felt just as many zings and pings and zoinks and quivers with Jayden this morning, and suddenly I mistrusted all the feels pulsating through my limbs. Too many conflicting, unidentifiable emotions and all of them equally risky.

"I remember," I said. "I was there for that." And I could see the details dawning on his face. His realization that, yes, I'd been there, and Tag had been, too. It wasn't an ideal thing to remember, and yet . . . it prompted me to ask the question that had been lingering in my mind since last night. Now might not be the best time for that, either, but I was going to go for it anyway.

"Matt, can I ask you something?" I asked after a pause.

He took a stroke with his paddle, doing an admirable job of keeping us next to each other. "Of course."

"Have you dated anyone since you've lived here?"

He moved ahead a bit. "Not really."

"Not really? Or no? No one."

He paused, but I could tell it wasn't because he was trying to remember. "Nope. No one."

"Why?"

"I guess no one has caught my attention. Until you came back home." He turned to grin at me, but for the first time ever, he seemed insincere, and maybe a little wary. I supposed I could just blurt out Wendy's name to see what kind of a reaction I got, but I didn't want Emily to be caught in the middle. And I didn't want Matt to feel obligated to share something he didn't want to share. Still, I persisted.

"So when is the last time you had a significant relationship?"

"I didn't realize we were out here for a fishing expedition," he said, plunging the oar into the water. I paddled to keep up until I was beside him again.

"Sorry, but you know all about me and Tag, and I have the distinct impression that the Lifetime TV-movie version you gave me of your past left out some stuff. There must have been a significant other here or there, and now you're being sort of mysterious. I'm starting to think a crime was involved. Is that it? Did you stuff your last girlfriend into a barrel and drop it in Lake Huron?"

The wariness faded as he chuckled. "You have a very vivid imagination, and my story is not nearly so sensational."

"Okay, give me the boring version."

He looked over at me, his blue eyes serious even as he smiled. "Okay, the short, boring version is that I was engaged, and my fiancée ran off with another man."

"Ohh . . . I'm sorry. That sucks." Though not eloquent, my response was accurate.

"It does. It did."

We floated for a minute before he finally said, "There is actually a longer, more interesting version, but it's more of a *sit down over a few drinks* kind of story. So how about I give you the director's-cut edition when we get back, okay?"

"That's fine, Matt. You don't have to tell me anything, if you don't want to." *Although, damn, now I really want to hear this story.*

"No, I'm fine with it. It's just . . . complicated."

Given what he'd already shared about his rather colorful history, I couldn't imagine what this next bit would involve. But he looked kind of sad, and so I said, "Complicated, huh? You do realize you're talking to a woman who dated her sister's fiancé's sixty-year-old father, right? And that I'm going to have to see him very soon at their wedding? How's that for complicated?"

"Well, when you put it that way, I guess my stuff isn't so complicated after all." His shoulders seemed to relax a bit. "Let's head out to the Pointe, and then we'll turn around and make our way back. Once we've landed, we can stop by the Palomino Pub for a drink or go to my place and you can see the kittens. Either way, I'd rather talk about this when we don't have to fight the currents."

I agreed, and we continued to head in the same direction, but the mood had dampened, and I wished I'd waited for a different opportunity to get my answers. While this morning's bike ride had been full of laughter and smiles, my afternoon had turned decidedly somber. Matt tried to lighten the conversation with some stories about Garth and Georgie's latest bickering match over which one of them had lost the good hammer, and a long, drawn-out anecdote about Tiny sharing his enthusiastic fascination with hearing his baby's heartbeat, and I laughed when I was supposed to, but it felt forced.

After an hour, we turned our kayaks back in to Zach at the shack. My ears and fingers and toes were cold, the wind had picked up significantly, and although there wasn't likely to be a big crowd at the pub late on a Sunday afternoon, I felt pretty certain that Dmitri Krushnic would be holding court with Sudsy Robertson, Monty Price, and a few of the other old guards. Matt's place with kittens sounded far more pleasant, and so we headed there. And I was right. The cottage was definitely cozier than the pub.

"This place is so cute," I said as I stepped over the threshold. "I thought you said it was a gardening shack."

"It was, but I've done an amazing job." He was teasing but the boast was accurate, because this little guesthouse was adorable. It was an efficiency style with wide wooden plank flooring, a big, comfy bed in one corner, and a kitchenette with cream-colored cabinets and a glass-tiled backsplash in the other. There was a tiny bathroom and a door that led out to a deck that was just big enough for four Adirondack chairs. As of yet, there was no railing on that deck because of the unforeseen kitten infestation.

"You have done an amazing job. What still needs to be done, other than the railing?"

"Some light fixtures and trim work. It's mostly finished. Now I'm just trying to stall because I don't want to move until I know where I'm headed next." He walked over to the narrow, vintage-style refrigerator and pulled open the door. "I have beer, oat milk, and water. What's your preference?"

"Are you having a beer? I thought you didn't drink."

"I usually stay away from the hard stuff, but honestly, it's not an issue. Since leaving Los Angeles, I've learned that the partying was more a by-product of my surroundings and the crowd I hung out with. Fortunately, not an addiction. I can take it or leave it. Right now, I think I'll have a beer."

"In that case, I will also have a beer."

He got one for each of us, popped the tops, and we went to sit out on the deck in the sunshine. He also brought me a soft knit throw blanket because the wind had picked up a bit. I hadn't told him I was cold. He just guessed, because Matt had that kind of insight, so I gratefully tucked it around my legs and feet.

Through the trees, I could just barely see the lake and a bit of the road that surrounded the island, but once the leaves were out in full force, this would be a completely private oasis. Even now, it felt very secluded. We sipped our drinks in companionable silence for a few minutes until I said, "I can see why you wouldn't be in a hurry to leave this little spot. It's very cozy."

"Yes, it is, and as long as the neighbors aren't making a huge ruckus, it's quite peaceful."

"A ruckus? You have noisy neighbors?" I looked around to see any nearby cottages, because this place was tucked into the woods behind the Dunnigan House, and the Dunnigans were far too rich to ever do something so gauche as be noisy.

"I'm referring to the infestation," he said.

"Oh, that's right. When do I get to see the kittens?"

"If we sit here for a bit, they'll probably come find us. There's one marmalade guy who is very inquisitive, and he's usually the first to show up. And he has a spotted sister, who shows up next. I'm trying to convince Emily to give one to Chloe for her birthday."

"Oh, that's too cute. Chloe loves Gigi's cats, and she's bummed to be giving them up when she and Emily move to the Peach Tree."

"Exactly. So tell your sister that Chloe needs a cat. Do you know of anyone else who needs one? I feel obligated to find them all homes, even though the mother showed up on my doorstep already in the family way."

"I'll ask around. Maybe Brooke is in the market. Or Leo. Or maybe even my dad. He hasn't had a pet in a while. We had to put down our old golden retriever about three years ago, and I've been expecting him to get another dog, but so far, he's resisting."

"Well, some people need to grieve relationships longer than others before moving on. Even with their pets."

This seemed like a decent enough segue. "Speaking of moving on . . ." I let that linger out there to see if he'd pick up the thread. He caught my meaning, and his chuckle seemed full of irony rather than humor.

"I guess you'd like to hear about *Wendy*, huh?" He said *Wendy* with the same dry, rhetorical tone someone wandering the desert might use when asking, *is it hot enough for ya?*

Trying to lighten the moment, I replied, "Well, given that you've told me the past only has power over you if you let it, I'm hoping you'd like to tell me."

"Did I say that? About the past?" His furrowed brow turned quizzical.

"You did."

He took a drink. "Yeah, that sounds like some kind of cheesy bullshit thing I might say."

An orange kitten popped his head up over the rim of the deck, and Matt pointed at him but kept talking. "Anyway, you already know the setup for this joke. She ran off with another guy. It happened about a week before we were supposed to get married."

"Ouch."

"Yes, ouch. See, I was having my bachelor party and she was having her bachelorette party, and since Traverse City just isn't that big, we ended up at the same bar. Seems fun, right?"

Clearly it was not fun.

"Everyone was pretty well lit, except for me," he said, the cadence of his speech slowing a bit for emphasis. "I haven't been drunk since moving back to Michigan, but I kind of wish I had been that night, because maybe then I wouldn't have spotted her in the bar parking lot. In the back seat of a car. Fooling around . . . with my brother."

My gasp was audible, and I nearly dropped my beer bottle.

"Your brother? I didn't even know you had a brother." Granted, that may have not been the most important part of this story—but it was a pretty significant point, nonetheless.

Matt shrugged like he was easing off a heavy, burdensome coat that scratched as he moved. "I don't. Not anymore. I mean, I didn't stuff him in a barrel and drop him into Lake Huron"—he gave me a sideways glance—"but I thought about it. He's still out in the world, somewhere, but I don't have anything to do with him. Or her. Obviously."

The orange kitten hopped up onto the deck, his fuzzy hair aglow in the sunlight as he came over to investigate things.

"I'm . . . speechless. Matt, I am so sorry. That's just so . . . unbelievably shitty." Again, eloquence escaped me, because any words used to describe this situation needed to be low-life and harsh.

"Yeah. Pretty shitty." He paused, and I waited because I simply didn't know what to say. He crossed his legs at the ankles, his posture relaxed, but his tone betrayed some thinly veiled and understandable melancholy.

"My brother, Cole, had been the only constant in my life, you know? There when my mother was missing. He's a year and a half older than me, so technically I was her *second* mistake." He took a long draw from that bottle of beer. "Even after moving in with my grandmother, he and I were a team. I felt like he was the only one I could really trust because he'd been with me through it all. When I ended up back in LA and kind of losing my shit, he was the one who came and got me.

Cleaned me up. Brought me back to the cherry farm. In some ways I felt like I owed him my life. So I guess one day he decided to collect."

He looked over at me and sighed all the way from his toes. I nearly got up from my chair to give him a hug. It was definitely what my heart wanted to do, but I stayed put because it seemed like he had more to say. And because the orange kitten had been joined by two others. A white one with orange and black patches, and a gray striped one with a mostly white face.

Matt noticed them, too, and his lips tilted into a small smile. "We have extra company today. There's two more, but they're shy."

"I'm going to need one of those kittens," I said. "Gigi will just have to deal with it."

"Sold," he said. We watched the little fluffballs as they grew more brave and came close enough to sniff our shoes.

"Can I pick one up, or are they too little?"

"Sure. My best guess is that they're about four weeks old, so you should be fine."

I scooped up the calico, who instantly began to knead at the blanket in my lap. "So, anyway," I said. "Your brother sounds like a giant, despicable asshole."

That resulted in a nod. "Technically he was my half brother. Different random dads, and I know Cole had his own issues. I realize that now. He tried to play it off like it was my fault because I'd gotten all the attention from the modeling and stuff, but that was just luck of the draw. He could've done it, too. My mom signed him up for all the same things she did with me, but he just wouldn't cooperate. I learned how to smile and stand still, and he just wouldn't do it. So . . . yeah. Wendy was my last relationship, and all this went down about a year and a half ago, about six months before I moved here."

He shrugged dismissively. "But hey, at least I caught them before the wedding, right? It would have been super awkward if we'd already been married." His joke fell flat, even as he rolled his eyes at his own misfortune. My urge to hug him grew harder to ignore.

"Are they still . . . together?" I asked tentatively.

"I have no idea, and honestly, I don't care. I've let all that go. I'm not going to waste my energy holding on to a grudge. I don't hate them, but I don't have the emotional bandwidth to wonder what they're up to or how they're doing, either. I don't owe them that."

I wasn't sure if that was incredibly healthy, self-actualized recovery or just good old-fashioned denial, but either way, I couldn't imagine that sense of betrayal. My sisters and I used to get angry with each other over who took the last brownie, so I couldn't in my wildest dreams fathom what any of us would do in a situation like this. Then again, none of us would have been in a situation like this.

The two other kittens began to meow near my feet, and soon all three of them were in my lap, and I was glad because I needed something to cuddle, and if I let my righteous sympathy get the better of me, that something was going to be Matt. I was feeling all sorts of feels. Anger and a sense of betrayal on his behalf, and a burgeoning need to erase that frown from his normally smiling face.

"Has your grandmother kept in touch with him?"

"I don't know. I've never asked her."

That part didn't seem quite so healthy. Totally justifiable, but maybe not so healthy. If nothing else, the curiosity would have gotten to me. "Do you think it might be good for you to find out?"

His blue eyes stared out at the trees, his voice contemplative, as if he were genuinely considering my question and not just giving an easy answer. "I don't really know what purpose that would serve. I mean, I don't feel bad about it anymore. Their journey is their journey and mine is mine. I mean, does it impact my ability to trust people? Of course it does, but so does my entire childhood." His follow-up chuckle was rueful but without a hint of self-pity. "I know my story has a few extra twists and turns to it, but everybody's got their baggage, right?"

He sat forward, leaning his forearms against his legs, and his expression when he turned to me was now cautiously open, as if he was measuring my reaction before sharing more. "And now you know all my secrets. For what it's worth, the only two other people I've told about this are Emily and Ryan. It's not really a story I'm interested in having go public, if you don't mind."

"Of course not. I won't tell anyone. Thank you for trusting me with it." I squeezed one of the kittens and wondered if Matt would've been happier to keep this part of his story all tucked away inside, but he smiled at me and seemed relieved, and I realized then just how sexy vulnerability looked on him. It was damn near irresistible.

We said our goodbyes shortly after that because I had to get home to Gigi's in time for dinner, a usually pleasant ordeal that I found I had no interest in today. Maybe I'd plead a headache and sit this one out, but if I did, Emily would think I was still mad at her. And I wasn't. I could see now why she wanted me to be careful with Matt's feelings—not that I wouldn't have been anyway. I wasn't prone to recklessly trampling over other people's emotions, but his situation was kind of big and kind of specific.

So, as Matt and I stood in the doorway of his little cottage, I gave him that hug. I'd thought to offer comfort, but wrapping my arms around him, I realized I'd been craving it as much for myself, and for a variety of reasons. Although I wanted to linger, I didn't. Because that hug felt a little too good and a little too comfortable and a little too . . . much. And if I wasn't careful, I might have ended up kissing him. And that would've just been too confusing for everyone. Well . . . maybe just for me.

Chapter 16

"Okay, people, listen up! Griffin will be here soon." Rashida was standing on a wooden bench just outside the Sugar Pie, Honey Bunch Bakery and shouting into a bullhorn—which almost seemed redundant because during the past few days of working as an extra, I'd come to realize that her voice could penetrate a cinder block wall lined with lead.

It was Monday morning, eight days since my bike-riding, kayaking Sunday, and since then I'd seen Jayden a handful of times, but only in passing. He always offered up a friendly smile and an enthusiastic wave, and I couldn't deny I'd felt like the coolest kid in the school cafeteria last Friday when he'd given me a high five as he walked by. But I'd had no more invitations, and although my ego did want him to make some kind of overture, it really was just that. My ego. We all wanted Jayden to invite us someplace, anyplace, to do just about anything. But I'd had my turn, and that was that.

Meanwhile, I'd seen Matt a few times as well while I did tasks for Emily. He'd seemed a bit more aloof the day after our long conversation. More reserved and perhaps a little wary, as if telling me something so deeply personal had left him feeling a little raw and exposed.

And unfortunately, when he'd asked if I wanted to meet him for a coffee on Thursday morning (after I'd skipped his sunrise yoga class—again), I'd had to turn him down because I was scheduled as an extra that day and said I didn't know when I'd be free again. And that was the truth. My schedule was jam-packed.

Gigi wanted me to restock the linens at her rental cottages on a daily basis, because Geena was selfishly not recovering from her hysterectomy at a rapid enough pace. Emily—with whom I'd patched things up, for the most part—wanted my help with making wedding favors, which involved cutting out circles of mint-green tulle and filling little tiny satin boxes with pastel-colored candied almonds and then having to tie tiny dark green satin ribbons into bows that were *just so* until my neck ached and my eyes went blurry. And even Brooke, Eva, and Marnie were pestering me for things because Emily's wedding shower was coming up this weekend, and they wanted my input on what games to play.

I'd never dreamed that being unemployed could be so damn much work.

But today, technically all I had to do was walk. At least according to the call sheet I'd been handed at seven o'clock this morning as I sat in the makeup chair in the middle of the Grand Ballroom. They were shooting a scene on the far west end of Main Street, which I already knew because I'd learned all about it at church yesterday morning.

Well, not so much at church but rather in the front yard of Saint Bartholomew's right next to the statue of Antoine Saint Antoine, where the congregation always congregated after the service to visit and gossip and whisper complaints about each other, the way all good Christians did.

"Harlan, how do you expect the good citizens of Trillium Bay to get their necessities on Monday if there's all sorts of movie shenanigans going on right outside my door?" wobbly, knobby old Mr. O'Doul of O'Doul's grocery store had complained, all but waving his cane in my father's face. "Give us this day our daily bread. That's what we ask of the Lord, and here you are letting those Hollywood people get in the way of people doing their shopping, and Mrs. O'Doul, she doesn't like it. Not one bit."

The chief was thoroughly accustomed to being accosted in such a manner by various members of the Wenniway Island community outside Saint Bart's on Sunday after church. Vera VonMeisterburger invariably brought him some issue concerning the library or the status of our fruit bat population, or Dmitri Krushnic wanted to share a scandalous story he'd recently heard from a very reliable source that never, ever turned out to be reliable in the slightest, or Judge Brian Murphy might amble over to ask if my father had, by any chance, seen his missing spectacles, when nine times out of ten they were on top of the judge's shiny, bald head.

These encounters were as much a part of our Sunday-morning ritual as dipping our fingertips into the holy water or fighting off a nearly debilitating dose of the drowsies as Father O'Reilly pontificated pointlessly about being a better person, even while knowing that he often cheated at cards, frequently swore like a drunken frat boy, and had no hesitation whatsoever about going into any one of the dozen fudge shops lining Main Street and helping himself to an entire plateful of free samples. Sometimes he even brought along a little plastic baggie so he could save some for later. He insisted that wasn't stealing because the samples were *free*—even if he did swipe about a pound at a time.

"Bob," my father had said to old Mr. O'Doul yesterday after church in the same droll tone he used with basically everyone on basically every occasion. "The folks around here are well aware that we have a movie crew on the island, and I feel quite confident that most of them are willing to postpone their shopping until later in the day if it serves the greater good. This production crew is bringing in a lot of money, you know, and the town council got your approval before we agreed to let them film. Remember signing that agreement?"

"I don't remember signing any agreement," the old man had groused. "You're just saying that because your daughter is the mayor.

Wait . . . is she the mayor? Or am I thinking of somebody else?" His heavily lined, age-spotted brow furrowed into an even more shar-pei-like cluster of wrinkles, his thick, bristly white brows nearly colliding. "Harry Blackwell is the mayor, isn't he? Is Harry Blackwell around here? Maybe I should go take this up with him."

Mr. O'Doul had turned then with all the alacrity of a nearsighted, three-legged turtle trying to navigate an obstacle course full of porcupines, and my father had made zero attempt to remind him that Harry Blackwell attended Saint Augustine's Episcopal Church over on Marquette Street on Sunday mornings and hadn't, in fact, been the mayor since last November.

Brooke had arrived at our sides soon after, and she and my father filled me in on the latest behind-the-scenes kerfuffles among the town council members as they'd negotiated the details of today's filming requirements with a cranky Griffin Boyle. Whatever the latest drama, however, somehow it must have all worked out, because here I was, early Monday morning, standing on the west end of Main Street, right outside O'Doul's grocery store with at least thirty extras, all of whom I was well acquainted with.

There were my friends Eva, Marnie, and Bethany, along with Dmitri, Sudsy, Xavier, and Percy and about two dozen others, all waiting for further instructions from Rashida. I was wearing a chocolate-brown satin dress with a high collar and long sleeves, so the fact that the air was cool and the sky cloudy was in my favor. A thick fog lingered in the air, and rumor had it that this had put the director in a good mood because he liked the spooky atmosphere it provided. I could hardly wait to see what Griffin *in a good mood* looked like.

All around us, the usual flurry of activity I'd come to learn preceded filming was happening. Crew members were scurrying here and there, camera rigs were being moved into position, and the video village—a term I'd learned from Jayden—had been set up off to one side and contained monitors from which Griffin could watch what the cameras were picking up.

Down the street, my father, Leo, and several other officers were standing near the wooden sawhorses painted safety orange that served as roadblocks to any equine, cycling, or pedestrian traffic. The ferry boats used by the general public wouldn't start arriving on the island for another hour yet, but boats from the marina still had access to the docks, so a few visitors were starting to show up and were being directed in the opposite direction.

A horse taxi arrived beyond the barricade, and we all watched with equal eagerness to see Griffin, Skylar, and Jayden climb down. They made their way up the street toward the extras, and as usual, Jayden waved and encouraged the cheers. Skylar's smile was more of the *she who smelt it, dealt it* variety, and Griffin hopped down and immediately began pacing around the area and scowling as if somehow, each and every inch of it offended him. Apparently *good mood* Griffin looked exactly like *cranky* Griffin. We extras had learned to never make eye contact with him, but as he strode in our direction, I felt his eyes bore into me.

"You," he said, pointing at me with his phone in his hand. "You're Skylar's costume girl, right?"

"Um, yes?" Not sure why I sounded like I was the one asking the question, but he was so damn intimidating, and I didn't want to somehow give him the wrong answer.

"Come here."

The group of extras, my dear friends who made no attempt to protect me, parted silently as I moved forward, as if the executioner had just summoned me to offer a final cigarette. I reached his side, and he all but glowered as he looked me up and down. He twirled his index finger in a horizontal circle, indicating that I should turn around, and so I did. Rashida came down from her perch and joined him. They murmured while I stood there wondering what was about to happen. Rashida nodded and tapped her chin a few times, then nodded again.

"She'll work, don't you think?" she asked.

Griffin stared at me for another long moment and then nodded. "Actually, I think she's perfect."

I wondered if they realized that I could hear them, or if they thought this was some kind of *Westworld* set where everyone except the two of them were actually animatronic robots just there to serve them.

"You ever done any acting?" Griffin asked me gruffly.

"No, not really, but I've been in a few pageants." I knew that was totally irrelevant, but when Griffin Boyle is staring at you and asking you questions, you want to give him *something*. At least I didn't resort to saying that I was a *really good* extra in the dining room scene or that Jayden had just bought my father's car. Fortunately, Skylar and Jayden had joined us by then, and he spoke up on my behalf.

"Lilly will do a great job, Griff," Jayden said, but Skylar's perfectly arched brows rose as much as her prematurely Botoxed forehead would allow.

"She's a little . . . wide, don't you think?" Skylar whispered loudly enough for everyone to hear. So not so much a whisper as a subtle roar.

Wide? What the fuck? I'm not wide.

Jayden actually chuckled as his eyes met mine before he turned to look at his costar.

"Skylar, she's your exact measurements, remember? So if she's wide, then so are you."

I could all but feel her sucking in her cheeks and stomach. The air around us shimmied with lack of oxygen for all the inhaling she'd just done.

"You guys do know I can hear you, right?" I said, testily. I'd been jabbed and prodded and poked with pins and treated like I was invisible long enough by these movie people. I could stay quiet when it suited me, but right now, they were just being rude. Fortunately, everyone but

Skylar laughed, and Rashida pulled me gently by the wrist to follow them to the other side of the street.

"Here's the deal," Griffin said. "In this scene, Jayden's character, Beau, is walking down the street. Consumed with grief, he's not really paying attention to where he's going. He bumps into you, and when you turn around, he thinks he sees his dead wife, but of course, you're not her. Do you think you can do that?"

"Do I think I can pretend to not be his dead wife?"

"Pretty much."

"Um . . . yes, I think I can do that."

"Good." Griffin turned to Skylar and suddenly put both thumbs and index fingers to his temples, his eyes going round. "Wait. This has given me an amazing idea. Skylar, go back to wardrobe and put on the same dress as this one." His head tilted in my direction.

I knew from my time as Skylar's mannequin that there were usually several identical costumes, since the actors often had to wear something for multiple days at a time. They definitely had another version of what I was wearing. And it probably had a few microscopic droplets of my blood on it from where I'd been stuck with pins.

"What? Why?" Skylar frowned, more than usual.

"Because I want to do a series of shots of the two of you in different spots on the street, and some with you in the foreground and this one in the background."

I guess I was *this one* now. I thought about telling him my name was Lilly, but it didn't seem all that relevant at the moment. Even to me.

"But I'm already dressed." Skylar pouted. "Why can't she go back to wardrobe and find the match to what I'm wearing?"

"Because this incredible fog isn't going to last all morning, and I need to get the shots of her with Jayden first." He flicked his fingers in an *off with you* manner, and even though she probably deserved it, I didn't like the way he was so dismissive. She looked at Jayden imploringly, as if hoping he'd back her up.

"Um, Griff, do they really need to have on the same dress?" Jayden asked. "What they already have on is kind of similar, don't you think? They're both wearing brown."

A tiny squeak emanated from Rashida's throat as Griffin slowly lifted his arm and put a patronizing hand on Jayden's broad shoulder. "Ah, Jayden. Jayden. My man. Remember all those great times we had together in film school?"

Jayden's expression soured, suggesting he knew exactly where this was going as Griffin continued. "Wait. What? What's that you say? You say you don't remember any great times together in film school? Maybe that's because you didn't go to fucking film school? That's right. You took tap dancing lessons and went on *Star Search* and hung around on film sets in your daddy's two-million-dollar trailer while he got high with Al Pacino. But I went to film school, so how about you let me make the call on this one so we can get some work done while this fog sticks around. Skylar, go change your dress."

Her mouth opened, but no sound came out as she thought better of it; then it clamped shut again as she spun around and pounded her feet back to the horse taxi, and I wondered if I was about to spend the day getting yelled at by Griffin Boyle. Something told me he'd not go easy on me just because I was new and clueless, but it was nice to see how Jayden had gone to bat for his costar. Even though he'd complained of her to me, he'd had Skylar's back when she'd needed it. For all the good it had done. Griffin had chewed up Jayden and spit him out, too. This was going to be a rough morning.

After Skylar left, we spent the next thirty minutes learning how to walk. Seemed like most of us had mastered the basics on how to get from point A to point B, but in this situation, it was all about pacing. Rashida and Griffin split all the extras into couples or clusters and had them stand at different spots along the sidewalks. When Griffin called "Action," everyone was supposed to move toward a specific location, but some people had to walk quickly, with purpose, while others needed to look as if they were just out for a relaxing stroll. Griffin wanted varied tempos to everyone's steps.

My job was to walk down Main Street, arm in arm with Percy O'Keefe, starting at O'Doul's grocery store and heading toward Anishinaabe Trail. But we couldn't walk too quickly because Jayden was starting down by the historic post office, and we needed to collide right outside the Mustang Saloon. It all sounded so easy, but it was much more complicated than one would have thought. I'd never watch another movie without noticing the extras.

"Okay," Griffin said to me when everyone else had received their instructions. "We'll do this a couple of different ways. First off, do you have a name?"

Several snarky responses popped into my mind, but I simply answered, "Lilly."

"Okay, Lilly. You are a nineteenth-century lady walking down the street with your sweetheart when a man you've never seen before bumps into you. You turn and look back at him, and you're annoyed by his clumsiness. Then he grabs your arm, and you're even more annoyed, so you pull away and then keep walking. I may tell you to move faster, or more slowly. Just depends on what I see. And don't forget to leave some room in that first reaction to give yourself something to build to when he grabs your arm. Does that make sense?"

"Yes." It mostly did, but even if it hadn't, I'm not sure I would've asked. My heart was pounding so fast I'm sure nothing would have come out except squeaks and gibberish.

"Good," he said. Then he spoke to Percy without bothering to get his name. "While this is going on, you just keep looking forward. When she stops, you stop, but don't turn and look at them. Then, when she pulls away, you start walking again. Clear?"

"Yes, sir," Percy answered, touching the brim of his hat in acknowledgment.

"Okay, good. We're not going to rehearse because there's no dialogue in this scene, and it'll be more organic if we just go for it. Like I said, Lilly, we'll start with you being annoyed, and then we'll do a few takes where you're more surprised than annoyed. After we do some takes of you, we'll reset the camera angles and then do shots of Jayden's reaction, but he'll be doing his thing every time. His reactions will help you with yours. Got it?"

"Yes." Still no real idea of what any of that meant.

I hoped I wasn't about to ruin this movie with my lack of acting chops, but Jayden was there and reached over to squeeze my forearm. "You'll do fine. But just a warning, I'm probably going to bump into you pretty square and solid. Griff likes to do a lot of takes, so I'll try not to bash you too hard, but it needs to look real. Let me know if you need a break or anything. Or if I'm hitting too hard."

"I will. Thanks. I'm sure my shoulder can take it."

"Okay. We got this." He gave me a wink and a thumbs-up and went to stand on his mark at the other end of the street.

"You are so frickin' lucky," Eva said to me as Jayden walked away and we took our starting positions. "All I get to do is cross the street and go down the other sidewalk, and you are literally bumping elbows with Jayden Pierce. I want your life."

Percy was next to me in a tweed suit and a bowler hat. "She is lucky," he said. "She gets to walk down the street with all of this fresh goodness." He smoothed his stable-stained hands over his puffed-out chest. "You know, you could get a piece of this, too, Eva. I'm very generous."

Eva rolled her eyes at the suggestion. "On second thought, crossing to the other side of the street doesn't sound so bad after all."

There was another flurry of activity around the cameras, and a collection of gawkers had gathered down by the barricade, a crowd of maybe twenty or so, but I was confident that as the morning wore on, there'd be more spectators. Both homegrown and visitors. At least they were far enough away that they couldn't see me or my reactions. It was bad enough that those enormous cameras would be aimed at me. A wave of panic washed over me as I stared at the equipment, and suddenly realized I was about to be *filmed in a scene with Jayden*. Not in the background or in a random, anonymous group, but *in* a scene with Jayden. I decided right then to change my mind. I didn't want to do this after all. But now it was too late because Griffin and Rashida were sitting in their chairs and staring at the monitors. Nothing but a meteor or a tsunami was going to save me.

"Places!" Griffin called.

A crew member stepped in front of one of the three cameras with the marker. "'Eternal Embrace.' Street scene number eight. Take one." He clacked the clacker and jumped out of the way.

A horse harness jingled in the distance. The fog continued to mist up the air near the water, and along the street I noticed that some of the storefronts had been altered to appear more historically accurate, so they looked almost the same, but not quite. Down by the barricades, I could see my father leaning against a post. It was all very surreal, and I wondered how he felt about me doing this—not that he'd ever offer up the information. If he was proud, he'd never say so.

"Quiet! Mark. Camera rolling!" Griffin called out. "And . . . action."

I clutched at Percy's arm like it was the only vine keeping me from plunging to my death over the edge of a precipice and was grateful that he took a step forward. Otherwise I might have stood outside O'Doul's grocery store immobilized, like Saint Bartholomew's statue of Antoine Saint Antoine, until Jayden came all the way to me. Down the street, he was striding toward us, his face a study of consternation and distress. Logical, since he was now Beau, a man heart-struck with grief, not to mention that little matter of his recently deceased wife potentially haunting him, too. That would certainly make a person look distraught.

After five seconds that felt like five minutes, I harnessed enough mental clarity to realize that staring at Jayden would probably ruin

Griffin's shot, so I decided to focus on Dmitri Krushnic's back instead. He was walking ten paces in front of me in a top hat that was far more distinguished than the beekeeping number he usually wore, and I hoped that by looking at him, I'd be genuinely surprised when Jayden made contact. As luck would have it, or maybe it was just his mad acting skills, I *was* startled when he made contact, because damn! He did hit me hard! The force was enough to turn me backward toward him.

And then everything seemed to move in slow motion as I watched his face take on its own look of astonishment. I felt him touch my forearm, and I had no idea what was happening with my own stupid face because I was so mesmerized by his and the way he was looking at me. As if I were his most cherished darling. His wife. The most precious gem in all the universe. He loved me. He missed me so desperately. Then Percy started walking again, and I remembered I was supposed to pull away—because I wasn't his dead wife.

"And cut!" Griffin called out brusquely, shoving the headphones from his head to dangle around his neck. He rose abruptly from his chair and strode my way. Something told me I hadn't done very well. Cranky Griffin looked even more cranky than usual.

"Lilly, was it?" he said, making it somehow sound like an insult.

I nodded.

"Did we, just a few minutes ago, chat about you looking annoyed? Because I seem to remember mentioning something about that over there."

He pointed toward O'Doul's, where we'd been standing before.

I nodded.

"Okay, good, because I thought maybe I'd gotten mixed up because what I just got from you in that scene was you being all dewy and lovesick. I know you think this guy is Jayden Pierce. But he's not. He's Beauregard Templeton Whitford III, and he may or may not have murdered that wife he's so distraught over. So, imagine a murderous widower bashing into you on the street. If that really happened, how do you think you'd feel?"

"Um, annoyed?"

"Yes, annoyed! And annoyed looks like this." He made a circle around his face with his index finger, and I giggled nervously, because Griffin Boyle was so chronically grumpy that it had gone past being intimidating and circled all the way around to being nearly comical. It was like being yelled at by a cartoon monster.

"Yes, annoyed. I'm sorry," I said. *It's just that gazing into Jayden's eyes is like staring into all the mysteries of the cosmos and getting every answer you ever dreamed of,* I wanted to say—but fortunately didn't—because I did not think Griffin was interested in that. Instead I said somberly, "I'll remember this time."

"Good. Take it from the top. Places, everyone!"

Jayden winked at me as I walked past him again to go stand near O'Doul's, and I felt my cheeks scorch with embarrassment. Maybe I could walk, but apparently I couldn't act. There was definitely a learning curve here.

Fortunately, we did the scene a dozen more times, and I felt myself getting infinitesimally more comfortable each time. In truth, my skills probably didn't improve all that much, but at least I was growing accustomed to seeing Jayden gazing at me with eyes full of heartbreak and longing without my knees going weak and my heart thumping so hard and fast that the trim on the front of my dress ruffled.

Then we had a brief break as the cameras were reset, and it was Jayden's turn to have *his* face filmed, and all my newfound resistance to his charms melted away, because before, he'd been *rehearsing*. But now the cameras were on *him*, and he was bringing it. Lord have mercy, the look of longing on his face was the most captivating thing imaginable.

And then, on the last take, he reached up and very nearly touched my cheek. His hand was so close to my face I could feel the warmth of it, but then he dropped it back to his side and turned to walk away, and once again, Percy had to tug me down the street and, darn it all, right back into reality.

Chapter 17

"I made the punch according to the recipe, but personally I think it tastes a little bland," I heard Eva say as I walked through the doorway into Marnie's house. It was Saturday morning, and we were gathering there to prepare for the biggest, bad-assiest wedding shower we could come up with because that's what Emily had requested. Since there'd been no shower the first time she'd gotten married, I believe what she'd said was, "I require hoopla," and so we were planning hoopla. And frivolity. And perhaps some shenanigans. We had a crowd of thirty or so people scheduled to arrive that afternoon, and there was a lot of work to be done. Apparently, hoopla was labor intensive.

To complicate matters, the weather outside was typhoonish and inhospitable, with gale-force winds rattling the rafters and rain coming down in torrential buckets. It wasn't an actual typhoon, of course, but about as close to one as possible without the folks at the Weather Channel showing up to do some live broadcasting.

This had made getting to Marnie's house a real chore. Unlike most of us, she lived in a thickly wooded bluff on the north side of the island, about as far from the downtown area as you could get. Only one narrow dirt road led to her tiny neighborhood, and the rain had transformed it to such muddy sludge that even the horse taxis were having a tough time getting in and out. I'd had to walk the last thirty feet while carrying two huge boxes of game prizes, not to mention a present I'd spent twenty minutes meticulously wrapping that was now as soaking wet as I was.

Inside the house, I set the soggy boxes and the gift down on Marnie's tiled entryway floor and shrugged out of my dripping-wet raincoat. My new sandals were caked in clods of muck. I needed a hot shower, a change of clothes, and a blow-dryer.

"The punch tastes fine," Gloria answered Eva from the kitchen. "You're just so used to the spiked stuff, and this doesn't have any alcohol in it, you lush."

Marnie came around the corner, looking adorable in a floaty black dress covered with tiny white dots, which only served to make me feel even more soaked and bedraggled.

"Oh my goodness," she said. "Did you swim here from Manitou?"

"It's raining," I answered, my tone ironically dry. "And the taxi got stuck in the mud. Sorry about your floor." I lifted one foot to show off all the extra bits of Wenniway Island clinging to my shoe.

"Don't worry about the floor. Come on in. I'll get you a towel."

I slipped off my shoes anyway, leaving them by the door, and then walked into the family room, which provided a clear view of the kitchen as well. Marnie's house was the bungalow variety, but she'd made the most of the space, and I loved her sense of style. It was decorated in pale shades of beachy blues and sandy tans, with whitewashed wainscoting surrounding the room, along with lots of rustic finishes like lamps with driftwood bases and antique vases full of polished beach glass.

Today her house was even more adorable than usual, with lots of wedding decorations already put in place. There were white paper bells hanging from all the light fixtures, balloons shaped like diamond rings and Cinderella's carriage, and dozens of pictures of Emily and Ryan in wooden frames, each with a number written on the glass in silvery marker.

"You guys have been busy," I said, doing a full turn to take in all the fun. I pointed at a photo of my sister and Ryan sitting on the porch of the Imperial Hotel with a number six written on it. "What are the numbers for?"

"It's one of the games," Brooke answered. "Each number corresponds to something significant to the bride and groom. We're going to give everyone a list of options, and they have to figure out which number goes with which thing."

I picked up the photo and looked more closely. "What's the six for?" I asked, giving up after about three seconds of contemplation. I was distracted by the water dripping down my back.

"Six is the number of people they'll have in their wedding party, since it's you, me, Chloe, Jack, and Bryce, and then of course Bryce's little boy is going to be the ring bearer."

I set the picture down a bit too hard on the bookshelf, the thought of seeing Bryce's sweet, pudgy-cheeked three-year-old in a tuxedo walking down the aisle giving my heart a twinge. Next to Tag, he was my favorite Taggert. Nothing against Ryan, of course, but back in Sacramento, Aiden had let me snuggle with him and read him bedtime stories, and he'd once offered to share an ice cream cone with me that I only pretended to taste because he'd pretty much drooled over every inch of it, including the cone, and I just wasn't ready for that kind of commitment.

"Cute idea," I said, accepting the towel that Marnie offered and wrapping it around my head.

"You might want to . . . uh . . . stop in the bathroom . . . ," she said haltingly, pointing rather awkwardly toward *her* face, which clearly indicated that something was actually wrong with *my* face instead. One look in the bathroom mirror confirmed it. My mascara was halfway to my chin in a look that could only be referred to as *oh no*. Fortunately, Marnie gave me a makeup wipe and handed over her trove of cosmetics to help me repair the damage. I was about halfway finished when a kajillion-watt flash of lightning nearly blinded me and a thunderclap ka-boomed so loud I felt like I was standing next to a cannon firing from Fort Beaumont. And a nanosecond after that, the lights flickered, and the electricity went out.

"Jumpin' G. Jehosaphat!" Gloria exclaimed. "That was a close one. Everybody saw that, right? I'm not imagining things?"

"Oh my gosh," Marnie exclaimed, clutching the front of her dress. "That scared the crap out of me."

Even typically calm Brooke was looking around as if to ensure that everyone was okay and that the house was still on its foundations. "Well, that was exciting," she said.

We all paused for another few seconds, waiting to see if the power would return. It wasn't unusual for things to flicker, the downside of living on an island with a moderately fragile but mostly reliable electrical system. Pretty fascinating, considering we got our power through cables that ran under the lake from Michlimac City. I stepped out of the bathroom, blush brush in hand, and after a full ten seconds, which was longer than it seemed when we were all standing around waiting for the next clap of thunder, we all came to the realization that the power was out for good. Or at least for a bit. So much for blow-drying my hair.

"Well then," Gloria said after another ten seconds, "I guess we're going to have this little shindig by candlelight and electric lanterns. I can roll with that."

"Awesome," Marnie said with a sigh. "I'll go gather some up."

As the storm raged outside, we worked like dervishes inside, putting up the rest of the decorations in the dimly lit house. It was the middle of the afternoon, so not completely dark, and of course we got a mega-dose of illumination every time the lightning flashed. We carried on about our business the way adaptable Trillium Bay folk did under circumstances such as this. A little rain wasn't going to ruin our party.

We arranged the trays of petit fours and finger sandwiches—since nothing says *badass bitches* like finger sandwiches—and Eva set about hiding little plastic penis figurines under sofa pillows and in nooks and crannies of Marnie's carefully arranged décor, because apparently that was another one of the games they'd planned. Whoever found the most penises won a fifty-dollar gift certificate to Wild Nights Lingerie compliments of Bethany Markham, who was still the island representative. Not to be outdone, Gloria had, of course, contributed a basket of Earth Harmony Love Me, Love Me, Love Me essential massage oils as another prize, which I secretly wanted to win, even though I had no one to get a massage from. They just smelled really, really good.

At one o'clock, Emily, Gigi, and Chloe arrived. The rain had let up a bit for them, and they had umbrellas and waterproof ponchos, so at least they managed to get to the door mostly dry. And by two o'clock, everyone else was there as well. Marnie had a full house, and the noise was nearly as deafening as the storm. We ate, and drank bland punch, and played silly games, and everyone found it simply hilarious that Chloe was the one who found the most mini-penises. Everyone except for Emily.

"Seriously, you guys. This is a wedding shower, not a bachelorette party," she'd admonished us, but then Chloe gave her the gift certificate for the lingerie, and so she stopped complaining. Then, in the light of the candles and lanterns, she unwrapped the presents and marveled over all the amazing gifts everyone had brought for her: more lingerie, some home décor, things for her new kitchen, and even a framed watercolor painting of the soon-to-be-finished Peach Tree Inn. It was nearly five o'clock when the party started to wind down. A few people had left, but at least fifteen of us were still sitting around sharing stories and commenting on how bad that storm had been. It had passed at last, but the power was still out.

In order to sustain myself in the prolonged darkness, I decided to get myself one more little finger sandwich. I got up and moved around a dozen people to make my way to the table, a tiny lantern in my hand.

"Oh, gee willikers," I heard Gloria murmur from the kitchen. She was standing there in the corner, her head lowered, with a cupcake in each hand. "Oh, good golly. Oh. Holy cannoli," she said breathily.

I held up my lantern, and she lifted her head and looked at me, her eyes big and wide behind her rhinestone-studded glasses, and I thought she was just feeling guilty about the cupcakes. But maybe it was more than that?

"Gloria, what's wrong?" I asked.

She lowered her voice and leaned forward slightly. "Lilly, um . . . I think maybe my water just broke."

She looked down again, and I lowered my light source, and sure enough, there between her sunny yellow size-eleven sandals adorned with big plastic daisies was a tiny puddle of . . . let's call it water . . . because calling it *amniotic fluid* was not a step I was willing to take, even though that's most likely what it was and even though it was the most natural thing in the world. Then again, lots of other liquidy things were technically *natural*, but that didn't mean I wanted to see them splashed all over a friend's kitchen floor.

"Are you sure?" I couldn't help but ask, even though the answer seemed fairly obvious. Still, I looked up at the ceiling to see if maybe the rain had caused a leak in the ceiling. But no. No leak from the ceiling. Just from Gloria.

Gloria looked back at me and shrugged, uncertainty painted all over her face, along with a fair amount of sparkly eye shadow. "Maybe? I don't know. I've never done this before. All I know is that I was standing here, and I took a step to get myself another cupcake—because those are delicious, by the way! Did you have one? Sugar Pie bakery did a phenomenal job on those. Try the red velvet, oh my gosh. So good!"

"Gloria," I said rather sternly, although I did have to admit those cupcakes were distractingly good. "What happened, exactly?"

"What? Oh, yes. I took a step to get another cupcake and then realized my legs felt drippy, and then I look down and then there was all this sploosh on the floor. I didn't feel it coming from my who-hah or anything. It was just sort of there all of a sudden." She took an enormous bite of her red-velvet cupcake, but I could see some concern pinching her features, and no wonder. She wasn't due for at least a month.

I had no real-world experience with this sort of thing. Emily had been in San Antonio when she was pregnant with Chloe, and I'd been a ways removed from any of the other babies born to friends or neighbors on the island. I'd heard stories after the fact, but this was up close and in real time. As in right here, right now.

"Are you having any contractions?" I asked, as if I'd know what to do if she said yes. Or if she said no. Honestly, I had no idea what to do. Where was that Lilly who was so eager to have a baby? That girl was nowhere to be found.

"I've had a backache today, but I thought it was from putting up the decorations. I'm still not sure. It's not like there's a pattern to the achiness. It's just . . . achy."

"Well, I think we should tell everyone else, don't you? And maybe call your doctor? And Tiny?" I said, talking calmly, even though my thoughts were jumping around like a teenager in a mosh pit.

She nodded slowly and shoved the rest of the cupcake into her mouth.

"Do you want me to tell them?"

She nodded, and I wondered if she was in a bit of shock, because I had to stop her from taking another petit four from the table as I turned to the rest of the group.

I held my lantern up high over my head and swung it like Paul Revere. Two if by land, and one if Gloria Persimmons-Kloosterman went into labor.

"Um, everyone? I'm wondering if we could get some help and advice over here because, um . . . we're pretty sure that Gloria's water just broke."

The level of activity and mayhem that ensued was like watching seventeen clowns all scramble to fit into one tiny yellow car, and Gloria just kept saying, "I'm so sorry, Peachy-keen. I didn't mean to upstage you at your own shower. I guess this baby loves attention as much as I do."

"Don't be silly, Glo. It's fine. We just need to focus on you right now, and that baby."

Women much wiser than myself, thank goodness, took over from there, and I was tasked with finding Gloria's purse and her phone so she could place some very important calls. And when Tiny didn't answer her call or respond to her 911 text, I was put in charge of tracking him down.

Naturally, I started with the chief, who promised to send out a search party of deputies, as well as contact the local coast guard about getting her to the mainland, because Gloria taking a regular ferry was not an option. It was good news that she wasn't in active labor, or so the ladies at the shower were saying, but she still needed to get to the hospital.

I texted Matt next and used lots of exclamation points.

R U WITH TINY? IT'S IMPORTANT!!!!!!!

And then, before he'd even had a chance to respond, I called him. "Are you with Tiny?" I asked as soon as he answered.

"Yeah, we're working at the Peach Tree. He's downstairs. Why?"

I quickly filled him in, and he reacted with surprise. "I thought she wasn't having her baby until next month?"

"Apparently no one told the baby that." I walked over to where Gloria was sitting on a towel and talking on the phone with her obstetrician. "Glo, I've got Matt on the phone, and he's with Tiny. What should I tell him?"

"Um . . . ," she said, looking up at me in a daze. "I'm not sure."

A dozen more calls were made before it was finally decided that Tiny would quickly stop by their place and pack her a bag of essentials, while Gloria, with help from Brooke and Eva, would make her way via horse taxi to the airport. As soon as Tiny arrived at the airport with Gloria's things, a coast guard helicopter would take them to the hospital in Michlimac City.

It wasn't an ideal plan because Gloria had no interest whatsoever in getting into a helicopter, and no one blamed her, but all things considered, she was just going to have to. Meanwhile the rest of us were all silently wondering if that ride had a weight limit, because Tiny could put them over the top.

A few minutes later, Gloria waved me over after ending a call. "Lilly-vanilli, I have a huge favor to ask," she said quietly, which for her was quite a feat. She must really be in shock.

"Of course, Gloria. Anything you need." I knelt down by the side of her chair.

"It's a jumbo request, because I know the roads out there are a mess-o-potamia, but I desperately need something fresh and pretty to wear, and heaven knows, nothing that tiny little Marnie has in this house is going to fit me, unless she lets me cut a hole in the center of her bedspread and I wear it like a toga. Not that I couldn't pull off the look, but anyway, I hate to ask you, but is there any chance you could run to my house and help Tiny pack my bag? And have him bring something that I can change into at the airport?"

"Of course. I can leave right now. How about you text me a list of what things you want so I'll have it when I get to your place?"

"Thank you so much, Vanilli. You have no idea how much this means to me."

"I'm glad to help."

I was glad to help, but doing this wasn't going to be a straightforward adventure, since getting from Marnie's place to Gloria's included a long, winding dirt road and several hills and I had no idea what condition things were in due to the storm, but I called my father again, who agreed to send a horse taxi to pick me up. That would help for at least part of the way, and at least it wasn't raining anymore. I was glad for that, but of course, the electricity was still out, so trying to find Gloria's stuff in the dark at her house, even with Tiny's help, could be another adventure altogether.

Chapter 18

I made it to Tiny and Gloria's house a few minutes after Matt and the baby daddy had arrived, but they hadn't made much progress other than to stuff an impractical chiffon nightgown (probably from the Wild Nights collection) and some tripping-hazard bunny slippers into a paper grocery bag. It was a good thing Gloria had sent me because these two were clueless, although the paper bag did come in handy when Tiny started to hyperventilate.

I'd gone to work finding a few more practical items, like a flowered duffel bag, a clean outfit for Gloria to wear, and the most preciously adorable teeny-tiny, ultra-soft sleeper for Baby Persimmons-Kloosterman, but Tiny took one look at that minuscule infant outfit and came completely unglued. Honestly, the man was like a thick-muscled Rottweiler with all the courage and emotional fortitude of a teacup Maltipoo. He was all but quivering.

So, Matt and I, with just a few meaningful glances between us, silently agreed that he'd deal with Tiny, and I would pack the hospital bag. I was the one with the list from Gloria anyway, and since Tiny seemed to have zero idea where anything was located even in his own house, including any of his wife's personal toiletry items, I was basically on my own.

And I was searching in the dark, using my cell phone as a flashlight. It was like being on the world's darkest, least fun scavenger hunt imaginable, especially when I had to dig around in the chest of drawers to find Gloria some sturdy cotton post-maternity panties and accidentally came across a menagerie of sex toys. Naturally I'd wrapped my hand all the way around one of the aforementioned gadgets before I'd figured out what it was, and when I realized what I'd grabbed, I dropped it like a hot, phallic potato, and it bounced—like a rubber dildo—under her bed. I was not about to go after it.

I loved Gloria. I really did. But after today, I felt as if I'd learned things about her that no one but she and Jesus should be privy to.

"Okay," I said, coming from the bedroom to find Tiny sitting on the couch holding a pillow and rocking slightly to and fro, while Matt sat next to him, rubbing his back in a circular, patting motion like he was a melting-down toddler instead of a soon-to-be father.

"I've got all her stuff. Tiny, do you need a few things? A change of clothes? A toothbrush? A razor? You'll be gone for a few days, at least."

"He's got his stuff," Matt answered, nodding at that paper bag. I grabbed it, stuffed it into Gloria's duffel bag, and soon we were back in the taxi on our way.

"You've got this, Tiny," Matt assured him as the buggy made its way toward Wenniway Island's modest airport. "You've read the books. You've powered through the videos. You took the Lamaze class. You're going to do fine. And you know Gloria is a powerhouse. She's going to do great, too."

"But we're not ready," Tiny said. "We still had a month to go, and I have to put the crib together. Where is the baby going to sleep if I haven't put the crib together? I'm not even officially a father yet and I'm already screwing it up."

Matt went pat, pat, pat on Tiny's broad back. "You're going to be a great father, and I tell you what. If you'd like me to put the crib together so it's ready when you and Gloria come back home, I can do that."

"Would you?"

I thought Tiny might say more, but he was too choked up. I wasn't sure if that was from gratitude or fear, but either way, he wrapped both tree-trunk arms around Matt and hugged so tightly I heard Matt wheeze for want of oxygen.

"I can help, too, Tiny," I added. "Matt and I can get the whole nursery set up for you, if you want. Gloria showed it to me the other night, and I know where she wants all the pictures hung and everything." I was volunteering Matt for more service than he'd first offered, but he smiled at me over Tiny's shoulder, and I knew I'd said the right thing.

"Yep," Matt answered. "It's all good, pal. We've got you covered."

"You guys are the best."

His phone rang. It was Gloria, and I could hear her voice loud and clear.

"How are you doing, baby-kins?" Tiny asked, his voice sounding deceptively confident. "Papa Bear is on his way."

"I'm not so sure about this, Papa Bear," she responded, a telltale quiver in her voice. "This helicopter is freaking me out. They expect to go right over the lake, and this thing looks like a giant dragonfly Transformer."

"Don't you worry about a thing," he said. "Those coast guard folks train all the time for stuff just like this, and they know what they're doing. It's going to be amazing, and just imagine the story we'll have to tell our baby when it grows up. I mean, lots of people have babies and lots of people ride in helicopters, but how many people do you know who take a helicopter on their way to have a baby? That's all you, Glo-Glo. Always making an entrance."

"You think?" she asked, sounding slightly less nervous.

"Oh hell yeah. You betcha!" He looked over at me, his face full of doubt, but he was doing his best to cheer her on. Thank goodness she hadn't seen him rocking on the couch fifteen minutes earlier.

Our airport saw a fair amount of traffic, given that many of the wealthier island inhabitants took charter flights to and from the island with regularity. Fortunately, this evening it was quiet, in part due to it being nearly 7:00 p.m., and also because the earlier storm had knocked out the electricity. The building and single runway were lit up with generator power, but all incoming flights would be canceled.

Unless you were a helicopter on your way to rescue a pregnant woman in distress wearing daisy-laden sandals and covered in cupcake crumbs.

I looked to the side of the hangar, and sure enough, the only activity was centered around the big military-looking monstrosity waiting on the gravel tarmac. Gloria was right. It did look like a dragonfly Transformer, and I was quite glad I wasn't the one who had to get into that thing.

I spotted my father and Leo, both in their uniforms; Eva and Brooke, who had accompanied the mother-to-be from Marnie's house; Dr. Pine, who must have been there to lend a hand if the situation called for it; and a handful of others, including airport staff and coastguardsmen.

Tiny jumped out before Henry the driver had even halted the horses and hit the ground at a sprint, dashing his way past everyone else to reach Gloria's side. She was sitting in an Adirondack chair next to the building, with everyone else hovering around her, looking apprehensive. Except for the chief, of course. He looked the same way he always looked.

There was a flurry of activity as Matt and I climbed from the buggy and said our hellos to everyone; then Brooke and I accompanied Gloria into the ladies' room so she could change her clothes.

"How are you holding up, Glo?" I asked through the metal bathroom door. "Crazy day, huh?"

"No shit," she said, and I realized just how nervous she must be because Gloria never swore. She was an *oh fudge, bejeebers, phooey* kind of gal. "And I'm about to load myself onto a fifty-ton piece of metal machinery that has the same propeller system as a beanie hat, and then I get to go have a baby a month ahead of schedule. This is awesome."

Brooke looked at me wide eyed and shrugged as if to say *she's not wrong.*

"Oh, honey. I'm sorry," I said. "I know this must not be how you imagined it, but I'm sure it's going to be fine. Tiny is so excited and proud, and you're going to get through this with flying colors."

"Please don't mention flying to me."

"Whoops. Sorry," I said again, for lack of anything else to add.

I heard Gloria sigh as she rustled around in the flowered duffel bag. "I know. It'll be good. Everything will be fine. I'm just scared. I wasn't quite ready, you know? But maybe it's a good thing."

"How so?" I leaned against the metal door, and Brooke continued to look both concerned and bemused.

"Well, given Tiny's physique," Gloria answered, "and mine, I was kind of expecting a twelve-pound baby. At least since she's showing up a little early, she won't be so darn big."

"So, you think it's a girl?"

"Of course. Only a girl would put me through this much drama before she's even born."

The door rattled and then swung open as Gloria stepped out of the bathroom stall and walked over to the sink. She gave her reflection in the mirror a once-over, fluffing her hair and adjusting the neckline of the soft, pink maternity top I'd brought for her, along with some stretch pants.

"Did you bring me a scarf? Or any accessories?"

"Um . . . no, that wasn't on the list."

"Well, that's no good. How's a gal supposed to feel her best with no accessories?" She reached back into the flowered duffel bag that was dangling from her shoulder and pulled out the triple-stranded turquoise necklace she'd worn to the shower. The stones were the size of grapes and marbles, and it must have weighed a pound and a half. "This will have to do, I guess," she said, dropping it down over her head.

"Do you think maybe you should leave your jewelry behind?" Brooke questioned. "I mean, they'll probably make you take it off once you get into a hospital gown, and you wouldn't want to lose it."

Gloria looked indecisive for a moment, her eyes sparkling with fresh tears. "I just want to look my best when I meet my baby."

"Your baby just wants to see your beautiful face, Glo," Brooke answered, and I was surprised by her sentimentality. Maybe there were a few soft spots in my sister's pragmatic armor, after all.

"You think?" Gloria asked, looking into the mirror again.

"I'm positive. Once she's home, you can show her all your fancy jewelry and talk about all the fun you're going to have teaching her how to put on makeup and which purses go with which shoes, but for now, I'd say keep things simple."

Gloria sighed and removed the necklace. "I guess you're right. That must be why they call you the smart one. And speaking of shoes, can you help me put mine on? I can't see my feet."

Brooke and I helped her slip into a pair of flats decorated with little beach balls, and in spite of her just acknowledging right in front of me that I was not the smart one, I offered to take care of her soiled outfit.

"If there's anything else you need, you just call. And at least this way you won't have to hang out with your cousin, right?" I said.

Her face brightened. "Hey, yeah. There's a silver lining! There's always a silver lining." She squared her shoulders, adjusted her rhinestone glasses, and smiled a warbly, trembly, unconvincing smile. Then she hugged Brooke and me simultaneously before saying, "I love you gals. Okay. Let's get on with it."

Brooke and I rejoined Matt and the others as we watched her waddle toward the chopper, escorted by Tiny and two of the coastguardsmen. The other two were already sitting in the pilots' seats, and I could see them pushing buttons and adjusting levers. Gloria turned and waved right before boarding, and Eva snapped a dozen photos with her phone, then caught the whole thing on video as the propellers twirled faster until the helicopter lifted into the air. The pilot offered a thumbs-up and a smile, which I found very encouraging.

"Well," my dad said as we watched the flashing lights move off into the sky and head toward Michlimac City, "if anyone was going to go big, it was sure to be Gloria."

We watched in silent agreement until the lights disappeared in the distance.

"I don't know about you, but I'm exhausted," Brooke said a moment later, looking around at the rest of us. "That was way too much excitement for me."

"You and me both," I said, even while thinking about all that Gloria and Tiny still had to face. It was hard to believe that only two hours had passed since she'd stared at me in Marnie's kitchen with the cupcakes in her hands and her sandals all wet. My dad had once told me that there were some moments in life that changed everything, that rippled out in every direction, and I was pretty sure this was one of them. We'd all just been a part of something amazing. Scary, stressful, awesome . . . and amazing.

Chapter 19

After leaving the airport, the taxi dropped everyone off at various locations until it was just Matt and me left. As we turned onto his road, Matt leaned toward me and said, "I'm feeling a little wound up. I think I'll head back to the Kloostermans' house and put that crib together. You up for it?"

"Tonight?" I was exhausted and drained and just wanted to take a hot, steamy shower before putting on pajamas and climbing into bed, but I could tell by his expression that he really hoped I'd join him, and something tugged at me. Something elemental. And since I'd turned him down for coffee the other day and had basically told him I had no idea when I'd have any spare time for him, I found myself saying, "Sure, but do you mind if we stop by my place so I can change my clothes? I've had on this dress since nine o'clock this morning, and I've been splattered with rain, mud, and a few other things that I'd rather not explain."

He chuckled. "Sure. Or you can just borrow some sweatpants and a shirt from me, since we're practically at my house."

That was a mostly logical suggestion, but if I disembarked from the taxi at Matt's house, Henry the driver would mosey straight to the Palomino Pub and start casting about tidbits of gossip. Then again, news of Gloria and Tiny's escapades would certainly be the biggest story of the day, so I decided I could risk it. The Kloostermans lived only a couple of streets from Matt's place, and we could easily walk from there, so we sent Henry on his way and walked into Matt's gardening-shed-turned-cottage.

Crossing the room in about four strides, he pulled some garments from his closet and handed them to me, indicating I could change in the bathroom. I briefly thought about asking if I could rinse off in his shower, but it seemed like too much. I was already feeling a bit awkward about wearing his clothes. Especially his pants, which turned out to be at least two sizes too big. I had to roll the waistband three times, and still they bagged around my ankles. I looked like a Clydesdale. The extra-large Traverse City High School T-shirt wasn't too stylish, but it was clean and fresh, and it made me feel a smidge better. So did the toothpaste that I stole from his medicine cabinet and swished around in my mouth, but oh, what I would've given for an actual toothbrush.

He smirked with good humor as I came out of the bathroom looking like a little kid playing the most depressing game of dress-up ever, so I gave him a fashionable twirl. "Do I make this look good?" I asked.

He nodded and opened the refrigerator door. "Definitely. Want a beer?"

"Oh my gosh, no. If I have a beer, I'll fall asleep in ten seconds. It's been a very long day, and I am seriously tired."

He looked back over his shoulder at me. "You are? Then why did you say you'd go back to Tiny's house with me?"

"Because you asked me to."

I didn't mean for it to sound quite so . . . personal, but there was really no way around that. I'd said yes simply because he'd asked, and a slow, satisfied smile crossed over his features, prompting me to add, "I mean . . . I didn't want you to have to go back there all by yourself and fumble around in the dark."

The smile got sexier as his eyes traveled over me. "Lilly. When I fumble around in the dark, I'm usually pretty successful."

I blushed and flushed and tingled at his reply, and finally turned away. "I'll bet."

"Anyway," he said after a pause, "if you're too tired to go build a crib right now, how about we just hang out here and watch a movie? I'm sure Tiny and Gloria won't be back for a couple of days. We could go tomorrow and set up the nursery."

I sighed with relief. "Really? I do like that idea much better. As long as I get to choose the movie."

"I'm willing to negotiate. And if you don't want beer, how about some water? Or some herbal tea?"

"Tea sounds goo—oh my gosh. You've done it. You've lured me into drinking herbal tea."

His laughter was as warm and comforting as the tea was sure to be. "Yes, that has been my elaborate ploy all along. To get you here and trick you into drinking my tea. Although the really complicated part was getting Gloria's baby to cooperate with my master plan."

"Amazing," I said, walking into the tiny kitchen, my borrowed sweatpants nearly tripping me. "But I only fell for it because I'm tired, so don't go thinking you're all that clever."

"Mm. If you say so."

He made us tea, which we drank from mugs that were certainly older than either of us, as we sat on a love seat in front of a twenty-four-inch television screen—the by-product of being in such a small cottage. It was either sit on the love seat or his bed, and that seemed like an even more precarious idea. I moved around a few times, trying to get comfortable without sprawling all over him.

"Are you okay?" he finally asked.

"Yes, I'm just . . . I had to carry some heavy boxes through the rain this morning, and it made me a little sore. I've got a twinge in my neck, and I'm just trying to get comfortable. Do you have some ibuprofen?"

"No, but I have these." He waggled his eyebrows like a cartoon villain and held up both hands with the panache of an arrogant neurosurgeon ready to perform a never-before-attempted brain transplant, and I chuckled because of course Matt would think he was some sort of neck-massaging miracle worker. It was all part of the no-meat-eating, yoga-teaching, herbal-tea-drinking, kitten-rescuing, nursery-finishing, nice-to-everyone persona. So how could I resist?

"Are you sure?"

"Of course. Turn around."

I swiveled on the love seat so my back was to him and my right leg was bent in front of me. I listened as he rubbed his hands together to warm them up, and then he touched me, and I felt my whole body sigh.

His hands were big and strong, and damn it all if he *wasn't* a frickin' neck-massaging master. Tag had been decent enough at this task, but he'd always either pushed too hard or grazed too lightly. Matt, however, was applying just the right amount of pressure in all the right spots. And I mean *all* the right spots. Even the places where he wasn't actually touching me. Maybe especially in the places where he wasn't touching me, because those were the spots that longed for attention.

"You're pretty tight," he said, and I found myself passing up an opportunity to make a joke about *that*.

"Well, like I said before, it's been a long day, and I carried those heavy boxes."

"You know, we carry a lot of emotional energy in our bodies, too. Especially in our neck, shoulders, and hips," he added.

"If you tell me that the cure for that is sunrise yoga, I'm going to punch you in the face," I said calmly.

He scoffed with exaggerated indignance, but I could tell he was not in the least offended. "Well, I've given up suggesting you try sunrise yoga, but clearly you've got some *hostility* stored in these muscle tissues," he teased. "Want to tell me about it?"

His hypnotic hands were making me sleepy—or sleepier—and exceptionally relaxed. "I live with Gigi and Emily, and Harlan is my father. Of course I've got pent-up hostility, but mostly I think I'm just stressed about life in general. Like most everyone. Except for you. You never seem stressed about anything."

"I get stressed. The trick for me is that I try to reframe stuff so it feels like growth instead of a burden."

I sighed. "I'm tired of growth. I'm twenty-seven. I want to be all grown up now."

His mild chuckle was full of understanding, even as he replied, "Yeah, I'm pretty sure life doesn't work that way. I think it's designed to make us grow every day with each new experience. That's the whole point of it. Once you stop learning, life gets dull."

"Mm-hmm," I said, not really listening anymore, because I just wanted to enjoy the warmth of his hands on my shoulders and the nape of my neck. It felt nice to be touched. Especially like this, and I tried not to imagine what it might be like to take this further.

"Please don't take this the wrong way," he said after another minute, "but if you lie down on the bed, I could do a better job." I could hear the humor in his voice, and I wondered if he'd read my mind, but then again, he was always so earnest about everything that I just wasn't sure. Was he sincerely offering me *just* a really good massage? Or was he actually suggesting something more?

In truth, I wasn't opposed to the *something more*, but I was kind of a mess tonight. I needed a hot shower and a toothbrush in the worst way, and although I knew guys really didn't care so much about that sort of thing, I did. And all things considered, after the day I'd had, I was emotionally unfit to make any sort of decision that involved us getting handsy with each other, or anything that involved the removal of clothing or kissing or sweet whispered nothings.

But a massage . . .

"Which would be the wrong way to take that?" I asked after a brief hesitation.

"I just don't want you to think I'm taking advantage. I'll be a perfect gentleman. I'm just suggesting that you might relax more if you lie down, and then I could get to these muscles in your lower back. Totally up to you."

Yes. He could be a perfect gentleman. I already knew that. The real question was, did I want him to be? Unfortunately, for tonight, the answer to that was yes. I wasn't ready for more.

"Um, I would probably love a more thorough back massage . . ." I let my voice trail off.

"Okay. Good. Come lie on the bed. I'll rub your back for ten minutes, and then we can watch a movie. How does that sound?"

"It sounds unfair to you."

He laughed at my answer. "It's not unfair to me. I offered. And anyway, my intentions are entirely selfish. You were fidgeting around on the sofa, and I'm hoping that if I work these kinks out of your muscles, maybe you can sit still and stop bouncing around."

"Well, when you put it that way, I guess I'd be doing you a favor."

"Oh, for sure."

We moved from the sofa, and ten minutes later, I was lying on top of Matt's super-soft, comfy comforter in his tiny, tranquil cottage while wearing his old high school T-shirt. And his pants. I was literally in Matt's pants, and with his hands on my back, it was hard not to think about being figuratively *in Matt's pants.* There was just no way he wouldn't be good in bed. With his hands, his emotional intuition, his yoga-induced flexibility? Fumbling around in the dark, indeed. But Henry the taxi driver was probably on his second glass of whiskey by now, telling everyone how he'd dropped me off at Matt's house and how Matt was trying to get me to shed my clothes.

Realistically, once word of that got around, no one would believe it had stopped at a massage, but I wanted to at least have some plausible deniability. Not that I cared that much what anyone thought, but after being fodder for the Wenniway Island gossip mill all last summer because of my relationship with Tag, I wasn't eager to replay that scenario. Better to keep people guessing. And better to keep my clothes on. Or rather, better to keep Matt's clothes on. Damn it.

I was so relaxed a few minutes later that I was nearly asleep when his hands slid up under the shirt and he touched the sensitive skin of my lower back. He stopped right then, rather abruptly, and pulled the shirt down, smoothing the fabric, giving me the distinct impression that the under-the-shirt business had been accidental. And I wasn't sure if he'd stopped because he was worried what I might think of it, or because of some reason of his own.

"Okay, how's that?" he asked, his voice matter of fact and efficient as he stood up from where he'd been sitting on the bed. Once again, he seemed full of vim and vigor, but as for me, it took every ounce of my energy to push myself up into a sitting position, and one look at my face made him laugh out loud.

"Have I ruined you for a movie?" he asked, crossing his arms and tapping his foot with mock impatience.

"What? No, of course not." And then a yawn nearly dislocated my jaw. "Maybe. But it's all your fault. I guess those cricks in my neck were the only thing keeping me awake."

He sighed, but I didn't sense any real frustration coming from him. "All right, sleepyhead. Let's get you home. We'll watch a movie a different night."

"Are you sure? Do you still want to put together the crib tomorrow?"

"Yes, absolutely," he said, grabbing me gently by the wrists and pulling me up. "Let's meet at the Kloostermans' house in the afternoon. Maybe around two o'clock? We might even have baby news by then."

"I hope so."

He walked me home after that because that's the kind of guy he was. Even though I'd walked home alone in the dark about sixty pachillion times over the course of my life on the island, he felt like he should walk me home. He said it was because I was so tired that he was afraid I'd curl up under a lilac bush and be ambushed by raccoons, and then, as I stood on the bottom porch step leading to Gigi's house, he said he'd only walked me home because he wanted to make sure that nothing happened to his favorite T-shirt.

"This is your favorite? Then why did you let me wear it?" I asked.

"It was on the top of the pile," he answered nonchalantly. "And for what it's worth, you do make it look good."

And then I thought for sure that he was going to kiss me, and I knew for *damn sure* that I wanted him to, but instead he just smiled and stepped backward, giving me a sort of awkward salute before turning around and heading off into the darkness.

Chapter 20

"So, how is it that you're wearing Matt's clothes?" Emily said smugly as soon as I came through the door and into the kitchen. She and Gigi were sitting at the table and appeared to be going over seating arrangements for the wedding. Although I felt as if it must be nearly midnight, it was actually only around nine o'clock. What a party animal I was.

I looked down at my Traverse City High School T-shirt and sweatpants combo. "How do you know these are Matt's clothes?"

"Well, for starters, Brooke called to ask if you'd heard anything from Gloria, and I said you weren't home yet, and she said the last time she'd seen you, you were with Matt; then Dmitri texted me and said Henry was down at the Palomino telling everyone how Matt invited you into his place to take off your dress; and then, last of all, we were just peeking through the kitchen window and saw him skulk away."

"If you already know all that, can't you figure out why I'm wearing . . . wait, no. *That's* not why I'm wearing his clothes. And he didn't skulk, for goodness' sake. He walked me home because I was so tired."

"And why were you so tired?" Gigi asked.

"Seriously? Have you guys forgotten about earlier today? Like, that part about Gloria and the baby, and me having to go get her bag, and then she and Tiny flying away in a helicopter? Aren't *you* tired?"

"Yes, I'm exhausted," Emily answered. "But I'm still wearing my own clothes, so I'm the one who gets to ask the questions here."

"Who made that rule?" I shuffled across the linoleum-floored kitchen in my too-long pants and pulled a whole-wheat bagel out of a plastic bag to pop in the toaster, because not only was I tired, but I'd suddenly realized I was hungry, too. Those little finger sandwiches from earlier had completely worn off, and Gloria had eaten all the cupcakes, so I never got one.

"I made that rule. Just now," Emily said. "So, tell us, how'd you get into Matt's pants?"

"Good one," Gigi said, giving my sister a high five.

I sighed and gave them the most succinct, unadorned answer I could, explaining about my dress and how Matt and I were going to go over to Gloria's house to put the crib together, but naturally I left out all the stuff about the massage. I didn't even mention the love seat or the herbal tea because the only exercise my grandmother ever got was jumping to the wrong conclusion, and I wasn't about to give her any more ideas. "But then we realized that going over there tomorrow afternoon made a lot more sense," I said.

"Oh ho ho. So you're going over there tomorrow afternoon?" Gigi said, as if she'd ingeniously latched on to some elusive piece of information, even though I'd literally just said I was going over there tomorrow afternoon.

"Yes. To set up the nursery. That's the forecast, and I'm sticking to it. Have you guys heard anything from Tiny or Gloria?" I asked, hoping to redirect their interest.

"Only that she's at Michlimac General, which is good news. It means they're not still flying around somewhere. I'm sure Tiny will text me as soon as he has any real news." Emily's expression turned from teasing me to concern for our friends. "I do hope everything goes okay. A month is kind of early. My due date is in January, so I'll almost certainly have bad weather to contend with when I go into labor. I may spend the whole winter in Michlimac."

"You'll be fine," Gigi said, patting her wrist. "All three of you girls were born right here on this island, and look how well you turned out. But Lilly is right. It was a long day, and I guess I am tired. And we've got church tomorrow. I'll see you gals in the morning. Don't stay up too late." Gigi got up from her chair and kissed us each on the cheek just as she'd done since we were little; then she headed up the creaky staircase to her room.

I spread some butter on my bagel and sat down at the table with Emily, who continued to stare at the seating charts strewn across the table like they were hieroglyphics she was trying to decode.

"Why don't you just let people choose their own seats? Then you wouldn't have to mess with all of this." I took a bite of my bagel and set it back down on a plate.

"Not a chance. You think I want Ryan's stuffy, pretentious family members and all of Tag's rich, snooty friends getting stuck at a table with Dmitri and Vera? Or Percy or Horsey? I'd rather his side didn't end up thinking we're all a bunch of whackadoodles around here." She sat back in her chair and stared at me. "Hey, wait a second. You've met some of them! How did I not think of that before? You can help me with this seating chart."

"Oh, joy. And by that, I mean no."

"Come on. I've tried to get Ryan to help, but he only knows which of his own relatives shouldn't sit by each other. Like his aunt Susan can't sit by his aunt Linda because Susan took their mother's good china after she died, and apparently everybody knew that it was supposed to go to Linda, so then Linda took their mother's diamond necklace, but that was supposed to be set aside for some random cousin. I can't remember which. It's a whole big thing, but anyway, Ryan can help with his family, but you've got the inside scoop on Tag's friends, and knowing who gets along with who would be so helpful. Please? It's what an assistant would do."

I should have read the fine print on those job requirements before I agreed to work with my sister, but if I argued, would she burst into tears? Because I simply could not deal with tears tonight. "Fine. Fine. I'll help you, but I can't do it right now because my brain is all done for the day. I can do it tomorrow."

"But tomorrow we have church, and then you'll be arranging the nursery."

"Then we'll do it Monday. You've still got time, Peach. Why the rush on this?"

"Because it's something I can finish and cross off my list." She frowned at the papers for a moment but then reluctantly started to stack them up. "But I guess as long as we do it sometime this week, that would be okay. Do you want help with the nursery tomorrow? I feel bad I wasn't more useful today, but honestly, the whole situation was kind of giving me a panic attack. What if that happens to me?"

I hadn't really thought about today from Emily's point of view, but it had been stressful all the way around, and it was no wonder she was worried. It was a risk we all took living in an isolated area. Most things we figured we could deal with, but pregnancy came with a whole other set of things to think about. And worry about. "I'm sorry if today was rough on you. At least the last part. You did have fun at the shower, though. Right?"

She smiled at last. "Yes, I had a wonderful time at the shower. It was so much fun. In spite of the rain and the storm and the crazy way it ended. You guys all did such a good job with the food and the games and everything, and I know Gloria was instrumental in making it such a great party. Which makes me even more certain I should go help you set up the nursery tomorrow. I bet Eva and Marnie would want to lend a hand, too. We should all go."

Yes, we should all go . . . except that I was kind of looking forward to it being just me and Matt.

"Everyone is looking at me like I did something naughty yesterday," I murmured to Brooke as we walked into Saint Bartholomew's Church at nine the next morning. "And I didn't."

"Well, that was your own dumb fault. You must've known Henry couldn't keep his mouth shut, and anyway, whatever happened at Matt's house last night, ninety-nine percent of these people are just jealous," Brooke whispered as we slid into the fifth row on the right, the same spot the Callaghan family sat every Sunday. Emily, Ryan, and Chloe were already there in the pew in front of us, but I'd waited outside to walk in with Brooke. And apparently so I could give everyone the opportunity to cast speculative glances my way. They all looked at me as if I were standing there still wearing Matt's T-shirt. And no pants. And a scarlet letter *A* on my chest.

"Nothing happened," I whispered back as Harlan and Gigi joined us, sitting down next to my sister.

"If you say so," Brooke murmured.

"You don't believe me?"

"Of course *I* believe you, but no one will believe *me* saying that nothing happened any more than they'll believe you when *you* say nothing happened. They'll just think I'm defending you."

"Why isn't everyone talking about how awesome I was to go get Gloria's bag yesterday? Or how awesome you were to help Gloria get to the airport?"

"Sorry, Lil. What can I tell you? Sex sells."

"Shhhh," Gigi shushed, reaching over and pinching Brooke on the arm.

"Ouch. What was that for?" Brooke grumbled back.

"That's for talking about sex in church."

Brooke gave me a dirty look as if the pinch were my fault, but I wasn't the one who'd pinched her, and I wasn't the one who'd said *sex* in church. And I hadn't done anything wrong last night, so why was I getting blamed for a whole bunch of stuff that I didn't even do? *Oh, that's right. Catholics.*

A minute later, scrawny Delores Crenshaw took her seat at the aged piano that was only slightly more rickety that she was, and as she started pounding out an up-tempo version of "Go Tell It on the Mountain," we obediently mumbled along. As we sang, I couldn't help but notice how much more on pitch the congregation seemed to be today without Gloria's glass-shattering soprano chiming in, but I found myself missing it. My ears didn't, but my heart did, and I spent the next hour wondering how she was doing, and how Tiny was doing, and if Baby Persimmons-Kloosterman had made an appearance yet, and how everything had gone after that helicopter took off last evening.

Emily had gotten a text message at about midnight last night from Tiny, saying that they were inducing Gloria's labor and that he'd keep us all in the loop as things progressed, but we'd had no updates since then. It was a little worrisome, and so I decided to take this time in church to stop fretting about people gossiping about me and Matt and instead focus all my positive prayer energy on ensuring that a new baby would be joining us soon and that Mom, Dad, and infant were all doing well.

And when Father O'Reilly ended his sermon, he reminded everyone else to do the same, which gave me a smug sense of being a good person, which also, ironically, completely disqualified me from actually *being* a good person. Again. Catholic. I was screwed either way.

"Have you heard anything?" Dmitri Krushnic asked as soon as our feet hit the grass in the front yard of Saint Bart's. For once I think his interest was sincere and not just eagerness to get the scoop before anyone else.

"I haven't," Harlan answered, then turned to Emily, since she was Tiny's boss and the most likely to be the first one he contacted. "Have you, Peach?"

She shook her head as she pulled her phone from her purse to check her messages, and as she did so, I saw at least a dozen other people pulling phones from purses and pockets as if everyone had had the same thought.

I spotted Eva and Marnie making their way toward us, and soon we were talking about the nursery and Emily was inviting them to join us in helping set it up. That made me irritable, which, of course, smote any good karma I'd accumulated with my piousness this morning. I didn't have any jurisdiction over this nursery, and I was sure that Gloria and Tiny would love knowing that everyone had helped, but Tiny had asked Matt to take care of it, and now everyone was sticking their noses into it.

And it took me only about forty-five seconds more to realize I didn't really care that much about the nursery itself. I was just annoyed because I'd been looking forward to an afternoon with Matt, and imagining what it would be like to play house with him, and that little bit of personal insight prompted far more questions than I had answers for.

I didn't have answers a few hours later, either, when I arrived at the Kloostermans' house, along with Emily, Eva, Marnie, Chloe, Brooke, and Gigi—all of whom had insisted they wanted to help. I wasn't sure how they all expected to participate, since the nursery just wasn't that big, but fortunately, Brooke put on her bossy pants and gave everyone a job. Gigi and Chloe were tasked with cleaning the kitchen and the bathrooms, Emily was put in charge of doing laundry since piles of it were everywhere, and Eva and Marnie were sent to tidy up Tiny and Gloria's room, including putting fresh linens on the bed. Fortunately, or perhaps UN-fortunately for me, in the light of day I was able to sneak into that room, find the bouncing dildo under the bed, and quickly toss it back in the drawer before anyone was the wiser. Then I went back into the family room just in time to see Matt arrive.

He looked surprised by all the activity, and I wondered for a brief second if he was as disappointed by the crowd as I was, but if that was the case, it didn't show as he gave everyone a smile and a hug, including me.

"I have your stuff," I said to him once we were alone in the nursery, because at least Brooke had discerned that we might need a few minutes to chat, just the two of us.

"My stuff?"

"Yes, your shirt and pants. I'll give them back as soon as they're washed. Thanks again for the loan, by the way."

"Of course. And you don't need to wash anything. You only wore it for, like, an hour."

That wasn't technically true, because I'd actually slept in Matt's T-shirt last night. I tried to tell myself it was only because I was so very tired. Far too tired to actually take it off and put on pajamas, but who was I kidding? It was always fun to sleep in a man's shirt, and even though he'd pulled that one from the top of his pile of laundry, it still had a bit of Matt-ness to it that had been inexplicably comforting to me last night for some reason.

"It's not a problem. I'll bring it back to you this week."

"That's fine. Whenever. How'd you sleep last night?" Did he know I'd slept in his shirt? Then I realized he was only asking because I'd been so drowsy at his house.

"Like a log. How about you? Did you watch a movie after I left?"

"No, I actually stopped by the Palomino Pub on my way home from your grandma's place. I figured Henry might be telling some tall tale, and knowing how this community loves a juicy bit of gossip, I decided that it was best to nip his story in the bud before people started hearing that we'd run around naked through my backyard or some such thing."

I smiled at him. "Were you defending your reputation, or mine?"

"Mine, of course," he said, but my heart went flippity-flop because it was obviously my reputation he was protecting, and that was about the sweetest thing I could imagine. Gosh, he was cute.

We made short work of putting together the crib, with me helping to hold pieces in place and Matt doing all the actual assembly. The
changing table took a bit more time, but before long, the furniture was
finished, and it was really starting to look like a baby's room, and just
in time, too, because as soon as I'd put an adorable mint-green sheet
covered with little yellow duckies onto the little mattress, Tiny texted.
Matt looked at his phone, and his smile spread, slow and steady, like
the sun rising. Without a word, he held it up for me to see the screen,
and there she was. A little pink bundle of baby joy with a text message that followed, saying, SHE'S PERFECT. SAY HELLO TO NORAH GRACE
KLOOSTERMAN, OUR DAUGHTER.

Everyone is sentimental when it comes to newborn babies—at least,
most everyone with a pulse—but I had a vested interest in this baby,
and so did Matt, because we'd been drawn into and immersed in the
drama and the worry and the hopeful outcome of this scenario, so
something about that photo and that caption and just how much she
meant to Gloria and Tiny . . . well, I lost it. I started to cry. I couldn't
help it. It was all right there, just under the surface, and seeing that baby
made it all burst out, like I was an overstretched water balloon flung
against a wall of sharp nails. I virtually exploded with tears, and Matt
pulled me into his arms. I could feel his chest moving, and I wasn't sure
if he was crying just like me. Or laughing. Turned out he was laughing.

"What's wrong? Is it Gloria?" Emily called out, dashing into the
room, her face etched with concern as she and everyone else rushed in
behind her until it was wall-to-wall women all demanding to know
what had happened. Keeping one arm around me, Matt held up the
phone with his other arm for everyone to see, and suddenly my unre-
strained wailing was drowned out by cries of delight and joy and elation
and squeals and squeaks and giggles and cheering. It all just made me
cry harder. Emily and her damned hormones must be rubbing off on
me, but Matt just hugged me tighter.

Chapter 21

"I was joking when I suggested the ghost tour," I said to Jayden as we stood on the gleaming parquet floor in the center of the Imperial Hotel Grand Ballroom.

Since their arrival, the movie people had used the Grand Ballroom for a multitude of purposes. It's where 90 percent of the Trillium Bay population had stood in hopeful anticipation of being cast as an extra. It's where we'd tried on woolen and silk costumes behind collapsible folding screens, and had our hair and makeup done by professional artists. It's where we'd eaten lunch and lounged around in between moments of being yelled at by Rashida and Griffin. But today it was serving its real purpose—as a ballroom—because today they were filming a much-anticipated dancing scene, and I was as giddy as if I were attending a real Cinderella's ball.

For hours yesterday, along with Dmitri, Sudsy, Eva, Marnie, Gigi, and a few dozen others, I'd practiced learning the steps of something called a quadrille. Fortunately, since most islanders spent their fair share of evenings square dancing at the community center or Saint Bartholomew's Church, the steps weren't all that difficult to pick up, and most of us caught on pretty quickly, with the exception of Vera VonMeisterburger, who always went left when she should go right or forward when she should go back, and Percy O'Keefe, who could not seem to stop himself from getting right in someone's face and demanding *so you think you can dance?* before launching into a flailing sort of thrashy freestyle that was not at all helpful, nor amusing. The dance master nearly kicked him out, but he was spared that indignity at the very last minute when Judge Murphy's back went out and we were a man down. In spite of all the antics over the course of the day, we became a fairly cohesive unit. At least good enough to be in the background, but heaven help us if the camera actually captured any of us up close.

Last night after rehearsal, I'd gone home bone-weary and limb-achy from being on my feet all day, but I was back at it now and full of eagerness in spite of the fact that today I had to do all that dancing again—while wearing a corset! But maybe it was worth it because, damn, I looked good. My dress was an elaborate champagne-colored silk ensemble that must have weighed twelve pounds, with all sorts of ruffles and ribbons and bows.

Meanwhile, Jayden looked ridiculously sexy and altogether at home in his crisp white shirt and bow tie along with his topcoat and tails. His hair was slicked back, and he had a red rosebud pinned to his lapel. Any other man in that getup might have looked like a snooty maître d' or a wannabe magician, while he looked naturally elegant and at ease. As if he'd just ridden in from his country estate for an evening of more refined entertainment.

Skylar was standing off to one side in a stunning gown of deep crimson with ivory lace trim and a neckline so plunging that I wondered if a wardrobe malfunction was imminent. In fact, a costumer was at this very moment pulling some double-sided tape from her bag, and it didn't take much deductive reasoning to guess where that was going. That looked like a job for duct tape, so I hoped that double-sided stuff had some superglue adhesive properties.

"I've been asking around," Jayden said, pulling my attention away from Skylar's remarkable and surgically augmented boobage back to his own delectable, God-given face. "And a bunch of people have said the ghost tour is a Wenniway Island must-do."

"Of course they've told you that. We all try to drum up business for each other, but I can guarantee that you will not find any ghosts on that ghost tour. You won't find spirits or demons or any sort of paranormal activity, and you most likely won't even hear any good stories about any of that stuff, either."

"Have you ever done the ghost tour?" he asked as if challenging me.

"No, but I have friends who've worked as guides, and I know what they're taught to say. They'll tell you some ho-hum, yawn-worthy, generic stuff about faces of little girls in windows and the sounds of heavy footsteps running down an empty hallway, and then they'll pretend to confide in you about the one story that they've been warned to never tell anyone that always involves some spot on the island where they've had their own personal ghostly encounter and how they'll never go back to that spot again."

His smile lit up as if he'd misheard me—because I'd just explained how dopey and not entertaining the ghost tour was. "That's exactly what I'm looking for," he said. "The more touristy the better."

"Why? Why would you want to waste an evening like that?"

"Well, for starters, I'm working eighteen-hour days, so any chance I get to not be thinking about this movie is a nice break for me. Secondly, you're fun to hang out with. And C, I can't do something like that in just any city, because people always recognize me, but around here, even if they know who I am, they don't make a big deal about it. I've never felt so *average* as I do here, and it's a nice change of pace."

Hmm. That was a bit of a slam, him toying with being average while the rest of us spent most of our lives trying to escape it. Sure, it was nice that he'd said I was fun to hang out with, but I couldn't help but wonder if by *fun*, in this case, he meant *average*. Because I was just an average girl—just another part of his whole *pretending to be a regular guy* Trillium Bay experience. It wasn't as if I thought I was someone special to him, but I didn't want to be common, either. No one wants that, and I felt kind of . . . used, like I was just a decorative pawn in his personal, private social experiment of dabbling in normalcy.

But then he added, "I don't think you realize what it's like to be hounded by the press everywhere you go. It's exhausting. Every vacation I've ever taken has been just one telephoto-lens picture away from being the latest click-bait graphic on some website. I have zero expectation of privacy. You have no idea how lucky you are to live in this bubble."

Again, not exactly a compliment, but being stalked by photographers didn't sound all that fun, either, and I was reminded about what he'd said about photographers even trying to take pictures through the windows of his house. Maybe fame and fortune weren't all they were cracked up to be, and maybe being average was a well-disguised blessing.

I guess I could give him a pass for that because I knew he'd grown up in a much different bubble, but still . . . the ghost tour? He'd just invited me to go with him, which had prompted this whole conversation, and while I could just encourage him to go on his own, he was now gazing at me with such earnest optimism, and truth be told, being under the magnetic spell of Jayden Pierce's baby blues, combined with his puppy-dog expression—oh my gosh—I wasn't made of stone. I had to say yes. It wasn't as if spending time with him was an actual hardship. Even if he had only invited me because I was *just a regular girl.*

"Okay. Fine. You're going to be woefully disappointed and wish you could get your ninety minutes back, but if you want to do the tour, I'll go with you."

He smiled again, and my sudden shortness of breath had nothing to do with the corset digging into my ribs.

"Okay, people! Listen up!" Rashida shouted, startling me. She was standing on a chair and pointing to the ceiling, her routine stance when calling us to order. "Here's how the next three hours are going to go." She gave us the list of usual instructions: *Don't talk to the talent. Don't get caught on the microphone. Don't make Griffin cranky.* It was the same old stuff we'd heard each day, and it struck me how desensitized I'd become to it all. Even the director's scowl as he stalked in and strode about the room glaring at everyone and everything didn't make me tremble in my silks anymore. Thanks to the day I'd spent getting bumped into by Jayden on Main Street, I felt as if I'd earned my place.

"You are in the wrong place," Rashida said to me as soon as she'd jumped down from the chair. "You need to be over there with that group." She pointed to the corner where Percy was doing his *so you think you can dance* twitch-a-thon. It looked like some of Dmitri Krushnic's bees had gotten into his tuxedo pants.

"Can't she be here in my group?" Jayden asked.

Rashida's answer was instantaneous and direct. "Nope, because all the extras rehearsed yesterday, and if people change spots now, everything will be messed up. We've hired professional dancers to be in your group, and it's their job to make you look good, so don't complain. And besides, if the audience recognizes Lilly from the street scene, it could impact the continuity of the storyline."

"I don't think it will," he said.

Rashida stood a little taller, and while at five foot five she was no match for Jayden physically, verbally, she was much bigger. "Don't be an asshole, Jay. I've got this whole scene blocked out, and I'm not changing it because of whatever this is." She wiggled her index finger, pointing from him to me and back again, bringing a blush to my cheeks and a spark to my curiosity.

He frowned at her dismissively, like, *Wut? I'm not doing anything.*

She made a fairly non-threatening *screw you, I'm not an idiot* face back at him, a sign of the easygoing, non-verbal shorthand they had, like they were rival siblings, and Jayden finally shrugged and smiled.

"You're the boss," he said, and I was all kinds of relieved as Rashida walked away, because while my dancing skills were adequate, they were not film-worthy. Definitely not professional quality, so I wanted to be in the background on this one, but before I could leave to go take my spot over in the corner, Jayden said, "So how about Saturday night?"

"Saturday?"

"Yeah, for the ghost tour?"

"Oh, I can't Saturday. It's the Lilac Festival."

"What's a lilac festival?" He crooked an eyebrow.

"It's a festival," I said patiently. "To celebrate the lilacs." I let that linger out there for a moment, just for effect.

"Ah, thus the name."

"Yes, thus," I answered. "You should come, though. It's one hundred percent touristy, and if you want the full Trillium Bay experience, this is definitely the place to get it. There's a parade at noon, and a pie-eating contest, and carnival games. And then at night, there's fireworks."

He looked happily intrigued, like a philatelist who'd just discovered a brand-new stamp, but Griffin barked, "Places, everybody!" and I had to scurry to my corner before I got kicked off the set for fraternizing.

The next three hours were a literal whirl of dancing with only a handful of breaks, and I was a hot, sweaty mess by the time we were through, but they let us extras stay in the ballroom and watch as just Skylar and Jayden danced. It was mesmerizing to watch the two of them gracefully gliding around the ballroom, and although Skylar typically had a slightly constipated expression on her face when the cameras weren't rolling, she was simply exquisite while they were focused on her. She fairly glowed and floated and oozed an innocent sensuality. No wonder they were such big stars. It was impossible to not feel their charisma and their chemistry. It was palpable.

"One of the makeup women told me that this is the scene in the movie where they fall in love with each other," Eva whispered to me as we sat off to the side, and I believed her, because they did indeed look like a couple falling madly, deeply in love. Jayden wrapped one strong arm around Skylar's tiny waist, and they twirled in a circle, around and around, somehow never breaking eye contact. And when the music stopped and Griffin yelled, "Cut!" Skylar giggled and fell against Jayden, and he wrapped his other arm around her and gave her a kiss on the cheek as the crew cheered.

"Oh my God! Please, do not make us do that again, Griff," Skylar said breathlessly, her face flushed with exertion, her smile incandescently bright. "I'm way too dizzy for another take."

"I think we got what we needed," the director answered. "That's a wrap for this morning, everybody. See you back here at one o'clock."

I wasn't an extra this afternoon and felt a twinge of disappointment, but in reality, that was good news because I had a million and one things to do. First, I had to call Gloria and check in on the progress of Baby Norah Grace, who'd spent her first week of life in the neonatal intensive care unit to give her lungs just a bit more time to develop. Other than that, she was a perfectly healthy baby. Then I had to meet Emily, Brooke, and Chloe at the Sew What Alterations Shop for a final bridesmaid-dress fitting, and then, because Brooke was super bossy *and* the mayor, she'd conscripted me into helping with some of the upcoming Lilac Festival chores. It was just two days from now, and we had plenty to do.

Honestly, how had anyone in my family functioned while I was busy working as a preschool teacher? It seemed as if every day one of them needed me for something. It was already the last day of May, and I had yet to make a connection with Mary Lou Baxter about a job in the fall. Time was ticking.

Jayden called my name just as I was about to exit the ballroom and then walked fast to catch up with me. "How about Sunday night then?" he said, as if our conversation about the ghost tour hadn't been interrupted by four-plus hours of dancing and filming, and I was reminded yet again of his tenacity about buying my father's car. It seemed that once he set his mind to something, there was just no dissuading him.

"Um, I think Sunday would work, but can I let you know? I need to check with my sister. She's the mayor, and there's festival stuff she might need help with after it's over. Cleanup and such."

"Your sister is the mayor? That's cool. But if we don't go on Sunday night, I'll have to check with Rashida. I know we've got some evening shoots coming up soon."

People were leaving the ballroom, weaving around us like we were traffic cones in the middle of the road while simultaneously casting inquisitive glances our way. Jayden seemed oblivious, but several of those squinty-eyed stares were coming from the very same people who'd given me squinty-eyed glares at church last Sunday when they'd thought I'd been doing something scandalous with Matt. You know, like drinking tea and putting together a baby crib? Me standing here chatting with Jayden would be all it took to provide more fodder for their bored, narrow minds, and I knew without a doubt that tonight around dinner tables and down at the pubs they'd be speculating and ruminating and conjecturing about this conversation and what decadent, mischievous, wayward plans Jayden and I were formulating.

We're just going on the ghost tour! I nearly shouted. Instead I asked Jayden quietly, "Can I text you when I know my plans for Sunday?"

"Yes," he answered, leaning closer, dipping his head toward mine, his expression serious. "But why are we whispering?"

"If you think a photographer with a telephoto lens is nosy, you should try living in a community with only six hundred people. They may be giving *you* some privacy, but I can promise you that I do not have any."

He nodded with instant comprehension and took a small step back, straightening his posture to look more professional and less like a guy inviting me to go ghost hunting with him.

"Understood. If you could get back to me with that information, it would be helpful," he said formally, but then he winked at me, so I knew he meant the information about my availability. And probably so did everyone else who'd overheard him.

Chapter 22

The Trillium Bay Lilac Festival, held the first weekend in June, was the official kickoff of our summer tourist season, and the island was always loaded with visitors. On Saturday at noon, rain or shine, a parade started near historic Fort Beaumont and traveled down Main Street all the way to Trillium Pointe. There were carriages decorated with signs and flags, bikes with streamers and bells, and the Wenniway Island Marching Band, which included several trombones, a few clarinets, some drums, a flute, a tuba, a bugle, a bagpipe, and even an accordion. Given that odd collection, it often sounded as if they were playing different songs, but no one seemed to mind.

All the ponies from Colette's Riding Stable were brushed until they gleamed, their manes braided and adorned with lavender ribbons, and all the businesses along the street flew lilac-adorned flags from the posts outside their doors. At the end of the parade route were food booths featuring famous Moose Tracks fudge from Judge's Fudge, apple dumplings from Eden's Garden of Eatin', and maple-lavender scones from Tasty Pastries. There were even dueling beer tents provided by the Mustang Saloon and the Palomino Pub, which I'd forgotten to mention to Jayden but were sure to be a draw.

He'd texted me last night to ask some details about the festival with a message that started with HEY, CHEVETTE, and ended with:

I HAVE NIGHT SHOOTS MON TUES SO IF NOT SUNDAY HOW ABOUT WED. U CANT BAIL ON ME. I'M AFRAID OF THINGS THAT GO BUMP IN THE NIGHT AND NEED YOU WITH ME. WILL C U AT FLOWER FEST. J

Matt had texted me soon after to ask where I'd be sitting during the parade, and I'd told him I wasn't sure . . . because I wasn't sure, but then I added:

NOT SURE WHERE BROOKE WILL NEED ME. WILL LOOK FOR YOU THO.

He'd sent me a thumbs-up emoji, which seemed kind of lame, but then again, so was my text to him. I thought about adding more, but Chloe and I had been in the middle of a cage-match, fight-to-the-death game of backgammon at the time, and so I'd set my phone aside.

"I think this might be the best the lilacs have ever been," Gigi said, drawing in a big, deep breath as we walked with Chloe and Emily down Anishinaabe Trail toward Main Street at nine the next morning. "I could even smell them while I was in the shower."

"Do you think that might have been from the lilac-scented soap you were using?" Emily asked, glancing at me over Gigi's head, because of course it was the soap since there were no windows in our bathroom.

"Nope, nope. I'm sure it was the real thing," Gigi said, adjusting the chin strap of her straw sun hat. She had on dark purple Bermuda shorts and a big T-shirt with an octopus on it, which only made sense because the octopus was also purple. And because he was holding a cocktail in each tentacle.

Emily and Chloe were adorable in coordinating sundresses of lavender and green plaid, which Chloe had agreed to wear only because Emily had given her ten dollars to go along with the matchy-matchy mother-daughter theme. I was sporting a sundress, too, but mine was covered in pastel flowers, which was the closest thing to anything purple or lavender I had that was clean. I hadn't had time recently to do any laundry, which was why Matt's T-shirt and sweatpants were still in my possession. And not at all because I continued to sleep in his shirt.

I wasn't entirely sure why I kept sleeping in his shirt, other than the fact that it was big and soft and comfy, but last night, as I'd climbed under the covers, I'd briefly wondered if there was any significant meaning behind me wearing it. Was it because it reminded me of him? I mean, of course it reminded me of him, but why did that make me want to wear it? And then I'd wondered, what if, somehow, I ended up with a T-shirt belonging to Jayden? Would I sleep in that one, too? Or instead?

The truth was it was hard not to compare them in my mind. The men—not the T-shirts. Not because they were in any real sort of competition with each other, though. I mean, sure, Jayden was utterly charismatic, and I wasn't so blind I didn't notice he treated me differently than he treated everyone else. He'd definitely grown more flirtatious lately, singling me out to talk to me every time we were on set together, and inviting me to do things—like bike rides and ghost tours—but he'd also made it clear he was interested in learning about the island, and I was an excellent resource. He'd said I was *fun to be around*, too, but so were puppies and kittens, yet that didn't mean you wanted to seduce them. More realistically, his attention to me was likely because he was an unabashed flirt.

Regardless, that didn't stop me from being attracted to him—even while knowing it was fruitless and pointless and probably delusional and maybe even a little self-destructive. How could I not be attracted to him? Jayden was . . . *Jayden*.

Ah, but then there was Matt . . . sweet, sexy Matt, who was so very *Matt-like*. So very *Prince Charming in a tool belt*, thoughtful and earnest and every bit as handsome as Jayden. And definitely interested in me in a romantic sort of way. After putting the crib together at Gloria's house the other day, and after he'd hugged me through my unbridled binge of blubbering, he'd kissed my temple—so softly that I thought I'd only imagined it, but Brooke had seen it. She'd said so later that evening when she asked me what was happening between us. I'd answered her honestly enough. I'd said, "Nothing," but we both knew the real answer was "nothing yet," because Matt seemed . . . inevitable, while Jayden was . . . unattainable.

I just couldn't deny it. I liked them both, which had my mind and emotions and hormones twisted into a dozen different knots because being attracted to Jayden was exhilarating and surreal, while my attraction to Matt felt . . . safe. If Jayden was a Ferrari, fast and flashy and impractical, Matt was . . . Matt was an F-150 truck. Useful, dependable, with lots going on under that hood. Ironic, these car analogies, given that I grew up on an island where motorized vehicles weren't allowed.

I continued walking with my grandmother, sister, and niece toward Main Street, wearing my flowered sundress and wondering about these men in my life while breathing in the sweet, heady fragrance of the lilacs. Gigi might be right. This year it did seem as if the blooms were extraordinarily spectacular, and the aroma triggered a dozen different memories of childhood summers spent playing outside, surrounded by the sweetly cloying scent.

"Do we have to drop off Gigi's blueberry pie first?" Chloe asked as we turned left onto Huron Street near Trillium Pointe, where, against the backdrop of shimmering blue water and bright sunny skies, I spotted the Buy-Buy Miss American Pie tent.

"I'll drop off the pie," Emily answered, taking the foil-wrapped plate from Chloe as we stopped under the shade of a big, thick oak tree. "Ryan and I are working in the tent this morning."

"You mean I wore this stupid, matchy-matchy plaid dress and we're not even going to be together?" Chloe asked, although her grin suggested she was far from upset.

"Well, you could come sell pies with me," Emily answered. "Last year you wanted to, remember?"

Chloe nodded and twirled one thick braid around her index finger. "Yes, but last year we'd just moved here, and I hardly knew anybody. Now I know everybody. Plus, last year I was only twelve, and this year I'm nearly fourteen."

I wasn't exactly sure how she was doing that math. She'd declared herself to be *nearly fourteen* since the day after she'd turned thirteen, but Emily just laughed and waved her away.

"Go find your people," she said to her daughter. "But you have to sit with Ryan and me during the parade so everyone can see how cute we look."

"Got it," Chloe answered before kissing her mom on the cheek. "See you guys later!" And then she was gone.

"Well, I have people to meet, too," Gigi said with a disdainful sniff. "Chloe isn't the only one with a posse, you know. I have to meet Maggie Webster to discuss a girls' trip we're planning for after the wedding."

"A girls' trip?" Emily said.

"Yes, we're going to the Seneca Falls casino. I've been told there's a lot of hot singles action over there."

Calling it a girls' trip seemed like a misnomer. Maybe they should call it a *Golden Girls'* trip, since I knew for a fact that the youngest member of Gigi's posse was sixty-three-year-old Myrna Delroy, and the last thing my grandmother needed was another man in her life.

"That's kind of far for you ladies to travel, don't you think?" I said. "And besides, Gigi, haven't you had enough husbands already? You need to leave a few for someone else."

"Honey, in the words of the great Elizabeth Taylor, you can never have too many diamonds or too many husbands."

"I've never heard that quote before," Emily said, tucking the foil more securely around the pie she was holding.

"Well, maybe she never said it out loud, but clearly that was her life philosophy. And since I only have three tiny specks for diamonds, I'm going to make up for it in men. Gus was a big disappointment, and I'm looking for my rebound affair. Speaking of rebound affairs . . ." She tilted her head back and peered at me from under the brim of her sun hat. "What's this I hear about you doubling up on dates yourself?"

Yep. When I said the people of Wenniway Island loved to gossip, my own grandmother was at the front of the line. My skin flushed, and it had nothing to do with walking in the hot sunshine. I stole a glance at Emily, who was looking back at me with equally unveiled interest.

"I'm not doubling up on dates. Why? What have you heard?"

"I heard you're two-timing Yoga Matt with Mr. Hot Stuff from the movie, and don't think I didn't see you batting your lashes at him during the dance scene in the Grand Ballroom the other day."

So much for family loyalty. "Gigi, I live with you, and you know for a fact that I've been home every single night, unless I've been working with Emily at one of her places. When would I even have time for all this alleged dating?" Was it getting hotter? It seemed like it was getting hotter.

Gigi scoffed dramatically. "You silly girl. People can get up to all sorts of shenanigans during the daytime. Haven't you ever heard of 'Afternoon Delight'? 'Skyrockets in flight,' and all that? How else could I have carried on such a torrid affair with Gus without realizing he snores at night?"

"Ew," Emily and I said in unison.

"Anyway," I added, "I can't be two-timing anyone when I'm not even one-timing anyone. We're all just friends."

"Does he know that?" Gigi asked, looking past me. I turned around, and there was Matt making his way toward us, and damn if he didn't look good. He was wearing basic khaki shorts and an equally basic navy-blue T-shirt. Nothing extraordinary. Nothing that half a dozen other guys in the nearby vicinity didn't have on, but somehow, he elevated the whole look, probably because it was so obvious that he wasn't trying too hard. He didn't need to. Maybe it was the days he'd spent as a model that gave him that easy, confident stride. Or maybe it was just that he was so stupidly good-looking. He might be as practical as an old pickup truck, but he still had shine, and damn it all again if that persistent case of the flutters didn't start low in my belly and flicker out in every direction the minute I caught sight of him. Maybe that's why I kept wearing his damn T-shirt to bed.

"Hi," he said as he reached our sides, gazing at each one of us in turn and saying our names in that meaningful Yoga Matt way of his. "Emily. Gigi. Lilly."

"Hi, yourself, good-lookin'," Gigi said. "Sure would love to chat, but my gals are waiting for me over near the beer tent. We're planning a mutiny."

"Sorry," Emily said. "I have to run, too. I'm working at the pie tent." She held up the pie as if it were evidence, and then she and my grandmother disappeared as fast as Chloe had.

Matt looked at me again. "Was it something I said?"

"No, Emily really does have to work in the pie tent, and Gigi is planning a girls' trip to Seneca Falls to find herself a new husband."

His nod was matter of fact—he knew Gigi and knew I wasn't trying to make a joke. "Gus still isn't over her leaving him," he said.

"Then Gus should've trimmed his toenails over a trash can rather than in bed," I responded.

"Seems legit. Anyway, let's talk about something else. Anything else," he added with a chuckle.

So we talked about Gloria and Tiny and their new bouncing baby girl, and about the progress of the Peach Tree Inn, and how he'd finally convinced Emily that she should give Chloe one of the kittens, although it was still a surprise. Then we talked about a handful of other things while wandering in and out of the food tents to see what looked good, and by then it was noon and time for the parade.

I hadn't planned to spend the morning with Matt, and he hadn't asked me to, but it just seemed to work out that way. And I didn't mind. The festival was always fun, but like most things lately, it seemed to be a bit more fun with him by my side. Then, when I said I was supposed to meet my family to watch the procession of buggies and bikes and bugles and bagpipes, he tagged along. And I didn't mind that, either.

We found a good spot on the shaded front porch of the Bay View Hotel and cheered and waved wildly at Brooke—our mayor—as she rode by in the front seat of the first carriage, next to Tandie Carmichael, this year's Miss Lilac Festival. They both grinned and waved back while Brooke's boyfriend, Leo, strode alongside videotaping the whole thing until he plowed headfirst into a lamppost and dropped his phone to the ground.

I heard a rumble of laughter coming from the chief, who stood beside me, and I knew that Leo would never, ever live that one down. Ryan had joined us, wearing a shirt made from the same lavender and green plaid fabric as Emily's and Chloe's matching sundresses, and I had a sneaking suspicion that he, also, would never, ever live that one down. Still, everyone made a huge, ridiculous fuss about the matchy-matchy outfits because what a cute family the three of them were, and soon there'd be a fourth, and Emily beamed with pride—and then threw up into a planter full of geraniums.

"Your family is really amazing, you know that?" Matt said to me later that afternoon as we sat at a long table under the Palomino Pub beer tent sampling many, many beers. We'd been joined by Marnie, Eva, Dmitri, and a handful of others who were ready for a break from the sun but not yet ready to leave the party.

"My family?" I asked. "How so?"

"You all have such different personalities and different outlooks on life, and yet you're all so supportive of each other. There's no jealousy between you. At least none that I've seen."

"Oh, there's some jealousy," I assured him with a laugh. "But it's pretty standard-issue stuff, I guess. I'm jealous of them for having careers, and they're jealous of me because I have the cutest feet." I stuck out my sandaled foot to prove my point.

"You have a career," he said. "It's just on hold for right now. Aren't you planning to go back to teaching in the fall?" He took a sip of a microbrew called Won't You Be My Trillium Bay-Bay and then passed it to me.

"I do want to go back to teaching, but if I don't ever call Mary Lou Baxter, she's going to think I'm not interested. I've just been so busy with other stuff I haven't had a chance."

"Do you think maybe you haven't called her because you're not sure that's what you want to do?"

That was a thought-provoking question. Far too thought-provoking for an afternoon beer-tent discussion, but I had my answer at the ready. "I'm totally sure. Teaching little kids is the only thing I've ever wanted to do."

"And why is that, do you suppose?" Again with the philosophical, but that was just Matt.

"Um, I'm not really sure. Teaching was just always what I planned for. I've always loved little kids. Being around them makes me happy."

He looked at me with a wistful smile, as if he wanted to ask more or had some insight he wanted to share, but then he smiled more broadly and tried another beer sample, something called Petoskey Stoned, and asked me which beer I liked best instead.

Half an hour later, we were on our next flight of samples and had been joined by Brooke, Leo, Ryan, and Emily when I heard the nasally, not-so-dulcet drone of Skylar's voice.

"Jesus, Jay. This place is like one of those towns in Epcot, you know?" she said. "Like, Yester-World or something. I don't really get it. There are people playing actual bingo, for God's sake."

I looked over my shoulder and recognized her instantly, although she had on coaster-size, onyx-colored sunglasses with a Trillium Bay baseball hat pulled down low, a man's white dress shirt over such teeny-tiny jean shorts that she looked as if she weren't wearing any pants at all, and gold, stiletto-heeled sandals that probably cost more than my father's car.

She teetered as she walked, those needle-sharp heels sinking into the grass with every step, forcing her to cling to Jayden's arm just to keep steady, or at least that's how she was making it look. I had a sneaking suspicion the shoes had been purposefully chosen for just this reason—so that she'd have an excuse to keep ahold of him. Word around the set was that she was getting twitchier and twitchier about trying to convince everyone they were an item. Partly because she liked him, and partly because her publicist thought it would make excellent PR.

Marnie had spotted Skylar, too, and leaned close to whisper in my ear. "I heard from one of the lighting crew that Skylar is pissed about the ghost tour because she's too scared to go, and she knows you're going."

"Why on earth would she care if I go?" I glanced toward Matt to see if he was paying attention, but he was now deep in conversation with Brooke's boyfriend about some novel Leo had allegedly been writing, and Marnie gave me an *oh, come on, seriously?* look in return. It came with a side-eye of *are you really that dense?* Dmitri stared at us from across the table, but I ignored him.

"What?" I whispered back. "She could go if she wants. I'm no threat, and it's not my fault she's scared of ghosts and bugs and snakes and probably bunny rabbits and butterflies. She's got a frickin' body-guard, for goodness' sake. Can't she make him go?"

"Who's got a bodyguard?" Matt asked, turning toward us, and I could have kicked myself with my really cute foot for saying that last part too loud.

"Skylar from the movie."

"Ah," was all he said, but I could tell from the murmurs rippling around the beer tent that everyone else was catching on to the arrival of our celebrities. Dmitri took off his beekeeping hat to get a better look, and I glanced over my shoulder again. Catching Jayden's eye, I gave him a minuscule wave, more like kind of a finger waggle, but it was enough.

"There she is. Hey, Chevette!" Jayden called out, and I could tell from his flushed cheeks and overly loud voice that he must have been hanging out in the *other* beer tent for a while. He walked toward us, with Skylar tottering along beside him like a flamingo trying to walk through muck, until they reached the table. It was awkward to look up at them, and so I stood, although everyone else kept their seats.

"Hi," I said. "Are you enjoying the Lilac Festival?"

"Yes," he said emphatically, but Skylar just stared. Those glasses were so big and dark they could've doubled as ski goggles, and I had no idea if she was actually looking at me. She could be cross-eyed and no one would be the wiser.

"So do you, like, live here *all the time*? Like, *live here*, live here?" she deigned to ask.

"Yep!" I said with about 200 percent more enthusiasm than necessary. "I love it here."

"Wow," she said, although it came out more like "Wwwwwwwwwwwow," as if she were a Chatty Cathy doll with the battery running low.

"I'm telling you, Sky," Jayden said. "You should have gone on the bike ride. This place is really pretty."

"Uh, prettier than where we filmed *Shangri-La*? I seriously doubt that." She swatted away a bug that I felt quite certain was imaginary.

"So, who's everybody?" Jayden asked, giving one of his signature big waves to the group at my table. "Which one of you is the mayor?" He took off his sunglasses and tucked one side into the neckline of his clingy T-shirt, and I heard Marnie's lovelorn sigh.

"That's me," Brooke said, raising her hand while Leo sat up straighter and didn't smile. The guy had been smiling all day, even when he'd bashed his head against that lamppost, but he wasn't smiling now, and I sensed a little machismo jealousy in the set of his jaw. Although his attempt to look menacing was somewhat diminished by the Scooby-Doo bandage he now had on his forehead. Lamppost—1, Leo—0.

"It's a very nice town you've got here, Madam Mayor," Jayden said with a wide grin. "Maybe we can film a sequel and come back again next summer." He was technically talking to her but ended that by pointing at me and saying robustly, "Ghost tour. Sunday night," and I wondered just how very long he'd been at that other beer tent. He seemed pretty sloppy, and since I didn't really want to discuss the ghost tour right now, I just smiled at him and observed from the corner of my eye as Dmitri pulled out his phone. To text *TMZ* undoubtedly.

Matt stood up then and turned to face the movie stars, the same set to his jaw that Leo had, and it nearly made me chuckle. If these guys were peacocks, there would be tail feathers everywhere. But then Skylar took off her sunglasses and gave him what the wardrobe ladies referred to as the "Full Sky," a look she'd perfected in front of the camera to portray all her campy, vampy, sex-kitten prowess.

She looked Matt up and down like he was a life-size Hershey bar that she wanted to devour and was willing to work off the calories for it.

"Who's this?" she asked no one in particular while continuing to nibble him with her eyes.

Since I felt like I was the most logical one to answer, I said, "Skylar, this is Matt. Matt, Skylar." He did his little head bow with his fingertips touching, just as he'd done that day I'd shown up at the Cahill house, and although he looked friendly enough, he didn't seem all that eager to pursue a conversation. In fact, he didn't say anything at all.

"Why haven't I seen you on the set?" Skylar all but demanded.

"I'm not an extra."

"Oh, I'll bet you are extra and then some," she replied with a tipsy giggle, and I watched his face turn a shade of pink I'd never seen on him before. "Are you going on the ghost tour?" she asked, running a finger along the edge of her shirt in a not-so-subtle way of exposing more skin. She wore a lacy black bra underneath and apparently wanted to make sure he knew that.

His pause was infinitesimal, the twitch of his left eye nearly indiscernible, but I knew him. It was the same subtle twitch I'd seen when he was aggravated with Garth Reynolds for being careless and screwing up something at work, or whenever Vera VonMeisterburger tried to lure him into a discussion about our fruit bat shortage, but in this instance I wasn't sure if he was annoyed by Skylar's comment or by the knowledge that Jayden and I were going on the ghost tour—for certainly, if he hadn't heard about it already, he'd just figured it out.

His demeanor gave me a twinge of guilt. Technically there was nothing wrong with me going on the tour. Jayden and I were *just friends*, and we certainly weren't keeping it a secret . . . but still, Catholic. We wore our guilt like Girl Scout badges, so whether I'd earned this one or not, I was going to wear it. And I didn't like the idea that I might be the cause of Matt's twitch.

"Not going on the ghost tour," he said.

"Well, good! Do you have other plans? Because if you don't . . ." She let that linger out there like it was a tempting morsel of bait waiting for Matt to gobble it up, but he didn't. He just smiled at her until her cheeks flushed and she jammed those post–glaucoma exam sunglasses back onto her face.

His lack of interest in her made me feel ever so smug, which was just as undeserved as the guilt, but I didn't have much time to ponder any of this before a chorus of dolphin-pitched greetings drowned out everything else, including my own thoughts.

"Hey, Jayden!"

"It's Skylar!"

"Oh my gosh! It's Jayden and Skylar!"

Chloe, who'd been scarce for most of the day, now suddenly appeared with a giggling gaggle of girlfriends. They arrived en masse, like a swarm of honeybees, all buzzing for attention. My niece had changed into shorts and a striped T-shirt after the parade, having done her due diligence by letting everyone see her, Emily, and Ryan together, and now was dressed like the other girls, although she was the tallest of the lot. And by far the prettiest, in my opinion.

Jayden gave her a fist bump as the swarm buzzed even louder, all talking at once, and asking the stars to autograph their arms or their shirts. Skylar took the glasses off once more and finally smiled as the girls doled out a fair amount of attention to her as well, saying how gorgeous she was and how much they loved her shirt and her shoes and her face and her hair and her everything.

Nothing I would ever do in my lifetime would earn me this kind of frenzied adoration from this cluster of chicks, or from anyone, anywhere, at any time, and I cast a glance over at the table of my peers as if to acknowledge our universal lack of achievement. Brooke shrugged, nonplussed, Emily looked only slightly envious but mostly bemused, while Marnie gazed upon the scene as if she wished she were one of the girls asking for an autograph.

Meanwhile, Matt leaned closer to me and said quietly, "I've got some stuff to take care of. I'll catch up with you later."

I tried to ask him what, but he stepped away from the fray before I had a chance. I watched him leave, and so did Skylar, and I'm not sure which one of us was more disappointed.

Chapter 23

I left the Lilac Festival not long after Matt. Once word circulated around town, especially among the visiting public, that Jayden Pierce and Skylar Tremont were holding court in the beer tent, it became a mad crush of people. All of a sudden it was too crowded, too hot, and too loud. I didn't think I could have gotten to Jayden's side even if I'd wanted to, and the truth was, I wasn't sure that I did want to. He was obviously a little drunk, and I was tired and full and needed a nap after sampling all that beer, and Brooke said she didn't need me for anything, which was both a surprise and a relief, so I decided to go home.

Gigi's place was quiet, a nice respite from the chaos of the festival. I took a shower to wash off the dust of the day, and I tried to take that nap, but for as tired as I was, my mind wouldn't let me drift off, and before long, I found myself with my phone in my hand, texting Matt.

He'd left rather abruptly, and I couldn't shake the feeling that it had something to do with me. Or more specifically, me and Jayden. Maybe I was imagining things, but it was a niggling sort of worry that was burrowing like a chipmunk, and the sooner I caught it and dealt with it, the less damage it would do. I tapped at my screen to send him a message.

R U GOING TO THE FIREWORKS?

He answered with:

NOT SURE. U?

I realized then how much I wanted to see him, in spite of having been with him all day, and that chipmunk of worry burrowed deeper. Because who ever skipped the fireworks? Everyone always went to the fireworks. I responded:

PLANNING ON IT.

And then I grew bold and added:

WANT TO WATCH THEM TOGETHER?

He didn't respond for nearly a full minute, which I'd learned from Chloe was a bit of a slam. Leaving someone unread or unanswered—especially in the middle of a conversation—meant they knew they were making you wait.

Then again, Matt wasn't a thirteen-year-old girl and probably didn't know the latest in texting etiquette and strategy. It was quite possible he was just doing something else at the moment because he had a life. Still, the waiting was hard, and the relief I felt when I finally saw some dots hovering on my cell phone screen was out of proportion to the actual incident.

DUNNIGANS ARE GONE AND SAID I COULD WATCH FROM THEIR BALCONY.

I read that and wasn't sure if he was inviting me or not—because apparently, I *was* a thirteen-year-old girl, so I felt relief again when I saw he was adding to his message.

WANT TO WATCH THEM FROM HERE? NOT TOO INTERESTED IN
THE TOURIST CROWD.

I made myself wait to respond, so as not to appear too eager, on the
off chance that he did know texting strategies, and responded exactly
forty-three seconds later. It was as long as I could wait.

THAT COULD WORK. WHAT TIME DO YOU WANT ME TO COME
OVER?

Ninety-seven seconds later he responded with:

HOW ABOUT NOW?

I looked at the clock and laughed. It was only 6:00 p.m. Hours
until the fireworks. And then he added:

MAKING SPAGHETTI FOR DINNER AND THE CATS ARE BORED.
COME AND PLAY WITH THEM.

And so I found myself, an hour later, happily sitting at the exquisite, marble-topped island of the Dunnigans' ultra-gourmet kitchen
watching Matt chop green peppers to add to a pasta sauce currently
simmering on the stove. The kittens were fine, and not at all bored.
Apparently, that was just a ploy. A well-played ploy, because they were
over at his little shack while he was, in actuality, staying in the big house
and taking care of the Dunnigans' two Weimaraners, Zelda and Gatsby.
The dogs looked virtually identical to me, and other than the obvious
differences, I was only able to tell them apart because Zelda had a wide,
rhinestone-encrusted collar, while Gatsby wore a black bow tie. Because
the Dunnigans were so rich that even their dogs were swanky.

"So, did you have fun today?" I asked him as I sipped a glass of a perfectly chilled pinot grigio that we'd taken from the wine fridge. Mrs. Dunnigan had left blue Post-it notes on a few bottles that said, *You can drink this*, giving us the distinct impression that this was the *cheap stuff*, which was just fine by me. I liked wine that came in boxes or had screw-off tops. This bottle had a cork, so . . . fancy.

"I did. Did you?" He'd changed into jeans and a plain white T-shirt that was so all-American sexy I found it utterly distracting. He was just one red bandanna in his pocket away from being an album cover. And I wanted to ask him about Jayden and Skylar and why he'd left when he did, but I needed this wine to do its work first. I was nervous and anxious, and I wasn't sure why. Matt usually had a calming, soothing effect on me, but tonight I was jittery and uneasy, so I sipped the wine and hoped it would relax me.

"Sure," I said. "The Lilac Festival is always fun, but as a native to the island, I'm morally obligated to enjoy it."

He smiled but didn't say more, so I decided to change the subject. "How long are the Dunnigans gone for?"

"A couple of weeks. They're in Tuscany. Sounds rough, right?"

"Awful. How miserable for them."

"Right? And I'm forced to spend my evenings in this dump." He gestured toward the immense expanse of kitchen around us, with the frescoed ceiling and the top-of-the-line appliances. Most owners of the larger, single-family homes on the island took pains to keep the décor and architecture true to the Victorian time period, but most of them also splurged when it came to their kitchens. For the right price you could get a high-end anything with all the modern features that only *looked* old-fashioned.

"I'm so sorry for your troubles," I said. "However will you manage?"

"Well, for starters, I'm going to drink all the wine with the blue Post-it notes on it," he said, lifting his glass in a toast before taking a sip. "And then I'm going to sleep in a room with a California king four-poster bed that must have been built on-site, because otherwise I have no idea how they would have gotten it in here."

"That sounds impressive."

"It is. Want to see it? I can take you on a tour of the house while we wait for the water to boil."

"Of course." I was not about to pass up the chance to see how the other half lived, although in reality the Dunnigans were not so much the *other half* as they were the 1 percent. This was technically their year-round home, but both of them were certified pilots and flew their own planes on and off the island with as much regularity as most people drove their cars to the grocery store. Rumor had it that she *came from money* and that he'd made a killing in the eighties by inventing some kind of software and then selling it for an outrageous dollar amount that included lots of zeroes.

"I cannot imagine having a house like this and still traveling as much as they do," I said as we trekked up to the third floor after seeing the solarium, the library, the den, the other den, and at least a dozen other rooms before finally arriving at the master bedroom. "Why would you ever bother leaving?"

Matt shook his head. "I don't know. Unless they go someplace to rob banks, because this house must have cost a fortune. But lucky for us, because here's where we get to watch the fireworks from." He walked across the plush Persian carpet in a room that was three times the size of his gardening-shed cottage and opened a set of mullioned-glass french doors that led to a white-railed balcony.

Following close behind, I stepped outside and nearly tripped—because the view was that spectacular. Even for a person who grew up on this island and had seen the landmarks from virtually every angle, this vantage point was amazing. Off to one side was Petoskey Bridge, along with the far shore of the Upper Peninsula and all the little uninhabited islands in between. I could see the lighthouse over near Leelanau Hill, and the rocky cliffs on the way to Beech Tree Point.

"Here's my favorite part," Matt said, pointing down to the yard below. I followed his gaze and saw the Dunnigans' intricately designed flower garden—except that calling it a *flower garden* was kind of like calling Buckingham Palace *the house where the queen lives*. It was huge and exploding with rioting colors and swirling shapes, and from here, I could see that the winding paths were actually three intertwined letters, like a monogram: *B*, *D*, and *O*, for Beth and Oliver Dunnigan.

"You can't see the patterns when you're on the ground," he said, "but from up here, you can. Apparently, Oliver did that without telling Beth the plan, and she kept complaining that his gardening beds didn't make any sense and that his paths were all screwy, but eventually she caught on. They each have their own version of the story, of course, but it's a cool garden, either way."

"It's amazing," I said. "If I ever manage to move out of Gigi's house, I want to find a place where I can have a garden. Flowers and vegetables, but mostly flowers."

"I'm sure you'll get out of there when the time is right," he said. "Maybe you should give Mary Lou Baxter a call."

"Maybe I should, although I'll never have a garden like that with my salary as a preschool teacher. And right now, I'm a little pressed for cash."

"My grandmother likes to say that enough is as much as a banquet, so I guess it's all relative. This house is impressive, for sure, but supposedly money can't buy happiness."

"Maybe not, but I'd be willing to give it a shot."

Matt chuckled, and I thought about how the opulence of this house reminded me of Tag's place back in Sacramento. Not the style, of course, because his place was a sprawling contemporary ranch with lots of shiny surfaces and abstract art, while the Dunnigans' *cottage* was pure, vintage Trillium Bay Victorian, but there was a similarity, in that it looked expensive—because it was expensive. But I'd hated Tag's house. No amount of money would've made me like it. So I guess

Matt's observation was accurate. Tag had been rich, but that hadn't been enough to keep me happy.

We admired the garden for another minute, then went back to the kitchen to finish making dinner, and decided to bring our plates of pasta back up to that fabulous balcony and eat our meal there. Matt brought along the bottle of wine, and as we sat on the cushy cushions of the rattan deck furniture and ate, and drank, and talked about a million little inconsequential things that felt meaningful simply because we were learning more about each other, I finally found the courage to ask him the one question that had been tapping at my mind all evening.

We'd finished our food, the wine was crisp and mellow, and the sun was just beginning to set on the horizon.

"Matt, can I ask you something?"

His chuckle was likely prompted by the fact that I always seemed to ask him *that* before asking him something *else*.

"Of course," he answered, just as he always did.

"Earlier today in the beer tent, why did you leave so suddenly? It seemed kind of abrupt."

"It was getting crowded," he said after a slight pause, and I knew that the usually honest and authentic Matt was being a little evasive.

"It wasn't that crowded when you left," I answered. "Unless you're talking specifically about Jayden and Skylar showing up." I decided to be direct, thanks to that wine making me bold.

He looked over at me, the lowering sun casting just enough glow to bounce off his tan skin and make him golden. "Well, I guess you caught me. I left because they showed up."

"Why?"

He paused again, his gaze as direct as our words. His eyes were intent on mine, his voice was quiet and calm, his chest rose and fell with a sigh, and my breath caught in my throat.

"Lilly, I like you," he said on that sigh. "It shouldn't come as a surprise that I'm attracted to you and that it's something I want to explore, but if you're not interested, if you're still tangled up in your feelings about Tag, or if you think this Jayden guy has something to offer, I'm not going to stand in your way. I won't stop being your friend, but I'm also not going to compete for your affection, because it's just not my style."

My heart ka-thumped like a square wheel inside my chest because I wasn't sure how to respond. "I'm not expecting you to compete, Matt. I didn't invite Jayden to the festival. He came with Skylar."

"Okay." He paused. "But you did go biking with him, and now you're going on the ghost tour together." He frowned as if the words weren't easy to say, but he was determined to say them anyway. "I'm sure that doesn't seem like a big deal to you, but I'm sorry, Lilly. You know how this island is. Everyone talks, and everyone is telling me—no, they're warning me—that you talk to him all the time and that there's something going on between the two of you. Honestly, that's your business, and maybe it's none of mine, but I don't want to get caught up in the middle of something and end up on the losing end. So, when Jayden showed up today, I just . . . I decided to take myself out of the picture before people around here started nattering on about seeing the three of us together."

He sighed again, more deeply, and for the first time since I'd known him, Matt seemed uncertain. For every rough and difficult story he'd told me about his past, he'd rarely shown any sense of injury or regret. Only Matt telling the story as he knew it, with no emotional embellishment. But now he seemed a little bit vulnerable, and it made my heart ache in a strange, unfamiliar way, a way loaded with both compassion and attraction because he was putting his feelings on the line, and I knew that wasn't easy.

"That was probably dumb and shortsighted of me," he continued. "But . . . I guess . . . given what happened with . . . given what has happened to me before, I just don't want to get caught off guard again. I don't want to fall for you if you're busy falling for someone else."

His declaration made that ache double and my attraction triple. "Are you falling for me?"

He turned to stare. "What do you think?"

I couldn't help but smile then as my pulse flickered and my heart fluttered. "I think you are."

A smile toyed at the corner of his lips as well. "I think I am, too."

The moment hung suspended as his gaze locked on mine, like he was trying to draw me closer with just the power of his sapphire-blue eyes, but then he blinked and looked away, breaking the spell.

"But," he said with a soft, sardonic chuckle, "you are a very busy woman, Lilly Callaghan. You have a lot of things and a lot of people in your life pulling you in different directions. I don't want to add to that noise. So you have to figure out what you want, and when you've decided, then you should tell me." He stood up and moved to lean against the railing of the balcony, turning to face me but from a distance, as if he needed that physical space between us, and I understood what he was saying.

And I wanted to tell him right then that there was nothing going on between Jayden and me. Not technically, anyway. But I couldn't deny that it was within the realm of possibility, that each time Jayden and I were together, there was the potential for *something* to happen, and I couldn't even swear that I didn't want it to. Even if it led to nothing. Because he was Jayden Pierce. And because he was fun and attractive . . . and he seemed a little interested in me, too.

"Does that make sense?" he asked at my hesitation.

"It does make sense."

I took a gulp of my wine as a butterfly floated by, and suddenly it hit me . . . what the hell was I doing? What the hell was I waiting for? There was Matt right in front of me, glorious, wonderful, *real* Matt, saying he was falling for me, while I took my own sweet time trying to figure out what to do about that—as if choosing a man were like perusing a box of chocolates.

Because that's all Jayden was. He was candy. For all the moments I'd spent over the past few weeks imagining fanciful scenarios of what-ifs with him, I'd always known, deep down, it was all just smoke and mirrors. A shallow, futile infatuation, and I needed to shut the door on those illusions because there wasn't really such a thing as a sexlebrity list. Not in real life. Matt didn't owe me a free pass with Jayden just because Jayden was a movie star, and he also didn't deserve for me to keep him wondering where he stood.

Or where I stood.

He'd been patient, and chivalrous, and a good friend, but I'd be a fool to keep him waiting in the friend zone for too long. Because Brooke was right. Matt was a hot commodity, and as much as I hated to admit it, Emily was right, too. A fling with Jayden would matter to Matt, and I could be throwing away a chance at my kind of perfect on something that wasn't even real.

Because the reality was it was Matt who gave me the tingles every time I saw him, and Matt who hugged me when I cried, and Matt who rubbed my shoulders when they were sore, and Matt who brought me food he'd made himself. It was Matt who asked questions that challenged me, and Matt who'd been nothing but honest and authentic. Giving up on the fantasy of Jayden was no sacrifice at all, really, because what I was reaching for was genuine and precious and definitely worth exploring.

I stood up and set my wineglass on the little table next to my chair. Then moved slowly in Matt's direction.

"Jayden is fun, Matt, and I can't deny that this movie stuff has been a bit of an ego boost, but it's all just pretend. I know Jayden's attentions don't have any substance. There are no real feelings between us."

"Pretend feelings can be just as confusing as the real thing, Lilly, and I'm still not sure where I fit in that scenario. For all my talk about life's hardships leading to growth, I'm not sure that me sitting around stewing in jealousy is actually doing me any good."

"Are you jealous?" For some reason that surprised me, because he always seemed like he was above that sort of thing, but his reaction proved me wrong.

"Of course I'm jealous. I don't give a shit about him being a movie star or being rich and famous. I don't care that he can drop five grand at the drop of a hat to buy some old car, but I do care that he's got you so distracted. And I hate that it makes me feel like I don't measure up."

He ran a hand through his hair and stared at me as if trying to see into my heart. "Lilly, I've spent a lot of my life trying to figure out where my value comes from, and right now, I hate feeling this mixed up. And I hate that I don't trust my own judgment when it comes to you," he added quietly. "That's why I'm just trying to step back and . . . protect myself until you decide what you want."

Everything inside me settled into place as I realized he was appealing to me as much as he was explaining. He was asking me not to toy with his emotions, and not to break his heart, and I knew in that moment that I wanted to make him feel safe and loved and valued in just the same way he made other people feel.

The way he made me feel.

I moved closer until I was right in front of him. With him leaning on the balcony railing, our faces were nearly level as I gazed into his eyes.

"I do know what I want," I said, my voice soft but certain. Because I did. It felt as if I'd just decided in that moment, but really, I'd known all along.

His eyes traveled over my face like a shy caress. "That wasn't supposed to sound so much like an ultimatum, you know," he said, his own voice husky but soft. "If you're not . . . falling, then you're not falling. You can't force it."

I smiled and leaned closer, certain it was time to give poor Matt Eastman all the attention and affection he deserved. He'd been very patient, and the truth was, I'd wanted to run my fingers through that

222 / Tracy Brogan

hair of his since the first day I'd come home and seen him standing on that overturned barrel. I'd wanted to press my palms against his broad, muscular chest and kiss his beautiful mouth and the curve of his neck and all the other places, too.

I reached up and ran my fingertips over his jaw, feeling the slight prickle of today's whiskers. "Are you trying to talk me out of this?" I asked.

"Definitely not."

"Okay, then. I know what I what." I said it decisively, and he inhaled sharply.

"Well, it had better be me, then, because if it's not, you're standing way too close."

I laughed then, and his own chuckle was full of optimism and relief.

"I'm right where I'm supposed to be," I said. "Here. With you. This is where I want to be and where I choose to be."

He smiled and pulled me close.

The night had grown dark all around us, with only the lights from the lampposts on the street below and the hallway light from inside the house giving us any illumination as I pressed against him and felt the dizzying heat of his body and the erratic thump of his heart. He wrapped his arms around my waist, then ran his hands up my back, drawing me even closer. I looped my arms around his shoulders as our faces were just a heartbeat apart.

This was the best part of a first kiss. The anticipation. The clamoring hearts and the tentative sighs. The searching eyes and the luxury of knowing that something wonderful was about to happen. And when Matt's lips grazed my cheek, I closed my eyes and knew that, yes, I was exactly where I was supposed to be.

And when he kissed me, ah . . . at last, I knew that in his arms was exactly where I planned to stay. All my senses swirled and merged into one big arc of longing as he held me tight. His kiss was perfect. Full of promise and hope and cravings that I couldn't wait to satisfy even while knowing I could never get enough of him.

The Universe, just to make sure that we'd gotten the message, sent fireworks into the sky overhead, bursting with shimmering light. Or maybe it was just Clancy and the guys from the fire station starting the Lilac Festival show, but either way, there were definitely fireworks.

Chapter 24

"And where were you until all hours of the night last night, young lady?" Gigi asked as I stumbled down the stairs and into the kitchen just in time to join her and Emily for the long, peccadillo-filled stroll to church. Chloe had spent the night at a friend's house, so she wasn't around, which was why Gigi felt so free to point out the fact that I, too, had slept over at a friend's house.

Well, technically I'd slept at the Dunnigan House, and technically there had been almost no sleeping, but explaining all that would've just complicated matters, and we were late for Mass. And I was so late for confession.

"I was out," I said primly. As primly as I could while suppressing an irrepressible grin. I was happy this morning. No denying it. One simple kiss on the balcony under the fireworks hadn't been so simple after all and had led to a blissful marathon of the best sex I'd ever had. Like *so very* the best sex ever.

I'd considered Tag skillful enough between the sheets, but my previous dating history had been sketchy at best and I'd had little to compare him to. Now I knew, and I sighed with latent satisfaction at the delicious memory of last night, because as it turned out—not surprisingly—Matt did not fumble in the dark. In fact, there wasn't a moment or a caress or a whisper or a stroke or a nibble or a kiss that I would've changed. It was perfect. Everything was perfect. Matt was perfect. Other than having Zelda and Gatsby standing next to the bed staring at us all night in canine curiosity, each second of it had been simply . . . perfect.

"I know you were out. Where were you?" Gigi said, all but waggling a finger in my face, although I suspected she was more proud than upset. Gigi loved it whenever anybody got some. Emily seemed suspiciously pleased as well, leading me to believe she assumed I was with Matt rather than Jayden. And of course she was right.

"If I keep living here, are you always going to be this nosy?" I asked, slipping my feet into the sandals by the front door before we all walked out onto the front porch and into the early Sunday morning sunshine.

Gigi scoffed at my question. "Honey, I'll be this nosy whether you live here or not, so I suggest you spill it. You look as smug as Mr. Whiskers does when he brings home a big, fat, dead mouse."

"Which one is Mr. Whiskers?" I asked, skipping down the steps toward the sidewalk.

"Oh my gosh! Stop avoiding the question!" Emily snapped good-naturedly. "Who were you with? Please tell me it was Matt."

I cast her a glance, and that was all it took to confirm her suspicions. She clasped her hands together gleefully as if her horse had just come in first at the Kentucky Derby, and I wondered if maybe she had put money on this race. It wouldn't be the first time. I'd grown up so sheltered on this island that I was the only chaste one in my entire dorm at college, and allegedly there'd been a wager on when I'd finally lose my virginity. Apparently one of my classmates won $200 from that pool, and all I'd gotten was fourteen very unsatisfying minutes with a kid named Dave who never bothered to take off his socks. I don't just mean during our lackluster sexual encounter. I mean he literally never took off his socks. Rumor was he had an extra toe—which I did *not* know about until afterward. Sadly, that was the only interesting thing about him.

But Tag and Dave and any of my previous quasi-mediocre partners were now solidly in my past. In fact, if I'd known then what I knew now, none of those guys would have made it past second base. Even

Tag, which made me feel just a little bit sorry for him. Emily had tried to clue me in on all this last summer, when she'd warned me against a relationship with such an older man, and she'd tried to steer me toward Matt even back then, but I'd refused to listen. No wonder she was feeling so victorious this morning. This was her ultimate *I told you so*. And this time, I didn't even mind.

Saint Bartholomew's was sparsely attended this morning. It typically was the Sunday after the festival, thanks to those dueling beer tents, but there were still ample holier-than-thou glances directed my way. Today, I didn't mind that so much, either. I wasn't exactly sure who knew what, because no one had seen me go to the Dunnigan House last night, and no one—to the best of my knowledge—had seen me walking home in the early-morning fog at five o'clock this morning so I could get at least a few hours of sleep. I'd left Matt without waking him because I knew he'd insist on walking me home, and then we'd be busted for sure. Maybe he could convince someone he was just up getting ready for sunrise yoga, but no one would believe that about me.

After the church service, it was the usual rigmarole in the yard of Saint Bart's, with islanders approaching the chief to complain about flower beds getting trampled as people found spots for yesterday's parade, Judge Murphy wanting to remind my father that Geezer Night Poker had been moved to Thursday at Sudsy's house, and Dmitri standing way too close, as if he was literally trying to sniff details off me about my evening's whereabouts.

"You've been doing a lot of work on that movie," he said after the usual greetings. "How's that going?"

"Good. It's been fun. How about you? Have you been enjoying it?"

"Sure. I've done a few scenes and enjoyed myself. Maybe not as much as you, though. Maybe you should head off to Hollywood when this one is a wrap and try your luck at acting."

"Mm, I don't see that happening."

"Why not? You've obviously made a good impression on the director. And that good-looking actor kid. Maybe tonight when you go on the ghost tour you can ask him about that."

I *could* tell Dmitri that I'd decided not to go on the ghost tour that night. That instead I planned to be back at the Dunnigan House with Matt, leaving DNA all over the floral velvet settee they had in the library while Zelda and Gatsby paced nervously on the Axminster rug next to us, but no. Any information I offered, even to confirm or deny Dmitri's interests, would only be used against me somehow. The less he knew, the better.

Fortunately, my sister Brooke showed up and pulled me away under the guise of discussing something of the utmost importance.

"Thanks for the rescue," I said as we walked from the yard of Saint Bart's and toward Joe's Cuppa Joe.

"You're welcome, but there is actually something I wanted to ask you about," Brooke said. "I hope you don't mind, but I promised Leo. Let me grab us each an iced coffee first, and then we can talk. Do you mind waiting?"

"Of course not." My curiosity was tantalized as I sat down on a bench in a shady spot overlooking the bay. Brooke joined me just a few minutes later and handed me a plastic cup.

"Leo doesn't think I've broken the law, does he?" I teased, even while wondering if the Dunnigans had inside security cameras that may have caught Matt and me standing naked in their kitchen during a midnight snack attack. That would be awkward.

But Brooke chuckled easily. "Nope, not as far as I know. This is actually a non-work-related question and more of a personal-favor sort of thing."

"Okay." My curiosity heightened. Since my relationship with Leo consisted of about a dozen encounters, all within the context of family gatherings, I could not imagine what kind of favor I could do for him. I was willing enough. I just didn't know what I'd have to offer.

"It's silly, really," Brooke said. "And probably not even worth mentioning, but . . . well, when Jayden said something yesterday about coming back to Wenniway Island and filming another movie here next summer, I guess it got Leo's creative wheels turning. You know he's been working on a novel, right?"

"Kind of. I think I've heard something about that."

"Well, he is. He's been writing it since he moved here last fall, and when we found out that movie people were coming here, he decided to turn it into a screenplay. Now he's almost finished with it."

"Okay. So what does that have to do with me?"

"He's wondering if you'd give a copy of it to Jayden or Griffin or basically anyone involved with the movie who might be able to give him some advice. Leo's a pretty grounded guy, and I don't think he's got any illusions of grandeur here, but I think there's a part of him that thinks if Jayden reads it, and likes it, maybe it could be turned into a movie. One that they could film here on the island."

"Seriously?"

"Yes."

"I don't think I have that kind of clout, Brooke. I mean, I could ask Jayden, but there's no guarantee he'd say yes, and if you'd ever seen Griffin in action, you'd know he's not the kind of guy to do anyone any favors."

"I know. I saw him at the coffee shop. He seems like an asshole."

"He is. The assistant director is okay, but she's not exactly warm and fuzzy, either. And I don't think she likes me very much."

"Why?"

"Because I fraternize with the talent," I said dryly. The irony of that statement was lost on neither of us because it was that very issue that made Leo think I had some inside access to Jayden. "Anyway, I'm certainly willing to ask him, and maybe he can ask them. We did sell him Dad's car, so maybe he'll feel like he owes us a favor."

"Can you ask him tonight? When you go on the ghost tour? Leo is really eager all of a sudden."

"Um, well, I wasn't planning to go on the ghost tour."

"Really? Why?" She took a sip from her straw, and I looked around to make sure we weren't being overheard. Dmitri was not above hiding in shrubberies to get a scoop.

Returning my gaze back to her, I said, "Because I had sex with Matt last night."

Her eyes went round. It was hard to surprise Brooke, so I counted this as a real score. She swallowed hard and slowly pulled the straw from her mouth. "You did? How was it?"

"Bendy and awesome."

She burst out laughing, and then so did I.

"Too bad I don't need any favors from Matt," she said once she'd caught her breath. "But at any rate, if you have a chance to ask Jayden about this on Leo's behalf, we'd both appreciate it."

I nodded. "I'll see what I can do."

Chapter 25

PLEASE CALL ME!!!! IMPORTANT!!!

I blinked a few times at the message on my phone, my eyes bleary from a deep, coma-like snooze because I'd fallen asleep on the front porch swing after coming home from church. It was about four o'clock in the afternoon now. I'd texted Jayden several hours ago saying I couldn't go on the ghost tour tonight because I had family obligations. It seemed like the best excuse. And although Matt had never specifically asked me not to go, I knew it would bother him, and I understood why. It just wasn't worth the risk, especially since I didn't want to go anyway.

But Jayden's response, though delayed, seemed a little over the top. And it had woken me up from a delightful, scorchingly hot erotic dream. Or maybe it was a memory? At any rate, I sat up, readjusted the chintz-covered pillows around me, and dialed Jayden's number.

"Hey, Chevette," he said. "Thanks for getting back to me so quickly."

"No problem, but I really can't do the ghost tour tonight. I'm sorry."

"What? Oh yeah. That's totally okay. There's actually something else I need to talk to you about. Can you come to the Imperial Hotel to meet with me, Rashida, and Griff?"

"When?"

"Right now."

"Right now?"

"Yeah. I know you had stuff you had to do tonight, but this shouldn't take too long. Maybe half an hour."

"Um, I guess. But why?"

"It's kind of hard to explain over the phone, but trust me when I say it's important."

"Um, okay. I can be there in thirty minutes. How does that sound?"

"Perfect. Meet us in the dining room, because I'm starving."

Of course he was starving. Jayden was always starving. And I wished he could've just told me what this was about, but he was being all kinds of mysterious. I hurried inside to freshen up and change my clothes. Matt and I had already agreed to meet at six o'clock, so no worries there. I could go right from the Imperial Hotel to the Dunnigan House and not be late.

I walked into the Grand Dining Room twenty-seven minutes later full of trepidation and curiosity. Were they going to admonish me for ruining their movie somehow? Had I done such a dismal job during those street scenes with Jayden that they needed to reshoot them? Had my background dancing been so very clumsy and awkward that I needed to sign a waiver saying I knew just how bad I looked before they could release the movie? Those were just a few of the myriad of worries running on a constant loop in my head, like the chain of my bike as I pedaled.

Jayden stood up when I reached the table and gave me a quick hug. Griffin looked up and grunted, and Rashida smiled at me. That's when I really started to worry—when Rashida smiled. I sat down in the empty chair next to Jayden, and he sat back down as well.

"Thanks so much for coming, Lilly. Especially on such short notice. We really appreciate it," Jayden said.

"Yes, we do," Rashida said, nodding and smiling even bigger.

And then Griffin said gruffly, "How do you feel about semi-gratu-itous nudity?"

Jayden let out an amused huff, Rashida rolled her eyes as her smile faded, and Griffin just stared at me, waiting for my answer like a lion homing in on the weakest gazelle of the herd. I was the weakest gazelle in this scenario, in case that wasn't obvious.

"Um, I guess that depends," I answered. "Can you give me some context?"

Rashida quickly tapped on her phone and then held up the screen for me to see. "Here's your context," she said. "That's Skylar's ass right now. Do you see anything wrong with it? What does that look like to you?"

It was a rather gruesome photo of an otherwise spectacular ass. "It looks like poison ivy."

"Bingo," Jayden said. "She's got it all over. Obviously, all over."

Rashida gave him an exasperated look. "Yes, all over. Thanks for that, Jay."

I looked to him, then Rashida, then Griffin, and back to Jayden, who shrugged with apparent chagrin. "It's sort of my fault," he said.

"How so?" I asked.

"Well, you may have noticed we were a little drunk yesterday." He paused to gauge my reaction.

"I'd suspected as much."

"Yeah, well, last night I was giving Skylar a hard time about being so afraid of the dark, and after the fireworks I sort of . . . dared her to go into the woods with me. And of course, being drunk, she had to pee . . . and she had on those ridiculous shoes, so then she fell . . . and then she rolled around a little bit before she could get up." He let out a little chuff of laughter, but both Rashida and Griffin glared at him.

He glared back. "Like I said, we were both kind of drunk."

"We took her to the Trillium Bay Medical Center this afternoon," Rashida said with a big, despondent sigh. "They gave her some ointment and a handful of steroid pills, but those won't kick in for a few days, and she could have the rash for weeks. It could actually get worse before it gets better. At least that's what the doctor said, but we have a shooting schedule to stick to."

"So what do you need from me? Are you asking me to fill in for her somehow?"

"That's part of it—" Jayden said, but then Griffin cut him off.

"About the nudity. We have to shoot a pivotal scene where Skylar's character kills herself by walking naked into the lake, but she sure as hell can't do it like that." He pointed to Rashida's phone, which now lay on the table between us like a cautionary tale. Of Skylar's tail.

I reached across and flipped the phone over. I was no fan of Skylar's, but she deserved a bit more respect than that, if only for the fact that she truly had an amazing ass. I wasn't sure if mine would measure up, and I thought that's what they were asking of me.

"Am I to understand that you want me to be her . . . her naked body double?"

"Yes," all three of them said at once.

I was not prepared for this. Jayden should have warned me over the phone.

"Can't you just, I don't know, shoot some other stuff until she's in better shape?"

"You know all that equipment the crew members have been bitching about? That stuff they had to haul up a hill and through the woods?" Jayden asked.

"Yeah?"

"It's for this scene, and the sooner we get it shot, the sooner we can get all that expensive stuff back inside. Right now, we've got security guarding it around the clock, and that's draining our budget. Not to mention what the weather and the moisture is doing to the cameras and the other electronics. As a producer, I can tell you that every minute of delay costs me money."

"Rescheduling the scene just isn't an option," Rashida added. "We've got perfect weather conditions tomorrow, and everything is in place. All we need is you."

"It would be a closed set," Jayden said, covering my hand with his own. "We've got permission to block off the area, so only the smallest crew would be there, and you'd be filmed entirely from the back. Easy as falling off a bike." He gave my fingers a squeeze.

"Did you say this is the scene where she kills herself?" I asked.

"That's sort of ambiguous," Rashida answered. "The audience will see her—or you—walking into the lake, but it won't be totally clear to them what happens next because the character is having a little break with reality. She's sort of hallucinating. Regardless, you'd only have to go in about waist deep. You don't even have to go all the way under."

I chuckled because getting my hair wet was the least of my concerns at the moment.

"Doesn't she have a stunt double or somebody for this kind of thing?"

"Her stunt double is a man," Rashida answered, a little impatiently. "And although he's a good sport, his ass doesn't quite cut it. We need a woman's ass. We need your ass because you're her exact measurements. We shoot in twelve hours, and we just don't have time to find someone else's."

"Tick-tock. Tick-tock. Ka-ching, ka-ching," Griffin added.

"Your ass would be perfect for this," Jayden said. I could tell he meant to tease, and I wondered if I should be flattered or insulted.

"We'll make it worth your while," Rashida added. She and Jayden were tag teaming me with hard-to-process information, while Griffin mostly scowled and stared at his watch.

Rashida handed me a slip of paper. "This is what we would pay you for a day's work, and it would probably only take a couple of hours. With any luck you'd be done by noon. In and out, with none the wiser. We'd want to keep this between us, by the way. Confidentiality is key because Skylar doesn't want anyone knowing she's got blisters on her ass, and Jayden seems to think you could keep this to yourself."

I pulled my hand from Jayden's grasp and opened the folded paper. Years of playing poker with my father had taught me how to not react, but this amount was more than I'd made in a month as a Trillium Bay preschool teacher. Maybe not life changing, but certainly enough to help me pay a few months' rent so I could move out of Gigi's place. Or take a very nice vacation, or maybe even set it aside for a rainy day. I was frugal by nature, and this was a lot of money to me, and all for just a few hours of work. Sure, I'd be naked . . . but still. That was a nice chunk of change.

Plus, in truth, I wasn't uncomfortable with nudity. After flashing my breasts to that auditorium full of spectators at my one and only beauty pageant, I'd learned how to be comfortable in my own skin, and showing it off to others didn't faze me that much. And if I had the same measurements as a sexy movie star and an ass nearly as good as hers, well, that was something to be proud of, wasn't it? I was strong and fit and not ashamed of my body. Why not make the most of it? I guess *the bottom line* here was that this was a compliment of sorts. At least it felt like one to me!

"I know it's a big ask, Lilly," Jayden said at my hesitation. "But you'd be doing us—doing me—a huge favor. We're working on a razor-thin budget, but if that amount isn't enough, we could negotiate. Maybe add another five thousand."

Another $5,000? Damn! How could I turn that down? It was just my butt, after all. Without being able to see my face, everyone would just assume it was Skylar. Until I was an old lady and decided to tell my grandchildren about the time my ass starred in a movie. What a story that would make.

I sighed as if I were truly torn, when in reality, I'd made my decision. The money and flattery and the fun factor were all just too much for my ego to resist. But their desperation had given me an idea. I was happy to take the cash, of course, but on top of that, these three had something more to offer. Something that gave me a gloriously altruistic excuse for saying yes.

"Five thousand more would make this seem a little more . . . acceptable, but in addition to that, I do have two requests."

"And what are those?" Rashida said warily.

"Well, first of all, I'd definitely want to keep this a secret, like you said. I don't need every person on this island seeing the movie and then giving my dad a hard time about me doing this. Do those nondisclosure forms apply to this situation?"

"They sure do," Rashida said, nodding. "And trust me, Skylar doesn't want this getting out any more than you do, so she sure as hell won't tell anyone."

"Good, and when you say *closed set*, do you mean it? Will your security people make sure there's no one spying on us?"

"Our security team is top notch," Jayden said. "No one will get within half a mile of where we are. We know how to account for telephoto lenses, and since there are no paparazzi around here, it'll be fine. Plus, we're shooting at the ass crack of dawn." His cheeks flushed. "Sorry. Poor word choice."

"What's the other request?" Rashida asked, eager to move on and hopefully close this deal.

"I have a screenplay you have to promise to read."

"A screenplay?" Griffin blurted loudly, as if I'd just confessed to having three breasts instead the standard two.

"You wrote a screenplay?" Jayden asked at the same time, equally loudly, as if that were more shocking and surprising than what they'd just asked me to do. These guys really did live in an alternate universe.

"I didn't write it," I answered. "A friend of mine did. He's a deputy here on the island, but he also writes . . ." I suddenly realized I had no idea what his screenplay was about. That would've been helpful to know, but never in a million years could I have guessed I'd have the opportunity to make this pitch quite so soon, nor in this particular manner. "Screenplays," I added. "He writes screenplays, so all I'd ask is that you read it and promise to give him some real feedback."

"Done!" Griffin said before the echo of my voice had even left my mouth.

Chapter 26

My mind was racing faster than the pedals of my bike as I rushed to the Dunnigan House to meet Matt. Now that I'd agreed to film that scene and had even signed a contract before leaving the hotel, remorse and uncertainty were kicking in on several different levels. I might have let the thrill of being asked go to my head and now was in a bit of a panic.

Being comfortable with nudity in general was one thing, but getting naked in front of a bunch of crew members was something else altogether. And I'd be the one in my all-together!

But Jayden, Griffin, and Rashida had promised that everyone involved was a consummate professional. They did this sort of thing all the time, right? I'd seen *Shangri-La*, and Skylar had been naked half a dozen times in that movie. Then again, Skylar was an *actress*. And I was a *preschool teacher*! I hadn't even thought of that before I'd agreed. What if I got my old job back, and then Mary Lou Baxter found out that was my butt on the screen and fired me? Would she do that? Had I just lost a job I hadn't even gotten back yet?

And what about Matt?

That was the thing weighing on me the heaviest. I'd agreed to keep this confidential. I'd signed my own NDA, but the guilt of potentially keeping this from him was already pulling on my mind like an albatross with an anchor around its neck and a monkey on its back. How had I not thought of him and how he'd feel before putting my name on that dotted line? It just hadn't crossed my mind in the moment, but if Matt hadn't wanted me to go on a silly ghost tour with Jayden, he sure as heck wouldn't want him seeing my butt.

Fortunately, that part was fixable. Since the scene was just Skylar walking into the water, I'd just ask Jayden to excuse himself. Problem solved. Producer or not, he was a good sport. He'd understand. He'd give me some privacy. I was doing him a favor, after all, so he owed me one, too.

Besides, he'd had his chance to see my butt, and he hadn't even acted interested. After we'd finished up in the dining room, I'd learned the last caveat to this agreement was that Skylar had to approve my ass personally.

Again, these people lived in an alternate reality.

So Jayden, Rashida, Griffin, and I had left the dining room and journeyed to Skylar's very plush, very palatial suite, where we found her lying on a chaise lounge, covered in red splotches and calamine lotion. She looked so miserable I could only feel sorry for her and decided then and there that if showing her my butt would make her feel better, I was willing to do that. I am the ultimate people pleaser.

Five minutes later, I was naked in her marble-tiled bathroom with her squinting at me like an art critic trying to discern if a Van Gogh painting was real or a forgery. I thought for a moment she might get out a magnifying glass to check the size of my pores, but at last, she nodded.

"You've got a great body. You may represent my ass," she said, reaching for more anti-itch cream.

I considered her comment quite a compliment, given the circumstances. It also probably helped that Dr. Pine had given Skylar something to *help her relax*, which had made her a much nicer person. In fact, after leaving the bathroom, she'd hugged me, and even invited me to stay and watch a movie with her, but I'd politely declined. Especially since it was a movie that she was in.

Now I was nearly to Matt's place and wishing I'd had a dose of whatever chill pill Dr. Pine had given her, because I was growing more agitated by the minute wondering how I'd last the night without telling Matt what I'd just agreed to. Could I do that? Could I keep it from him? He wasn't my husband. He wasn't even technically my boyfriend. We'd had one night together.

Oh, but it was one amazing night! And one I hoped would lead to a series of other amazing nights, and maybe even some lazy mornings and blissful afternoons. The truth was, even though we'd only been physically intimate since yesterday, our relationship had started the day I'd come home and seen his smile. Since that moment, we'd been moving toward something inexplicably genuine, so as I rode my bike toward the Dunnigans' place, I realized I needed to tell him.

It was the right thing to do, and hopefully he'd be okay with it. After all, it wasn't the movie he had an issue with. It was Jayden, and I would just make sure that Jayden wasn't there. And besides, Matt had been an *underwear* model. So surely he couldn't object to it based on the skin factor.

Yes, I definitely planned to tell him, but from the moment I arrived at the Dunnigan House, he kept my mouth busy with things far more pleasurable than talking, and it was hours later, after we'd traumatized poor Zelda and Gatsby in a dozen different ways, before we settled in for some food and conversation.

"Which kitten do you think Chloe would like?" he asked as we reclined on the sofa of the Dunnigans' sunporch. We were eating leftover spaghetti, drinking another bottle of what Matt referred to as *blue-label white*, and watching the sun go down over the lake. I was wearing one of his T-shirts, and he had a fuzzy green throw blanket wrapped around his waist like a kilt. It was a good look on him.

"I think she'd like any of them, but I'd like the spotted one for myself, unless you had other plans for her."

He turned to look at me. "You really want one of these kittens?"

"Yes, I do." I really did.

"You don't think Gigi will mind having a fourth cat in the house?"

"She won't even notice," I said. I could mention that I'd be getting a place of my own soon, but I wasn't quite ready to divulge that yet. Soon. But not yet.

He smiled at me as if he really felt paternal pride over these scruffy, illegitimate alley kittens. "Okay, then. The spotted one is all yours. In that case, I think Chloe might like the curious orange tabby, don't you? He's got the best personality."

"I think so."

"Me too. I told Emily I'd take one over to the Peach Tree tomorrow and get things all set up, so he's already there for the big reveal."

"The big reveal?"

"Yes, Chloe's big reveal. Since her room is all ready, Emily wants to bring her and everybody over and make a big production of it tomorrow afternoon. Didn't she tell you?"

The last twenty-four hours had been such an emotional tilt-a-whirl ride that any mention of the Peach Tree Inn had flown from my mind completely.

"Oh, maybe she did mention something about that, but we were on the way to church and I was kind of distracted. I guess I didn't realize she was talking about tomorrow. I'm supposed to be on set as an extra in the morning, but I should be done by noon." Yet another chance to tell him, but I still wasn't quite ready, and the fact that I was hesitating was not a good sign.

"You're an extra tomorrow?" There was a hint of something in his tone, something edgy that he was obviously trying to disguise, and it made me that much more nervous.

"Yeah. They kind of sprang it on me at the last minute, but I told them I could do it." I felt his body tense, but it was just as subtle as the change to his voice. Or maybe it was all just my imagination, my anticipation of him not wanting me to be a part of it. But I wouldn't know what he thought or what he felt until I came clean.

I cleared my throat. "But there's something I wanted to ask you about first."

"Okay."

"When you were a model, you did underwear ads, right? Because word on the street is that you were an underwear model."

"Oh God," he said, covering his face with his hands, and his chest rumbled with an even deeper chuckle, making me that much more glad. "Yes, I was an underwear model. Please don't remind me."

I grasped his wrists gently and pulled his hands away, and he didn't resist. I was pleased to see him smiling, even if he did seem a little embarrassed.

"How did that make you feel at the time? I mean, did you feel sort of, I don't know . . . exposed? Or did it make you feel bold and sexy?"

His answer was quick, with none of his usual pondering. "Neither, really. I mean, I guess I got used to it, but it was just a job, and I was just another guy. They shot dozens of models at one time, and nobody paid any attention to who we were, and the paycheck was always nice. Why?"

His answer was just what I needed to hear, because that's the way I was looking at this scene for tomorrow. It was just a job, the paycheck was phenomenal, and in the grand scheme of things, it wasn't particularly scandalous, especially since so few people would even know it was me. This was fine. Everything was going to be fine.

"That's good to know," I said, relief washing over me. "Very good. And it leads me to something I need to tell you. Something you have to keep private, just between the two of us, because legally I'm not allowed to tell anyone."

"Okay," he said again, his smile fading as cautious curiosity overcame his expression.

"You know this scene I'm supposed to shoot tomorrow?"

"Yeah . . ."

"Well, this one is kind of . . . wait. Let me back up a minute. Do you remember Skylar?" That was a stupid question because of course he remembered her. She was hard to forget.

"Yes, I remember Skylar." A frown creased his forehead.

"Okay, well, long story short, she's got a raging case of poison ivy."

Frown slightly diminished. "That's lousy."

"No kidding, and it's all over her butt and everything." I needed to stress just how incapacitating this rash was.

"That's awful. She must feel wretched."

"Yes, it is, and she does. But anyway, here's the deal. She was supposed to do this scene tomorrow where she walks into the lake, but because she's covered in oozy, red blisters, they've asked me to be her . . . body double."

He was looking at me with interest now, like he was trying to understand why I was making such a point of telling him this. "Okay. And?"

"And, well, it's a nude scene. She's supposed to walk into the lake naked, but of course, she can't because, you know, poison ivy on her ass."

"Wait. They've asked you to do a nude scene?" Frown definitely back now.

"Sort of. I mean, I'll only be shot from the back, so it's only my butt, and no one who sees the movie will even know it's me because we all had to sign an NDA, since Skylar doesn't want anyone to know. Even I had to sign one, so I wasn't supposed to tell you, but I felt like I needed to."

"Huh," he said softly, letting that sink in. "Sounds like you've already agreed to it."

"Like I said, they sprang it on me this afternoon, and we film tomorrow at dawn. I didn't have much time to think about it, and the amount of money they're giving me is ridiculous. Between you and me, that's why I can get a cat. Because with the money, I can afford to get my own place." That should make him happy. Me having my own place was a good thing.

Matt stood up from the couch, and the cushions shifted right along with the mood in the room.

"Are you . . . does this bother you?" I asked.

He walked over toward the window. "I don't know. I don't love it. I mean, I'm trying not to be a caveman here, but my first instinct is to think it's a potentially bad idea." He turned back around. "I feel like they might be trying to take advantage of you, Lilly. The movie industry doesn't have that great of a reputation, you know."

"Oh, I'm not worried about that at all. I've kind of gotten to know Griffin and Rashida, and even though they're not friendly, they're not . . . creepy, either. And this is really just a case of them urgently needing someone who looks like Skylar, and they can't use her stunt double because he's a dude."

I thought that might elicit a smile out of him, but no such luck.

"But . . . you and Jayden doing a nude scene?"

"Oh, Jayden won't even be there," I responded quickly, feeling certain he'd agree to steer clear. "It's just me and the director and a handful of other people."

Matt paused again before saying, "It sounds pretty sketchy to me, Lilly. Once you agree to be on film, you don't have much control over what's done with it. And how do you know they won't get you there for one reason and then try to talk you into doing something you're not comfortable with?"

Now, that was adorable, and I couldn't help but smile at the fact that his concern wasn't so much from jealousy as it was about my safety and reputation.

"I appreciate you wanting to protect me, Matt, but it's just not necessary. There's no ulterior motive here. They literally just need a butt, and I'm the butt they've asked for."

"And it's just you in the scene?"

"Yep. I just walk into the water and that's it."

He was quiet for another few seconds but finally looked at me again, his smile forced. "It's your decision, of course. I support you if this is something that's important to you. I just want you to be cautious."

I rose from the couch and crossed the room to wrap my arms around him. "I appreciate that, and I just want to know that you're okay with this. If you're not, well then, I'm not sure, because I've already signed the contract. But I didn't want to keep this a secret from you."

"Thanks."

"So . . . we're good?"

He paused before pulling me closer. "We're good. I do have a request, though."

"What's that?"

"I would never ask you to step back from this movie-extra stuff, because I know you're having fun with it, but . . . I can't deny the whole Jayden thing still has me on edge. I wish it didn't, but it does."

I leaned in and kissed him. "I understand that, and as I said, he won't be there. And I won't go on the ghost tour, and no more bike rides or anything like that. You can trust me, Matt. There's nothing to worry about as far as Jayden goes."

He squeezed me tight, as if to seal in that promise. "Okay," he said after a pause. "Thank you for telling me and for being so honest. I admit I'm not a fan of this whole idea," he said with a sigh. "But I'm a big fan of yours, so . . . I guess it's movie time."

I smiled up at him. "It's really pretty funny when you think about it. I mean, my butt's going to be on the big screen, and no one will even know it's me except for you and me. I'm not telling anyone."

"Not even your family?"

"Oh my gosh, especially not my family. You think Gigi could keep this to herself? I may as well tell Dmitri."

Matt smiled at last, and relief flooded through me. "Do not tell Dmitri. And don't tell Percy because, well, I think that's self-explanatory."

I laughed even as I grimaced. "Definitely not telling Percy, either. This is our little secret, and since I'm filming at four thirty in the morning and it should only take a few hours, I'll be at the Peach Tree in plenty of time to be there for Chloe's big reveal."

He pressed his lips against the curve of my neck and murmured, "Technically, it sounds more like you're the one having the big reveal."

Chapter 27

Four thirty in the morning felt very much like the middle of the night as I biked my way to the Imperial Hotel. It was a good thing they were only filming my backside, because my face looked so haggard, I could've played the ghostly version of Jayden's wife with no help from the makeup crew. I'd stayed at Matt's until almost midnight, lavishing him with attention to make sure he was feeling all kinds of love and affection and erase any lingering concerns he might have had about me and Jayden; then he'd walked me home so I could get at least a few hours of sleep. No one had seen us together strolling hand in hand down the middle of Main Street, and I was, quite frankly, a little disappointed. Where was Dmitri when I needed him? I was with Matt and didn't care who knew. But it was a drizzly night, and no one was around to notice.

In the Imperial Hotel lobby, only a handful of lamps glowed from a few small end tables, and Clark the night clerk was sitting at the front desk watching *Game of Thrones* on his cell phone while eating a banana.

"Good morning, Clark," I said, startling him.

"Oh, mornin', Lilly. What are you doing here so early?"

"Movie stuff. Have you seen anyone around yet?"

"Yep, that red-haired fella just bolted into the kitchen to see if he could find anyone to make him some coffee. I told him Miss Leticia doesn't make the coffee until five a.m., but he was pretty determined."

"Hey, Chevette." I heard Jayden's voice drift softly from the wide, carpeted staircase. He had on gray sweatpants and a dark sweatshirt, and with the lights so dim, it took a minute for him to appear. When he finally did, his eyes looked as puffy as mine, so it was a good thing he wasn't on camera this morning, either.

"Hi," I replied softly. "It's too frickin' early to be awake. Can I just rip up that contract and go back to bed?"

"Nope. We need you. Griffin promised he'd find us some coffee, so once that's down the hatch, we'll be ready to get this scene shot."

"Yeah, so about that . . ." I pulled Jayden by the front of his sweatshirt away from the front desk so Clark the clerk wouldn't hear our conversation, but he was already back to staring at his screen, so I probably didn't need to be too concerned. "So, this is kind of awkward to ask," I said quietly, "but do you think you could, you know, excuse yourself from the set today?"

"Excuse myself?" His puffy eyes widened a little.

"Yes. I just feel like the fewer people who are there, the more comfortable I'll be, and since you're not in the scene, can't you just, you know, skip it?"

His smile was hesitant, and he almost seemed uncomfortable. "Lilly, I'm in the scene."

That woke me up, and fast. "You are? I thought it was just me walking into the water."

He spoke slowly, as if not certain I quite spoke the language. "It's you. Walking into the water. Toward me."

"Toward you?" My suddenly loud voice reverberated around the empty lobby, and Clark shushed me like he was an obnoxious librarian instead of an oblivious clerk. I lowered my voice again, but my heart was suddenly thumping very loudly. "I'm supposed to walk naked into the water. Toward you?"

Now it was his turn to steal a glance at Clark the clerk, who was back to ignoring us.

"Yes, you walk up to me, and I put my arms around you, and then . . ."

"And then what?"

"And then I kiss you."

"You kiss me?"

Wow, that came out loud, and now we had Clark's full attention. "Just joking," I said with a strained smile and a wave to the clerk before pulling Jayden by the shirt farther away from the front desk.

"What the hell are you talking about? You guys never said anything about kissing. I thought this was the scene where she drowns herself." He'd told me during our bike ride that he had a nude scene, but I didn't realize *this* was it!

"Yeah, she drowns because she's having a nervous breakdown and thinks she sees her husband in the water."

"How the hell was I supposed to know that? You guys never said anything about that part of it."

He stammered for a minute. Now he was the one having trouble with the language. "Well . . . uh . . . I just . . . it's in the script."

"So?" I demanded. "I've never read the script, Jayden. I'm an extra, remember?"

He seemed confused now, like he was still waking up and none of this was tracking for him, but he put his hands gently on my shoulders and squeezed, which I imagined was supposed to be reassuring but in no way was. "Okay. Okay," he said calmly. "So I'm getting that this is a bit of a surprise to you, obviously, but . . . what's the actual problem?"

"I'm going to be naked."

He nodded, his face now a study in concentration as if he were trying to solve an invisible puzzle as he replied, "Now, that I'm certain we told you yesterday."

"Sure, and we talked a lot about my backside, but I didn't realize I'd be flashing you all of my . . . front side."

He smiled then with reckoning. "Ah, I see. Well, here's the thing. If you want, we can cover up the fancy bits you have in the front here." He waggled his fingers at my breasts and then made a very discreet motion to signify my lower half. "We have tape and little fabric flap things, so you'll be covered up, for the most part."

That was not reassuring and handled only a portion of my concern, because he said there'd be hugging, and no little bit of fabric was going to change that. And kissing? We would be kissing? Why couldn't they have asked me to do this a week ago, when Matt wasn't an issue? Because now he was very much an issue!

Jayden surmised my continued concern. "I promise this is how it's done, Lilly, and everyone will be entirely professional about it. And I'll do whatever I can to make you feel comfortable with all of it, okay?"

"How could you guys not mention the hugging and the kissing?" I murmured again.

Jayden shrugged good-naturedly. "It was in the script."

Fuck that script. If I'd known all this yesterday, I wouldn't have agreed to it. I wasn't an actress. I was a teacher. This was a lot to process. And it would be a lot for Matt to process, too, because of course I'd have to tell him. Or maybe I could just hope he'd never see the movie? That was a long shot, for sure. Damn it!

I was suddenly nauseated with worry.

I liked Matt. So much. He was my guy. And he would not be happy about this.

"I'm still sensing some distress here," Jayden said. "Which part of this has you so rattled? Because I'm wondering if I should take it personally."

"I'm a preschool teacher."

His gaze darted around his head as if seeing cartoon birds circling as he tried to catch my meaning. "And?"

"And you're a movie star, and I'm nervous and I have a . . . I have a new . . . situation."

"A situation?"

"Yes. I've just started dating someone, and he's not a fan of any of this." I pointed back and forth between the two of us. "He's not even crazy about us being friends."

"Ahh, I see." Jayden's smirk was full of sass but little disappointment, which I tried not to take personally. "Can't you just tell him I'm on your sexlebrity list?" he asked with an innocent shrug.

My spontaneous chuff of laughter had a slightly deranged, embarrassed quality to it. "You know about those?"

"Of course," he said with a shrug. "Everybody has one."

"See? That's what I tried to tell my sister Brooke, but she doesn't have one."

Then I shook my head because we were definitely getting off topic. "Anyway, he's a very understanding guy, but he's got some trust issues. Not with me necessarily, but from his past, and now he and I are just starting to figure things out, but when he finds out that you and I spent the day . . . canoodling, he's going to take it pretty hard."

"It's not canoodling, Lilly. It's acting. It's . . . performing, and once we're on set, you'll see the difference. And anyway, he never has to know because we're not supposed to talk about the movie or any of the scenes to the public anyway, so you'll just need to keep this under your hat. Even if he sees the movie later, he'll think it's Skylar, right? Problem solved."

Ugh. My problem was not solved. Matt would know it was me because it had taken me less than three hours to tell him everything last night, even though I was legally bound not to. But I couldn't explain that to Jayden because I wasn't supposed to tell anyone that I was in this scene. *This is why secrets are bad, Lilly.* They just always, always come back and bite you in the ass. Literally this time.

Unfortunately, I didn't have much time to fix this because I'd signed a contract and made a promise. The crew was getting ready, and Griffin and Rashida—and Jayden—were all counting on me. They needed me, and quite frankly, I wanted the money. So, for now, I simply had to make the best of it because there wasn't time for them to find another ass.

After a golf cart ride—a perfectly acceptable mode of transportation while on the hotel grounds—and a cup of coffee so strong it nearly disintegrated my plastic spoon, I was now wide awake, but unfortunately even more nervous. We were now at the location of the shoot, a conveniently secluded spot of beach with rocky outcroppings on either side and nothing but a bluff above us. The sky was a dark gray, with the sun still half an hour from rising.

In the wardrobe tent, I stripped down so the makeup gal whom I'd met a few times before could spray me all over like I was getting a spray tan. She was very thorough. I'd be washing off that makeup for weeks to come.

"Are you interested in the fig leaves?" she asked, and I couldn't help but giggle because that was a ridiculous thing to call them. But then again, it was pretty much what they were. She gave me two silver dollar–size circular adhesive patches that went over my nipples, for all the good they did, and a beige triangle that covered up my bikini area. Looking in the mirror, I realized that these pointless little patches were probably worse than being naked because all they did was draw attention to the parts I was trying to be discreet about.

"Do most actresses use these?" I asked.

She shrugged. "It's about fifty-fifty," she said. "Skylar never uses them, but that's only because she's showing off. Then again, if I looked like her naked, I'd flaunt it, too." She looked me up and down. "You could flaunt it, if you wanted to."

"Um . . . thanks?" I guess?

I accepted the fluffy white robe she offered and stepped outside the tent to find Jayden stepping out of a second tent, and he was also wearing a fluffy white bathrobe. I could just see a hint of chest hair in the V of his neckline, and my senses tingled. Whether it was from nerves or involuntary attraction or the three thousand and one grams of caffeine in that coffee I'd just had, I couldn't tell.

"Want to see something that's going to put all your fears to rest?" he asked, a mischievous smile tilting the corners of his mouth.

"I'm not sure. Do I?"

He grinned, and with a sway of his broad, sexy shoulders, he slowly, oh so slowly, opened his robe as if he were doing a striptease just for me while softly singing *bow-chicka-bow-bow*, and I got to see just exactly what Jayden Pierce was hiding under that fluffy white terry cloth. Which was all magnificent Jayden Pierce. Muscles and angles and more muscles . . . plus a sturdy pair of beige Spanx. His chest was still a sight to behold, and his legs were long and muscular, and that smattering of hair I'd seen a hint of trailed tantalizingly over his abdomen, but oh my. The stretchy, flesh-colored man shorts ruined it all.

Well, not ruined it. There was still a lot of something impressive going on there. He was still fabulous, but I burst out laughing, which had clearly been his intention.

"Right?" he asked with a broad grin. "I make this look hot as fuck, don't I?" He did a little gyrating with his hips, which only made us laugh harder. I did not know that was even possible at this time of the morning, but then he said, "Okay, your turn. Show me what you've got."

I sobered up instantly. "What?"

"I'm serious. Get it over with, because you have to walk into that water toward me with confidence. If you're slouching and trying to cover up, Griffin is going to get all cranky, and you know how he is when he's cranky."

I didn't actually know how Griffin was when he wasn't cranky, but that didn't mean I wanted to flash all the goods at Jayden while we stood in between two makeup tents.

"I'll walk with confidence when the time comes," I said, feeling my skin flush so hotly I must be burning away all that makeup I'd just had put over me. Odd how the generic notion of being filmed from a distance felt so much less intimidating than showing my body to Jayden. This felt far more intimate.

He stepped a little closer. "I know it seems crazy or extreme, but I've done nude scenes before, and there's just no way around the awkwardness, even for professionals. I realize this is not the kind of thing a preschool teacher does every day. At least not at any of the schools I ever went to." His expression was only half-teasing, the other half being full of patience. "I'll be in character out in that lake, you know, and looking at you like I'm all hot and bothered, which is just going to make you feel that much weirder. So let's give it a go right now. I promise not to laugh."

"Laugh?" He thought seeing me naked would make him laugh?

"I just mean because of the fig leaves, or did you decide to go without?" He arched an eyebrow optimistically, and for one brief, shining moment, I wished I'd had the courage to be like Skylar and go all full monty on him. Just for the shock value.

Alas, I did not. I was proud of my body, sure. But this was all proving to be a mile outside of my comfort zone.

"Fig leaves," I said with a nod. "Definitely fig leaves."

"Okay," he said. "Let's see what you got."

I sighed, realizing that Jayden was right. Better to get it over with now rather than when Griffin was already yelling at me. Opening my robe right then was probably the most embarrassing, awkward, difficult thing I'd ever had to do. And also, the most bold and courageous thing, too. I had nothing to regret and nothing to be ashamed of.

I undid the belt slowly, but then—like ripping off a bandage—I flung it open, and Jayden's eyes went wide in feigned astonishment.

"Wowza!" he exclaimed loudly. "Ah-ooo-ga! Those are the most amazing, big, American breasts I have ever seen. Unbelievable. Holy shit!" He went on and on, hopping from one foot to the other with his smile huge, and it only took me about half a second to realize he was doing this to make me feel more comfortable, not less. He was showing me just how silly it all was, and he was right. If you couldn't laugh at a little bare skin, then you had no sense of humor. I was a badass, and I could handle this.

"Guys, guys," he said, waving over some imaginary friends, "come and get a look at these boobies. They are glorious."

"Okay," I said, smiling back and drawing my robe closed. "You've made your point. And you are an asshole." But he just laughed harder and stepped forward to hug me.

"Don't you feel better now?"

"Yes, because now I know that no matter how foolish I might feel, you're the biggest dope here today."

"Exactly."

Chapter 28

Jayden's questionable pep talk was only modestly helpful, but when the cameras were rolling and Griffin called "Action!" I was able to do my part. I walked into the lake, shoulders straight back and chin held high in the air as if I was fierce. The water temperature being about forty degrees was a nice distraction from both the fact that I was missing my bathing suit and the fact that Jayden was indeed looking at me like a man who was madly in love. And when I got to him, and he put his arms around me, and then kissed me—well—nothing could have prepared me for that. And I decided to just roll with it.

He was big and warm and strong, and when he ran his hands up to my shoulders and then cupped the back of my head for a better kissing angle, who was I to complain? He was the professional actor, after all. I was just a wallpaper-hanging preschool teacher. Honestly, it was hard to believe they were actually paying me for this. I probably would've kissed him for free.

I'd have to explain to Matt how all this had happened, of course, and that conversation would certainly be difficult, but he'd been supportive last night, so surely he'd understand this. I'd figure it out somehow. We'd figure it out. Together. Because even though kissing Jayden Pierce was fun, it was still Matt who made me sizzle. It was Matt who made my pulse race and my heart beat faster. It was Matt I wanted to share things with, like spaghetti and garden paths and kittens. Jayden was like a toy on Christmas morning that you desperately wanted to unwrap, but after an hour or so of playing with it, you'd move on.

But Matt was my constant. And my future.

Back in the lake, Jayden and I did a dozen takes as the sun rose until he complained that his legs were numb from the cold water.

"You've cost me my fertility, Griff," he groused as we stumbled from the lake and crew members wrapped us in warm blankets and gave us cups of coffee.

"Then I've saved you from millions of dollars in child support payments," Griffin answered. "You're welcome."

"How'd I do?" I asked Rashida quietly, and she gave me a thumbs-up.

"You did good," she said. "I daresay that your ass is just as talented as Skylar's, but you didn't hear that from me."

We did a few more shots of me walking into the water without Jayden there, because according to *the script*, he was just a hallucination drawing the poor woman out into the lake to her doom, and then we were done.

"So, that's it?" I asked as I came back out of the lake. It was nearly 8:00 a.m. by now. I was entirely desensitized to having the crew see me as I came back out, which was a thought that had not occurred to me until after the first take, but they all seemed far too busy adjusting their equipment to pay any attention to me. And by that, I meant adjusting their actual equipment, like cameras and microphones. Not their *equipment*. It reminded me of what Matt had said about the underwear photographers being so disinterested, which gave me some peace of mind. Nonetheless, I was grateful to be handed my white robe once more.

"And that's a wrap," Griffin said. "We got everything we need."

"Well, what I need is breakfast," Jayden said. "Now that this nude scene is over, I can finally eat something. You hungry, Chevette?"

"You've got two hours," Rashida said to Jayden. "We need you back in hair and makeup by ten."

Jayden nodded and looked back to me. "There's a killer breakfast buffet at the Imperial. You up for it?"

I was hungry, and I had a long day still ahead of me while going on almost no sleep. The coffee and adrenaline had long since worn away, and food might be the only thing to get me through, so I agreed. I'd add that to the list of things to tell Matt, but surely in the grand scheme of things, this wasn't going to be the thing his mind snagged on.

I got dressed in the tent, the golf cart whisked us back to the hotel, and half an hour later we were back in the Grand Dining Room and I was trying to remember the last time I'd eaten breakfast at the hotel. It was the go-to buffet for Mother's Day, but we didn't celebrate that, other than to do some yard work for Gigi, so this was a rare treat.

"So, how do you feel about all that from this morning?" Jayden asked as he ate his twenty-eighth piece of bacon. Maybe it was only his fifth or sixth piece, but all I knew was that he'd eaten a *lot* of bacon. And a lot of french toast and scrambled eggs and hash browns.

"I feel okay about it. Do you think I did okay?"

"I think you did great, especially considering you don't have any formal training."

"Walking doesn't usually require any formal training," I answered, taking a bite of my eggs. And the kissing part had come pretty naturally, too. Since they were only filming the back of my head, I didn't have to worry about what my kissy-kissy face looked like, which was, of course, a huge relief.

Jayden smiled. "You know there's more to it than just being able to walk and hit your marks, and you've caught on to all of it really quickly. I don't just mean today. I mean all the other days, too. The scene on Main Street and everything. You could make a job of this, you know."

"A job of being an extra?"

"Maybe being an actress. The camera loves you. Even Griff said so."

"He did? He never said it to me. In fact, he's never said anything to me at all other than to tell me what I was doing wrong."

"Griff's a tough-love kind of guy, but his bark is way worse than his bite. He never would've asked you to do that scene this morning if he didn't think you could cut it."

"I guess I'm glad to hear that, but I hardly think the little bits of stuff I've done in the last few weeks qualify me to be an actress."

"Everybody has to start someplace. For what it's worth, we'll still have another month's worth of interior shots to do for this film when we get back to Los Angeles, so if you want to come along, we can keep you busy."

"In Los Angeles?"

"Sure. There's a kick-ass séance scene coming up, and a love scene in a bed instead of in an ice-cold lake, if you're interested." He winked at me in such an exaggerated fashion that I knew he was kidding.

"I don't think Skylar would go for that."

"Probably not the love scene, but she doesn't have any say about the rest of it, so what do you think?"

"About what?"

"About coming out to LA and finishing up the movie with us."

"Um, no."

"Why not?" He posed the question as if he were asking nothing more out of the ordinary than inviting me out for a cup of coffee. Like I could just pick up and go. Then again, this was the guy who'd tried to buy my car out from under me at a gas station.

I smiled patiently. "Because I have stuff going on here, in my real life, and LA is three thousand miles away. Plus, it's expensive out there. Where would I even stay?" We weren't seriously discussing this. It was a rhetorical question.

But Jayden responded with, "You could stay with me. My place is huge. You could have a wing all to yourself."

His invitation was flattering, and if he'd asked the Lilly I was a few weeks ago, I might have said yes, intrigued by the adventure and the pull of Jayden's charm.

But I knew now that that's all this was. Flattery and charm. Just like Tag, he thought I could just step from my life right into his and make a place for myself. But I had a place. Here. Because Trillium Bay wasn't just where I was *used* to being. It's where I *wanted* to be. I was *home*, and there was nothing about acting or stardom or the LA lifestyle that appealed to me. Not down deep where it mattered. What mattered to me now was the life I could create on Wenniway Island.

I set down my fork. "Remember that guy I mentioned this morning?"

"Vaguely." His smile said he was teasing.

"I'm pretty invested in that, and I'm pretty invested in getting my old teaching job back. I spent almost a year following around a different guy and ended up in California for months on end, and it taught me a very important lesson."

"What's that?"

"You can take the girl off the island, but one way or another, she's always going to find her way back. I'm happy here. I like my life. So thanks for the offer, but that's a pass."

He shook his head. "Okay, but if you change your mind, you have my number."

Chapter 29

The big reveal at the Peach Tree Inn that afternoon included more than just showing Chloe her room. I arrived to find Emily, Ryan, Chloe, Matt, Horsey Davidson, and Garth and Georgie Reynolds—the whole work crew, with the exception of Tiny, because he and Gloria were still staying with her cousin while Baby Norah Grace grew big and strong enough to come home from the hospital. Brooke, Leo, the chief, and Gigi were at the inn, too. It was a full-on family affair, and Emily and Ryan delighted in showing us all the progress that had been made, even though most of us had seen it at various stages.

The lobby was full of vintage-style furniture and polished wood-work. The kitchen, while not nearly as gourmet as the Dunnigans', was still gorgeous enough to satisfy all my sister's epicurean fantasies, and the eight guest rooms were each decorated with a different theme that still fit the overall aesthetic of the inn. In the back was a master bedroom and living space for Ryan and Emily. There was also a nursery, of course, just a tiny room off the master that had yet to be decorated. They had time for that, and it was pure joy to see their excitement. Ryan and Emily had created something wonderful here for their growing family, and I felt a little tear well up in my eye at the thought of it. I could see Christmases and birthday parties and winter nights playing card games. That was our kind of fun. And I was glad I'd be here to see it.

I stole a glance at Matt, who smiled back. He'd been a little distant since I'd arrived, and I assumed it was because my family and the work crew were around, and he and I hadn't really discussed how public we were yet. I appreciated his discretion. I also appreciated that he seemed happily surprised when I pulled him behind a door during our tour and gave him a fast, hard kiss when no one was looking.

But we'd had no time to talk, other than for him to say, "How was your morning?"

And for me to answer, "Awkward."

"Any regrets?"

"Like you said, a paycheck is a paycheck." I'd fill him in on the rest later. This wasn't the time, because it wasn't going to be a fun or simple conversation.

We'd rejoined the group in time to hear Chloe ask, "Um, where's my room?" She looked a little concerned that they'd forgotten her.

"Your room?" Emily said, as if it were an afterthought. "Oh yeah. I guess we do have one more room to see."

"We saved the best for last, Niblet," Ryan said reassuringly, tugging on her braid, and she smiled, but I could tell she was uneasy. Which would only make the surprises in store for her that much more thrilling. And as we walked back up to the third floor, I heard my niece say, "Oh, no you didn't."

"Yes, honey, we did," Emily said, smiling broadly as she flung open the door to the Princess Turret Room, now fully decked out with the four-poster bed, furry pink floor rug, and every gloriously tacky thing that a nearly-fourteen-year-old girl could want, right down to the hammock chair hanging in one corner and the disco ball hanging in the other.

"Oh my gosh, oh my gosh, oh my gosh!" Chloe exclaimed. If any bats were snoozing nearby, she'd most certainly just woken them up with the pitch as she examined each corner of the room and everything in between. She kept looking back at my sister and Ryan as if to make certain they weren't just teasing her, and when her own squeaking dissipated, she got the most unusual look on her face.

"What is that noise?" she asked.

Matt had disappeared and then reappeared with a large cardboard box, so at her question, he stepped forward. "This room is pretty big, so your mom thought you might need some company in here."

"Nooooo," she said in disbelief as he set the box on the floor and lifted off the top. The orange tabby meowed, and I thought my niece was about to spontaneously combust with happiness. Then, in much the same way that I had when seeing the picture of Gloria and Tiny's baby, she burst into tears.

We Callaghans are a weepy people.

"You have Matt to thank for the kitty," Emily said once Chloe had regained some measure of composure. "He talked me into it, so when it walks across your face at dawn and wakes you up, or when it's bouncing off the walls in the middle of the night because it wants to play, blame Matt."

But Chloe scooped the orange fuzzball from the box and beamed up at Matt with tear-shining eyes. "Thank you, Matt. You're the best. Thank you. Oh my goodness. And Skittles is the best."

"Skittles?" Emily asked.

"Yes! I've been dreaming of this moment for so long that I already know his name. It's Skittles McKittycat."

"Damn it, that's what I was going to name my kitten," I murmured to Matt under my breath, and he winked at me.

"You've done an amazing job here, Peach," Harlan said as he gave my sister a hug. "I'm proud of you." Naturally, this caused my sister to burst into tears, so my father patted her back distractedly with one hand while reaching out with his other to shake one of Ryan's. "Good luck, kid."

The *you're gonna need it* was implied but left unspoken.

"Thanks, Chief. I appreciate that," Ryan responded with a grin.

"It's simply marvelous," Gigi added. "So marvelous I hardly even mind that you'll be stealing customers away from me."

Emily dabbed at her tears. "We won't be stealing any customers, Gigi. Your rental cottages are perfect for families, and this place is more a romantic getaway for couples."

"Hmm, for romantic getaways, huh?" Leo murmured to Brooke. "Maybe we should book a room?"

This prompted her to ask loudly, "Peach, do we get a family discount?"

"Maybe, but we're not quite ready for lodgers yet," Emily answered. "We've got our hands full enough as it is. I can't believe we're moving in here this week."

"And then we get married the week after that," Ryan added, sounding mostly enthusiastic but maybe just a little apprehensive, too. I could hardly blame him. In less than a year's time, he'd gone from itinerant bachelor to husband, new father, and stepfather, not to mention bed-and-breakfast owner, in addition to his regular job with Taggert Property Management. It was a lot.

"Yep, in ten days I'll be an innkeeper's wife," Emily said with a smile, but there was some anxiety in her voice, too. Not because it wasn't all good stuff coming her way, but because she was transitioning from being an independent, house-flipping single mom to a wife, innkeeper in her own right, and the mother of both a newborn and a teenager. That was a lot, too.

"And then my family shows up," Ryan added, his comment giving me a bit of a start.

The plan was for Emily, Ryan, and Chloe to move their belongings into the Peach Tree Inn this week; then early next week the Taggert clan would arrive for a few days of prewedding festivities, including sightseeing, hiking, golfing, and plenty of time for the two families to mingle—which meant I'd be encountering Tag. A lot of Tag, for several days, and in close proximity, which was a thought I'd all but blocked from my mind.

Now it was hitting me, and a glance at Matt told me it was hitting him, too.

Like my friendship with Jayden, I knew my past relationship with Tag wasn't something he needed to worry about, but I understood this was a lot for him, as well. Which made telling him about kissing Jayden this morning an even bigger and more delicate conversation that we needed to have, and I wondered if maybe I should explain everything *after* the wedding and *after* the Taggerts had left, because there was just a lot of *a lot-ness* going around, and suddenly I wasn't sure of the best course of action.

Chapter 30

"Lilly Jane Callaghan, I have been waiting and waiting for your call." Mary Lou Baxter came scurrying toward me the next afternoon as I stood outside O'Doul's grocery store, her twiggy birdlike legs carrying her round little body like a sandpiper's. The woman was high on energy and short on attention span, and the much-beloved principal at Trillium Bay School.

"Mary Lou," I responded with a smile. "I'm so sorry! I have absolutely been meaning to get a hold of you, but it's been a crazy time for me. I've been helping my family with remodels and rentals and weddings—"

"And keeping time with that handsome devil from the movie," she interrupted with a mischievous twinkle in her eye, "not to mention dallying with our very own Yoga Matt. It's no wonder you haven't called me. You're a busy girl! And a lucky girl!" She shoved at my shoulder playfully.

Trying to explain all the current dynamics would take far more time than I had, so I simply said, "Yes, I'm a lucky girl."

"So, are you going to Hollywood to become an actress?" she asked.

"What? No, of course not. I'm staying right here, especially if I can get a teaching job. What are the chances of that?"

Mary Lou looked surprised. "I'd say the chances are pretty good if you really do plan to stay. That temporary replacement we hired after you left last fall did not work out. She started counting down the days to the end of her contract around Valentine's Day. Too much snow, she said, just because her front door kept getting drifted shut, but it's not like the chief didn't go on over there each and every time she called him and shovel out a path for her. Nope. She said this place was like *The Shining* and she'd never make it through a second winter."

"I'm sorry to hear it was so rough for her, but does that mean you'll take me back?" Could I be *that* lucky of a girl?

Mary Lou tapped her chin as if weighing the pros and cons with immense gravity; then she burst out laughing and shoved my shoulder again. "Well, of course I'll take you back, you silly girl. You can have the preschool through second grade group, unless you wanted something different. We might be able to shift a few others around, but you always were the best teacher for the littles. You've been sorely missed, let me tell you."

"Oh, Mary Lou, that is wonderful news! I desperately want my old job back, but I've been putting off thinking about it because I was afraid the answer would be no. You are the best." I grabbed her for a long, tight hug. It was good to be home.

"Of course, it's not just up to me," she said once I'd let her go. "I'll have to run it past the school board, but April Mahoney owes me a favor, and Sudsy Robertson will vote however I tell him to, so you're as good as hired. It's good to have you back. I'll be in touch."

"Thank you. I'm so excited."

I was excited. So very excited I practically skipped into the mayor's office, but my euphoria was short lived.

⌒◎

"I recommend you tell him everything, Lilly. Tonight, before he has a chance to hear it from someone else," Brooke said bossily some twenty minutes later as I sat in her office after having accidentally broken my nondisclosure agreement. Again.

I couldn't help it. I'd been so eager to tell her about getting *the movie people* to read Leo's manuscript that I'd stumbled right into the part about doing a nude scene. And once she'd heard that, I figured I may as well tell her the rest.

"I am going to tell Matt everything, but don't you think maybe I should wait until after both Jayden and Tag are gone? Then we can officially put them both in our rearview mirror and be done with them."

"*Rearview mirror?* Interesting choice of words, but my answer is still no, because if you wait, he'll think he's only getting you by default because they're both gone."

I hadn't really thought of it that way. Maybe Brooke was the smart one.

"And anyway," Brooke continued, "there's no way people won't find out. What the hell made you agree to do a nude scene, anyway?"

"Ten thousand dollars."

"Ten thousand . . . are you kidding me?"

"Nope. It was five thousand at first, but then Jayden doubled it. They were that desperate, and I figured the money would make a nice little nest egg for me now that I'm back home to stay. And it's just my anonymous butt. Certainly not worse than flashing my boobs to an auditorium full of pageant parents."

Brooke bit back a reluctant smile. "That was really something," she agreed. "And ten thousand dollars is a lot of money, but even so, you had to know there'd be repercussions."

"Not really. It's all supposed to be on the hush-hush down-low, so if you and I can keep this to ourselves for a few days, then at least I'll have some time to figure out exactly how to explain the Jayden part to Matt."

"I'll keep quiet, Lil, but you might want to work on that yourself, too. We can't have Judge Murphy throwing you in jail for breach of contract."

Right. That's all I needed. To have Skylar Tremont suing me.

Brooke got up from her desk and moved over to the coatrack to grab her jacket. We were headed to Gloria and Tiny's house to see the new baby, and as we walked, I thought about those potential repercussions.

I hadn't really considered those. And in my defense, if Jayden hadn't been there, if it had been a simple case of a little gratuitous butt footage, everything would still be fine. Even if word got out about that, I could handle the island gossip. It wouldn't be the first time I'd been sent through the wringer for one thing or another, but knowing that this time I'd be dragging Matt through it with me? That filled me with remorse.

"Holy bejeebers, it's good to be home," Gloria said as she eased back into her denim-covered rocking chair with the tiny bundle of her and Tiny's daughter in her arms. "I don't ever want to ride on another helicopter for as long as I live. Isn't that right, Norah Grace?" she said, adjusting the blanket so we could see her little miracle baby, who was already plumping up and perfectly healthy.

"That was a wild day for the rest of us, so I can only imagine what it was like for you," Brooke said, sitting next to me on the sofa.

Tiny was off checking on the progress at the Cahill house, so it was just the three of us, plus the baby, and I was dying to get my mitts on her, but Gloria was being understandably greedy.

"It was fucking bazonkers," Gloria said. "And pardon *moi* my Frenchy-poo, but there is not a combination of Earth Harmony essential oils on the planet that would've calmed me down in that situation. I would've chugged the stuff just to keep from hyperventilating if I thought it would've worked, but I'll tell you what," she continued, pointing at us with her free hand, "that man of mine, my Tiny, he was solid as the Rock of Gibraltar. He talked me through every single minute and every single breath. He was ah-and-amazing. I couldn't have done any of this without him. Well, I wouldn't have needed to, of course, if he hadn't knocked me up in the first place, but I'm glad he did." She grinned at us. "Totally worth it. Do you want to hold the baby?"

"Yes," Brooke and I said in unison, and I let her have the first turn because she was the oldest.

As I waited impatiently, my phone buzzed. Pulling it from my purse, I saw it was a text from Matt—which made me smile—until I read it.

WE NEED TO TALK. CAN YOU MEET ME AT CUPPA JOE'S?

"What's wrong?" Gloria asked.

I looked up from my phone. "Um, I'm not sure. Cryptic message from Matt."

I looked to Brooke, and her expression was equal parts *I told you so* and sympathy. My palms grew clammy as my heart started to race. Had he heard? Some of it? Or all of it? Or was this something else entirely? Regardless, it must be important if it couldn't wait until tonight, when we were supposed to have dinner. And tonight, when I'd planned to tell him everything and then cover him with kisses until he was convinced that Jayden meant nothing to me, and Tag meant nothing to me, and that he, Matt, meant everything.

I texted him back.

OF COURSE. I'M AT GLORIA'S BUT CAN MEET YOU IN HALF AN HOUR. DOES THAT WORK?

He sent the okay symbol back, and that was that.

It wasn't encouraging that he wanted to meet at the coffee shop rather than at his place. Maybe he'd suggested Joe's because he wanted a cup of coffee . . . except that he never wanted coffee. He only drank tea.

Damn it. I was screwed.

Chapter 31

I ordered two cups of organic green tea with lemon, Matt's favorite, and was waiting in a booth when he arrived. I'd selected a spot in the far back corner, hoping we'd have a bit of privacy. If I ended up crying, which suddenly seemed within the realm of possibility, I didn't want to be next to the big picture windows for all of Trillium Bay to see.

Walking here from Gloria's, I'd held out hope that I was stressed for nothing. That his message, although seemingly urgent, wasn't anything negative. But I knew, deep down, that it must be something dire. No good conversation ever started with *we need to talk*, and as he entered Joe's and approached the table, his expression wasn't all that welcoming. The stone in my gut grew sharp edges. He didn't look angry, just . . . indifferent, which for some reason was far more disturbing. Anger or agitation I could handle, but apathy would be much harder to fix.

"Hi," I said as he slid into the booth.

"Hi." He glanced at me, unsmiling, and seemed more interested in the mug in front of him.

After a long, heavy pause, he said formally, "Thanks for meeting me on such short notice."

"Of course."

I could—and probably should—just launch into my explanation of everything, put all my cards on the table right up front, but since he was the one who had called this impromptu meeting, it seemed like I should let him start.

"So . . . ," he said after another long pause. "I'm going to head home for a little while."

"Home? You mean, like, the cottage behind the Dunnigans' place?"

"No, I mean home to Traverse City. My grandmother called this morning and reminded me I haven't been back in a while, and this seems like as good a time as any for a visit." He shrugged as if to knock that cow chip of bullshit right off his shoulders. Living a life of authenticity and honesty had made Matt Eastman a lousy liar.

"Now seems like a good time to leave?" I asked, my voice involuntarily rising an octave. "With us just getting started and Ryan and Emily's wedding right around the corner?"

"Us just getting started . . . yeah, about that. I think we need to tap the brakes a little bit."

My heart went thunk as he leaned back in the booth, his expression . . . expressionless.

"Tap the brakes? I don't want to tap the brakes. I want to go full speed ahead. With you. I thought we'd had this conversation," I said.

"I thought we had, too, Lilly, but now I'm not so sure."

"Why?"

"I think you know why."

The flutters that Matt triggered every time I saw him turned to big, flapping moths, leaving me breathless and hollow. Time to put those cards down on the table after all.

Gosh, how I wished I'd told him yesterday. Or better yet, hadn't done that scene with Jayden at all. I could've backed out. But I hadn't, because I'd wanted the experience. I'd wanted it for me. To prove I was brave and bold and that something about me was unique—even if being unique meant pretending to be someone else.

And now I needed to tell Matt all the details. Or rather, confirm what he'd likely already heard. Time to tell him my truth, the whole truth, and nothing but the truth, so help me God.

"Matt, there were things I wanted to talk to you about yesterday afternoon, but I didn't have a chance because my family was around. I was planning to tell you everything tonight. Obviously, you've heard something elsewhere, so how about you hear my version next, and then we can talk about it."

"Okay." He was calm and detached, as if I'd just said, *O'Doul's has a sale on grapes today.*

Big breath in. Big breath out. "When I told you about doing that scene for the movie, the one in the lake, I didn't think Jayden would be there, but . . . there was some miscommunication. And he was."

"Okay." *Bananas are three for a dollar.*

Big breath in. Big breath out. "There was some miscommunication about exactly what they needed me to do, too. Just like you said might happen. I heard one thing from them, but once we were on set, things were a little different."

He took a slow sip from his cup, his posture stiff, although it seemed as if he wanted to appear casual. When he didn't prompt me for details, just toyed with the string of the tea bag, I sighed and forged ahead.

"They needed me to walk into the water, just like I thought, but Jayden was in the water, too. And we had to . . . well, we had to kiss."

His eyes crashed into mine for a split second before he tore his gaze away to glare at the far side of the room, exhaling sharply.

Annnnd shit. It looked like he *hadn't* heard that part yet. Shit, shit, and shit. If I'd realized that, I might have tap-danced around it a bit rather than lobbing that information at him like a grenade. It was flung like monkey poo now.

"I'm sorry, Matt. I wouldn't have agreed to do it if I'd known that's what was going to happen. You know that, right?"

He looked back at me, his eyes dark, his jaw uncharacteristically tense. "I don't really know that, Lilly. I'm glad you think that's what you would've done, but either way, it's not really my business."

That cut to the quick.

"Of course it's your business. You and I are starting something here that's important to me. That's why as soon as I was done with the scene, I rushed right over to the Peach Tree to see you."

"Right after?"

"Yes."

"Right after the scene? Or do you mean right after you and Jayden had breakfast at the Imperial Hotel?"

Ahh . . . so *that's* what he'd heard. Fuck. Of course I'd *meant* right after breakfast, but that's not what I'd said, and now it sounded like I was making excuses or deliberately leaving things out. The man practically had a tattoo on his forehead that said *trust issues*, and now he wasn't going to believe me no matter what I told him. But I had to try anyway.

"Right after breakfast because I'd been up since four a.m., and I was starving and tired and I needed something to eat. There honestly wasn't more to it than that."

"Okay. So, let me see if I've got this right. You were naked. And kissing. And had breakfast, but other than all of that, there was nothing to it?" Sarcasm was a new look on him. I didn't care for it.

"You're making it sound like something it wasn't."

"I'm not the only one, Lilly. Like I've told you before, people are coming to me with stories about you and Jayden. I'm not asking for that and I'm not trying to spy, but the gossip is deafening. And it's everywhere, just like when rumors of Wendy and my brother started circulating. Because I'd been warned about them—long before the night I caught them—but they both just kept denying it until it was right in my face, and then no one could deny it any longer."

Well, *that* was certainly new information that would have been helpful to know sooner.

"I'm not her, Matt, and this situation is completely different. In fact, when Jayden asked me about coming to Los Angeles, I said no because I'm very happy right here with you."

That was supposed to make him feel better, but his jaw dropped for a second before clamping shut, and I realized I'd just stuck my head in a bear trap. What the hell was wrong with me? I'd just insinuated that there was in fact some kind of relationship with Jayden, but there wasn't. Shit, shit, shit.

"He asked you to come to Los Angeles?"

"Yes, but in a totally casual 'crash at my place and do your own thing' kind of way. It wasn't a romantic overture."

"He invited you to stay at his place?" His tone was growing more incredulous with each question, because oh my God. I was so bad at this. No wonder people didn't tell the truth. It was hard! Everything I said just threw more gasoline on this dumpster fire.

"Um, yes, but you know how movie people are. They have people stay with them all the time. It doesn't mean anything. And the point is, I told him no because I don't want to be in Los Angeles. I don't want to be with him. I want to be here with you."

"Okay," he said again, his voice flat, and I could tell he was only acknowledging what I'd said without really believing me.

I stared at him, and he stared back, and I felt like all the connections we'd made over the past few weeks were as fragile as a spider's web, so frail they were nearly impossible to see, yet strong and sticky enough to entrap me.

"Do you believe me?" I finally asked.

"I don't disbelieve you."

Well, that was some passive-aggressive fuckery, and I wasn't sure what to do with that. Was he mad? Or hurt? Did he have questions? Or even some accusations? How could I know what to say if I wasn't sure what he needed to hear?

I reached across the table, but he slid his hands away.

"I'm sorry, Matt. Yesterday morning didn't go the way I'd expected it to, and I wasn't sure what to do then, and I'm not sure what to do now. I don't know what else you want me to say."

He regarded me steadily for a moment. "I don't know, either. I'm not sure how I feel about any of this. I need some time to get centered."

"I don't know what that means."

"It means . . . it means I need some time. Away."

"Uh-huh. Time away. So that's why you're leaving town?"

"Yes," he said firmly. "There's just too much noise around here, and I can't think."

I looked around. Joe's Cuppa Joe was nearly empty at 4:00 p.m. on a Tuesday afternoon and all but silent, other than the occasional whoosh and hiss of the cappuccino machine. He caught on to my confusion immediately.

"I don't mean that kind of noise. Not literal noise. I mean spiritual noise. Emotional noise. I'm all jumbled up inside. With the movie people everywhere, and Jayden around all the time, and now Tag and his family coming, there's too much talk, and no place to find quiet."

He paused while I tried to come up with a solution that didn't involve him leaving. "Tag is truly not an issue, and neither is Jayden," I said emphatically, to no avail.

"So you say, but as I've told you, I try to keep my expectations pretty fluid. I don't plan things too far in advance, and all I know right now is that I need to recalibrate. I think you called that decompressing back a few weeks ago, right? I can't do that here. I need to go home for a bit."

"You are home." My voice was just as firm as his was when he'd said he was leaving, but he just shook his head.

My sigh was decidedly frustrated. I wanted to look at this objectively and try to see his point of view, but my own emotions were a jumbled mess, too. Had I really screwed up that badly? Was he overreacting? Or did this situation land somewhere in the middle?

"Is all of this emotional turmoil you're experiencing really because of me?" I asked.

His gaze was unwavering as he paused, then finally said, "Yes. I guess I just wasn't ready to trust someone."

Ouch. Never ask a question if you're not ready for the answer, but at least I had a handy defense. "So . . . maybe this isn't so much about me as it is about the people from your past?"

His expression turned patronizing. "Lilly, this is about your choices and your actions. You did something that you knew would hurt me once I found out about it, and I'm not sure how to process that."

That hurt, too. "I'm sorry, Matt. I truly am, but do you really think you can't trust me? I've been as honest with you as I can possibly be. I broke a nondisclosure agreement just to make sure you were in the loop on what I was up to. And I was planning to tell you everything about breakfast and the scene with Jayden tonight at dinner, and that's the God's honest truth."

It was all I could do to not place a hand over my heart. If I'd had a Bible handy, I would've sworn on that, but this was Joe's Cuppa Joe Coffee Shop, and the only books around here were décor.

Matt gazed at me for a moment. Evaluating. Measuring. "I believe you," he said at last, but the truth didn't seem to cheer him up in the slightest. Wasn't the truth supposed to set you free? If that was the case, why did it bludgeon people with its weight?

"If you believe me, then don't leave right now. Stay so we can work through this and figure things out."

He shook his head again. "I told you, Lilly. There's too much noise, and I need some quiet. And for the record, I've been honest with you, too. I've told you everything. More than I've ever told anyone else, but what good did it do? You still ultimately made choices that served you first."

"What? Wait a minute. That's totally unfair. Maybe I made choices that were right for me, but I didn't do anything malicious. And you have to know I never meant to hurt your feelings."

"I know," he said with weighted resignation. "But I got hurt anyway."

He started to move from the booth.

"So that's it, then?" I asked, my voice edged with frustration. "You're just . . . leaving? With no resolution here? When are you coming back?"

"I'm not sure."

"In time for the wedding, though, right? Emily and Ryan will be so disappointed if you're not there. And you know I will be, too. I was hoping you'd be my date."

My last-ditch effort at levity soared through the air and landed like a brick.

"I'm not sure," he said again. "Now I need to grab my bag from home and catch the next ferry if I'm going to make it to Traverse City tonight before my grandmother goes to bed." He shifted again in the booth, although we'd solved absolutely nothing. Speaking of bricks. This was like talking to one because I hadn't changed his mind about leaving, nor had we cleared the air. In fact, all we'd done was stir up sludge.

"Wait, seriously? You won't even say when you'll be back?"

"I can't give you an answer if I don't know what it is," he said calmly. Too calmly.

"Okay . . . will you at least text later to let me know you got to Traverse City safely?"

He paused in his motions to gaze at me once more. "It's a ferry ride and a two-hour drive straight down Route 31 in a rental car, Lilly. I think I can navigate that all right, so . . ." He let that linger out there.

"So . . . no? You're not going to text me? What the fuck, Matt?"

Now his sigh was as frustrated as mine, an annoyed huff that came with an eye roll that was completely unexpected. "Okay," he said dismissively. "I'll text you when I arrive, but then I'm turning off my phone because the whole idea of shutting out the noise is to, you know, shut out the noise."

"So I'm noise now?"

He gazed at me for a moment and my world stood still, and then it crashed when he said, "At the moment? Kinda."

Wow. Just . . . wow. That was uncalled for. And it pissed me off.

"You know what?" I said tersely. "That's just fine. You go on home to Traverse City. Turn off your phone and pretend like we never happened, if that's what makes you feel safe, but all this crap about *noise* and *space* is just you being a chickenshit. That's right," I said to his surprised expression. "You have feelings for me, and that scares the crap out of you because you know other guys are interested in me, too. But here's the thing, Matt. I don't care about them. I only care about you. I care about you more than any other man I've ever known. And I'm not Wendy and I'm not cheating on you. So all of this"—I waved my arms around in the air to signify the invisible free-floating emotional cargo surrounding us—"this isn't noise. This is life. And it's messy and complicated and nuanced and painful and exquisite, and it's in motion all the time. We can't make it stop, so for all your aspirations of achieving emotional enlightenment, you still have to *live* in the world. That's where the people are, and that's where the love is. So you can go hide in your yoga bubble or at your cherry farm or whatever. Or you can decide to take this ride with me, where it's fun and it's fast and it's exciting. It's up to you."

I stood up before he could. "Safe travels. Maybe I'll see you at the wedding."

I walked out of Joe's Cuppa Joe with my heart thundering and my palms sweating. I had no idea where all that ragey stabbiness had come from. Exhaustion? Stress? Cerebral hemorrhage? Demonic possession?

Regardless, I'd just thrown down the gauntlet, and it was up to Matt to decide what to do next. Meanwhile, I had shit to do.

Chapter 32

"Where does this go?" I asked my sister as I carried an armload of blue-flowered bedding into the lobby of the Peach Tree Inn. It was day two of moving her, Chloe, and Ryan into their new digs, although they'd agreed that, for the sake of appearances, they wouldn't start sleeping there until after the wedding. Given that she was visibly pregnant, it seemed that ship had already sailed, but denial and propriety were first cousins around here.

"That goes in the Marquette Room," she answered, holding an ornate Tiffany lamp knockoff in each hand.

"Which is the Marquette Room?"

"It's this way," Chloe answered. "Follow me."

My niece led me to the second floor, second room on the left, and opened the door. She followed me in and shut it behind her.

"What's up with Matt?" she asked as soon as it closed.

I set the bedding on the mattress. "With Matt? He went to visit his grandma in Traverse City."

"Yeah, I know that part," she said impatiently while helping me spread out the comforter. "But why did he leave right before the wedding? I hear things, you know. Did you two have a fight?"

"Kinda, sorta. I'm not really sure." I could've played dumb and pretended not to know what she meant, but my skirting-of-the-truth days were behind me. From now on I'd be a walking, shining beacon of full-frontal honesty at all times. "I think he felt a little threatened by my friendship with Jayden."

"Because you made out with him in the lake?"

I stopped smoothing the bedspread and looked at Chloe. "Where'd you hear that?"

She shrugged and plopped down on the bed, undoing all the smoothing. "Susie Mahoney heard from Constance Messner that Skylar Tremont told a bunch of hotel workers that you and Jayden had to do a nudie-nudie scene in the lake and that it was supposed to be her kissing Jayden, but she had poison ivy on her butt."

"All of that is supposed to be a secret," I said.

"Well, then maybe Dr. Pine shouldn't have loaded her up with Xanax. That stuff is like truth serum. So it's legit then? You made out with Jayden Pierce. Oh my gosh, how was it?"

She suddenly seemed less concerned about Matt, and I wondered at the appropriateness of discussing someone's kissing prowess with my young niece.

"Everything was handled in a very professional manner," I said.

"Handled? There was handling?"

"Geez, Chloe," I snickered, against my better judgment. The kid was growing up too fast. "What I meant was that everything was very professional."

"Okay, sure, but you still got to kiss him, right?"

"Yes."

"And you've been kissing Matt, too, haven't you? Gosh, I wish I were you."

Now that was definitely awkward. "Don't you have someplace else to be?" I asked.

Her grin was broad and sassy. "Nope. I'm here all day. So anyway, what are you going to do about your boy troubles?"

I sank down on the mattress next to her. "Honestly? I have no idea. Matt's gone radio silent. No text messages or phone calls. I haven't heard from him since Tuesday night, and I'm not sure when he's coming back."

I thought for sure he'd check in again after letting me know he'd arrived safely, but nope. Nothing. Not a peep. I'd decided to go the optimistic route and sent him a heart emoji every morning, but so far they'd prompted no response, and I didn't even know if he'd gotten them. Had he really turned off his phone completely? Who did that?

On Friday, after all their stuff had been moved into the inn, we hosted Emily's bachelorette party in the lobby. It was very much like Drunk Puzzle Night, except with a dozen extra gals and a puzzle shaped like a penis. And then we played Pin the Penis on the Cover Model, Draw a Penis While Blindfolded, and Penis Ring Toss. No one should ever let Marnie be in charge of games.

On Saturday, while I was mildly hungover from too many Penis Coladas, the Taggert clan arrived, and seeing Tag was every bit as weird and awkward as I'd imagined. Even weirder than walking into the lake naked, and I wasn't sure why. Maybe because we had so much history together and yet everyone was pretending that we didn't. No one mentioned our past association, including Tag and me.

Ryan's brothers, Jack and Bryce, and Bryce's wife, Trish, were all cordial but not overly familiar, as if those months I'd spent in Sacramento had never happened. Maybe that was for the best. Because what was there to say? My relationship with Tag was recent enough that reminiscing would hurt, but long enough ago for everyone to be fairly certain that no sparks were about to be reignited.

And they weren't. No sparks at all. In fact, Tag looked . . . older to me. So much older that I pulled up some pictures on my phone from our trip to Portugal last spring just to see if my eyes were playing tricks on me, and realized he actually looked pretty much the same. It was just a change in my perspective. Apparently, my love goggles had foggy lenses. He was still handsome, for an old guy . . . but no sparks.

The days progressed. We all did wedding-y things, and family things, and touristy things. The inevitable roar of rumors about me doing a nude scene and kissing movie star Jayden Pierce spun around the island like a dervish. Gigi gave me a high five; my father gave me a stern look. That was about it. I didn't bother to confirm or deny anything but simply said I'd signed a nondisclosure agreement that prevented me from talking about the movie, which satisfied no one except for me. Because I didn't want to talk about it. I wasn't embarrassed or ashamed, but I wasn't interested in adding fuel to that particular fire, either.

Rumors about Matt having left the island spun around, too, but few people asked me about that directly. I'm sure there was speculation and conjecture and suspicion. Undoubtedly there were assumptions and suppositions and a vast amount of guesswork. No wonder Matt had left. He didn't like people prying into his personal affairs, and yet his departure only added ammunition to the rapid-fire gossiping.

On Wednesday, I did one more stint as an extra, but Jayden wasn't there. He sent me a text on Thursday, though, asking if I could meet for lunch at the Imperial Hotel. With Matt gone, I had no reason to say no. Who cared if people talked? Plus, I was pretty sure the movie gang would be leaving soon, and I did want a chance to tell him goodbye. We'd had fun, and it wasn't his fault my new boyfriend couldn't handle a little emotional noise.

"We did our final shots yesterday, so we're officially done with filming," Jayden confirmed as he snarfed down a club sandwich and then asked if I was going to finish my baked potato soup. I shook my head and pushed my bowl in his direction.

"Is Griffin happy with how things went?" I asked.

"He's as happy as Griffin ever is. He's not more cranky than usual, and I might even go so far as to say he's infinitesimally less cranky, so let's say . . . yes, I think he's happy."

"And how is Skylar's ass?"

"Her ass is splotchy and she's remorseful."

"Remorseful?"

He paused with a soup spoon halfway to his mouth. "I assume you know by now that everybody on this island heard about our lake scene, right?"

"Oh yes. I'm well aware. Everyone at church was super nice to me about it."

"Really?"

Leave it to Jayden to miss the obvious sarcasm. "No, they were not. Delores Crenshaw has started a petition to have me publicly shunned. But this, too, shall pass. As my grandmother said, 'You can bet your bottom dollar they couldn't get a dollar for their bottoms.' She says the ones crowing the loudest are just jealous."

Jayden chuckled. "Well, they should be. You have a great ass."

"Thanks. Hope it looks that way on film."

"It does. Griff showed me the dailies. You have nothing to worry about."

"Really? So I look okay?"

"Phenomenal."

I laughed then because there surely wouldn't be many times in my life when a movie star paid me a compliment. In fact, this might be the very last time, so I decided to take it as a win. Sure, it was superficial, but in the moment, I was okay with that.

"I'm glad to hear it. And don't forget you guys all promised to read my friend's screenplay."

Jayden dipped a french fry into the ketchup on his plate. "Already did. It's good. I'll make Griffin read it on the plane. Who knows? Maybe we'll be back here someday." He crooked an eyebrow at me suggestively.

"On behalf of Deputy Leo, I hope so."

"Just on behalf of Deputy Leo? What about you? Do you want me to come back?" His grin was charming as ever. "Maybe things won't work out with that new guy."

If anyone else had said that, it might have sounded crass, but I knew him well enough to understand the teasing behind it. That was just Jayden being Jayden. He probably had a line of girls waiting for him back in California.

Nonetheless I said, "I'll keep you posted."

He dunked another fry. "Good, because just for the record, if Rashida hadn't threatened me with bodily injury, I totally would've hit on you."

"You would have?"

"Of course. And the offer still stands, just so you know."

"So, in other words, I'm on your list?"

"Exactly."

Chapter 33

Ryan and Emily's rehearsal dinner was Friday evening at Tate's Tavern on the Bluff. The sun was low and golden in the sky, and the cocktails had been flowing since early afternoon. Everyone was feeling happy and mellow and loving, and I wanted to sink into the warmth and enjoy myself. This was a wonderful and special occasion. But I missed Matt. His absence was like a fog all around me.

While I'd been annoyed after he'd first left, I'd tried to appreciate his need for space. Now, after ten days of hearing nothing at all, I was, quite frankly, getting worried. Was it possible we'd seen the last of Yoga Matt? My heart bounced between fracturing at the thought of that and steadily thumping with the certainty that he'd come back. Eventually. Then I'd get annoyed again, and so the cycle continued.

I did a pretty commendable job at playing happy around other people. Only Brooke seemed to sense my distress. She wasn't usually that intuitive about people's feelings, but since she'd all but raised me, maybe she had a special sort of substitute-mother's intuition.

"He'll be back," she said to me that evening as we sat on a bench under a shady tree on Tate's patio.

"He'll come back to the island, probably. I think. I'm just not sure he'll be coming back to me," I said with a sigh.

"He'll come back to you," she said decisively. "I've seen the way he looks at you. He's in love."

I shook my head. "He may love me, but he doesn't trust me, and you can't really have one without the other." I wanted to tell her all about his brother and his ex-fiancée and his mother, but I didn't. That wasn't my story to share. But if I did, Brooke might realize that once Matt left someone, he really left them. It was the thought that made my heart go cold every time it crossed my mind. Had I broken something that couldn't be fixed?

"It's true you can't have love without trust," Brooke said with a nod, "but sometimes trust can take a bit of a beating and still bounce back."

"What makes you think so?"

"Well . . . Leo wasn't exactly honest with me when we first met, and look at us now. Solid as a couple of rocks."

I chuckled at her analogy. "Rocks, huh? That sounds super romantic."

She cuffed me gently on the shoulder. "It is if you like rocks, and we both like rocks, so shut up."

Leo joined us a few minutes later.

"How's it going?" he asked pleasantly.

"Good," I answered. "Looks like those crazy kids are going to make it down the aisle tomorrow."

"Yep, looks like they are."

"Feeling inspired?" I teased as he sat down next to my sister. Brooke blushed and pinched me discreetly at my indiscreet question, but Leo chuckled.

"Maybe. This is where we had our first date, right, Brooke?" he asked, causing her blush to deepen.

"Yes, it is." They exchanged a glance so loving that I couldn't suppress a forlorn sigh.

Leo tore his eyes away from my sister and looked back at me. "Hey, by the way, I wanted to thank you for asking your movie friends to read my screenplay. I don't imagine anything will come from it, but it's worth a shot, right?"

I nodded. "Absolutely. Jayden already read it and said he really enjoyed it."

"He did?" Now it was Leo's turn to blush, and I noticed that his scar from walking into the lamppost was fading nicely.

I nodded again. "He said he'd have Griffin read it on the plane. Who knows? This could be your big break. Stranger things have happened."

"Let's hope. There's something else I wanted to mention to you, too," Leo said, still looking at me.

"Yes?"

"Matt's back."

"Oh." I gulped and didn't know what else to say. I'd given up sending the morning heart emojis a few days ago and had settled into a kind of resigned holding pattern. If he wanted to ignore me, I wasn't going to beg. But if he was back . . .

My longing turned back to annoyance. He was back, and still he hadn't bothered to contact me?

"He got home this afternoon," Leo continued. "But he didn't want to bug you because he figured you were in the middle of wedding stuff."

"How thoughtful." My tone was beach-sand dry, and Brooke gave me an arched-brow *I told you so*.

Leo chuckled. "Right. Anyway, I got the impression that if you were to be available anytime later this evening, he's probably available, too. I know he wants to see you."

"Oh," I said again.

"He had a pretty interesting visit with his grandmother, so . . . yeah. There's that."

"Could you be more cryptic? Because I'm not quite agitated enough by the fact that he's back and still hasn't called me." I crossed my arms and glared at the messenger.

But Leo laughed and stood, pulling Brooke up with him. "I'm a little beyond the *passing notes in study hall* phase. I think you two need to talk to each other. But I will say"—he lowered his voice conspiratorially—"after spending a week with your old boyfriend, Tag, Matt's a way better guy. Tag's kind of an asshole."

Brooke snorted in agreement, and I smiled then, because I'd been noticing the same thing. Not sure how I'd missed it before, but I knew Leo was right. Tag was pretentious.

Matt was a far better guy.

Even if he had left me high and dry and *unread* for ten freaking days.

"Come on," Brooke said, gesturing to me. "We should all get back."

She was right, of course. We were in the middle of Ryan and Emily's rehearsal dinner extravaganza, but now my mind was thoroughly and entirely on Matt.

I checked my phone when we got back inside the restaurant and realized he'd left me a message after all.

HI. I'M HOME. I KNOW YOU'RE BUSY WITH FAMILY BUT VERY MUCH WANT TO SEE YOU. ANY CHANCE YOU'VE GOT A FEW MINUTES FREE TONIGHT?

I waited half an hour before responding—because he'd kept me waiting for over a week, and texting strategy demanded it. I did have some pride, after all, but as soon as I told Emily he was back in town, she shooed me away to go find him.

"Go," she said. "Go make nice. I can't have two of your old boyfriends moping around at my wedding."

So I walked onto the patio and sent him a message . . .

I'M AT TATES.

He responded immediately.

I KNOW. ME TOO. BEEN WAITING FOR YOU TO RESPOND.

I looked around and spotted him sitting on a bench identical to the one I'd been on earlier, but it was near the end of the long cobblestone driveway leading to the restaurant.

There was no avoiding him now, and all the feelings I'd been keeping inside started to swirl. The longing, the frustration, the uncertainty. He was wrong to have left me for so long without so much as a word. It wasn't fair. Noise or no noise, he owed me more than that. And then there was the worry and the agitation and the ache of missing him. My heart and my head were at war, and it was quite possible that only Matt could declare which was the victor.

I walked down the path in my flowy flowered dress knowing I looked good and wanting him to notice. I wanted him to remember what he'd been missing. I wanted him to set aside all those concerns of his and take a leap of faith with me. After he'd apologized profusely, of course.

He stood up and watched as I approached, a tentative smile on his face, but I didn't lean in to hug him. I crossed my arms instead. I was a rock. But not a romantic rock like Brooke and Leo. I was an impervious rock that wasn't about to fling myself into his arms just because he'd *finally* bothered to come back. Even though he looked so very good with his tan skin and his hair tousled by the breeze.

"Will you sit with me for a minute?" he asked, gesturing to the bench.

"I guess," I said, plopping down and staring straight ahead.

I heard his soft chuckle, and for a man who should be full of remorse, he was not off to a good start.

"I screwed up big-time," he said at last, and I stole a glance in his direction. He was sitting sideways on the bench, fully turned toward me.

"Ya think?" I asked.

"Yes. Very much yes." His pause made me glance at him again, and his open expression made my heart tumble involuntarily in my chest.

"Lilly, I missed you like crazy. The whole damn time. I tried not to, but it was just no use. When I finally told my grandmother everything that was on my mind, do you know what she said?"

I shrugged with feigned indifference. "I'm sure I have no idea."

Matt chuckled again. "She said you were totally right and that I was a chickenshit."

I plucked at the fabric of my dress. "She sounds very wise."

"She is, and so I'm back, but there's a couple things I need to explain and I hope you'll understand."

I deigned to look over at him.

"Lilly," he said on a sigh, "I've spent the past year and a half trying to process old, destructive feelings while not letting myself be controlled by them, but I realize now all I really did was shut down and avoid feeling anything at all. But when you walked into the Cahill house that day, I couldn't *not* feel it. I couldn't ignore my attraction to you, and the more we talked, the more time we spent together, well, everything about you woke me up. It cracked me open, and suddenly everything was spilling out, and you're right. It scared me. A lot."

I uncrossed my arms and looked his way and saw all the earnestness he had to offer. He was getting better at apologizing. So far.

"Being around you made me want things again," he continued. "Looking at you, I could see all the stuff I craved but thought I wasn't worthy of. The house and the family and the dogs and the cats. A garden with our initials in it. Then I saw you willing to commit to caring about me and standing by me. That was the scariest thing ever. You were calling my bluff."

He reached out and trailed a finger softly down my arm until it rested on my hand. "But there was also Tag floating over you like a shadow, and then there was Jayden tapping on your shoulder and constantly pulling you away, and I guess that was just too much for me. Wanting you and wanting all you had to offer was just too much. Because . . . what if I lost you?" He took hold of my hand then, and I let him grasp it as he stared into my eyes and said softly, "What if someone smarter, or richer, or better than me comes along and I lose you?"

Tears welled in my eyes, and the hurt I'd felt at his absence slipped away like a morning mist. He was back, and he was back *for me*.

"You won't lose me, Matt, because when I look at you, I see all of those same things. The house and the kids and the pets and the gardens. Those are the things I want, and you're the man I want to share them with."

"Still? Even now? After I ran off like a jackass?" His smile was sheepish but hopeful as he squeezed my hand more tightly.

"Still. And always. But promise me you won't do that again. This was the longest ten days of my life, and from now on, if there's a problem or an issue or if there's something that scares us, we need to talk to each other about it and work through it together. Like a partnership. There's no relationship if we're not honest about how we feel, Matt. And there's no relationship if we don't trust each other. So . . . are you ready, willing, and able to trust me?"

He nodded solemnly. "I am. I do trust you. I was carrying around a lot of old hurts, but I think I've finally faced all that. I'm looking forward now. I guess the question is, are you ready, willing, and able to trust me back?"

Boy, was I. I squeezed his hand in return and answered emphatically, "Yes."

"Good. I like the sound of that. Do you know what else I like?"
"Me?"

"God, yes. So damn much." He moved closer to me on the bench. "Did you know that it's possible to think about someone twenty-four hours a day? Because that's how much I thought about you. The more I tried to shut out the world, the more thoughts of you consumed me. It was aggravating."

I smiled because I knew it was a compliment.

"Well, you did a pretty good job of keeping *that* a secret," I said. "You didn't call me one single time." Yes, I'd forgiven him, but that still stung.

He twined his fingers around mine. "I know. I'm sorry to have left you worrying and wondering. I just knew if I heard your voice, it would be all over for me and I'd come back before I'd figured everything out."

"And have you figured everything out now?"

He pondered that for a moment and then answered in that thoughtful way of his. "No, because like you said, life is always in motion. There's always going to be some other riddle to be solved, but I did figure out the most important thing."

"Which is?"

"That I'm crazy about you. I realized that even if I came back here and you gave me a boot to the backside, I had to tell you exactly how I feel. I realized there's no risk I wouldn't be willing to take for you. Even a broken heart."

He reached up and placed a warm, work-roughened palm to my cheek, and it felt so good.

"I won't break your heart," I said, even as mine thumped erratically inside my chest. I covered his hand with one of my own. "You won't break mine, either, right?"

"Of course not."

"Then can I ask you something?"

"Always."

"Will you kiss me, please?"

"Always," he said again, and before his lips met mine, I watched a butterfly land on the arm of the bench right behind him, and I smiled. I didn't believe in ghosts or signs, but if I did, I might just think that my mother approved.

Chapter 34

My sister was a beautiful, glowing bride as she glided down the aisle of Saint Bartholomew's Church on the arm of my father, her gently rounded belly a sign of even more happiness to come. The church was full of happy attendees, the flowers smelled like heaven, and the chief was beaming from ear to ear.

"I'm not sure I've ever seen his teeth before," Chloe whispered to me from near the altar, where we stood waiting with Brooke, bouquets in hand. I smiled back at my niece and hoped the wedding photographer got about a hundred images of that joy on my father's face before it reverted to his typically bland expression. As he handed Emily off to Ryan, I even saw a tear sparkle from the corner of his eye.

Who knew Harlan Callaghan was such a sentimental fool?

Standing at the front of the church, I looked out over the crowded congregation. There was Gigi, resplendent in fuchsia with a matching feathered hat that could have nicely doubled as an Easter basket. I spotted Gloria and Tiny and their sweet baby, Norah Grace. There were Marnie and Eva, Percy and Dmitri, and dozens of others. So many familiar faces, all smiling, too. This was a happy day.

And there, next to Leo, was Matt in a navy-blue suit and a striped silk tie. I'd never seen him dressed up before. He'd always made scruffy clothes look good, but damn, the things that man did to a suit! Although, if I was being really honest, nothing looked as good on Matt as nothing at all. I blushed as I caught his eye, and he winked at me, sending the flutters out in every direction.

We'd left Tate's Tavern on the Bluff last night and headed to his tiny gardening-shed cottage. The Dunnigans were still traveling, but I didn't want to be in their space. I wanted to be in Matt's space, surrounded by his things, in his bed, where we whispered urgent sweet nothings and made plans that would take a lifetime to complete. We kissed and caressed and confessed to all the deepest feelings we shared. All the old hurts were healed, and new promises were made. Promises I knew for certain that we'd keep.

As the moon rose, sending beams of light over the covers of Matt's cozy, comfy bed, I fell asleep wrapped in his arms with the echo of his words in my ear.

"I love you," he'd whispered.

And I'd kissed him and whispered it back. "I know. I love you, too."

∽

"Mom! Aunt Lilly! Look who I found. Can he stay?" Chloe trotted into Emily and Ryan's reception at the Grand Ballroom with a casually dressed Jayden Pierce in tow. She was pulling him by the wrist, and he had on jeans and a Trillium Bay T-shirt, just like a tourist.

"Sorry. I don't mean to crash your wedding," he said to Emily with a smile, "but the kid wasn't taking no for an answer." That was ironic, coming from the guy who'd once tried to buy a car at a gas station.

Emily gave me a glance as if to make sure it was okay, and I smiled with an easygoing shrug. I didn't mind, and after last night, I didn't think Matt would care, either.

"You sure about that?" Brooke murmured into my ear.

"Yep," I said with a smile. "Matt and I are rock solid."

And we were, so perhaps it was to no one's surprise when I caught the bouquet and walked right past wealthy businessman John Taggert and right past mega-movie-star Jayden Pierce and pulled the island's very own Yoga Matt from the crowd. I leaned in close and gave him a kiss that left doubt in no one's mind who I wanted for myself.

There may have been some cheering, and perhaps some applause. Maybe it wasn't for us. Or maybe it was. Either way, I didn't care. I just wanted to kiss him.

And when Jayden of all people caught the garter, he just handed that to Matt, too.

"You're a lucky man," Jayden said to him.

"I know," Matt responded with a smile.

The night wore on, and everyone ate and drank and danced and laughed. They wished Emily and Ryan well and talked about how wonderful it all was. The love and the baby and the happily ever after.

"You know," I said to Matt as the hour grew late and we were dancing cheek to cheek, "Peach and Ryan got engaged at Gloria and Tiny's wedding."

"You don't say," he murmured against my hair.

"Yep, so I'm wondering if maybe they started a tradition. Maybe Leo will propose to Brooke tonight."

"That would be very romantic," he said.

"Wouldn't it?"

"Mm-hmm."

"Matt?"

"Yes?"

"Can I ask you something?"

"Always."

"Are you going to ask me to marry you?"

His feet halted as he leaned back to look down at me, an intrigued smile on his face. "Do you mean, like, right now or eventually?"

I shrugged in his arms. "Eventually, I guess. Or right now. Whenever. Because I'd really like to marry you someday, and I just thought you should know that."

His smile broadened. "Okay. In that case, Lilly Callaghan, will you marry me someday?"

I smiled back. "Yes. Yes, I will. And we can live in a little house and have a lot of babies and plant a garden and get a dog. How does that sound?"

"It sounds perfect," he said. "That's exactly what I want."

"Me too," I said. "You're exactly what I want."

ACKNOWLEDGMENTS

First and foremost, a heartfelt thanks to all my readers. Your continued support means the world to me. To everyone who sends a lovely note or takes a moment to leave a review, big squeezy hugs for you! Writers may work in isolation, but we live on your praise.

Thanks to Anh Schluep for being an ocean of calm in an otherwise crazy business, and to Lindsey Faber for helping me navigate this journey while making it so much more fun than it would've been going alone.

Thanks to Nalini Akolekar, my friend, confidante, and all-around kick-ass agent who, among many other things, always makes the time to discuss with me the finer points of our favorite TV show.

Thanks to Jane for the innumerable beta reads and all the wise and welcome feedback. You're the best.

Thanks to author (and movie extra!) Jean Willett for telling me all about your experience on the set of *North and South*! You sure made it sound exciting! Wish I'd been there, too!

Many, many thanks to Sally Kilpatrick, Jamie Beck, Sonali Dev, Priscilla Oliveras, Falguni Kothari, Kwana Jackson, Virginia Kantra, Barbara Samuel, Liz Talley, and Hope Ramsay. You are all amazing writers, and I'm grateful for everything that I've learned from you.

And finally, the biggest, most heartfelt thanks goes to my daughters, Webster Girl and Tenacious D. Without you, nothing else matters. I love you bunches.

ABOUT THE AUTHOR

Photo © 2017 Kristy Berands Photography

Tracy Brogan is the *USA Today*, *Wall Street Journal*, and Amazon bestselling author of both the Bell Harbor and Trillium Bay series. Her debut novel, *Crazy Little Thing*, has sold more than a million copies, and her books have been translated into more than a dozen languages. A three-time finalist for the Romance Writers of America RITA® Award, she writes fun, funny stories full of family, laughter, and love. Brogan lives in Michigan and loves to hear from readers, so contact her at tracybrogan1225@gmail.com or check out her website at www.tracybrogan.com.